PRAISE FOR

# The Midnight Queen

"A fresh and inventive historical novel . . . I can't wait to see what Sylvia Izzo Hunter does next."

—Marie Brennan, author of the Memoirs of Lady Trent

"Elegantly written, fast-paced, and highly original—a stunning story of magic, scholarship, and true love. Sylvia Izzo Hunter brings both rural Brittany and an alternative Regency England to vivid life. A remarkably assured debut."

—Juliet Marillier, national bestselling author

"Sylvia Izzo Hunter has crafted an impressive debut novel and begun a provocative series."

—SFFWorld

"Great for readers of historical and fantasy lovers alike . . . I think you will enjoy the rich and detailed story and world that Sylvia Izzo Hunter has created."

—Book Briefs

"An imagination so inventive as to come up with [as] enchanting and riveting a novel as The Midnight Queen will be sure to produce untold wonders . . . Deliciously complex . . . An absolute page-turner . . . The Midnight Queen is a fresh new story unlike anything else in its genre."

—Black Dog Speaks

continued . . .

D0377131

"A breath of fresh air, recalling books as they used to be—stories to be savoured . . . *The Midnight Queen* is a long journey through mistaken identities, conspiracies, and finding the limitations of magic capabilities, and a journey that was highly satisfying in the end."

—*Nyx Book Reviews*

"In *The Midnight Queen*, Izzo Hunter pulls from a multitude of mystical tales and myths to create her own magical version of Britain that is both innovative and intriguing. The plot is creative and suspenseful—and never predictable. Your affection for the dynamic heroes will only grow as Hunter's characters face challenge after unexpected challenge. *The Midnight Queen* is a novel that readers will be unable to put down."

—*RT Book Reviews*

"An interesting and exciting story, full of magical spells and skills, which easily kept me intrigued . . . The characters are well developed, and I enjoyed seeing Gray and Sophie, in particular, grow both personally and magically."

—*Bitten by Books*

*Ace Books by Sylvia Izzo Hunter*

THE MIDNIGHT QUEEN

LADY OF MAGICK

# Lady of Magick

✳

### SYLVIA IZZO HUNTER

ACE BOOKS, NEW YORK

**ACE**

**An imprint of Penguin Random House LLC**
**375 Hudson Street, New York, New York 10014**

This book is an original publication of Penguin Random House LLC.

Library of Congress Cataloging-in-Publication Data

Hunter, Sylvia Izzo.
Lady of magick / Sylvia Izzo Hunter.
pages ; cm
ISBN 978-0-425-27246-6 (trade)
I. Title.
PR9199.4.H8684L33    2015
813'.6—dc23
2015007896

PUBLISHING HISTORY
Ace trade paperback edition / September 2015

PRINTED IN THE UNITED STATES OF AMERICA

10   9   8   7   6   5   4   3   2   1

Cover illustrations: Owl © Dn Br / Shutterstock Images;
Leaf © Aleks Melnik / Shutterstock Images;
Grey tree drawing © SoftRobot/Shutterstock Images.
Cover design by Diana Kolsky.
Interior text design by Tiffany Estreicher.
Maps by Cortney Skinner.

Penguin
Random
House

# ACKNOWLEDGEMENTS

I owe a general debt of gratitude to my family, my friends, and my colleagues of all sorts for the many hours (or possibly weeks) they have collectively spent listening to me complain about why on earth my characters behave the way they do and bewail my lack of progress in writing and/or revising, and for just generally being patient, lovely, and kind.

More particularly, I am indebted to my beta readers, Anne Marie Corrigan, Tawnie Olson, Antonia Pop, Jeannie Scarfe, and Kim Solga, for encouragement, critique, new angles of view, serious discussions of the psychology of fictional persons, and of course tea and milk shakes; to Latinista-in-chief Michael Appleby for saving me from incomprehensibility; to Alex Hunter for blocking help and chess strategy, and to Rhiannon Davies Shah for conversational Welsh (even though the chess game and that conversation ended up on the cutting-room floor); and to the nice people at the Butterfly Conservatory in Niagara Parks, Ontario, for answering my questions about *Lepidoptera*. Books consulted in the process of writing this one include Robert D. Anderson et al., *The University of Edinburgh: An Illustrated History* (Edinburgh: Edinburgh University Press, 2003); Thomas Hope, *Household Furniture and Interior Decoration: Classic Style Book of the Regency Period* (reprint, New York: Dover, 1971); and (on Google Books) R. A. Armstrong, *A Gaelic-English and English-Gaelic Dictionary* (London, 1825). All linguistic, geographical, biological, and other errors that remain are, of course, my own.

Thanks also to Carleton Wilson, my website guy, and Nicole Hilton, who kindly took my author photos. The beautiful maps are the work of Cortney Skinner.

And thanks once again to the fantastic team at JABberwocky Literary

Agency; to my agent, Eddie Schneider, and my editor, Jessica Wade, who between them pushed and pulled me in the right directions to make this a *much* better book; to Isabel Farhi, able editorial assistant and fellow Wholockian; to copy editor Amy J. Schneider for saving me from many a continuity error; to Diana Kolsky for the stunning cover, and Tiffany Estreicher for the gorgeous interior design; and to Michelle Kasper, Julia Quinlan, Erica Martirano, and Nita Basu for shepherding the book the rest of the way into your hands.

Finally, ALL THE THANKS to Alex and Shaina Hunter for all the times they did extra household chores so I could write, brought me tea or ice cream, came to my choir concerts, and gave me helpful hugs, and also for all the times they said, "Shouldn't you be writing?"

The plot of this book plays fast and loose with the history, genealogy, and mythology of Scotland, and to some extent even its geography, and personal names and some place-names have been Anglicized for ease of reading in English. The songs sung by the characters in the course of the story, however, are real ones. They are, in order of appearance, the student hymn "Gaudeamus Igitur"; the Somersetshire ballad "The Trees They Grow So High"; two eighteenth-century (as far as I know) Gaelic love songs written by women, "Ailein Duinn" by Annag Chaimbeul and "Fear a' Bhàta" by Sìne NicFhionnlaigh; Robert Burns's "Ae Fond Kiss"; and the Oxfordshire ballad "Oxford City." The long spell in chapter XXXIII is borrowed from a thirteenth-century liturgical poem, with apologies to its various possible authors.

# Lady of
# Magick

✳

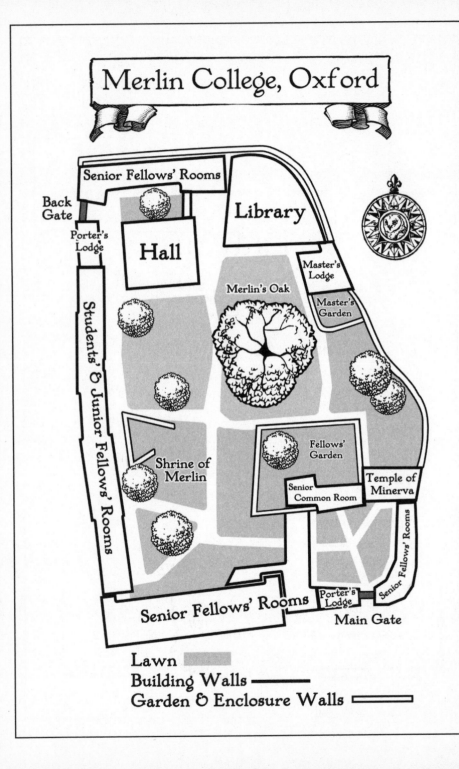

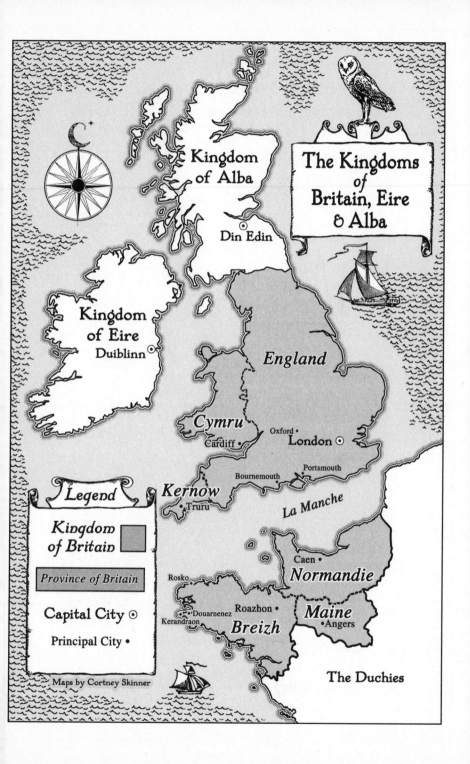

PART ONE

# Oxford to Din Edin

## CHAPTER I

# In Which Gray
# Receives an Invitation

*Weaving her way* slowly through the stacks of the Merlin Library with an armload of histories and grimoires, her chin resting on the dull-green leather of the topmost, Sophie Marshall smiled to herself. From one pocket of her black scholar's gown trailed a long scrap of writing-paper, on which an equally long list of abbreviated notations—such as *M. Domitianus on G.A.*, *"Aves Tenebrae," Trevelyan Hist. Mag. Brit.*—had been neatly written, and tidily scored through; the pile of codices in her arms representing the morning's final foray into the scrum of undergraduates revising for their Finals, she could now retreat to her carrel to pass the balance of the day in solitude and study.

As she passed a shelf of Roman histories, another black-gowned figure erupted from a gap in the stacks, its face invisible behind another tottering pile. Sophie checked her advance, but too late; a moment later two undergraduates and more than a score of books lay scattered in the narrow aisle.

"Oof!" said the young man cheerfully, picking himself up and beginning to sort through the litter of codices. "A hazardous business, this! Now, let us see: Mine are the Greeks, you know, and these therefore will be yours, I think—"

Peering short-sightedly at Sophie, he held out a battered copy of Trevelyan's *Historie of Magick in Britaine*. He wore a vague, amiable smile to match his voice, but as her hand closed on the spine of the codex, their eyes met, and a masque of politeness descended over his face. "I beg your pardon, Your Royal Highness," he said repressively. "I hope you have taken no hurt."

Sophie's answering smile faded into a sigh. "None whatever, I assure you," she replied, and busied herself in collecting up her books.

She reached her carrel with no further *contretemps*, and finding it—thanks to her warding-spell—still blessedly undisturbed, attempted to lose herself in contrasting the varying accounts of the lives of several famous British mages. But the encounter had flustered and annoyed her, and she found herself dwelling on it far more than she knew it deserved.

How could she have been so foolish as to expect a welcome here? Beyond each summer's brief visits by the families of Merlin men receiving their degrees, no woman's foot before her own had ever trod the paths and lawns of Merlin College—and few were those, as she had since discovered, who wished it otherwise. Her own wilful blindness had led her here, her determination to judge the College by her husband and by her tutor, Master Alcuin, who took her as she was; why had she not understood that it was not they but her stepfather, Professor Callender—with his nostrums about the dangers of advanced study to the delicate female mind—who exemplified the Merlin man? And her circumstances were not helped by the tendency of her fellow students to perceive the Princess Edith Augusta in place of Sophie Marshall.

And yet . . .

The lonely, isolated, often unhappy Sophie of a few years since, whose life was made bearable by her illicit forays into the Professor's library, could have imagined no greater prize than this. After the astonishing revelation that Sophie was in truth the daughter of the King of Britain, her hasty marriage, and the chaotic night on which she and her friends had saved the King from his advisors' plot to poison him, the promise of a place at Merlin had come, like a gift from the gods themselves, to save her from a life of useless idleness, isolation, and acrimony in the royal household, or of wandering penury with Gray. And for all the ceremonious politeness of her fellow undergraduates, the tongues stilled and faces averted at her approach, the glares, the naked resentment, she was more often happy here than she had been in her stepfather's house—now Gray's and hers, at least in name—in Breizh. Having once accustomed themselves to her, Gray's friends treated her as one of themselves, no longer seeming conscious either of her sex or of her rank; the men of Breizh, with few exceptions, had made it a point to demonstrate their friendship. The rest resented her presence, but just often enough did they forget their hostility in the heat of debate that Sophie held out hope of a future thaw. And everywhere one went at Merlin, was there not some new discovery waiting to be made? If only there were fewer game-pits and cowpats along her path . . .

Sophie fetched a wistful sigh, twisted a curl of dark hair around one finger, and applied herself to the *Aves Tenebrae.*

At length she was recalled to the present by a soft tapping on the wall of her carrel. Turning in her seat and tilting back her head, she beheld her husband, looking slightly rumpled and bearing a covered basket.

"Have you time to spare for luncheon?" he inquired, depositing the basket and perching dangerously on one corner of the desk.

"It is not noon already?" said Sophie, startled.

Gray's hazel eyes crinkled in silent laughter. "Indeed it is," he said, "and high time you were dragged away from your books, evidently. Your hands are all over ink."

Sophie examined her fingers. Then, casting an eye at her husband, she said, "Whereas yours, on the contrary . . ."

Gray looked down at his own hands, and registered the palimpsest of ink-stains—the fresher, darker blots overlaid on older ones half scrubbed away—with a rueful grimace.

Sophie grinned at him.

Then she pushed back her chair and allowed Gray to take her hands and pull her up out of it. "What have you got in that basket, then?"

"I have wheedled a picnic luncheon from Mrs. Haskell," Gray explained happily, as he and Sophie emerged arm in arm into the Garden Quadrangle. "She is in one of her cheerful humours today, and allowed Nessa Strout to pack it up for me. Had you rather eat in the quad, or in the Fellows' Garden?"

Sophie paused and began to look about them. Having thoughtlessly made the suggestion, Gray at once saw it had been a foolish one; there was scarce a foot of space not already occupied.

All about the grassy quad, undergraduates—and even a few Junior Fellows—basked in the hesitant March sunshine. A few made some pretence of studying, drowsing over a codex under a willow tree or reclining on the lawn amidst a litter of papers and books, but most were simply and unashamedly lolling about in various stages of undress, gowns and coats and even one or two neck-cloths abandoned in little heaps on the grass. The place was so still that the progress of any person across the quad was spectacle enough to draw the attention of the less somnolent, and wherever Gray looked, some curious eye returned his gaze.

One rather undersized first-year had gone so far as to open his shirt; he met Gray's eye with happy equanimity, but a moment later, his glance alighting on Sophie, he flushed to the roots of his tow-coloured hair and scrambled to retrieve his discarded gown.

Discomfited, Gray looked away—directly into the face of a Junior Fellow who was eyeing Sophie with curling lip and supercilious eye. Under the massive oak-tree in the centre of the quad—the one which generations of matriculating students had believed to be planted by Merlin himself—a trio in commoners' gowns had their heads together, muttering; a moment later the knot of black silk exploded in laughter like a murder of crows, and one by one they swooped down to make extravagant, mocking bows.

"Clear off, the lot of you!" Gray ordered. They scattered, obedient to his scowl and his Master's robes but howling with derisive mirth.

Sophie stood motionless, all her attention apparently on the springing buds of the nearest tree, until the last of them had taken himself off; only the tightening of her fingers on Gray's arm betrayed her. "The quad seems rather overpopulated," she said then, in a calm and distant tone.

Outraged on Sophie's behalf—and mortified at having thought-lessly delivered her to such abuse—Gray drew her closer to his side, looking determinedly straight ahead as they resumed their interrupted journey.

The Fellows' Garden was occupied only by the Regius Professor of Magickal History, sound asleep on a stone bench quilted by creeping thyme, with a fat codex splayed open upon his breast. It was not difficult to avoid waking him; the first anger over, they consumed Mrs. Strout's cold collation almost in silence. When they had eaten all they could, and fed the rest to an intermittent procession of chipmunks and an elderly hedgehog, Gray said, "We need not stay here, *cariad*, if you are unhappy."

Sophie did not look at him, but went on twisting a sprig of bee-balm between her fingers. "And where else should we go?" she inquired.

It was an old dispute, and he had not really expected her to yield, but it dismayed him to see all her lovely colours faded in dejection, that had bloomed so happily a few hours since. "I am not so very unhappy, Gray," she continued. "Or, at any rate, I am as happy here as I should be anywhere else."

When his sister Jenny had spoken these words to him, or something like them, on her wedding-day, Gray had wished for power to give her some better assurance of happiness, and hated his father for promising Jenny to a man she did not love. *How young and foolish I was, to believe that where love leads, happiness must always follow!*

"There is the house in Breizh," he ventured, and was perversely cheered by Sophie's answering flash of temper.

"I do not choose to be an object of pity to Lady Maëlle and

Amelia," she said tartly, "and I have not endured the disapproval of my fellow undergraduates for five terms, only to retire like a wounded fox when the sixth is scarcely begun." Two years of her life, or nearly, devoted to this undertaking: not, Gray conceded, an effort to be lightly abandoned.

The Regius Professor of Magickal History stirred on his makeshift bed, gave a tremendous snore, and muttered, "Asparagus washtub!"— making Gray and Sophie start, and then snicker, until finally they were cramming their gown-sleeves into their mouths to muffle their laughter. Staggering a little, they packed away Mrs. Haskell's picnic-cloth, china, and plate and left the Fellows' Garden as quietly and quickly as they could.

"Do you see?" Sophie said, prodding Gray gently with her elbow, as they emerged at last, still chuckling, into the Front Quad. "Life is not so very grim. I beg you will not fret yourself so over my well-being; I am sure you have work enough without."

Gray set down the basket and drew her into his arms. "You are my wife, *cariad*," he reminded her; "I can hardly be expected to do less."

She rose up on tiptoe, and her hand came up to rest against his cheek; the touch set the air about them humming softly, Sophie's magick and his own in the strange communion that they no longer thought to question—from which Gray deduced that her feelings on the subject were more forceful than she wished him to see.

Temple bells began to toll the hour—two after noon—and for some time the air was filled with the plangent bell of the College's shrine to Minerva.

"I have left the day's revising half done," Sophie said at last, draw-ing away from him with a fond smile, "and you have Bevan and Ran-some at the third hour, have you not?"

She stood on tiptoe again and drew his head down for a fleeting kiss, and then she was striding away across the quad, her black gown billowing behind her.

Gray watched her go, troubled. *She chose to come here,* he reminded himself, *and chooses to remain; neither I, nor her father, nor any mage living, could have kept her here, if she did not wish it.*

*But Sophie deserves a happy home, not merely one less miserable than her last.*


"Magister," said Ransome, "were you at Professor de Guivrée's lecture yesterday afternoon?"

"I was not," Gray said; and then, startled, he asked, "Were you?"

"Certainly!" Ransome's air of affront—as though attending lectures had been a settled habit of his—was so comical that Gray had difficulty in suppressing a smile. "Bevan saw me—did not you see me, Bev?"

Bevan, a little grudgingly, admitted that he had.

Gray suspected a ploy to draw attention from the deeply inadequate essay Ransome had produced for this afternoon's session. The boy had natural talent in plenty, but no patience whatever for his books; his parents had sent him to Merlin to read magickal theory rather for the prestige of the subject than because he had any real interest in it. Gray privately thought that he had much better have trained in some more practical branch of magick—alchymy or botany, perhaps—where his talent might have been a greater help to him, and his aversion to the library a lesser hindrance.

Ransome was thus equally an object of sympathy and exasperation to his tutor—often both simultaneously; today's effort to summarise the theory of summoning-, finding-, and drawing-spells had been particularly exasperating, set beside Bevan's careful and thorough synthesis. Knowing Ransome as Gray did, however, only made the digression more irresistible: What had made him choose *that* lecture, of the hundreds given in any College term, to grace with his presence?

"Well," Gray said, therefore, "and what did you think of the lecture?"

Ransome's guileless face screwed up in concentration. After a moment he ventured, "I thought . . . it seemed as though he had an axe to grind."

"Yes," said Bevan unexpectedly, "and I know why, too."

"Do you?" Ransome looked impressed, and rather relieved. "Why?"

"There was a . . . an uproar at his lecture last term," Bevan said. He cast a cautious glance at Gray, who knew very well what he meant but did not like to curtail this rare manifestation of scholarly discussion between his students. "Old—er, that is, the learned professor had described his study of temples to Neptune and Ceres in Petite-Bretagne—your pardon: Breizh, I mean—and said that the introduction of altars to local gods has rendered many of them inefficacious as offering-places. He did not go quite so far as to call the local gods mere superstition, but—"

If Guivrée had stopped short of asserting that the ancient gods of Britain's provinces were not fit to lick the metaphorical boots of the gods of Rome, Gray suspected, it was only because he chose not to set that particular cat amongst a set of pigeons so many of whom were Breizhek, Cymric, or Kernowek born and bred—not because he did not himself believe it true.

"There was a great deal of muttering," Bevan went on, "but the only student who dared put a question at the end of the lecture was Soph—was Mrs. Marshall," he corrected himself, colouring a little at Gray's silently raised eyebrow, "and it was a very good question, too, to which he had not a good answer. He began to bluster about women's fancies, instead, and there was nearly a brawl between his supporters and—"

"A *brawl*?" Ransome exclaimed. "And I *missed* it?"

Gray contrived to keep his countenance by carefully *not* looking at Bevan.

"Well, *this* time," said Ransome, in a rather disgruntled tone, "his lecture was nothing but a dispute with a book by a Fellow at the University in Din Edin, which I daresay no one else present had read—"

"*I* have read it, at any rate," said Bevan irritably. "It is a treatise on the theory of zoomorphic shape-shifting," he explained, aside to Gray; "you know, sir, that I am particularly interested in—"

"Yes, yes, Bev, all of Merlin knows it," Ransome interrupted, rolling his eyes.

No observer of this conversation, Gray reflected, could have guessed that last term Ransome had blacked the eye and bloodied the nose of a second-year student who had mocked Bevan's patched boots, or that what progress Ransome had made in Old Cymric was due almost entirely to Bevan's patient tutelage.

"But you see, Magister, he insisted—Professor de Guivrée did, I mean—that the author is quite wrong about things; I am not perfectly sure what things," Ransome confessed cheerfully, "but it seemed to be all of them. It all sounded reasonable enough to me at first, but *then* he said a perfectly absurd thing, and that is what I wanted to ask you about, sir."

He shook his flaxen hair off his face and sat back in his chair, looking expectantly at Gray. Beside him, Bevan closed his eyes briefly and put a hand to his brow as though his head ached.

"And," said Gray, after a moment, "what, Ransome, was the perfectly absurd thing?"

"Oh!" Ransome flushed a little. Then he sat up straight, folded his face up into a scowl, hooked one thumb into his waistcoat pocket, and produced a startlingly accurate approximation of Professor de Guivrée: "'It should surprise no one, however, to find such entirely wrongheaded ideas propounded by one who freely confesses to collaborating with . . . *females.*' I mean to say, Magister . . . !"

Gray smiled at him. "I do believe the tone of your mind improves, Ransome," he said. Ransome, he now recalled, had mentioned a large number of very clever sisters at home in Cirenceaster; perhaps they had had more influence on him than he allowed.

*Din Edin. Collaborating with females. That sounds very much like someone I know . . .*

"Bevan," said Gray, "what was the name of this shockingly broadminded scholar? I believe I may be acquainted with him."

On the morning of the first of June, having sat up very late with her books the previous evening, Sophie awoke much later than was her custom, and was in danger of entirely missing a lecture which she very much wanted to attend. She was hurrying out the door when her attention was caught by the stack of letters which she had brought up the previous afternoon, and which had lain all night forgotten on the rather unfortunate hatstand; and she paused, one hand still ungloved, to riffle through them. One directed to herself, in her sister Joanna's hand, she tucked into her reticule for later perusal. The rest were all directed to Gray, but only one (which looked rather the worse for its journey from Alba) seemed likely to be of immediate interest.

Gray himself emerged from the bedroom in his dressing-gown, yawning, as Sophie was pulling on her other glove. "Where are you off to so early?" he inquired.

"You remember," said Sophie; "Doctor Richardson, from Marlowe, is giving a lecture today—with illustrations—on his travels in Egypt." She made a grab for the letters and handed them up to him. "Look! There is a letter from your correspondent in Din Edin!"

Gray took the letters and frowned at them, in the manner of a man who has not yet eaten his breakfast.

"I overslept, and had not time to make tea," Sophie said, "but the kettle is on the hob—I must go, love, for I shall be late if I do not leave this moment."

Standing on tiptoe, with a hand on each of Gray's shoulders, she hastily kissed him, then darted out the door and down the stairs.

"You will never guess what was in that letter from Din Edin," said Gray, when they sat down to their rather spartan dinner that afternoon. He retrieved the letter from the pocket of his coat, together with a broken pen, two silver coins, a scrap of writing-paper scribbled all over with magickal formulae, and an owl's tail-feather.

"A translation of that very puzzling account of the Battle of the Antonine Wall?" Sophie hazarded, inhaling soup and exhaling suggestions, Joanna-like. "An antidote for wolfsbane poisoning? Another list of books which you must send northward at once, with all possible speed?"

"I said you would never guess," said Gray, laughi
invitation from Rory MacCrimmon, on behalf of the
tical Magick at the University, to lecture there all next yea
practice of shape-shifting."

Sophie put down her spoon with a clatter, looking satisfyingly
gobsmacked. "An invitation . . . an invitation to *you*?" Then it seemed
to occur to her that her astonishment might be taken amiss, and a
becoming pink flared in her cheeks. "That is—"

Gray grinned at her. "I can scarcely credit it, either," he said,
which was entirely true: He had hinted very hard over the course of
several months, but until now he had not thought he should succeed
in his object. "But it is so, indeed. And look!"

He passed the letter to her, pointing out the second paragraph on
the second page, and watched happily as she read:

> *As you have mentioned your wife's interest in magickal*
> *study, I wish to assure you both that she is of course*
> *welcome, should she wish it, as a student either in my own*
> *School or in the School of Theoretical Magick, whichever*
> *may be the most suitable . . .*

Sophie, round-eyed, put the letter down very nearly in her soup-
plate, from which Gray rescued it with the ease of long habit.

"And it *is* true that there are other women at the University?" she
demanded.

Gray nodded. "Several hundred of the undergraduates are women,
MacCrimmon says. He seemed surprised at my asking, though I had
told him of the dispute regarding female scholars when Bevan and
Ransome first brought it to my attention. You should be entirely unremarkable there, I daresay."

"You intend to accept his invitation, I hope?"

"I should very much like to do so, yes," said Gray. "Of course there
will be all manner of administrative and political details to sort out,
but if the notion pleases you—"

But as Sophie was not much interested in administrative or

political details, Gray was spared the danger of revealing that one of them consisted in securing her father's permission to undertake the journey, and another in arranging conveyance and accommodations for some at least of the quartet of Royal Guardsmen (two posing as undergraduates, one as a journeyman baker, and the fourth as a banker's clerk) presently responsible to His Majesty for Sophie's safety.

Sophie looked almost dangerously gleeful. "I should like it of all things," she said.

## CHAPTER II

# In Which Joanna Receives a Declaration

*"My dear,"* *said* Sieur Germain de Kergabet to his wife, "have you any objection to my taking Joanna with me today?"

Joanna sat on her hands in tense and hopeful silence. Though Sieur Germain, in his capacity as Lord President of His Majesty's Privy Council, seemed truly to value her assistance as a sort of unofficial undersecretary, he deferred always (or nearly always) to Jenny's wishes in the disposition of Joanna's time; Jenny having now attained that advanced stage of gravidity at which the slightest exertion fatigued her, who could deny her claim to Joanna's companionship and support?

"No, indeed," said Jenny, cheerfully; "Agatha and I will go on splendidly together, I am sure. Do you dine at home tonight, my dear?"

Without waiting to hear Sieur Germain's answer, Joanna excused herself and ran upstairs, lest Jenny should suddenly change her mind.

When she emerged from her bedroom, with her bonnet-strings dangling and a sheaf of her memoranda from the previous day's meetings in one gloved hand, she nearly collided with the nursery-maid bringing little Agatha downstairs to her mother.

"Aunty Jo!" said Agatha, putting up her arms. "Aunty Jo!"

Joanna therefore descended the stairs slowly and awkwardly, with Agatha on one hip and her papers and reticule under the other arm.

Sieur Germain was below in the hall with Mr. Fowler, putting on his hat. Joanna handed Agatha back to the nursery-maid and thrust her head into the breakfast-room to call a hasty farewell to Jenny; then she clattered down the stairs and, after taking a moment to tie her bonnet-strings and compose herself into the picture of a dignified young lady of good family, followed Sieur Germain and his secretary out of the front door.

The morning's meeting with the Alban ambassador was interrupted by a page bearing a message.

The outer sheet was directed to Sieur Germain and proved, on Joanna's unfolding it, to be a perfectly unobjectionable—though also perfectly unnecessary—memorandum. Folded within, however, was a second sheet of paper, directed to herself. With growing dread, she unfolded it and beheld what was unmistakably a sonnet:

> *In those dear eyes of soft and wintry hue*
> *Within whose depths my heart is daily drown'd—*

Flushing with mortification, Joanna stuffed the sonnet into her reticule and handed the memorandum along the table to her patron.

The meeting dragged on for a further hour, whilst Joanna took precise and dispassionate notes on Alban marriage customs for Sieur Germain and inwardly wrestled with the problem of the sonnet. She did not doubt its author, for it was by no means the first such . . . tribute . . . she had received; as feigning ignorance seemed only to have made her admirer more persistent, the time had clearly come to take a firmer hand.

When at last the conclave was adjourned, therefore, she touched her patron's arm and murmured, "I shall be with you shortly; I must just have a word with Prince Roland."

"Certainly," said Sieur Germain. "I shall be with His Majesty in the audience chamber."

Joanna smiled pleasantly at the Crown Prince, who could have no notion what his brother had been up to. "Ned," she said, "where might I find Roland?"

"Why, out in the gardens, I suppose," said Prince Edward, looking puzzled. "Or perhaps the library."

It took her some time to locate Roland, having first to shake off his elder brother's earnest escort and elude the assistance of a series of pages and stewards. At length, however, she ran him to earth in the Fountain Court, where he was engaged in teasing a peacock by imitating its gait.

Joanna stood for some moments unnoticed, watching him and shaking her head in affectionate exasperation; though a great trial to her at present, Roland had not lost his talent for making her laugh.

"Roland!" she said at last, waving his latest poetical effort at him. "Whatever do you mean by this?"

The Prince turned towards her with a glad cry of "Joanna!" Then seeming to register her general failure to fling herself into his arms, he said, somewhat deflated, "Did not you like my sonnet?"

"Roland," said Joanna, exasperation once again overriding amusement, "you have no business to be writing sonnets to me! Or to anyone else, for that matter—but most especially to me. What would your mother and father say?"

Roland looked down and scuffed at the turf with one shoe. "I do not see that it is any of their business," he muttered.

"Of course it is their business!" said Joanna. "You are second in line to the throne of Britain, until Ned has a son."

"But Sophie—" Roland began.

"I should not take Sophie as a pattern, if I were you," said Joanna. "Unless of course you have been yearning all this time for a draughty garret in Oxford, and said nothing about it to anyone."

Roland had, Joanna remarked not for the first time, a very stubborn set of the chin.

"She would not give up the man she loves, for any consideration," he said; "I call that noble and admirable."

With an effort, Joanna refrained from rolling her eyes. "You may call it what you like," she said, "so you do not attempt to follow her example. You had much better take up a less dangerous pastime than writing sonnets to unsuitable young ladies."

"I do not write sonnets to *unsuitable young ladies*," said Roland, visibly stung; "only to you."

Joanna's face heated, whether in outrage or embarrassment she hardly knew. "Roland, you cannot—"

"My dearest Jo!" He strode forward and, before she could retreat, had trapped both of her hands in his and was gazing earnestly down into her face. "You must let me tell you—"

"*Let me go.*" The words emerged with surprising firmness, considering the flailing panic of her thoughts, and he obeyed her at once, stepping back a pace with a look of some alarm. Immeasurably relieved, Joanna drew a breath and said more calmly, "I am going to give you some good advice, such as you might receive from your wise and sensible elder sister, if you had one."

*Instead of which, you have got Sophie,* she added, to herself. *The gods help us all.*

Roland groaned, but Joanna persisted: "If you must write love-poetry, choose some other object—the Lady Venus, perhaps, or the beauties of Gaia."

"I am not in love with Venus, or with Gaia."

Joanna nearly laughed aloud. "And you suppose yourself in love with me? Roland, you know I am extremely fond of you, but you have not the *least* idea what it is to be in love."

"Well, no more have you," said Roland, looking wounded.

"In any case," said Joanna, "even were your father inclined to let you choose your own bride without interference—which, for very sound reasons, he is not—there is not the least possibility of your ever being permitted to marry me. I must conclude, therefore, that you wish to persuade me to some dalliance; and that, I tell you plainly, you shall never do."

"That is not what I—that is not at all—" Roland stammered, crimson-faced. "I wish to persuade you to an engagement."

Joanna was so shocked that she laughed aloud. Surely, *surely*, he could not be serious? Quite apart from the far grander marriage which his father was already secretly arranging for him, how could he possibly imagine such a thing?

Roland's stiff posture grew stiffer, and his red face redder, at this effrontery.

"I do not see why my father should object," he said. He began to pace, forward and back around the near rim of the fountain. "My father likes you very much, in fact."

"As the Kergabets' protégée, and Sophie's sister, he may," said Joanna, who was herself rather fond of King Henry. "I daresay he finds me amusing. But your mother does not; and in any case it does not follow that I should for one moment be tolerated in the character of your wife. Roland, the daughter of a convicted traitor! You cannot seriously suppose it. But this is all beside the point, because *I do not want to marry you.*"

This, at last, seemed to make an impression; he stopped in his tracks and regarded her with a gobsmacked expression that nearly made her choke.

"Why not?" he demanded.

"Firstly," said Joanna, "because I am very fond of you and your brothers, and wish you every happiness, which is exactly what you should *not* have, if you married me. And, secondly"—raising a hand to forestall his protest—"because it is my dearest ambition not to be a princess."

This was not strictly true, in that Joanna had many ambitions more definite and positive than that one, but it was true enough for present purposes.

Roland, inexplicably, appeared heartened by what she had intended as a thorough set-down. "I shall say no more at present, then," he said cheerfully, and gave her his best courtly bow, with a brotherly kiss to follow.

And then, whistling, he strode away, leaving Joanna alone in the Fountain Court with the peacocks and her own exasperation.

The following day brought a letter from Sophie, the first in more than a fortnight. Joanna—suffering still under some irritation of spirits, as a result of her conversation with Roland—had gone for a ride in the park in lieu of both breakfast and morning calls. She had been particularly eager to avoid a planned call upon Mrs. Griffith-Rowland, with whom Jenny felt obliged by Kergabet's position to maintain an acquaintance, but whom both she and Joanna cordially disliked; having seen Jenny's carriage and pair in the stables, she was hopeful that she had succeeded in this object.

And, better still, a letter from Sophie! She snatched it up from the salver in the hall and broke the seal at once.

"Din Edin?" she said aloud, upon reaching the middle of the second page. Was it wise of His Majesty to be sending Sophie to Alba whilst he himself (or, at any rate, Lord Kergabet) was in the midst of negotiating Roland's betrothal to the Alban heiress? Did he, in the teeth of all evidence to the contrary, imagine her in the role of envoy? Surely not. But then, King Henry had a blind spot where Sophie was concerned, the size of the boulder of Sisyphus.

"Jenny!" Joanna bounded up the stairs to the first floor with no thought to propriety, or to the smell of horse which clung to her skin and clothing. "Jenny, you will never guess—"

She stopped short on the threshold of the morning-room, staring at the stranger who had taken possession of her accustomed seat.

"Why, Jo, dear!" Jenny turned, smiling, and beckoned her in. "I had nearly given you up for lost. Come in and meet our guest."

Joanna approached warily; the stranger rose to her feet, at which she seemed inclined to stare. She was tall—at least as tall as Jenny—

and the gown she wore, severely cut from some stiff, heavy fabric in an unflattering shade between mustard and chestnut, emphasised her bony wrists and elbows.

"Miss Pryce, may I present my sister-in-law, Miss Joanna Callender; Joanna, Miss Gwendolen Pryce."

Miss Pryce raised her head just long enough to meet Joanna's eyes as they exchanged ceremonious curtseys. The face thus glimpsed was all planes and angles and wide dark eyes: An interesting face, Joanna thought, which might have stories behind it.

This thought did not prevent her frowning when Miss Pryce resumed her former seat on the sofa, leaving Joanna to perch on the edge of a hard chair lest Madame Joliveau, the housekeeper, scold her for covering the furniture with horse-hairs.

"Miss Pryce has come to stay for a month or two, perhaps," Jenny continued, in the light, almost careless tone which (to Joanna's experienced ear) suggested that a great deal lay unspoken beneath her words. "Jo, as you are on your way upstairs, perhaps you will save me the climb, and show Miss Pryce her room? Madame Joliveau has had her things put in the small bedroom on the second floor."

"Of course," said Joanna. "If you will follow me, Miss Pryce?"

"Thank you, Miss Callender," said Miss Pryce, faintly; "thank you, Lady Kergabet."

"What brings you to London, Miss Pryce?" Joanna inquired, as they climbed the stairs to the second floor—this being the least intrusive of the many questions which presented themselves to her mind.

"My stepmother has persuaded my father that I ought to be a governess," said Miss Pryce. She glanced sidelong at Joanna.

Joanna frowned. "But Agatha is rather young for a governess, surely?" she said, puzzled. "She is not yet three." And Jenny had said *our guest*, not *the new governess*.

"Agatha—that is Lady Kergabet's daughter? No; to the Griffith-Rowlands, who are my father's neighbours in Clwyd, when they are not in London. They have got four children, and—"

She stopped abruptly, and shut her mouth into a tight straight line. Joanna revised her assumptions, and began to regret that she had not gone out with Jenny after all; evidently this had been no ordinary morning call. "I am a little acquainted with the family, yes," she said.

By now they had reached the small bedroom—it was the one Sophie had slept in, briefly, before her marriage to Gray, with the same kingfisher-blue coverlet still upon the bed—and Joanna opened the door and stood aside politely for Miss Pryce to enter it. A sad little trunk and threadbare carpet-bag, she saw, had been stacked beside the dressing-table.

"Oh!" said Miss Pryce, in a tone of gratified surprise. "How lovely!"

She stood in the centre of the blue-and-ivory carpet, gazing about her at the small, prettily furnished room that was to be hers, as though it had been a palace; and for the first time she smiled. A small and hesitant smile it was, but it gave her narrow, rather saturnine face the spark of animation which had hitherto been lacking. *Yes*, thought Joanna at once; *I rather thought so.*


Joanna left Miss Pryce to her unpacking and descended the stairs to demand explanations of Jenny.

Jenny, however, was not to be drawn.

"Her father and stepmother placed her in a very unfortunate situation," she said, "and I am helping her to get out of it"; and no more would she say about the sudden advent of Miss Gwendolen Pryce in Carrington-street, except to adjure Joanna to be civil to her.

"I hope I am civil to all your guests, Jenny," said Joanna, a little affronted—but only a little, for it was true that she was often quite uncivil about them after they had gone.

Jenny patted her hand in silent apology. "But what were you coming in such a hurry to tell me, Jo?" she said.

"Oh!" said Joanna, diverted instantly, though only temporarily, from Miss Pryce. "You will never guess: Sophie and Gray are going to Din Edin!"

* * *

Governess or no, Miss Pryce, it transpired, was very fond of children. Agatha—for whom Miss Pryce represented that almost magickal thing, a new and interesting person who did not speak to her as though she were a simpleton—was instantly smitten; and no sooner had Miss Pryce made Agatha's acquaintance than she was dragooned into a game of hunt-the-slipper in the nursery.

Joanna had other concerns to occupy her—chief amongst them, at present, the implications of Sophie's visit to Din Edin, which she must lose no time in bringing before Sieur Germain and Mr. Fowler; it was no hardship to be spared an afternoon of pretending to be baffled by Agatha's entirely transparent hiding-places, and she told herself sternly how absurd it was that she should begrudge Agatha's worshipful attention.

She penned a brief reply to Sophie's letter and, setting it aside, sat down again with her notes and Mr. Fowler's from the previous day's meeting with Oscar MacConnachie, which she had still to read through, transcribe into longhand, and copy out fair for Lord Kergabet's files. The first two of these tasks required her full concentration, but the last left her ample attention to spare for the puzzle of what—for it was evidently not a distaste to other people's children, and surely the owner of that dreadful gown and that pitiful carpet-bag was not the woman to abandon her situation on a whim—should have made Miss Pryce's situation with the Griffith-Rowlands so very unfortunate as to lead her to seek refuge in a household of complete strangers.

After dinner that evening, when the gentlemen joined the ladies in the drawing-room, Joanna at once sought out Sieur Germain; Mr. Fowler, she remarked with some amusement, appeared to be paying awkward court to Miss Pryce.

"And is it true that His Majesty has given his permission for this venture?" she demanded, having given him a précis of Sophie's letter.

"So it would appear," said Sieur Germain. "You know of course that His Majesty finds it difficult to deny your sister anything; and in any case I saw no compelling reason to advise him against it, as things stand. Of course she shall be guarded, as she is in Oxford—and Lord de Courcy will keep an eye, and can dispatch both of them back to Britain at once, should the need arise."

"I think you underestimate Sophie's capacity for attracting trouble," Joanna muttered—almost, but not quite, under her breath.

Sieur Germain smiled grimly. "Her father may, but I assure you that I do not."

"She has invited me to visit them in Din Edin next spring," said Joanna. "I thought, perhaps, we might turn such a visit to our own purposes . . . ?"

"I expect so." Sieur Germain's smile curved up in approval. "I expect so."


It soon became apparent that Miss Pryce was very fond of horses, as well as of small children; when not embroidering baby's gowns and bonnets for Jenny, or inventing tales for Agatha, or playing melancholy Cymric songs upon the pianoforte (to Joanna's ear, at any rate, they sounded very melancholy, but that might be only because they were very slow), she soon took to trailing after Joanna into the stable mews, and making friends with both the grooms and their charges.

Whilst driving out with Jenny in the carriage and pair one afternoon, Miss Pryce persuaded the Kergabets' coachman to let her take the reins briefly and, on the strength of this and subsequent trials, was permitted to drive Jenny without other supervision than Harry the footman. Joanna rather fancied that Miss Pryce hankered after a riding-horse; the Kergabets kept none in Town, however, but Joanna's own mare, Kelvez, and the surly gelding on which the grooms were mounted, for the purpose of escorting Joanna—and no gently bred young lady (Joanna included) was likely to wish to tackle Old Spider-Legs.

It was with considerable astonishment, therefore, that Joanna, upon entering the stable mews one morning, beheld both Kelvez and Spider saddled and bridled, and Gwendolen Pryce standing between them, both sets of reins clasped in her gloved left hand. Her ordinarily saturnine face wore an expression of unalloyed delight, which rendered her almost unrecognisable.

"What are you doing?" Joanna demanded. "Where are Gaël and Loïc?"

"I am going riding with you," said Miss Pryce. "Gaël and Loïc are gone out on an errand for Mrs. Treveur. Gaël is expecting to ride out with you when he comes back; I offered to tack up for both of you whilst they were out."

Spider snorted and tossed his head sharply, yanking on the reins; Miss Pryce, holding her ground without apparent effort, said, "None of that, you great lummox."

Spider snorted again, more quietly, shifted his great hooves, and was still. With her free hand, Miss Pryce reached up to gently rub his nose.

Joanna stared. She did not know how much of Miss Pryce's tale to believe—Gaël and Loïc surely were not such fools?—but many a young man's head was turned by a lovely face, and Miss Pryce's was very lovely when she smiled like that, with the flush across her sharp cheekbones and her dark eyes shining. That aside, Joanna was torn between an impulse to snatch the reins of her own mare from Miss Pryce's hand and leap into this adventure with both feet, and a dread of the likely consequences to Miss Pryce, to Lord Kergabet's grooms, and to herself if she did so. Perhaps, if they did not stay out too long . . .

"I like to ride very fast," she said, after a long moment's contemplation. "Gaël can sometimes keep up with me; I don't expect you can."

"We shall never know unless we try," said Miss Pryce.


To Joanna's further astonishment, Miss Pryce proved to possess a riding habit with split skirts, and rode astride—though upon reflection, it would have been more astonishing had she been able to find a lady's saddle to fit Spider, or to persuade him to be ridden sidesaddle.

"Many ladies ride so, in Clwyd," she said with a little shrug, when Joanna ventured to comment.

"In Breizh, also," Joanna conceded. "But I never learnt, because my father would not allow it."

In London, however, it was not at all the done thing, and they drew not a few stares on their sedate amble to the gates of the park, from the tradesmen and errand-boys who populated the streets at this early hour. But once on the bridle-path—where today it appeared they were the only ladies present—Joanna quite forgot to notice whether they were being looked at, for it seemed that Miss Pryce could keep up with her after all.

"Where did you learn to ride like that?" she demanded breathlessly, when they slowed to a walk on a gently curving stretch of the path to let the horses breathe.

Miss Pryce gave another of her little half shrugs. "My stepmother is frightened of horses," she said; "the more time I spent in the stables, or on horseback, the less I saw of her. And, of course," she added with a sort of determined nonchalance which invited Joanna to treat the thing as a most entertaining joke, "it irked her that I should be making friends with the grooms and stableboys, and not with the dull daughters of her horrid friends."

This was perhaps the longest speech Joanna had ever had from Miss Pryce, and certainly the most revealing; she was not altogether certain how to reply to it.

"Has Spider got his wind back?" she said instead, leaning down to lay a hand against Kelvez's flank. "We had best be getting back, before the Watch is called out after us."


"Joanna Claudia Callender, what in the name of Hecate were you *thinking*?"

Jenny was apparently too angry to sit still—or perhaps, just now, she found the advantage of height appealing—for she paced to and fro before Joanna and Miss Pryce, like a Breizhek fishing-yawl in a storm.

"If you like to make a spectacle of yourselves in public," she continued, "that is your own affair, and there are certainly worse means of doing so than by galloping through a public park at dawn. But to go there unescorted, against Kergabet's express instructions, and to involve Gaël and Loïc—not to speak of Mrs. Treveur—knowing that they should be held responsible, if you were to be hurt, or worse—"

She dropped onto the sofa, now, with a pained huff, and smoothed one hand absently over her belly.

"Please, Lady Kergabet," said Miss Pryce. "It was not Miss Callender's idea, and certainly not the grooms'; it was mine."

"I see," said Jenny, regarding her with narrowed eyes; turning once more to Joanna, she added, "And Miss Pryce forced you to accompany her, I suppose? Coerced you into the saddle at knife-point, perhaps?"

"No," said Joanna. She dropped her gaze to the carpet and the muddy toes of her riding-boots. "Of course she did nothing of the kind."

"I rather thought not," said Jenny.

She sighed, then, and said nothing at all for such a long time that Joanna had to fight a strong compulsion to fill the silence with explanatory and apologetic babble.

Miss Pryce did not resist so successfully. Joanna could see her hand twitching fretfully, and the sway of her skirts as she shifted from foot to foot; at last she burst out, "I only wanted to go riding. Mrs. Griffith-Rowland would not let me—she said I must remember my place, and astride a horse was not it—and Spider is a dear boy really—he would never hurt me, any more than Kelvez would hurt Miss Callender—and the weather was so fine this morning—I *am* sorry, Lady Kergabet, truly."

Her voice hitched; Joanna, looking up at her sidelong, saw her throat work. "I . . . I shall go upstairs and pack my things."

She curtseyed gracefully to Jenny, and turned away.

"Gwendolen," said Jenny.

Miss Pryce turned back towards her, face carefully blank.

"If you wished so much to ride," Jenny said, "why did you never say so?"

After a long silence, Miss Pryce said doubtfully, "I beg your pardon, ma'am?"

"Gwendolen, come here."

Miss Pryce hesitated—glancing aside at Joanna, who attempted an encouraging smile—and slowly, haltingly, crossed the room to stand before Jenny.

"When you spoke of packing your things," said Jenny, "where did you intend to go?"

Miss Pryce hung her head and spoke to her toes: "To the Griffith-Rowlands', I suppose, if they should consent to take me back. Or to my father's house, if he will have me." She paused, then raised her chin defiantly. "Had I any coin for the passage across the Manche, I should go to my sister Branwen, in Rouen. Though," she added, and here defeat crept into her tone once more, "I expect her husband would only send me back to Papa again."

"Sit by me," said Jenny, patting the sofa seat.

Miss Pryce sat, clasping her hands tightly in her lap. Joanna looked away from the flare of hope that lit her face; it felt wrong to witness this conversation, but worse to flee the room without Jenny's having dismissed her.

"I have welcomed you to my home," Jenny said, "and I did so because I wished to help you, and felt you might be . . . less unhappy here."

Joanna gripped her elbows in an effort to keep still; plainly, Jenny's words were not for Miss Pryce alone.

"I can do nothing for you if we cannot trust each other," said Jenny. "I recognise that your trust is not easily won, and I understand, I believe, why that should be so. But you have now lived a month in this house, and I think have had no cause for . . . alarm?"

"No, indeed, ma'am," said Miss Pryce, her voice so low as to be nearly inaudible. Joanna, by a sort of sympathetic instinct, shook her head.

"If any thing distresses or alarms you, you must tell me," said

Jenny. "And if there is anything you need, or that you wish for, you have only to ask, and I shall see what can be done. I do not wish to treat you like a child; you have had enough of that, I think. And no one here will pry into your secrets. But there must be no more trickery and sneaking, and certainly no more taking advantage of the servants. I wonder that you should have done so, being so recently in a like circumstance yourself."

Joanna peered sidelong at the occupants of the sofa, and saw that Miss Pryce was hanging her head.

"I did not think it through," she murmured.

"Jenny," said Joanna, "you will not punish Gaël and Loïc? I am sure they will not be so gullible again."

Miss Pryce's head snapped up, the better to glare at Joanna. Jenny, however, continued as though Joanna had not spoken. "You will apologise to Gaël and Loïc for involving them in your scheme," she said, "and to Treveur for the trouble he and his staff were at in searching for you; and then I think we need say no more about it."

Miss Pryce blinked. "I . . . I thank you, Lady Kergabet."

"Go upstairs and take off those horsey things," said Jenny, patting her hand.

Miss Pryce rose from the sofa; when Joanna made to follow her, however, Jenny's voice—soft, but with steel beneath—stopped her in her tracks: "Joanna, a word."

Joanna sat down again. "I know what you are going to say," she began. "I ought to have known better."

"You certainly ought," said Jenny. "And I ought to punish you—though it is something of a relief to see you behaving more like yourself."

Joanna blinked in surprise, but did not quite dare to demand an explanation.

"But you must understand, Jo, the position in which you should be putting Kergabet, if such . . . pranks were to become generally known. If we cannot rely upon you to behave with discretion—"

"I do understand," said Joanna. The spectre of some form of house arrest loomed before her: no rides in the park, no excursions to the

Palace, no useful or interesting work—nothing but morning calls from ladies who sought Jenny's influence and patronage—and edged her voice with desperation. "And I am very sorry. Truly, Jenny—I promise I shall not do anything of the sort again."

Jenny studied her a long moment, and at last said quietly, "I shall hold you to that promise, Jo."

The day's surprises were not yet at an end, for when Joanna opened the door to her bedroom, she found Miss Pryce—still dressed in her dishevelled riding-clothes—sitting before the unlit fire with her arms clasped about her drawn-up knees.

"What—" Joanna began, but Miss Pryce interrupted: "I am sorry, Miss Callender. It was wrong of me to attempt such a, such a *prank*, and foolish besides, and worse to involve you and the boys in it."

Joanna crossed the room and dropped to her knees on the little hearthrug, bringing her face level with Miss Pryce's. "It was very wrong, and very foolish," she agreed, "and I was wrong to connive at it." And then, setting aside Jenny's disappointment and her own self-reproach, she allowed the memory of the morning's gallop across the park to bubble to the surface of her mind, and to produce a rueful, reminiscing smile. "But the gods know when I last had such fun!"

Miss Pryce raised her eyes, and her startled expression gradually gave way to a hesitant smile. "I am glad you are not angry with me, Miss Callender," she said.

"I did not say so," said Joanna, honestly, "but I should be a hypocrite indeed, to blame you for a thing I did myself. And I wish you might call me Joanna, as my friends do," she added, "now that we have got into a scrape together, and lived to tell the tale."

Miss Pryce, improbably, blushed; a faint flush of rose across her sharp cheekbones. "Joanna, then," she said. "I should like that exceedingly; and you must call me Gwendolen, or—or Gwen."

"Gwen," Joanna repeated, grinning. "I wonder—when the fuss has died down a little—will you teach me to ride astride?"

## CHAPTER III

# In Which Sophie
# Makes a New Acquaintance

*Sophie looked about* her in mingled satisfaction and regret, surveying the trunks, crates, and bandboxes that filled what had so recently been her sitting-room. So different was this orderly, carefully planned departure from the hurried, stealthy dead-of-night flight that had been her leave-taking from Callender Hall that the two scarcely seemed to belong to the same category of ideas. Yet now, too, she was about to leave the comfortably familiar for the utterly unknown, and the disquieting echo reminded her what high hopes she had once had for her life at Merlin College.

Her year's examinations having been successfully concluded, and her life and Gray's tidily packed away and labelled, variously, for conveyance to their lodgings in Din Edin or for stowage in Merlin's attics, Sophie had nothing much to do but await the arrival of Sieur Germain's carriage, which was to convey them to London. She prowled restlessly through the denuded rooms and up and down the stairs, adjusting and readjusting the disposition of trunks and valises, peering out of the window in anticipation of the carriage, and attempting to quell the mixture of trepidation and delight that the prospect of a journey always kindled in her heart: not only their visits to her mother's kin in Naoned and to Gray's family in Kernow, but even the more frequent journeys to London, less than sixty miles off. Din Edin was nearer four hundred, and, moreover, in quite another kingdom. Sophie wavered between joyful anticipation and dread at the prospect of once again starting over in a strange city full of strange people.

*But it must be better to be at Din Edin, where there are others like me . . .*

Though, of course, even in Din Edin she should still be a princess, and it could not take long for the fact to be found out.

*Well, perhaps the Albans will not set so much store by it,* she told herself bracingly. *And I shall have Gray with me; that, at least.*

Gray himself at this point appeared at the door of the sitting-room, a little pink in the face—it was past Midsummer, and the day was already warm—and grinning broadly. "Your chariot awaits, *domina mea,*" he said, with a courtier's bow; then spoiling the effect entirely, he crossed the room in two long strides, caught her hands, and swung her about in a sort of impromptu gavotte.

"Gray!" Sophie protested, laughing. "What are you about?"

"I came up to warn you," he said; "they have all come to see us off in style."

"Who have?"

"Why, Evans-Hughes and Crowther and Pryce, and Master Alcuin, and Bevan and—"

Sophie ran back to the window, which she was sure she had been watching all the morning, and flung it wide to peer out into the street once more, but saw no one she recognised. "Gray, what—"

But even as she turned away from the window, a small thundering of booted feet sounded in the corridor, and a moment later a crowd of young men, seasoned by a very few white beards, erupted into the room—which suddenly seemed impossibly small—and burst into a reasonably tuneful chorus of "Gaudeamus Igitur."

Except that someone, Sophie recognised halfway through the first stanza, had improved it for the occasion: instead of *let us therefore rejoice whilst we are young,* their friends were singing *let us therefore rejoice in the Marshalls' good fortune,* and then, *may their road be smooth, may their beds be soft . . . may they detest Din Edin and soon return to us.*

Sophie laughed through a sudden lump in her throat.

She had ventured once to suggest a visit to Glascoombe, to take their leave of Gray's parents and his brothers; but the hour subsequently spent in reminiscing upon their previous visit, in the summer following their marriage, reminded her why the trial had not been repeated.

Instead they passed a pleasant se'nnight in London, with Lord and Lady Kergabet and Joanna, which allowed them to renew their acquaintance with Agatha and to be introduced to their new nephew, Yvon. Sophie was very fond of Jenny's children, and also very glad that they were Jenny's and not her own. As usual when the latter idea presented itself, she considered the example set by her own several parents—Mama, doting upon her at poor Joanna's expense; King Henry, torn always between love for his children and duty to his kingdom; Professor Callender, tirelessly self-interested and prone to forbid his daughters whatever thing they liked best—and by Gray's, to whom he was such a disappointment, and despaired.

Joanna appeared much subdued, both more sober and less voluble than on their previous visit, and much taken up with errands and tasks for Sieur Germain, and with the young Miss Pryce, whom Jenny declined to explain except as a guest of her house. Joanna resisted Sophie's attempts to discover what might be amiss by turning the conversation (to the children; to the recent betrothal of Edward, the Crown Prince; to Jenny's mother's most recent visit, and her tiresome celebration of Yvon over his elder sister), by requests to hear this or that song which only Sophie could sing for her, or by avoiding her sister outright. Sophie did succeed in extracting a promise from Joanna that she should make the Marshalls a visit in Din Edin in the spring; and from Jenny, a promise of regular reports on Joanna's welfare.

Joanna and she had spent so much of their lives apart—Joanna at school in Kemper more than half the year, whilst Sophie languished under her stepfather's interdiction-spell at Callender Hall; Sophie at Merlin College whilst Joanna was here in London, nearly sixty miles away—that it had not occurred to Sophie till now how different a separation of hundreds of miles might be. Of course she should not dream of giving up such an opportunity, for Gray and for herself, only because she missed her sister; but miss her she would, though Joanna seemed in no danger of missing Sophie.

Sophie's other duty whilst in London was to call upon the royal family, and upon the whole, the visit went off rather well. Her father and brothers were genuinely happy to see her, whilst Queen Edwina appeared to have grown either more reconciled to her stepdaughter or more skilled in concealing her resentment thereof, so that Sophie was able to converse with her, almost without guilt.

She was received in one of the Queen's private sitting-rooms, a chamber resplendent in blue watered silk and rosewood, and fed on cherries, redcurrants, strawberries and gooseberries arranged in gleaming pyramids, *petits fours*, profiteroles, and jam-tarts; for half an hour she patiently answered again a series of questions already asked and answered in her correspondence with her father.

"Must you go so far away, Sophie?" said Prince Henry, a little wist-fully, when the fruit and patisserie had all been eaten. He had shot up alarmingly since Sophie had last seen him, but had still the same round boy's face and mop of golden curls, and the same sweet treble.

"It is not so very far," said Sophie, as much to herself as to Harry; "not much farther than Rouen, and nearer than Breizh. And it is only for a year, after all. We expect to return by the end of next summer."

"But Alba is quite different to Britain," said Roland. "Mr. Hawkins—our tutor in history and Cymric, you know, Sophie—spent a year in Alba when he was young and has told Harry and me all about it. He is from the Border Country, and his grandmother came from Alba."

"It sounds a perfectly *savage* place," put in Harry, enthusiasm now kindling in his blue eyes. "Not civilised at all. In the mountains, he says, the men do not even wear trousers!"

Sophie blinked at the mental image thus conjured, and was glad that Gray had not come with her, for she could not have met his eyes without exploding into laughter.

The Queen said, "Harry!" in a reproving tone, and Henry's round face flushed.

"I meant," he said, "I did not—that is—Mr. Hawkins says that they wrap themselves up in woollen blankets, instead, so that they seem to be wearing skirts."

Sophie kept her countenance with some effort. "The Romans did not wear trousers, either," she pointed out, "but you would not call them uncivilised, surely?"

"No-o," said Harry.

"Oscar MacConnachie wears trousers," said Ned.

"Who?" said Harry.

"The Ambassador from Alba," said Roland, witheringly. "Idiot."

"Roland, for shame!" exclaimed Queen Edwina.

"Roland, Harry may not know all the same things you do," said Sophie quietly, "but that does not make him stupid."

Roland, who had shrugged off his mother's sharper admonition, went rather pink and reached out a hand to ruffle Harry's curls.

"I should quite like to go to Alba," he said, after a moment. "What an adventure it would be! But I am not at all sure it is a proper adventure for a lady, let alone the Princess Royal."

Sophie looked at him in surprise.

"Fortunately," she said, "I shall not be undertaking my adventure as the Princess Royal, but only as an ordinary undergraduate."

This repudiation of her ancestry she regretted almost immediately, and she glanced at her father to see how he bore it; he, however, was looking at Roland with a worried frown.

Sophie was still pondering what this might portend when the door at the far end of the room opened to admit a slight, hesitant young person in a rather elaborate gown, who proved to be the Lady Delphine d'Evreux, the Crown Prince's affianced bride.

"Oh!" she said, her voice so low and diffident as to be nearly inaudible, regarding stranger-Sophie in evident alarm. She made a neat little curtsey to the Queen and continued, "I beg your pardon, ma'am! I did not know—"

"Of course you are welcome, Delphine!" cried Ned, jumping up from his seat beside Sophie. "Do come in and meet my sister!"

It was quickly apparent to Sophie, first, that Lady Delphine had had only the haziest notion, before this, of Ned's having a sister; and, second, that if she was not (as Joanna had once said of Gray, to Sophie's chagrin) "violently in love" with Ned, she certainly admired him exceedingly.

A walk in the gardens was then proposed, and though the Queen excused herself, bidding Sophie a remarkably civil farewell, the rest of the party were soon strolling (or cavorting, in the case of Harry) amongst the perennial beds in the Midsummer sunshine.

Sophie found herself walking with Lady Delphine and attempting without success to picture her as the future Queen.

"I do think you are *terribly brave*, ma'am," she said to Sophie, staring up at her with enormous blue eyes. "To be going so far from home, to such a wild place as Alba."

"Do you so?" Sophie inquired, amused. "Indeed, I think you must be much braver than I. For"—she glanced over her shoulder at her father and lowered her voice—"all the kingdom knows that I ran away with an impoverished student rather than risk marrying an Iberian prince one day; yet you seem quite equal to the challenge of marrying Ned."

Lady Delphine's eyes opened still wider, and she seemed at a loss for words. Sophie, instantly repenting her mischievous impulse, said more soberly, "I am sorry, Lady Delphine; my tongue is apt to run away with me. Ned is a good, kind young man, and I am sure you shall be very happy together."

Lady Delphine gave her a diffident, rosy-cheeked smile. "I shall certainly do my best, ma'am," she said.

★    ★    ★

An alarmingly royal carriage and pair returned Sophie to Carrington-street, rather pale and silent, in time to dress for dinner.

"Was it very trying?" Gray asked, bending to kiss her as she sat pinning up her hair before the glass.

Sophie sighed. "Only moderately trying," she said. "I met Ned's bride-to-be; she called me *ma'am*, though she cannot be more than two years younger than I am, and when she admired my bravery in going off to live amongst savages who *do not even wear trousers*, I—"

But at this point she observed Gray's expression of amused bafflement in the glass before her and collapsed into silent laughter, tilting her chair back so far that it, and she, must have gone sprawling had Gray not caught and righted them in the nick of time.


In the drawing-room, Joanna was waiting to demand her sister's impressions of Lady Delphine d'Evreux.

"I hope," she said severely, when these had been decanted, "that you did not fill her head with romantical ideas. She may not be very much to our taste, but she is the very bride for Ned, and—"

"As Ned's wife she may do splendidly," Sophie interrupted. "They seem very taken with one another, and I wish them joy. But as Queen of Britain, Jo? What *can* my father be thinking of?"

"Perhaps," said Gray, "he may be learning from experience."

He had intended no insult to the late Queen Laora, but both Sophie and Joanna turned on him such coldly outraged looks that he at once saw, to his dismay, in what light his words had been understood.

"I meant," he amended hastily, "that perhaps Sophie has cured him of making political matches for his children, without regard to their temperaments."

This explanation sufficiently mollified Sophie, that she smiled briefly at him and tucked her hand into the crook of his arm; but Joanna only looked ironical, and turned away to speak to Sieur Germain.

## CHAPTER IV

# In Which Sieur Germain
# Receives a Letter, and Sophie and
# Gray Make a Journey

*On the morning* of the Marshalls' departure, the family's early break-fast was enlivened by the arrival of an express from Carlisle, bearing a letter for Sieur Germain from Lord de Courcy in Din Edin.

Sophie and Gray appeared not to remark this particularly, and having noted with passing interest the coincidence of a letter's com-ing from Din Edin on the very day when they were themselves to begin their journey thither, they returned to their tea and bread-and-butter. Gwendolen, arriving in the breakfast-room almost on Treveur's heels, had not so much as glanced at the thick letter in his hand, being more concerned with claiming her share of Mrs. Trev-eur's excellent bramble jelly.

Joanna, however, watched Sieur Germain, covertly but very closely, as he opened the Ambassador's letter and read it. Lord de Courcy habitually sent his ciphered dispatches by the dedicated cou-riers who rode once every fortnight or so between Din Edin and Newcastle-upon-Tyne (weather and other circumstances permitting), whence they reached London by the Royal Mail; it must be something very particular that led him to send an express from Carlisle, and she yearned to know what it might be.

By the set of Sieur Germain's lips when he laid the letter down again, the news it contained was less than welcome. "Joanna," he said quietly to her, "when you have finished your breakfast, go up to the library and make a fair copy of this letter, please."

Joanna glanced at her half-finished third helping of breakfast, and then at the sheaf of writing-paper in Sieur Germain's hand. Then scooping a last mouthful of bread-and-butter and bramble jelly into her mouth with one hand, she held out the other for the letter, and rose from the table with alacrity.

When Joanna returned to the breakfast-table not half an hour later, a moral struggle was going on in her mind, between her express promise not to discuss the details of Roland's Alban betrothal with anyone outside the close circle of those presently involved in its negotiation, and the question of whether to let Sophie and Gray take up residence in Din Edin at present was to send them into difficulty, and perhaps even into danger. When she had sat down with the cipher key and Lord de Courcy's letter, she had been thinking only of its possible implications for Roland; by the time she had finished deciphering and copying it, however, this new worry had taken possession of her thoughts.

Deciphered, the Ambassador's letter was brief and bald:

> *My Lord President: Be circumspect in your dealings with*
> *MacConnachie, and do not tarry about the business.*
> *Donald MacNeill*—ruler of Alba, and prospective
> father-in-law of Roland—*favours the match, but some in*
> *his court, of whom see list appended, are united and bitterly*
> *earnest in opposing it. They can imagine no other reason for*
> *H.M.'s interest than that the marriage is a bid to place his*
> *son on the throne of Alba, and thus absorb their kingdom*
> *into our own; and what is only bluster now, I fear will soon*
> *take some more concrete form. It is difficult to gather news*
> *from the remoter parts of the kingdom, but it seems clear*

*that the poor crops and the livestock plagues which have
been reported here and there will not be helpful to our cause,
being rumoured to be of either divine or magickal origin.
The attempted secrecy which H.M. and D.MacN. appear to
consider necessary, has only lent fuel to the fire of these
men's suspicions; therefore I hope that the business can be
concluded satisfactorily without loss of time, and the news
made public by official means* [this last underscored], *so
that all may proceed openly and aboveboard, and this
rumour-mongering be put to rest.*

> *I remain, &c.*
> *Courcy*

She could not, must not, betray Sieur Germain by telling Sophie
of the King's plans for Roland. Leaving aside all considerations of
honour and trust, to do so would expose her patron to attack by all
those who disapproved of her presence, even peripherally, in the discussions of the Privy Council; and, furthermore, she would be dis-
graced and, in all probability, sent away to live under the eyes of her
mother's cousin, Lady Maëlle, eye in the depths of Finisterre, where
she would go slowly mad with only Amelia and the housemaids for
company.

But if Lord de Courcy was correct in predicting . . . what? Joanna's
imagination at once flew from palace coups to civil war to bloody
riots in the streets of Din Edin—

"Jo?" Sophie's voice, a little sharper than was usual, jarred her
back to present reality.

"I . . . I am sorry," Joanna said. "I was thinking."

"Thinking something very unpleasant," said Sophie, sotto voce,
"to judge by the colour of your face."

"Sophie," said Joanna, looking down at her clasped hands, "will
you come upstairs with me for a moment? I am afraid there has been
some mistake about your books."

★  ★  ★

"You know that I am a great deal with Sieur Germain," she said, when she had closed the door of her bedroom behind her sister, "in council meetings and the like; and from time to time one hears things. I have lately heard—" How to convey her warning, without betraying the trust of others?

*When embroidering a falsehood, work in as many threads of truth as you may.*

"There have been poor crops in parts of Alba," she went on, "and cattle disease and the like; and there are rumours of unrest, which is not to be wondered at in the circumstances. I . . . I do not like to think of your going where there may be trouble."

Sophie's dark eyes widened; she sank into the carved chair before the dressing-table and folded her arms along its back. "Truly?" she said. "But cannot we help them, then? There has been no war between Britain and Alba for some years; is not the present King . . . if not our ally, at least not our enemy? Their gods are not ours, I know, but surely he would accept any help we might usefully offer, if his people are starving?"

"His people are not starving," said Joanna hastily. *Yet.* "I am only remarking that when Fortuna turns her wheel, and one finds oneself under it, one is apt to seek someone to blame. If what I have been hearing is true, it seems some in Alba believe there is magick behind their misfortune, and mages behind the magick."

Which was true enough, in some lights, with the wind in some quarters: Donald MacNeill was a mage, after all, and his daughter also—not to mention Prince Roland.

Sophie's face was very still as she thought all of this through. "Thank you, Jo," she said at last, "for looking before we leap."

"But you intend to leap nevertheless," said Joanna.

"Jo, you know what an opportunity this is for us!" There was a faint edge of pleading in Sophie's tone, which anyone less well acquainted with her could not have discerned; Joanna rather wondered that she did not bolster her argument by reminders of Joanna's own past leaps into hazardous circumstances. "And I cannot think that Rory MacCrimmon would invite us if there were any danger. And besides that, Jo, I . . . I have tried never to mention it, but things have not been altogether easy at Merlin."

"I know that." Joanna spoke before she thought.

Sophie blinked. "You know it? How?"

*By what you did not say.* But Joanna was spared the necessity of formulating a reply by Gray's choosing that moment to call up the stairs, "Sophie? Have you nearly finished?"

"Nearly," Sophie called back. She had clearly no intention of cutting this conversation short, but she could not—or, at any rate, almost certainly would not—physically restrain her sister, and Joanna was on her feet and out the door before Sophie had even left her chair. She paused on the threshold to say, in an urgent undertone, "Sophie, do please be careful!"

"I am always careful," said Sophie, primly and, in Joanna's opinion, most untruthfully.

Joanna stalked away, down the stairs and past her brother-in-law, lest she say something Sophie might find difficult to forgive. It was cold comfort to reflect that even had she divulged the entire truth, it was very unlikely to have done any good.


Gray had been very firm and tediously specific in negotiating with his father-in-law's equerry the details of their conveyance to Din Edin. He was glad of it when, emerging from Jenny's front door in her sensible travelling-dress, Sophie regarded the sleek black barouche with its pair of bays, and the solidly built coachman standing by the near-side horse's head—all, as eventually agreed, quite free of the royal arms and livery—and gave a just-audible sigh of relief. If she also remarked upon the familiar faces of the two outriders—Tredinnick and Goff, whom Gray had last seen dressed as Oxford undergraduates loitering along the Broad—she gave no sign;

Gray nodded at them, however, in his customary manner, and they returned his acknowledgement with a pair of cheerful salutes.

Joanna came bounding down the front steps, followed more sedately by Miss Pryce, and stood at Sophie's shoulder; Miss Pryce hung back, as she had done throughout their stay at Jenny's—as though she should have liked to imagine herself a full participant in whatever was going forward, but could not quite bring herself to believe it.

"Good morning, Cooper!" said Joanna, addressing the coachman. "How are you? I hope your lumbago is quite gone away?"

"Why, Miss Callender!" Cooper produced a frank, engaging grin. "Yes, thank you, I am very well."

Joanna looked him up and down approvingly, then stood back a little to examine the carriage. "I half expected to see the royal arms upon the door," she remarked, sotto voce.

"That is because you have no faith in my powers of persuasion," said Gray.

Joanna snorted.

"Sophie," she said, "Gray, this is Edwin Cooper. Cooper, Mr. and Mrs. Marshall."

Then, her social duty discharged, she wandered away towards the horses.

"Your servant, madam. Sir." Cooper's nod, Gray was pleased to note, was respectful but in no way servile.

"Well met, Cooper," said Gray.

Sophie caught Gray's hand in hers and squeezed it. "We are going to Din Edin," she said, so softly that he had to duck his head towards hers to catch her words. "Really going."

"Yes," he said, smiling down at her. "Our great adventure."

Her answering grin broke over her face, transforming it from sober thought to sudden, luminous beauty. Out of the corner of his eye, Gray saw Cooper rock back in astonishment, and he tensed warily. But in an eye-blink Cooper had recovered himself, smiling benignly at Sophie.

"I think we shall get on very well together," said Gray.

★  ★  ★

"I like your sister," said Gwendolen, in a considering tone, as the Marshalls' carriage retreated. "She does not give herself airs."

Joanna bristled. "Of course she does not!"

"You need not puff up like an angry hedgehog, only because I paid your sister a compliment," said Gwendolen, now sounding quietly amused. She was holding Yvon in her arms, and absently kissed his soft fair hair.

"A compliment, was it?"

"Anyone would think, to hear you, that you had not been at Lady Brézé's evening party with Lady Kergabet and me last Luneday," said Gwendolen, "or had somehow failed to hear her dropping Queen Edwina's name in every other sentence, because her daughter was at school with Her Majesty. At present, I can think of no higher compliment to bestow."

Joanna tried her best not to chuckle at this, and failed.


The early part of the journey north passed uneventfully enough for even Gray's taste. Their borrowed carriage was well-sprung and comfortable; Cooper knew his business, and treated both passengers and horses with appropriate care; Tredinnick and Goff were polite and unobtrusive. They went leisurely, with frequent pauses, leaving (as Cooper put it) no local sight unseen.

In the Peaks of Derbyshire, Sophie scandalised Cooper et al. by scampering about on rock outcrops from which she might easily have fallen to her death. Once or twice even Gray was rather alarmed, but when she came hurtling down from one such promontory, assuring him that he had never seen such a prospect, he was helpless to resist her plea that he come up at once and look at it, and soon found himself scrambling after her.

"There!" Sophie exclaimed breathlessly, flinging out her arms. "Is that not the finest thing you ever saw?"

It was a fine thing, indeed. The sun shone, and a fresh breeze chased towering cloud-ships across the brilliant summer sky; spread out below their rocky perch, the hills and valleys made an ocean of velvet-green and gold, dark-shadowed where a cloud passed overhead, then suddenly flaring into brilliance.

Gray glanced sidelong at Sophie, poised no more than a foot from a sheer drop, her bonnet dangling by its strings from one hand, and was suddenly reminded of their voyage from Rosko to Portsmouth, when she had stood in the prow of a fishing-yawl and wrestled with her conscience. He shivered.

"Come away from the edge, *kerra*," he said. "The prospect is equally splendid from here, I assure you."

She turned and gave him an odd, impenetrable look, but reached amiably enough for his outstretched hand, and allowed herself to be drawn back from the precipice and into his arms.

"I thought nothing could be as magnificent as the Breizhek coast on a windy day," she said, "but this country is quite as magnificent, in an altogether different way. Truly the gods who made this kingdom are to be admired."

Gray smiled fondly down at the top of her head. "You have found some new source of magnificence nearly every day of this journey," he said.

Sophie turned in his arms and looked up at him, a puzzled frown creasing her brow. "Have not you?" she asked. "But then, I suppose you have done more travelling than I . . ."

Gray reined in half a dozen fatuous or dangerous replies—beginning with *I have no eyes for magnificent landscapes when I am looking at you* and ending with *It makes me furious to think how long you were caged and miserable, when you might have been storing up memories full of joy*—and instead said, with perfect truth, "You have more capacity for wonder, Sophie, than anyone else I know."

She gazed at him for a long moment, her head on one side, and finally said, "I love you very much, Gray Marshall, but sometimes I cannot at all understand you."

Then she grinned, pulled his face down to hers, and kissed him.

"I think," said Gray rather breathlessly, some time later, "I think we understand one another well enough."

They arrived late that afternoon, by prior arrangement, at the Plough and Pipes. Cooper, as was his habit, disappeared with the landlord to see to their several accommodations; Gray had long ago concluded that his object was, at least in part, to shield Sophie from the frank discussion of such matters as His Majesty's requirements for her security, which must be necessary at each halt. On this occasion, however, he reemerged into the inn-yard at a rapid walk, wearing a thunderous frown; Gray at once caught Sophie's arm and murmured, "Be careful. Something's amiss."

Cooper strode across the inn-yard to stand by the carriage door, as though meaning to open it. "Mr. Marshall," he said in a low voice, "ma'am, I think it best we don't remain here. I believe the landlord has been telling all the neighbourhood about his illustrious guest, and I'm thinking you'll not be very pleased with the results."

Sophie scowled.

"What other choices have we in this neighbourhood?" Gray asked. "I seem to remember passing another inn along the road . . . ?"

"The Drowned Man, aye," said Cooper. He glanced sidelong at Sophie. "The horses have got another few miles in them, once they've been fed and watered and rubbed down. With your permission, sir, I thought to ask for a meal to be put up, in case you should be hungry before we reach the Drowned Man."

Gray strongly suspected that Cooper had ordered the said meal already, and was only couching the information as a request for permission in an effort to avoid ruffling anyone's feathers. If so, the effort was successful, for Sophie at once said, "That is very well thought of. Yes, please do so. And be sure they put up enough for five; for you know that inn at Hathersage, when we asked for a cold collation, gave us scarcely enough for two, and we were all as ravenous as—as my sister Joanna, after scrambling about all afternoon."

Cooper nodded gravely and went away to see to the horses.

"We may as well stretch our legs whilst the opportunity offers," said Sophie philosophically, and they descended from the barouche and strolled arm in arm about the inn-yard.

It was not long, however, before murmurs and flashes of movement began to catch at the corners of Gray's eyes, and not much longer before it became clear that they were already the object of highly unwelcome attention; the inn's upstairs windows were lined with inquisitive faces, and stableboys and serving-girls peered around posts and door-frames to stare. Sophie's gloved fingers bit painfully into his arm; a shimmer of magick, intimately familiar but not his own, ran through him; and from one moment to the next the faces grew puzzled, and the murmurs changed in tone from agitated interest to bewilderment, then died away: Sophie had caused herself and him to become . . . unremarkable.

"I am so tired of hiding," Sophie sighed. "I wish we need not do it."

Gray stopped walking and turned back to face her. "I hope you are not hiding on my account," he said.

Sophie raised her face to his, wearing an expression of the utmost bafflement. "Of course not," she said. "No one would stare and point at *you*, if you were not in my company."

From anyone else, this statement could only have been construed as insulting. Gray considered its source, however, and—after counting ten—said only, "And I should not object to being stared and pointed at, if you did not mind it."

Gray remembered how self-conscious he had once been about his height, and considered how much less trying it was to wear his six feet and three inches with confidence and authority than to be continually attempting to fold himself out of everyone's way. Sophie, he thought, would be happier when she had learnt to wear her title as though it belonged to her, rather than putting it on, like an ill-fitting garment and a pair of boots that pinched, only when some particular occasion obliged her to do so.

"But I do mind it," said Sophie, in a tone of such finality that Gray could find no purchase for argument.

They sat together in the barouche, gazing in opposite directions, until Cooper returned with the horses and a hamper, and were conveyed in near silence to the more modest comforts of the Drowned Man.

The official letter of invitation provided by the University, and letters of reference from Lord de Courcy, Lord Kergabet, and Oscar Mac-Connachie, smoothed their passage from the Border district into Alba proper; Gray deduced from the nonchalance of the guardsmen and officials on both sides of the Roman Wall that they had taken the *Mr. and Mrs. Marshall* mentioned in these documents at face value, and was glad to have been spared both any repetition of their reception at the Plough and Pipes, and the strop from Sophie which was likely to follow.

The green or golden fields and sheepfolds, tidy cottages, and occasional great houses, the shepherds and the gangs of harvesters working in the fields, continued very like—if differing in style—from England on the one hand, to Alba on the other; until, on a sunny August day some forty miles past the frontier, they passed a field of what might have been barley, lying black and blighted. After it came another, and another; the air grew hazy, and the horses snorted at the oily smoke and stench of what proved at length to be a farmer burning half a hundred carcasses of sheep upon a pyre; so many blighted fields were there that for two hours or more, there was nothing to be seen but blackened stalks of grain, and withered marrows, and wasted beasts. The grim farmer cremating his flock aside, they saw no people at all.

"Joanna was not exaggerating," said Sophie, as Cooper urged the nervous horses past a paddock in which three shaggy, rheumy-eyed ponies chewed listlessly at the remains of a stand of clover. "But she said the people were not starving; I am not sure I can believe it."

She shivered; Gray tucked one arm about her, drawing her in closer to his side. "You must write to your father, when we are come to Din Edin," he said. "I am sure something can be done."

"Yes," said Sophie, "I suppose so."

She did not point out, though she must see the implication as well as Gray did, that what Joanna knew of Alba's circumstances, surely His Majesty must know also.

The blight ended as abruptly as it had begun, some few miles onward, and they saw no more such sights before they reached Din Edin.

## PART TWO

# Alba

## CHAPTER V

# In Which Gray and
# Sophie Land on Their Feet

*September had almost* begun by the time the wheels of the Marshalls' borrowed equipage clattered onto the streets of Din Edin. Gray stared around at the bustle and hum of the great city—no match for London, of course, but many times as populous as Oxford, and a dramatic change from the tiny villages and small farming towns through which they had been passing. Beside him, Sophie was blending in, or so he judged by her intent listening stillness and carefully expressionless face.

"Is all well, *kerra?*" he asked, as the barouche slowed to allow the passing of a heavy waggon piled high with barrels that sloshed.

Sophie turned and looked up at him; her dark eyes were wide and fathoms deep. "There are so many people," she said, wonderingly, "and not one of them knows or cares who I am, or who my father is."

Gray grinned and squeezed her hand. "It is fortunate that I know you so well," he said; "you must be sure not to say such things to strangers."

"You do not know me at all, if you suppose for a moment that I should," she retorted, but though she attempted a scolding tone, she was smiling. Then something caught her eye and she sat up straight, all eager attention: "Look there! It is one of Harry's *men without trousers!*"

Gray turned his head sharply, startled. But though the man in question indeed wore no trousers, he was fully clothed in some sort of wrapped and gathered garment, in a colourful woven pattern of scarlet and green and gold. This together with a splendid head of ginger hair, and a beard to match, made him stand out in the crowded street, but no one apart from themselves seemed to find him an object of interest.

They drew up at last before a modest house in Drummond-street, the door of which was opened, before Gray's upraised hand had let the knocker fall, by a young woman in a green gown. Tall and slim, with auburn hair and a constellation of freckles across her fine straight nose, she smiled at Gray and Sophie as though perfectly delighted to see them.

"You are Magister Graham Marshall?" she said, and to Sophie, "and Domina Sophie Marshall?"

Gray, bemused, nodded.

"Welcome to Din Edin, Magister, Domina. I am Catriona Mac-Crimmon—Rory MacCrimmon is my brother," she added, by way of explanation. She spoke in a softly accented and curiously formal Latin. "I feared that I should not recognise you, but the moment I saw you I was altogether certain. My brother described you very precisely."

"How could he?" demanded Sophie, startled into speech. "He has never met either of us!"

"I should imagine that he asked his friend Mór MacRury," said Miss MacCrimmon cryptically. Then she smiled again. "Now, do come in and be welcome to our house! You have been travelling; I am sure you must be weary."

The business of dispatching Cooper and their baggage to their own lodgings in Quarry Close, and consulting as to the location of the nearest stabling for the horses, took some little time. At length, however, Gray and Sophie found themselves comfortably ensconced in a cluttered, welcoming sort of library-*cum*-sitting-room, partaking of tea and oatcakes whilst their hostess decanted from them, with an efficiency which Gray felt Joanna might have envied, the tale of their journey.

Catriona—for so she at once insisted they address her, almost before they had finished drinking from her chased copper welcome-cup—seemed so much au fait with the life of the University that Gray was unsurprised when Sophie asked her, rather hesitatingly, whether she was herself a student there.

"Oh! No," Catriona laughed. "That is, I did study along with Rory for a year—you may not know that we are twins?—but I have not the patience to make a proper course of study in one subject; I much prefer to keep house for him and be left to read whatever I will. But you are to be a student, I understand?"

"Yes, indeed," said Sophie, with one of her slow-blooming smiles. "Though perhaps I may also be insufficiently patient. I suppose we shall find out!"

"I hope at least you will come to all of my lectures," Gray said, "though I dare say you will find them very dull."

Catriona looked uncertainly from one of them to the other, as though she did not altogether know what to make of this remark.

"He means," said Sophie, with a brief reproachful glance at Gray, "that he has nothing to say which I have not already heard. But I trust that may not be so, for you have a prodigious library here, have not you? And I dare say it has a great many books in it, Gray, which even you have not read."

Catriona's enthusiasm for the University Library carried the conversation happily forward until a bustle at the front door and a bass-baritone hail in which Gray could distinguish almost nothing but Catriona's name announced the arrival of some other person.

"Ah! Here is Rory," Catriona exclaimed, jumping up from her seat on a sofa the other end of which held a tall, precarious stack of codices and a glossy ginger cat.

She ran lightly out of the room. When she returned a few moments later, she was towing by the hand a young man a little taller than herself, with hair like rings of polished copper and the same freckled nose and bright, dancing green eyes.

"Welcome!" he said, turning on Gray the widest, most disarming grin the latter had ever seen. "I am delighted to see you both arrived here in one piece—that is to say . . . well! You will forgive my clumsy Latin, I am sure."

Rory MacCrimmon shook Gray by the hand—his hand was large and calloused, his grip confident—but made Sophie a very creditable leg, which performance made her blush becomingly.

"I hope you have got something splendid for dinner today, Catriona," he said.

If the dinner was not so splendid as those they had eaten in London, the simpler fare was plentiful, well seasoned, and delectable, and Sophie thoroughly enjoyed both the food and the society.

"My colleagues are agog to meet you," said Rory MacCrimmon to Gray. "A true shape-shifter! And the students, also. I predict you shall have a train of apprentices stretching from the University to Castle Hill."

His sister smiled gently at Sophie. "I hope you are not inclined to jealousy, Domina," she said.

"Of course not," said Sophie at once—though as the conversation moved on, it occurred to her to ponder whether this was only because she had never had the least cause, and whether things might be different at the University, where clever women with an eye for Gray's (to Sophie's mind, very considerable) charms were likely to be all about them.

She was not long left to ponder, however, for Rory MacCrimmon turned to her with his engaging grin and asked, "Have you ambitions in the shape-shifting line yourself?"

"Not as such," Sophie replied, cautiously, "though I confess I should rather like to be able to fly, as Gray does."

Catriona shuddered.

"Should you, indeed?" said Rory. "I have not much head for heights, myself. My own project, as I have explained to your husband, is the form of a wild cat—now, wait a moment, where have I—"

And over his sister's protests, he leapt up from the table and ran out of the room, to return an awkward few moments later brandishing a sheaf of anatomical drawings and watercolour sketches; and the next quarter-hour or more was enthusiastically devoted to the physiology and physiognomy of the Alban wild cat.

Sophie entered gladly into the men's enthusiasm, but Catriona, she saw, did not; perhaps keeping house for her brother had given her her fill of wild cats.

"Have you any projects in train at present, Miss MacCrimmon?" Sophie inquired, when a spirited discussion of the relative merits of feline and strigine camouflage, to which she could contribute nothing, offered her an opportunity for escape.

"Catriona, please," her hostess reminded her. "I have been dabbling in historical research; some of the clan histories make very interesting reading."

"Oh!" said Sophie, her interest piqued. "Have you any recommendations for a newcomer to the field? Though of course," she added, more doubtfully, "I suppose the books will be all in Gaelic?"

Catriona patted her hand in a familiar and (if it was not only Sophie's fancy) rather condescending manner. "I shall look you out some books tomorrow," she said kindly, "and bring them round when I come to call on you. And of course there are many more in the Library, in all manner of languages! Though you shall begin learning Gaelic soon enough—you know, do you not, that the University holds a daily tutorial for the foreign students and the visiting Fellows?—you must not be discouraged, however, if you find it does not come easily to you; Gaelic is not so easily learnt as Latin or Français."

The admixture of kindness, condescension, and pity in this speech left Sophie blinking in confusion, and she did not know quite how to answer it; there had been, however, an offer of books, to which there could be no other response than heartfelt thanks.

"I am much obliged to you," she said, therefore.

\* \* \*

It was late in the evening when, escorted by Rory, Sophie and Gray set out on foot for Quarry Close. The day had been fine and warm; the evening was crisp, clear, and still, portending chilly days and frigid nights in the darkening of the year. The streets around the University were lit by magelight lanterns mounted on iron or wooden poles, so that their progress along the pavement took them from light to shadow to light again.

Sophie, warm in the circle of Gray's arm about her shoulders, listened attentively to Rory MacCrimmon's account of a scandal in what would seem to be the University's equivalent of Merlin's Senior Common Room, involving the theft of a manuscript and a series of unpleasant insinuations relating to an undergraduate. It did not seem to occur to him (and certainly should never have occurred to Gray) that she ought not to hear such a scurrilous tale; this lack of constraint completed the work begun by Catriona's enthusiasm for the University Library, leaving Sophie feeling taller and broader of shoulder as well as (perhaps paradoxically) comfortably invisible. *Perfectly unremarkable, Gray said, and so I shall be!*

*At least, until someone here learns the truth.*

She put that thought resolutely away from her—it was bound to happen, and the gods knew that she had lived through worse!—and raised her face to smile at the midnight-dark sky.

Lamplight and magelight gleamed in the windows of the narrow stone-faced houses of Quarry Close. To one of these, with a grin and a flourish, Rory conducted them, handing over a heavy brass door-key which, when Gray tried it in the lock, stuck only a little.

Then he was striding away in the direction of Grove-street, calling a cheerful good-night over his shoulder, and Gray and Sophie were alone in their new home.

"Our own house!" cried Sophie, in high delight. "Or very nearly.

Oh, but, Gray, I am afraid I shall be a shocking housekeeper. I ought to have watched Cousin Maëlle more closely . . ."

"You forget," said Gray, grinning down at her, "that I was an impoverished student for many years before I met you. What I do not know about subsisting on bread-crusts and rinds of cheese is not worth knowing."

For just a moment, he saw, she feared he might be in earnest, and the idea of his living for years on crusts of bread wrung her tender heart. Then she caught his intent and frowned at him for jesting on such a subject—but with a smile dancing in her dark eyes.

"Besides," Gray went on, more practically, "Miss MacCrimmon has engaged a daily woman for us, and I am sure we shall have no difficulty."

Perhaps more to the point, Sophie's father had made them a very generous allowance, delivered via Edwin Cooper—to Gray, who was not too proud to accept His Majesty's help, rather than to Sophie, who should certainly have protested—together with the promise that Lord de Courcy, His Majesty's ambassador in Din Edin, might be applied to for the relief of any financial difficulties arising during their sojourn there. Gray had no notion of their falling into any such difficulties—their wants were not extravagant, and the stipend provided by the University to its visiting lecturers more generous than he had expected; in addition to which, he had still his Fellowship from Merlin—but he had welcomed the assurance all the same.

Sophie was soon flitting about the tiny house, a little globe of magelight hovering at her shoulder, peering through windows and opening cupboards. There was, unsurprisingly, no pianoforte, but Gray studied the sitting-room and dining-room, calculating angles and clearances under his breath, and soon saw where, with a little judicious rearrangement of the existing furnishings, one might be installed (if it could first be got through the front door). He made a mental note to discover as soon as possible where an instrument might be hired or, if that were impossible, purchased.

Sophie's bright laughter rang out somewhere overhead.

"Gray!" she called. A small magelight came bouncing down the staircase and hovered at Gray's shoulder. "You must come up and see this ridiculous bed!"

Gray smiled, barred and warded the front door, and took the stairs two at a time.

The bed was indeed a trifle absurd: set into a sort of loft, so that it must be reached by a small ladder, and hung with curtains so heavy, and so hideous, that they might have been designed to repel armed attack. A massive brass warming-pan hung beside the hearth, and a row of deep drawers was set into the wall beneath the bed; Sophie knelt and pulled two of them open, revealing at least three tightly folded eiderdowns. Stooping to pull open the third, Gray was not entirely surprised to discover a stack of woollen blankets.

"All of this does make one suspect," said Sophie, rising and dusting off her skirts, "that winters in Din Edin may be colder than we are accustomed to."

"If that is so, I am sure we shall find ways to keep warm," said Gray, resolutely straight-faced. To his great satisfaction, Sophie burst into delighted laughter.

"I was never in the slightest doubt," she said, and, leaning her hands on his shoulders, bent to kiss him. "We both are capable of some cleverness, after all."

Gray felt that he could never tire of that particular juxtaposition of solemn face and slyly laughing eyes.

When they ventured downstairs the next morning, Catriona's daily woman—by name Donella MacHutcheon, Catriona had told them—was sweeping the kitchen floor and singing in Gaelic, and the small table was set with a round brown teapot and a breakfast of what proved to be oatmeal porridge, butter, and cream.

Conversation with Donella MacHutcheon was greatly hampered by their having no language in common but Gray's few words of

Gaelic. Sophie, however, broke the ice by at once taking up the melody of the song Donella MacHutcheon had been singing and asking, in Latin but with eloquent gestures, to be taught the words. When she sang back the first strophe and refrain in her clear, pure soprano, note-perfect, and was rewarded with a wide, astonished smile, Gray smiled too, in pride and no little relief; nothing could be less like the expression which Sophie and he had been accustomed to see on the face of Mrs. Haskell.

After breakfast and some desultory attempts at unpacking, they sallied forth into the streets of Din Edin. The day was bright and crisp, and the neighbourhood of the University filled with people variously loitering, strolling, and hurrying in every direction, exactly like the streets of Oxford on a brisk September morning—but for the preponderance of spoken Gaelic.

"We must find a bookshop, first of all," said Gray decidedly; "tutorials or no, we shall need books to learn Gaelic from. And then, *cariad*, should you like to look about the University proper?"

"I should quite like," said Sophie, "to see the Library which Catriona MacCrimmon spoke so fondly of last night. And, Gray—"

She paused, and they walked on in silence for some moments before she said, "Might we inquire whether somewhere in the University buildings there is an instrument that I might practise on? Somewhere where I should not be in anyone's way?"

It was on the tip of Gray's tongue to say, *I have a much better idea than that*; but it occurred to him that it would be better still to surprise Sophie with a pianoforte of her own, and so instead he said, "Of course!"

They found three bookshops within a stone's throw of one another. The first was dusty and smelt very strongly of cats; the second was so aggressively clean and well ordered that they scarcely dared take any book down from the shelves to look at. The third, however, possessed only one resident cat ("So important for the mice, you see") and just that small degree of disorder which seemed to invite serendipitous discovery.

"So you are the famous Sasunnach shape-shifter!" the proprietor exclaimed, when Gray had explained their errand; observing Gray's astonished expression, he continued, "The one whose praises Rory MacCrimmon has been singing all summer."

"Then I suppose I am he," Gray said; he blushed to the roots of his sandy curls, and Sophie concealed a grin.

They left the shop with their arms full of codices neatly bundled with twine, and, by unspoken agreement, turned their steps towards Quarry Close rather than continue their explorations thus burdened. Donella MacHutcheon had gone home, they found, but she had left their dinner on the table, covered by a linen towel, together with a bowl of apples, green-gold streaked with red. Sophie was abruptly transported to the kitchen of her childhood, and bit into an apple with a pensive sigh.

Gray for once did not seem to remark her distraction; he palmed two apples, dropped them into the pocket of his coat, and held out his hand to her, saying, "The University Library, *cariad*? What say you?"

Or perhaps, Sophie reflected later, having spent the afternoon happily engrossed in a four-hundred-year-old grimoire, Gray had been perfectly conscious of her mood, and had known the best means of holding it in abeyance.


The introductory tutorials in Gaelic began on the first day of September. The rank beginners—Sophie and Gray amongst them— met at the second hour before noon and were instructed by a kindly woman with a good deal of silver in her dark auburn hair, who introduced herself to her pupils as Dolina MacKinnon and listened patiently as, one by one, they struggled to introduce themselves in return.

Catriona MacCrimmon's arch warnings notwithstanding, Sophie found the language no more difficult than the Cymric she had been studying with Master Alcuin since first arriving in England, though she was forced to concede that its variety of spelling put both English and Français in the shade. Dolina MacKinnon—clearly well accustomed to the wide linguistic variety of her charges—followed up the introductions by requiring each person present to list the languages in which he or she already had some proficiency; the great majority could speak (or, at any rate, read) some Cymric, and Dolina MacKinnon accordingly spent most of their remaining hour mapping upon a large blackboard the connexions and branching distinctions between the two languages. Master Alcuin and Gray had made use of the same approach in helping Sophie to learn Cymric—to which her native Brezhoneg was even more closely related—and to her great satisfaction, as the lessons progressed she began to recognise connexions almost before Dolina MacKinnon pointed them out.

Though the Gaelic lessons were not productive of much local acquaintance, they proved an excellent means of becoming acquainted with other newcomers to the University—from undergraduates to a visiting professor newly arrived from Rome, all more or less equally at sea amongst the mysteries of Gaelic lenition.

Rory and Catriona MacCrimmon declared that as sojourners in Din Edin, Sophie and Gray must see the view from the top of Arthur's Seat, and before the weather turned; and accordingly the four of them set out one bright morning with a picnic luncheon to climb the city's great hill.

"I have heard," Sophie began, hesitating a little, as the path began to grow steeper, "that you have had some troubles here of late—poor crops, and the like. We saw some signs of it on our journey—a long stretch of blighted fields, and a man burning a whole flock of dead sheep."

Joanna's reluctantly extracted warning had nagged at her all along their journey from London, but particularly since seeing those blighted fields after the crossing into Alba. She had seen no obvious signs of hunger, disease, or unrest elsewhere, or here in Din Edin either, but being so little familiar with the city and the ordinary run of its inhabitants' lives, she could not be certain of recognising such signs when she saw them.

"That is true," Catriona said, "but I was not aware that Alba's troubles were of such interest to our neighbours. Mind that rabbit-hole, Sophie."

Sophie paused, looking down, and stepped around the hole. There was a hint of coldness in Catriona's tone that surprised her; by Rory's slight frown, he was in the same case as herself.

"Well, naturally one is more apt to hear these things when one is known to be travelling to Alba," Gray said reasonably. He had paused when Sophie did, and was now looking up at the blue sky and white puffs of cloud with a satisfied expression; he had not been very eager to leave his books this morning, but after all he seemed to be enjoying himself.

"It is a strange thing, indeed," said Rory. "Poor crops of every sort, and sick beasts of every description—there seems no pattern in it. Of course it is inevitable that some should call it a punishment from this god or that, and others should call it the effects of malicious magick."

"Of course," Gray agreed. His eyes met Sophie's; she was sure he was thinking, as she was, of the plot they had helped to foil, which had been meant to convince an entire kingdom that the sudden death of their king was the will of their gods. "And has anyone any evidence in either direction? Or in any other?"

"If anyone had," said Rory, with a wry twist of his lips, "I should not expect to be the first to be told." He shifted Donella MacHutcheon's picnic hamper from one hand to the other. "In any case, we shall not starve; the priests of the Cailleach—she is our goddess of autumn and winter, you know, as Brìghde is of the summer and spring—have storehouses, and the clans also, which will be opened at need; we are not at the mercy of a single season's crops."

"My dear Sophie," Catriona said, in a rallying tone, "this is not a very cheerful subject you have started! Tell us instead what you think of our Library, now that you have been to see it."

Sophie did not much like to be dictated to so blatantly, during an outing which she had organised herself, but even less did she wish to offend Catriona, who had been everything helpful and welcoming since their arrival—and even before it, as the picnic hamper in Rory's hand attested. She acquiesced in the change of subject, therefore, as gracefully as she knew how, and was able (with Gray's assistance) to praise the University Library even to Catriona and Rory's satisfaction, with no need to misrepresent her true opinion; it was, in fact, the largest and finest library she could ever have hoped to see.

The views from the top of Arthur's Seat, too, were everything the MacCrimmons had promised. The whole of Din Edin spread out below them: to the east, the golden walls of the Castle, and to the west the deep blue of the firth. They amused themselves for some time in rambling over the hilltop to admire the various views, and in attempting (without much success) to pick out their own lodgings from the warren of rooftops below; and then, happily fatigued and ravenously hungry, they spread their picnic-cloth and attacked the contents of the hamper.

"Local legend says," Rory remarked, as he reached for another slice of Donella MacHutcheon's pigeon pie, "that this place was a crossroads of Ailpín Drostan's great spell-net."

"History, I think you mean," said Catriona. She was smiling, but it was, Sophie rather thought, the sort of smile that is intended to masque something decidedly more dangerous. "This was a crossroads of the spell-net, indeed, though by no means the greatest of them."

"Oh," said Rory, carelessly, "the spell itself I grant you; but I do not see how anyone can pretend to do better than guess at the details."

"No; you I suppose do not," said Catriona. Sophie could not be certain whether she had imagined the slight emphasis on *you*.

"What do you mean by *spell-net*?" said Gray. His eyes were alight with the spark of scholarly curiosity; if there was any chill or awkwardness in the conversation, he seemed not to have remarked it. "And who is Ailpín Drostan?"

"Ailpín Drostan was the first chieftain to unite all the clans of Alba under a single banner," said Rory, "so that he is regarded—accurately enough—as the father of the kingdom. He was a great warrior, and a great mage; to which of these attributes his success is principally owing, historians of the period have long disagreed," he added, with a wry half smile, "and will, I expect, continue to disagree until the end of time."

"That is a quality of historians, I am told," said Sophie, and the half smile broadened out into a grin.

"It is certainly a salient quality of all those I have ever met."

Catriona said, "It was through the spell-net that the kingdom was created, and was sustained for generations after Ailpín Drostan's death, under the rule of Clan MacAlpine, to whom he gave his name."

She spoke rather as though reciting a lesson, and Rory turned to her with eyebrows raised in astonishment; but whatever he had meant to say was forestalled by Gray's asking eagerly, "How so? What sort of spell was it—a protection, perhaps? But one man could not cast a protective spell over a whole kingdom; no mage has ever had such a range, or so much power. A group of mages, then—but how—"

"*How* is of course the great mystery," said Rory; "no one knows. Or perhaps I ought to have said that it is one such, for no one truly knows what or why, any more than how. I must say that had I been present at the time, I hope I should have kept better records than Clan MacAlpine appears to have done—"

"Rory!" said his sister reprovingly. Sophie could not see what cause there was for reproof; it was not disloyal, surely, to utter so mild a stricture upon such a long-ago king.

"But Clan MacAlpine do not rule Alba now," she said, testing this hypothesis.

"No," said Rory. "Not for many generations."

"And the spell-net itself—whatever it may have been, or been for—I suppose decayed along with the fortunes of Clan MacAlpine," said Gray, thoughtfully. "I should have liked to understand how it was made, and why. It is a great pity, indeed, that they did not keep better records."

Sophie looked at him, smiling at his scholarly censure—he and Rory MacCrimmon were birds of a feather, truly!—and in so doing discovered that Catriona MacCrimmon was also smiling at Gray, in a manner that put Sophie distressingly in mind of her elder sister, Amelia: smug and acquisitive and very slightly predatory.

The hot wash of fury that swept over Sophie was, she told herself, both unwarranted and absurd: Gray was not looking at either of them, was not even returning Catriona's smile, much less inviting any inappropriate attentions on her part. Her anger was swift, and as swiftly mastered; but though deploring the impulse, and the impression it might give that she did not entirely trust her husband, she could not help leaning closer to him and laying a proprietary hand upon his arm.

## CHAPTER VI

# In Which Joanna
# Enters Unfamiliar Territory

*Joanna prodded irritably* at the spun-sugar cage of glazed profiteroles on her plate. What was the use of a dish which one could not eat without first attacking it with a pick-axe? A covert glance up and down the long, elaborately decorated table suggested that her fellow dinner-guests were similarly reluctant to engage in this gastronomic battle, and that those who had dared were faring poorly. Across the table and to Joanna's left, an irate dowager duchess was surreptitiously removing fragments of spun sugar from her décolletage; several places to her right, an unfortunate young man was staring down in bewilderment at the wide, flat circle of puff-pastry, spun sugar, and cream that now surrounded his plate. Joanna suspected an attempt to extract the profiteroles from their cage by magick.

She repressed an exasperated sigh. Her next neighbours, with whom she had been conversing, turn-about, throughout this endlessly elaborate dinner, were Lord Havery, younger son of the new Earl of Wessex, whose painful shyness, gradually subdued by nearly a dozen glasses of wine, had unfortunately given way to an unstoppable flow of poorly informed opinions on the politics of the Duchies, which Joanna longed to correct but dared not; and the octogenarian,

nearly deaf, and highly inebriated Viscount Somersby, who was labouring under the delusion that Joanna was his granddaughter, and
recounted in excruciating detail all of the clever things she had apparently said at the age of three. It had been a trying meal, and the evening promised to be more trying still, for it was to be devoted to a
ball in honour of the Queen's birthday.

Joanna had once longed to go to a ball—had, in point of fact,
schemed and connived her way into one, when her elders had (perhaps rightly) decreed her attendance too dangerous—but now, in the
midst of her first real season of ball-going in London, could scarcely
remember why the idea had held such appeal. True, there was generally plenty to eat, and of a high standard; there was of course plenty
of dancing, provided that one did not mind whom one danced with,
and were willing to persevere for half an hour together in the most
insipid sort of conversation; and from time to time there was an opportunity to speak to someone genuinely interesting. No assembly
since that first one had been so dramatically disrupted by attempted
poisonings, calls for rebellion, duels, or magickal catastrophes; this
must of course be accounted a blessing, but Joanna could not help
feeling that a ball featuring none of these elements lacked excitement.

And Roland was certain to ask her for a dance, which prospect she
presently dreaded above all things.

She had in fact done her best to cry off from this long-standing
invitation, but Jenny had first employed reason and logic—"It will
cause all manner of talk, Jo, if you are not there"—and finally resorted to bribes, promising to let Joanna drive her phaeton around
the park whenever she should wish for the next month.

After the ordeal of dinner, upon the gentlemen's rejoining the ladies,
the company moved into the Green Ballroom, where every available
surface had become a riot of summer blooms and a company of
musicians were assembling themselves with much scraping of chairs
and adjusting of instruments.

Joanna did her best to hide behind Jenny, but her efforts availed her nothing; the couples had scarcely begun to form up for the first two dances before Roland, resplendent in a coat of blue velvet precisely matched to the shade of his eyes, had found them out and was kissing Jenny's hand and paying her absurd compliments. Jenny— who, Joanna grudgingly supposed, could not strictly speaking be accused of betrayal, having no idea how very much Joanna wished to avoid dancing with Roland—laughingly stepped aside so that he might speak to Joanna; despite the few moments' warning, Joanna could think of no excuse likely to pass muster, and, when he requested the first two dances, was forced to acquiesce.

Joanna had danced with Roland so often before, when he had been her friend instead of her chief tormentor, that it was perfectly absurd to feel that the eyes of all the room were upon them as they went down the dance. To be fair—and Joanna hoped she was capable of being fair, even to persons with whom she was deeply annoyed— Roland was in his best looks tonight, all bright blue eyes and shining golden curls and aristocratic nose and cheeks flushed with excitement and dancing, which, she supposed, might naturally draw attention. She had taken care herself to dress in a becoming but retiring manner (wishing all the while that Lady Maëlle had not taken Queen Laora's charms of concealment back with her to Breizh), so that when the inevitable occurred, she should at least not be accused of *enticing* Roland to dance with her.

"You are very quiet this evening," said Roland, as they met, clasped hands, and turned about. "Is something amiss?"

As this was hardly the place for Joanna to tell him once again that he was himself very much amiss, she merely lifted her chin and looked down her nose at him.

She had found a new sonnet in her reticule two days since, full of absurd allusions to wood-nymphs and the goddess Proserpina. This had so annoyed her that even the reliably oblivious Mr. Fowler had been moved to ask whether Miss Callender was quite well, and every shred of self-control Joanna possessed had been necessary to save him from a vicious telling-off. She was beginning to wonder whether she was entirely sane; Roland's behaviour was exasperating, certainly, but he must tire of it eventually, and she ought not to be so foolish as to mind it.

*I wish Lucia MacNeill of Alba may give him what he deserves.*

"I think you had better not dance any more at present," said Roland, eyeing her suspiciously across the set. "You are very pale. I shall get a glass of wine for you and find you a seat on the terrace."

Joanna, to her infinite chagrin, flushed to the roots of her hair. How *dare* he! "I am *not* pale," she hissed, furiously and now with perfect truth, "and I shall *not* let you fetch me wine and conduct me to the terrace." In a more publicly audible tone she said, "Your Highness is very good! I am quite well, however, I assure you."

Roland, stymied, stared at her with furrowed brows; Joanna returned her very best carefree smile and ignored him.

The first two dances ended at last—surely there had never been such long ones!—and Roland tucked her hand into the crook of his arm and led her away towards, so far as Joanna could determine, that corner of the room which was farthest from where she had left Jenny. She allowed herself to be led; she had nothing to gain by making a scene in front of all of these people, and if she had not, then Roland had not either.

"People are looking at us," she murmured, behind a blandly acquiescing smile. "You ought not to pay me so much attention."

"They may say what they please," he retorted. "I must speak to you, Jo."

"You—"

A potted pear-tree—*How perfectly absurd!*—loomed up before them, and Roland released her hand, caught her elbow, and turned her swiftly to propel her behind it.

"*Roland!*" Joanna hissed, jerking her arm away. Before she could escape, however, he was gripping both of her elbows and dipping his face towards hers, so close that he might have kissed the tip of her nose, or even . . .

It was not, *decidedly* not, the fear of being kissed by Roland, but the prospect of being discovered in this absurd and deeply incriminating circumstance, that made Joanna's pulse accelerate and brought the flush back to her face. "Let me *go*, Roland. What can you mean by—"

"My father is plotting something," Roland whispered, harsh and urgent. "Something to do with me. Ned will not tell me anything, and I do not know what they are about, but *you* know, I am sure of it. You must tell me, Jo. As you are my friend, you must tell me."

This was so very much not what Joanna had expected, that for a panicked moment she nearly told him all. But it was only for a moment. This, *this* was what all of Sieur Germain's enemies in the Privy Council expected: that, faced with the choice between keeping His Majesty's confidences and ingratiating herself with a handsome young man, she should betray her patron and her King as easily as breathing. *Well, that I certainly shall not.* Yet she was, as Roland had said, his friend, and to keep this truth from him was another sort of betrayal.

But no one should ever say of Joanna Callender that she did not know where her duty lay.

"I should like to know," she said, with a laugh that came very near to sounding natural, "why you imagine that I am privy to all your father's secret plots."

Roland waved this away impatiently. "You live in the same house with Lord Kergabet, who is well known to tell his wife everything." This was unfair, but Joanna did not say so. "And you always do know whatever there is to know. If something *is* afoot that concerns me, you must *tell* me!"

Joanna looked up into his bright blue eyes and lied as convincingly as she was able. "There is nothing to tell."

## CHAPTER VII

# In Which Gray Gives a Demonstration, and Sophie Is at a Loss to Explain Herself

*The schedule of* lectures for the first fortnight of the new term was posted on the day before the Autumn Equinox. By this time Sophie's faithful adherence to Dolina MacKinnon's programme of study enabled her, upon spying Gray's name halfway down the list, to puzzle out that the entry read, *Magister G. Marshall (Merlin Coll., Oxon.)—On practical shape-shifting: Lecture the first (to be read in Latin).*

She carefully noted down the time and place, and set about working out the titles of other listed lectures.

> *Magister N. Ferguson (School of Healing and Healing*
>     *Magick)—On the philosophy of healing: Lecture the first*
> *Professor D. MacAngus (School of Theoretical Magick)—*
>     *Fundamental magickal ethics: Lecture the first*
> *Professor D. MacAngus (School of Theoretical Magick)—*
>     *Fundamental magickal ethics: Lecture the first (to be*
>     *read in Latin)*
> *Magistra M. MacRury (School of Practical Magick)—*
>     *Legal and ethical considerations in the use of scrying*
> *Professor A. Maghrebin (University of Alexandria)—On the*

> *Osirian Books of the Dead: Lecture the first (to be read in Latin)*
> *Doctor M. Ní Sabháin (College of Magick and Alchymy, Duiblinn)—A survey of alchymical discovery, with special reference to the Erse School (to be read in Latin)*
> . . .

*How provoking,* thought Sophie, *that so many particularly interesting lectures should be read only in Gaelic!* Then, recollecting that she was standing in the middle of Din Edin, she laughed at herself, and putting away her pen and commonplace-book, set off for her library carrel to work on her list of Gaelic verbs.

Some three days later, Sophie pushed open the door of a Library reading-room one afternoon to find a tall, imposing woman a few years older than herself, with a great plaited coronet of russet hair wound about her head, just looking up from the reading stand where she was consulting an enormous codex. Sophie halted on the threshold, daunted by the stranger's penetrating stare.

After a moment the woman said in Latin, "You must be Sophie Marshall," and offered Sophie a flashing smile that, for a moment, lit her shuttered face like sunshine glinting through storm-clouds. "I am Mór MacRury."

The name was familiar; it had been on the list of lectures, Sophie remembered.

"I am pleased to make your acquaintance, Miss— Magistra—" She floundered; the stranger laughed, a clear alto chuckle.

"You Sasunnachs!" she said. "Always seeking to be strangers to one another. You must call me Mór." Her Latin had the same soft, musical tilt that Sophie was becoming accustomed to hear from Rory and Catriona, and from Dolina MacKinnon.

Sophie, delighted, grinned in return and said, "Then you must call me Sophie. And I am not English."

"No?"

"Well," Sophie conceded, "I suppose I am *half*-English. But my other half is Breizhek, and I was brought up there."

"Like the Lost Princess!" said Mór. Sophie stiffened a little, but perhaps this was no more than the idle remark it appeared, for her new acquaintance at once went on, "And now you are come to Alba. Do you find Din Edin very different from Oxford?"

"Sophie? Are you there?" Gray's voice, softly calling, floated in at the door.

Sophie sprang to her feet and ran to meet him. "Hush," she admonished, taking his hand, "and come with me; I have made a most interesting new acquaintance!"

Mór MacRury looked up from the scroll she was copying. Her brief, startling smile flashed over her face again; then she blinked several times. Her eyes narrowed, and her face creased into a puzzled frown. "Brìghde's tears!" she said softly. "And what does that mean, I wonder?"

"What does what mean?" Sophie demanded. "What makes you look so baffled, Mór?"

Gray, meanwhile, had disentangled himself from Sophie's grip and was gazing shrewdly at Mór. "May I ask," he said, "forgive me for addressing you when we have not been introduced—"

Mór glanced aside at Sophie with a wry twist of her lips. "You will not deny that *he* is English, I suppose?"

"No," Sophie conceded, suppressing a smile. "Gray, this is Mór MacRury, who is a lecturer in practical magick; Mór, my husband, Graham Marshall."

"The Sasunnach shape-shifter, yes."

Gray ignored this—Sophie supposed he was grown quite used to it by now—and forged ahead: "Magistra MacRury, may I ask: Have you the talent of seeing others' magick?"

"Like Master Alcuin!" Sophie whispered, and studied Mór with new interest.

Mór's arched russet eyebrows flew up. "I have," she said. "And since you have so quickly guessed it, perhaps you may be able to explain to me what it is I am seeing? For I confess I am, as Sophie puts it, baffled."

"I regret that I cannot explain it," said Gray. "But—"

Despite having asked the question, however, Mór MacRury did not appear to be attending to his answer. "Sophie has a deep well of magick," she said, tilting her magnificent head and studying the pair of them with narrowed eyes. "Almost the deepest I have ever seen. It lay quietly all the time we were speaking together, waiting to be called upon, which she did not have occasion to do. Then you came in"—she looked sharply at Gray, and narrowed her blue eyes still farther—"and Sophie's magick leapt up like a great flame feeding on dry wood, though she seemed to be calling upon it as little as ever. And yours, which is nearly as deep, boiled up as though to meet it. I have never seen such a thing, though I have lived so many years among mages."

Sophie looked up at Gray, and found him regarding her with a troubled expression. Master Alcuin, who had observed what was presumably the same phenomenon, had never satisfactorily explained it; perhaps, like herself, Gray was torn between avid curiosity and a desire to avoid notoriety.

"It is true," he said slowly, as though testing each word before he spoke it, "that we are much in the habit of working spells in concert."

"Perhaps that may account for it," Mór conceded. Her thoughtful frown remained, however, and Sophie—feeling rather pinned under glass—was not altogether sorry when the approach of the dinner hour obliged them to part from their new acquaintance.


The University term proper began on the following day. A senior member of the School of Practical Magick having died suddenly in the first week of September, Gray—though invited only as a lecturer—found himself applied to by the head of the School to take on several of the students thus left without a tutor; and Sophie, for her part, threw herself into undergraduate life with the same enthusiasm that had characterised her first term at Merlin.

Together with two other young women, she met her tutor on the fourth morning of the term, in a cluttered, cosy study comfortingly reminiscent of Master Alcuin's rooms in Oxford. Throughout this first meeting she was perpetually on her guard, equally fearful of giving offence and of attracting attention; gradually, however, it became apparent that though her recent arrival, her still halting Gaelic, and her unfamiliarly accented Latin made her a curiosity to her fellow students, they saw nothing else in her to occasion extraordinary interest. Still, she kept a tight rein on her concealing magick—just enough, and not too much—glad now of the long hours she had spent in learning to make it answer to her will and not merely to her instincts and emotions.

Her tutor, the redoubtable Magister Cormac MacWattie, she observed with a more wary eye. Their first meeting, he explained, would be devoted largely to gauging where Sophie and her companions stood in their course of study, Sophie being a newcomer and the others having had other tutors the year before. Though Sophie felt she acquitted herself reasonably well in respect of matters theoretical—allowing for the rather dismaying number of important works in Gaelic with which she was yet unfamiliar—she began to wonder whether there was any possibility at all of her catching up her year-mates.

In deference to Sophie, Cormac MacWattie spoke slowly, or spoke in Latin, except when beginning to be absorbed in a subject, when he forgot her handicaps altogether and her head began to ache with the effort of parsing his rapid Gaelic—by turns lulling her ear with its similarities to Brezhoneg or Cymric and baffling her by its differences.

When they passed on to matters practical, Sophie—knowing now how much more emphasis was placed on practical magick here than by most tutors at Merlin College—was rather apprehensive. In fact, however (thanks to having been Master Alcuin's student, as well as to Gray's less formal tutelage), it was in the practical tasks that she more easily held her own, demonstrating without much difficulty her ability to direct the size, height, and direction of a globe of magelight;

to summon objects up to the size and weight of Cormac MacWattie's Gaelic translation of the *Greater Mabinogion* without upsetting the intervening furniture or causing injury to herself or anyone else; and to use a finding-spell to locate one of her own hair-pins, which Cormac MacWattie had concealed on the top of a bookcase whilst she and her fellow students waited in the corridor outside. The calling and control of fire—though on the very small scale of a candle flame—presented a greater challenge: not because it required more magick, more self-control, or significantly more finesse than the other tasks (it did not) but because Sophie had never yet succeeded in separating this relatively small and ordinary magick from the horrors of the night in the Master's Lodge at Merlin when she had first seen fire-magick used in battle. Eithne MacLachlan's flame was tiny, but steady and obedient; Una MacSherry's larger and less tidy, but still firmly under her direction. Sophie's, however, lurched from spark to conflagration and back again so rapidly and erratically that Cormac MacWattie was moved to step in and put it out altogether. He waved off Sophie's halting apologies, but above his kindly smile his eyes were shrewd and thoughtful.

"One last task," he said, "before we part. Look closely at this cup." He held up the little silver goblet with which he had welcomed them at the beginning of the session. The three students passed the cup from hand to hand.

"Now that you know what it looks like," he rumbled, remembering again to speak slowly, "give it back to me."

He held out his hand, and Sophie returned the cup. Then with a barked "Eyes front!" Cormac MacWattie strode around the half circle of chairs until he stood behind his students. Sophie heard the rustle and scrape of books moving along a shelf, and a faint metallic clink, and then heavy footfalls as her tutor returned to seat himself in his armchair.

"Eithne MacLachlan!" he said. "Summon me that cup, if you please."

The afore-named, a plump and pretty young woman, abundantly freckled and exceedingly shy, started in her seat. When she made to turn towards the bookcase at her back, Cormac MacWattie brought her up short with a pointed cough. Biting her lip doubtfully, Eithne MacLachlan closed her eyes and, after a moment, began to mutter a spell. Sophie clasped her hands in her lap and held her breath.

Eithne MacLachlan, it appeared, could not perform an unseen summoning, and Una MacSherry, though she seemed to have a large store of elaborate summoning-spells by heart, did no better. They both appeared so much chagrined by this failure that when it came to Sophie's turn, she felt almost ashamed of the ease with which her muttered *Accedete!* made the welcome-cup sail over her shoulder and onto her outstretched palm—though, after the debacle of the candle-flame, she could not help feeling some pride in it, too.

Eithne and Una gaped.

Cormac MacWattie raised rather shaggy grey-gold eyebrows and nodded at Sophie. "Well done," he said, reaching to take back the cup. "Who taught you how to do that?"

Sophie flushed and dropped her eyes. "I . . . taught myself it," she said, uncertain and awkward in Gaelic.

"You may speak in Latin, Sophie Marshall," her tutor reminded her, himself shifting into that tongue. "You taught *yourself* the skill of unseen summoning? May I ask how?"

Sophie shrugged uncomfortably and fought a strong urge to disappear. Why had she not dissembled, pretended to be less adept? She could not tell the truth; suppose she said, *My husband was in danger of his life, and I could help him only by summoning a weapon I could no longer see for smoke and dust*—these people could not possibly believe her, and indeed it would be almost worse if they did.

"The circumstances . . . urgently required it," she said at last. "I am not altogether certain how I succeeded the first time, but once I had got the trick of it, the next time was very easy."

Cormac MacWattie's expression—lips pursed, eyes narrowed, head tilted on one side—suggested that he found this explanation insufficiently specific, but to Sophie's vast relief he chose not to pursue it for the present. "The magicks we learn because we must," he said mildly, still in Latin, "we seldom afterwards forget;

but it does not follow that learning ought always to occur under duress."

"No, indeed, sir," said Sophie feelingly.

The session ended with stern instructions for their subsequent meeting: for Sophie, an essay upon the theory of elemental magick, with particular reference to the magick of fire, and for the others, upon the theoretical differences between seen and unseen summonings. Sophie tried to flee to her carrel in the Library, but Eithne and Una crowded round her outside the door of Cormac MacWattie's study, so that she could not escape unless by actually pushing past them.

"How *did* you learn to do that?" Una MacSherry demanded. Her Latin was heavily accented, but so much more fluent than Sophie's Gaelic that Sophie could scarcely fault it.

They were both regarding her eagerly, expectantly, and she wanted nothing more than to erase herself from their notice; but that was one of the things she had promised herself never to do here, in light of the questions it must raise.

"It is as I told Cormac MacWattie," she said at last, haltingly; "there was a thing I needed very much, but I could not see it. It seemed to me that it could not be worse to try and fail, than not to try at all. That I succeeded was . . . a surprise to me."

She did not add that it had surprised Gray, also, and greatly (and unpleasantly) surprised their enemies. She did not add that when she recalled that moment of desperate wanting, she could feel again the smoke burning her eyes and her throat, the rough weight of the pikestaff slamming against the palm of her hand, and that it was all of a piece with the panic that seized her when she attempted any spell involving flame. There were few people in the world to whom she could imagine saying any of these things, and all of them but one were very far away.

Eithne MacLachlan looked rather disappointed that Sophie could not (or would not) be more specific; Una MacSherry, however, was directing at her a narrow-eyed gaze that reminded Sophie uncomfortably of her sister Jenny in a suspicious humour.

"Sophie Marshall," she said thoughtfully. "Marshall is the name of that very handsome new lecturer—the tall one they say is a shapeshifter. And he is Sasunnach, too. You are . . . I suppose you must be his sister?"

Sophie, ruthlessly suppressing another hot and perfectly absurd stab of jealousy, laughed. Gray would laugh, she knew, at being called *very handsome*, whatever might be her own thoughts on the subject. "No, indeed," she said. "He does have two sisters, but I am his wife."

"His *wife*," Una repeated. She frowned. "Then why do both of you use the same family name? Or are you cousins?"

"Oh!" said Eithne MacLachlan, looking a trifle smug, Sophie thought, at knowing something which Una MacSherry did not. "Because that is the Sasunnachs' custom, Una, for a bride to take the name of her husband's family."

"That is our custom, indeed," said Sophie, a little puzzled, "but what is yours?"

"You must be very lately married," Una said, ignoring the question and raising her eyebrows; "you cannot be more than seventeen."

Sophie's face flushed hot. "I am *twenty*," she said—which was essentially true—ignoring, in her turn, the first of Una's implied questions. "Not that my age is any affair of yours."

"And you are not cousins?" said Eithne MacLachlan.

"Certainly not," said Sophie.

"My mother and my father are second cousins," said Eithne MacLachlan, in an explanatory tone, "but my father has forbidden me to marry any of my cousins—*if the MacLachlan blood ran any thicker,* he says, *it would stand still*—and I think it a great pity, for my cousin Niall MacLachlan—"

"Eithne, enough!" cried Una MacSherry, clapping both hands over her own ears. "We are all sick to death of your cousin Niall MacLachlan!" Eithne subsided; Una dropped her hands and, turning to Sophie, said in an only slightly less belligerent tone, "Your husband—is he a shape-shifter, truly?"

"Certainly he is," said Sophie, "an excellent one. Why should you think he is not?"

Una flushed, now, and her blue eyes darted away from Sophie's. "I beg your pardon," she said. "I ought not to have mentioned it." Her voice was tense and defensive, however, rather than contrite; Sophie had unknowingly given some manner of offence.

"I . . ." Acutely uncomfortable, Sophie cast about her for a peace-offering. "Should you like to be introduced?"

Eithne and Una exchanged an unreadable look. It was Eithne who finally spoke: "If we are to spend all this year together with Cormac MacWattie," she said, with a return of her earlier diffidence, "I wish we might be friends."

Sophie swallowed hard and essayed a smile. "I should wish the same," she said. "I have not many friends in Din Edin yet."

Eithne grinned at her briefly and rather startlingly, white teeth and green-grey eyes glinting in her freckled face, and Sophie could not help grinning back. Perhaps Eithne was not naturally shy, but only intimidated by Cormac MacWattie?

"Una," Eithne said, and nudged her companion gently with one elbow.

Una was not to be so easily won over, it appeared; she did raise her eyes to Sophie's again, however, and repeated her earlier apology in a discernibly less hostile tone.

"I don't presume to speak for Una MacSherry," Eithne said, perfectly cheerful now, "but I should very much like to meet your famous husband."

Sophie considered the angle of the sun. "He will be in his study now, I expect," she said; "I believe he has students at the same hour as Cormac MacWattie."

"Well, then!" Eithne linked one arm through Sophie's elbow and the other through Una's. "Lead on, Sophie Marshall."

★   ★   ★

Gray, absorbed in recording his impressions of his new students, started at Sophie's firm knock at his study door—the same quick syncopated rhythm with which she had always announced herself in Oxford—and sprang up to open the door. Why was she here now, when they had arranged to meet in the library and walk home together to eat their dinner? Had she already fallen into some sort of trouble? Surely not—

He was more startled yet to find, in the corridor outside, that Sophie had brought with her two Alban girls perhaps a little younger than herself. Sophie gave him a small, half-apologetic smile; her companions stared up at him in frank curiosity.

Despite her evident embarrassment she introduced her new acquaintance very gracefully. Eithne MacLachlan shook Gray's hand with a diffident smile, and Una MacSherry with a grave, measuring look.

"I am delighted to make your acquaintance," he said, and beamed at them as though they had really been Sophie's friends—a supposition of which he was not at all persuaded. He tried to read in her eyes and the angle of her chin whether she wished him to invite all of them in and serve them tea, or to concoct some excuse to send them on their way.

"Sophie says you are a shape-shifter," the grave, auburn-haired one—Una MacSherry—said. "You would not care to give us a demonstration, I suppose?"

Gray swallowed back the incredulous laugh that rose to his lips; Sophie had flushed scarlet in agonised embarrassment, and he did not wish to add to her discomfiture.

"Una!" Eithne MacLachlan exclaimed, laughter and outrage warring in her soft contralto voice. "How can you say such a thing? Anyone would think—"

She cut herself off abruptly, and there ensued a brief, whispered argument in rapid Gaelic. Sophie made a tiny stifled sound; Gray, glancing at her over the bent heads of her fellow students, could see that she was trying hard not to simply flee what was becoming a hideously awkward conversation. He tried to imagine what sequence of events might have led to this unexpected visit: Had Sophie been boasting of him? It seemed unlikely, though admittedly more likely than that she should have been showing away on her own behalf.

Sophie blinked rapidly, and her lips silently formed the words *I am sorry*. Now, at last, Gray understood her: She feared that she was embarrassing him, as well as making a spectacle of herself.

He grinned briefly at her and said, "I do not make a habit of displays for strangers; but as you are friends of Sophie's—"

And as all three of them stared at him in openmouthed astonishment, he shrugged off his coat, handed it to Sophie, and summoned up his magick.

The sensations of the shift—the compacting of muscle and the lightening of bone, the unfurling of long flight-feathers from his outspread arms as they became his wings—were as familiar by now as the weight of Sophie's head upon his shoulder or the rough-smooth slide of paper under his fingers. It was tidier to remove all of his clothes first and fold them up ready to put on again afterward, but of course one could not do such a thing in a public corridor, before the eyes of two young women one had only just met.

It could not be denied, however, that clothing—and the presence of a neatly tied neck-cloth, in particular—made things rather more difficult. Fortunately Sophie was not unfamiliar with the problem, and in a matter of moments the confounding folds of linen were swept away and Gray was blinking up at her, on her knees amidst the abandoned garments.

Sophie wrapped his shirt about her forearm and held it out, low; Gray hopped and fluttered onto the proffered perch, feeling awkward and ungainly as he always did in the interval before going aloft. Sophie climbed to her feet and turned to face Una and Eithne. Though Gray could not see her face, he imagined an expression of quiet triumph.

Una MacSherry and Eithne MacLachlan, whose faces he could certainly see, looked satisfyingly gobsmacked.

"May I," the latter said, looking at Sophie, "may I—"

"Gray?" Sophie turned her head, and Gray turned his, so that their eyes met; he bobbed his head once, an established signal, and Sophie turned back to Eithne and said, "You may."

Eithne MacLachlan put out a cautious hand and drew one finger gently along the slope of Gray's folded left wing.

Una MacSherry—the more sceptical of the pair—hung back, staring.

"Have you never met a shape-shifter?" Sophie asked, in a tone of honest curiosity. "Is this talent very unusual in Alba?"

It was very unusual everywhere in the known world, as Sophie well knew, though primarily—in Gray's opinion—because learning to shape-shift required more patience, determination, and research than most mages could be bothered to devote to mastering a skill which was not, for the most part, of much practical use. He sidled towards her elbow and nudged his head reprovingly against her shoulder.

"I have never met one, that I know," Eithne MacLachlan admitted. "Though of course one cannot know without asking, and asking would be dreadfully rude."

Gray and Sophie exchanged a look.

"I have heard Magister Rory MacCrimmon lecture about shape-shifting," Una MacSherry said, "but I do not believe he can do it himself."

And there, Gray suspected, was the spark that ultimately had led to his perching on his wife's arm in an upstairs corridor in the middle of the afternoon for the entertainment of undergraduates. He blinked his eyes at Una MacSherry and hooted in annoyance; then, because it seemed foolish to waste all the effort of a shift for no more reward than this, he gripped Sophie's wrist through its makeshift wrappings to signal that he meant to fly.

Sophie blinked in surprise, but it was short-lived: Gray had not gone flying for nearly a se'nnight, and it was not to be supposed that he should waste this opportunity to do so. She looked about her for a convenient window, and finding none along the corridor that could be opened, she instead made for the top of the staircase that descended into the broad, high-ceilinged hall below, and tossed Gray over the rail.

Una gasped, and Eithne choked back a protesting cry; they crowded against the railing, peering anxiously down into the hall.

Sophie did not trouble to join them; instead she tripped lightly down the steps, and at the foot of the staircase paused, one hand on the newel-post, to watch the fun.

Gray's colleagues had presumably known themselves to be sharing their premises with a shape-shifter, but this seemed in no way to mitigate the astonishment with which those presently passing through the hall greeted the arrival in their midst of an owl whose wingspan measured more than four feet. A lecturer with an impressive white beard dropped his armful of scrolls and sat down abruptly on the floor; a pair of women walking arm in arm cried out in astonished delight as Gray glided past them; a fair-haired young man wearing a wrapped plaid and a severe expression blanched, turned on his heel, and fled at a rapid walk.

Gray did not follow him out into the crisp autumn air, but flew two leisurely circuits about the hall and then, having apparently made his point, alighted on Sophie's shoulder and waited to be carried in state back up the stairs.

"Lazybones," she scolded him; but as the weight on her shoulder was in fact rather less than a newborn baby's, it was difficult to summon up any genuine affront.

## CHAPTER VIII

# In Which Catriona MacCrimmon Renders Assistance, and Sophie Makes an Unexpected Acquaintance

*In the course* of the succeeding fortnight, Sophie attended Gray's lecture and nearly a dozen more. Those read in Gaelic she found rather a frustrating exercise, until Catriona MacCrimmon, calling in Quarry Close to return a borrowed codex, found her struggling to decipher her notes and said, "Shall I come with you from time to time, and help you with the difficult words?"

Sophie tried to demur—it was such an imposition, surely much more than hospitality demanded—but Catriona was so cheerfully persistent that continued refusal seemed churlish. "I thank you," she said therefore, "very much indeed."

"Oh! I beg you will not think of it," said Catriona. "It will prevent me from stagnating, you know."

As Rory MacCrimmon had predicted, Gray's first lecture was so greatly oversubscribed that Sophie had no choice but to cram herself in amongst those standing at the back of the hall, for both the seats and the aisles between them were entirely occupied—the front two rows, at least, not by students but by other lecturers, readers, and professors. She could see from Gray's face, when he emerged to take his place at the lectern, that the size of his audience surprised him; he took it in stride, however, and delivered his remarks as confidently as if he had been speaking to half a hundred sleepy undergraduates at Merlin College.

Having noted that the course of lectures on the fundamentals of magickal ethics—which all undergraduates in both theoretical and practical magick were required to attend, and upon which they should all be examined—was offered both in Gaelic and in Latin, Sophie attended both, and, with Catriona's help, made a linguistic exercise of comparing her notes from each iteration and attempting to fill in the gaps. The substance of the first of these lectures presented no particular novelty—Sophie hoped that she did not need to be told that magickal ethics forbade her to work a sleeping-spell without the subject's consent or to make use of a summoning to pick a man's pocket—but gave her many an uncomfortable moment, by bringing to her mind instances in which she had, either unknowingly or from desperate need, violated a wide variety of the tenets elaborated in Dougal MacAngus's lecture.

She was particularly grateful for Catriona's murmured translations when Mór MacRury's lecture on scrying devolved into legal details which, rooted as they were in the unfamiliar laws, customs, and legal vocabulary of Alba, must otherwise have been entirely lost to her.

"Courts of law have long tended to dismiss or discount the evidence of scry-mages," said Mór MacRury, nodding at the blackboard on which, before beginning, she had inscribed the headings of her lecture: *Scrying on trial / The scry-mage as expert witness / Compromising evidence / Reliable, fallible, or both?*

"Scry-mages and those who rely on their findings may see this as nothing more than unreasoning prejudice," she went on. "There are, however, sound reasons for magistrates to demand independent corroboration of evidence obtained by scrying. Many of these are outside the scry-mage's control—it is not possible, for example, to prevent tampering with the aetheric echoes which attach to an object, though methods can be learnt to detect some forms of such tampering. Unfortunately, however, the collective reputation of all scry-mages has also been damaged, perhaps irreparably, by the unscrupulous practices of a few, practices which are justly considered to compromise the integrity of evidence derived from scrying. The most insidious of these is that of scrying objects acquired without the knowledge or consent of their owners, for the purpose of obtaining evidence justifying an arrest—because in so doing the scry-mage taints what is otherwise incontrovertible evidence, and thus calls into question every link in the chain . . ."

Sophie left Mór MacRury's lecture silent and thoughtful, and replied to Catriona's remarks somewhat at random, remembering with disconcerting clarity that once she had tried to persuade Jenny to secretly scry her guardian, Lady Maëlle, and had nearly succeeded.

Several days later, Sophie arrived in the Central Refectory, where she had arranged to dine with Gray, at the agreed-upon hour, and could find no sign of him. She had waited, gazing around in search of the familiar shock of sandy curls hovering slightly above the heads of every other person present, long enough to feel the beginnings of real annoyance, when she was hailed by none other than Mór MacRury, half rising from her seat at a table midway down the room.

*Gray may find me, if he chooses,* she told herself rather crossly, and wove her way through the thronged tables.

"Sophie," said Mór MacRury, "I believe you know Eithne Mac-Lachlan and Una MacSherry?"

"Yes," said Sophie, smiling shyly at them.

Mór gestured at the other three occupants of the table, and named them in order: "Ringan, Lucia, Fergus: This is Sophie Marshall of Oxford; Sophie, Ringan MacAngus, Fergus MacCallum, and Lucia MacNeill."

Sophie controlled her instinct to bow, and instead put out her hand, in the local style, to each of the Alban students. The two men—scarcely more than boys; they seemed of an age with her brother

Ned—gripped her hand cheerfully enough and, having made her acquaintance, returned to their mutton and their conversation. Lucia MacNeill, however, regarded her with bright interest and, as soon as Sophie had sat down, said, "I understand you are but lately come from Oxford, Sophie Marshall?"

"I am," said Sophie, inclining her head with a small smile. Which questions would follow next, she thought she might guess, but she was pleased that Lucia MacNeill did not speak of Britain as though England were the whole of it, as so many of the Alban students did.

"Din Edin sees very few travellers from Britain," said Lucia MacNeill, "though our kingdoms are such near neighbours."

It was not a question, exactly, but clearly she expected some reply.

"Crossing the frontier is not always a simple matter," said Sophie cautiously, wary of giving offence. "We were fortunate in receiving a formal invitation from the University, and in obtaining letters from the Alban ambassador in London, as well as from our own ambassador in Din Edin, and from the Privy Council, permitting us to leave Britain and to enter Alba, and I do not think any of the latter had been possible without the first. Even the post is not at all reliable; such a state as I have seen letters arrive in!—and sometimes they do not arrive at all."

Lucia MacNeill had listened patiently to all of this, her blue eyes intent and her delicately pointed chin resting upon her hand; now, sitting up straighter, she said in a thoughtful tone, "Well, we must hope that it may not always be so."

"Indeed," said Sophie.

Lucia MacNeill then inquired as to Sophie's tutor; and having herself been, it transpired, Cormac MacWattie's student the previous year, they passed a happy quarter-hour with Eithne and Una in comparing notes upon his methods. They were not the first to be caught off their guard by the challenge of an unseen summoning, and Sophie's shyness receded with Lucia MacNeill's admission that she had also been the only one of her tutorial to pass this test.

By the time Gray appeared at last, Sophie was pleasantly full of roast mutton, root vegetables, and goat's cheese and was laughing madly at Lucia MacNeill's impression of a preternaturally solemn Dougal MacAngus. Though still rather cross with him, she made introductions with perfect cheerfulness—no one should say of her that she was guilty of hanging out her dirty washing in public—but thereafter she turned back to Lucia MacNeill and Fergus MacCallum, with whom she had been debating whether Gaius Aegidius or Conor Òranach MacAlasdair were the more useful source of elementary spells, and left Gray to fend for himself.

If she had meant this for a snub, however, it was a singularly in-effective one, for Gray seemed perfectly content to discuss lecture schedules with Mór MacRury. Sophie, increasingly cross with herself and growing not a little jealous, found herself stealing glances at him, and blushed with embarrassment when their gazes crossed.

"I like Lucia MacNeill," Sophie said, merely to break the awkward silence, as they made their way back to their lodgings after dinner. Gray had not offered her his arm as he usually did, and she had made no attempt to take it. "She seems very clever, and she does not mind laughing at herself. But there is something odd—I wonder whether you remarked it?—the others at the table all seemed inclined to defer to her, even Mór MacRury rather."

Gray laughed.

"What are you laughing at?" Sophie demanded.

"Lucia MacNeill is heir to the throne—no, not the throne—the chieftain's seat of Alba," said Gray. "That is, when Donald MacNeill dies, or chooses to yield the throne—Donald MacNeill is—"

"I know who Donald MacNeill is, I thank you, and what it means to be heir to his throne," said Sophie, now very cross indeed. She drew a deep breath and let it out, and was able to say more calmly, "It had not occurred to me that I might cross paths with the heiress of Alba over dinner in the Refectory. She certainly appears to have made a better success of her studies than the Princess Royal did at Merlin."

"Sophie—"

"I suppose," she continued, overriding Gray's attempt to speak and ignoring his simultaneous attempt to take her hand, "I suppose you will say that this shows what a goose I am, to dread being found out."

Gray sighed quietly and said nothing. Sophie found she had been half waiting for him to answer back—to say something calm and eminently sensible—and was perversely disappointed at being given no opportunity to rail against his perfectly reasonable arguments. Risking a glance up at him, she found him looking carefully straight ahead, his hands now vanished into the vast pockets of his great-coat.

They walked on in silence for some time. It was a chilly evening, and between the pools of lamplight the street was very dark.

"Gray," said Sophie at last, sotto voce, inching closer in wordless apology, so that her pelisse brushed against the skirts of Gray's great-coat.

"I am sorry for laughing at you," said he, "and for having been so late to dinner. The great Doctor Balfour was in a tremendous strop, you see, because someone had rearranged his mammalian skulls; I ought not to have let it detain me."

"And I ought not to have sulked like a child," Sophie conceded. "I apologise."

He drew his right hand out of his pocket and curled his arm about her shoulders, drawing her in against his side: *Apology accepted.*


*You will never guess who I met yesterday,* Sophie wrote to Joanna the next morning.

> *The heiress of Alba, sitting at a table in the Central Refectory like any ordinary undergraduate, discussing Gaius Aegidius and the uses of Atropa belladonna! You may imagine how envious I was when I learnt whom I had been speaking with. I hope we shall meet again, for I should like to ask her about the blight we saw on our journey. She*

*seemed remarkably well informed about Britain, which in
general the students here are not; but if she is to rule Alba
after her father, I suppose that must account for it . . .*

At the close of their fifth session, as Sophie made to leave her tutor's
rooms with Una MacSherry and Eithne MacLachlan, Cormac Mac-
Wattie said quietly, "Sophie Marshall, a moment, if you please."

"Sir?" Sophie turned back, her arms full of codices. The others
went out; the door closed behind them.

"You are thoroughly conversant with the theoretical aspect of
fire-magick," said Cormac MacWattie, without other preamble. "Your
essay upon the subject was . . . I should not say a model of its kind, for
you might have greatly improved it by a third draft, but certainly it
demonstrates a thorough knowledge of the topic at hand. And yet
you struggle with its practical application, as I have not seen you do
in any other area of practical magick thus far. Even the little magick
of a candle-flame, which any talented child ought to have mastered
by the age of six."

He regarded Sophie in expectant silence, whilst she battered her
thoughts into some sort of order—for all the world as though he were
prepared to wait all afternoon for her reply.

"I . . . do not much like working with fire," she said at last; at Cormac MacWattie's sceptical expression, she added, "Very well: I am
frightened of it. In Français we say, *chat bouilli craint l'eau froide*, the
scalded cat fears cold water, and I am the scalded cat."

"An interesting metaphor," said Cormac MacWattie. "And how
did you come to be scalded?"

Sophie thought for a long moment before she spoke. "I have seen
at first hand the harm which can be done by mage-fire," she said at
last. "I do not wish—"

"That is a fool's argument, Sophie Marshall," said her tutor, "and
you know as much, I think. You are a powerful mage—ah, I see you
do not pretend not to know it—and any magick of yours which

you do not learn to master, will one day master you. To your own destruction, it may be, and certainly to the detriment of others. To believe otherwise is a dangerous indulgence."

Sophie swallowed. It was true that Gray and Master Alcuin had indulged her in this, had allowed her to direct her studies towards other aspects of magick—there were so many, after all!—and that the almost purely theoretical course of study for a Merlin Mag.B., together with the habits learnt over sixteen years' ignorance of her talent, had abetted her in concealing her aversion to even the simple act of calling fire.

"I am not in the habit of indulging my students," Cormac MacWattie continued, "and particularly not such a promising one as yourself. I have refrained from calling attention to your . . . difficulties before your fellows, but they have not gone unremarked."

Sophie cleared her throat. "May I—may I ask what—"

She stammered to a halt; Cormac MacWattie studied her, his eyes widening in astonishment. "Sophie Marshall, you surely cannot suppose that I am threatening you?"

"I . . ."

Her tutor cast up his eyes. "Brìghde's tears!" he muttered. "What ideas these children do invent!" And turning again to Sophie, he said, "You are my student; your progress, or lack thereof, is in part a reflection upon my tutelage. I should be doing neither of us a service by allowing you to face an examination jury without having learnt to perform such an elementary magick. Have I made myself clear?"

"Yes, sir," said Sophie.

"Now: You have been attending Dolina MacKinnon's morning lessons, have you not?"

Sophie nodded.

"Very well. You will come here every morning, then, before going to Dolina MacKinnon; there are no lectures so early, and I have no other students at that hour. If you are willing to put your knowledge into practice, I daresay we shall not be about the task longer than a fortnight."

"I . . . I thank you, sir," said Sophie.

Cormac MacWattie waved this away, and, when she did not at once turn for the door, he flapped one large hand at her and said, "Go, go! You shall be late for your lecture on ethics."

"Oh!" said Sophie, and hastened away.

The next morning Sophie knocked at the door of Cormac MacWattie's study, and when the door opened, she was confronted with a very forest of tallow-candles, lanterns, and lamps. Behind them sat her tutor, drinking tea.

"Oh," she said, nonplussed.

At his gesture she threaded her way through the assemblage of combustibles, perched gingerly upon her accustomed chair, and accepted a cup of tea, poured from a pot around which a warming-spell hummed gently, almost below the threshold of her hearing.

"A few precautions, I think, before we begin," said Cormac MacWattie. He rose from his seat and paced a small circle about an occasional table, in whose centre, set upon a mat which appeared to have been woven from fine wire, reposed a large, fat tallow-candle. "Set me a ward about this table, if you please."

Warding-spells—for reasons which she should not have dreamed of disclosing to her tutor—were a speciality of Sophie's. By the time she had completed her own circuit of the table's perimeter, with herself and Cormac MacWattie inside it as well as table, mat, and candle, she felt both entirely confident in the integrity of her wards and rather more inclined to optimism with respect to the purpose of this lesson.

Cormac MacWattie prodded with one finger at the invisible barrier and gave a surprised huff. "Yes, indeed," he said. "Now: We have at our disposal two sand-buckets"—he pointed them out—"and whatever water-spells we may see fit to deploy; the air is quite damp this morning, which is all to the good. Shall we begin? Light me this candle, if you would."

Sophie drew a deep breath; let it out; closed her eyes and sank into the consciousness of her magick, the many-petalled flower of cold blue-white flame by which it represented itself to her reasoning mind. Seek, find, catch the end of a petal between metaphorical fingers: The process was so familiar by now as to be the work of a breath. And then came the tension-taut moment when, having gathered up her magick and focused it on the candle-wick, on the tiny shimmer of heat always present in the air, she said, *"Flammo te!"* to strike the spark.

In the next breath, she was shouldered aside, and Cormac MacWattie was dousing the half-melted candle in a bucket of sand.

"Well," he said. "I see the difficulty now, I think."

"Oh?" said Sophie. Despite her best efforts, her voice shook, and her breath came too quickly.

"Your metaphor—the scalded cat—was apt," said Cormac MacWattie, scraping the sand back into the bucket. That done, he set the candle upright again—now a little less than half its original height, and deeply cratered. "What does the cat do, when the object of her fear threatens? She arches her back, she extends her claws, she hisses and spits—in short, she makes herself a threat in return, so far as she is able."

He looked at Sophie expectantly.

"Sir, I do not see . . ."

"Do you not, indeed? That spell of yours, Sophie Marshall, used as much magick as you could put into it, and was flung at its target with sufficient force—so to speak—to light a candle on the other side of the Firth: not the force of sober thought, calculated from the facts at hand, but the force of unreasoning fear."

Sophie wished very much to deny this, but she could not.

"We shall have to go back to the beginning," said Cormac MacWattie. He frowned thoughtfully. "Suppose," he said, "that instead of lobbing your blazing Yule-log into a drought-stricken forest and fleeing the conflagration, you held a candle-flame on the end of a lamplighter's pole, and touched it lightly to the wick of a lamp."

*Another metaphor,* thought Sophie. Master Alcuin had been fond of telling her that to use magick was to deal in metaphors, made concrete in the world.

"Yes, sir," she said aloud, **and set about** constructing the image in her mind's eye.

The next attempt could **not be called** a success, precisely, but certainly it was less destructive than the first. By the end of their allotted hour, Sophie was drooping with fatigue—not from drawing too much upon her magick, but only from the effort of restraint—and Cormac MacWattie's stock of candles had been reduced by four; but her progress was visible, if slow, and he seemed pleased with her efforts.

"Fire is like magick," she murmured, as she smoothed her hair and gathered up her books. "Controlled, an invaluable tool; uncontrolled, a catastrophe."

"I beg your pardon?" said Cormac MacWattie.

Sophie, who had not meant to be heard, repeated herself. "It is a saying of my husband's," she explained.

"Indeed?" said her tutor. "I have heard it said before, or words to the same effect, but always in the opposite direction. But then," he added, in a thoughtful tone, "one does not often meet a mage who is capable of teaching herself unseen summoning, yet has reached the final year of her undergraduate education without discovering how to call fire to light a candle."

In the second month of the term, Cormac MacWattie turned his students' attention to what he called *the magick of the land*. For the first time, the reading required was entirely in Gaelic, which made Sophie's preparation something of an ordeal, and each successful navigation of a page of text a small triumph to be celebrated. Before long, however, she had become sufficiently engrossed as to feel the work no hardship.

The magick of the land, Cormac MacWattie had told them, was a key to Alba's history, or a legend propagated by the early clan chieftains, or a gift of Alba's gods, or a tale to mislead the credulous, or some combination of all these, depending upon the particular scholar consulted. He had charged Sophie, Una, and Eithne to read through the list of sources he had assembled for them, as well as any others they might lay their hands on, and draw their own conclusions, which they should then debate at their next meeting.

Might Rory and Catriona MacCrimmon's tale of a great spell-net woven across Alba by a long-ago king, Sophie wondered, be such another source? But as Cormac MacWattie had also asked that they each form an opinion without reference to one another or to anyone else, she refrained from raising the question with either of them.

"Well?" Cormac MacWattie inquired, when next they gathered in his study. "What have you to teach me today? Una MacSherry: Enlighten us, if you please."

Una MacSherry came down firmly on the side of those scholars who considered the magick of the land no more than a charming folktale, invented by farmers and husbandmen of generations past to explain what they themselves could not—why a field cleared of stones in one season should sprout a new crop of them the next; why fields must sometimes be left fallow; why some sicknesses spread from beast to beast, or beast to man, whereas others do not.

Eithne MacLachlan, whose grandparents were farmers, was inclined to the view that some clan chieftain or chieftains unknown, undoubtedly with the connivance of the priests of the Cailleach (and perhaps of the Cailleach herself), had invented the idea out of whole cloth, for the purpose of cementing their own position of power over the smaller landholders.

"But the clan chieftains favour enclosure, while the priests oppose it," Una objected. "Why should they act together against the smallholders?"

"We are speaking of a time long before enclosure was thought of," said Eithne. "And, in any case, not all of the chieftains agree—when have they ever done?—so there is nothing in that, Una."

Sophie, when it came to her turn, was a little hesitant to unfold her own conclusions, for she had not expected to differ so wildly from the others, and as an outsider she felt that perhaps she ought not to opine at all.

"I think," she said, "of course it is not for me to say, but—I should not be surprised if there were such a form of magick, once. Perhaps not now, but long ago."

Eithne and Una looked sceptical; Cormac MacWattie merely nodded and said, "Go on."

"I have found—perhaps I have not understood everything correctly—but I have read half a dozen separate accounts, collected by several scholars over half a dozen parts of the kingdom, of workings which had some observable effect, and these accounts seemed to me to tally remarkably well . . ."

"But so they should do, of course," said Eithne, "if all had heard the same tale from the priests of the Cailleach, and were merely repeating what they had heard, or were bending their observations to suit it."

"That is so, of course," said Sophie.

"Perhaps the scholars themselves invented it!" Una said.

"Perhaps, indeed," said Cormac MacWattie. "When next we meet, I shall ask you each to defend a conclusion other than the one you have put forward today; and then we shall see where we stand."

As this time Cormac MacWattie had said nothing against their discussing the magick of the land with whosoever they chose, Sophie took up the subject with Mór MacRury on her way home from the University that afternoon, with Lucia MacNeill after Dougal MacAngus's lecture two days later, and with Catriona MacCrimmon when the latter called in Quarry Close on the morning after that. Mór was noncommittal—*The gods have their ways, of which men know nothing*—and Lucia MacNeill, Sophie thought, rather evasive; perhaps this was a matter on which it was politic for the royal family (as Sophie could not help considering them) not to opine.

Catriona MacCrimmon, however, proved an inexhaustible wellspring of knowledge—or, at any rate, of commentary—on the magick of the land.

"Of course it is difficult to understand, here in the city," she said; and when Gray, returning from an outing with a colleague, was drawn into the conversation, she insisted on their all going out to the nearest unbuilt place—in the event, they found themselves halfway up towards the crest of Arthur's Seat—in order to observe.

Catriona knelt amid the damp, straggling grasses—it had been raining for the better part of three days, and the air was chill—and, stripping off her gloves, pressed both palms flat against the soil. Sophie and Gray exchanged a look of mild alarm and followed suit.

"Do you see?" said Catriona. "It is faint and difficult to hear, surrounded as we are by the city and its noise—Din Edin was built from the land, of course, from its stones and timbers, but as it grows, the connexion weakens." Her voice grew wistful as she added, "I wish I might live on Leòdhas again, where the land and the people are better acquainted with one another."

It was a sentiment with which Sophie had some sympathy—for all that her childhood home had been more than half a prison, she was a creature of the countryside, far more than of the crowded, clattering town—and diverted her momentarily from the disconcerting question of what it was Catriona could see, or hear, or feel, that she (and, by his baffled frown, Gray also) could not.

"Can you not go home to Leòdhas, if Din Edin does not suit you?" she asked.

Catriona looked at Sophie as though, for a moment, she had forgot her companions' presence. Then she blinked, and smiled, and said, "But Rory is here, and I have my own work to do. Besides, I should miss the Library; there is nothing anywhere else in Alba to compare."

Sophie nodded, slow and thoughtful, and stared down at her bare hands splayed against the ground. *Perhaps the seeing and hearing are metaphorical,* she thought, *and I have been going about this in the wrong way.*

She closed her eyes, sank into her magick, and turned her perceptions inward; then—feeling her way awkwardly, for she sought an unknown destination and had neither map nor guide—she curved her fingertips into the soil and listened with her hands.

For what seemed a long time, there was nothing in her mind's ear but the slow beat of her heart. Then, faint and far away, just on the edge of . . . ought she to call it *hearing*? . . . a soft sighing that tasted of sandstone and the sea.

Then skewer-sharp, a rent in the sound, like a gull's shriek breaking an incantation, quivered through her, stealing her breath.

Then silence, and the too-rapid beating of her heart.

The sound had been there and gone in a moment, and try as she might Sophie could not catch hold of it again.

She opened her eyes, blinked dizzily for several breaths, and looked down at her hands. There was dark soil under her fingernails.

When she looked up again, Catriona was speaking—Sophie struck the heel of one hand against the side of her head, sharply, to clear away whatever metaphysickal cobwebs might be clogging her physical ears—and Gray was shaking his head.

Catriona turned to Sophie. "And you?" she asked eagerly. "Did you hear it?"

"I . . ." Sophie hesitated. "I think . . . perhaps. Just for a moment. But I may be quite mistaken."

"It is difficult here, as I told you," Catriona said, with a kindly, condescending smile that made Sophie squirm. "Or perhaps it is because you are not children of Alba."

They dusted off their fingers with their handkerchiefs, and put on their gloves, and made their way down the slope to the footpath (where her father's guardsmen fell in behind them, as though they were two strangers who happened to be taking the same way home), and back to Quarry Close. Their muddied clothing drew a few stares, but no one spoke to them, nor did they speak to one another, until Catriona paused at the turning for her own lodgings and turned to Sophie.

"I hope you understand a little, now, how the land lies," she said; and, bidding them farewell, she turned away.

Sophie watched her out of sight.

"I think," she said at last, "that I understand less now than I did before."

"Did you hear something, truly?" Gray said. "I did not, but I should have sworn that you did. Your face had that look."

"I believe I did hear it," said Sophie, slow and thoughtful. "Not with my ears, you know." Gray nodded; with so many more years' experience of magework, he must, she thought, have understood this before she did. "I have not the least idea what. It was not . . ."

Her voice trailed away; Gray hummed inquiringly.

"It was not a happy . . . *sound*, let us say, for lack of a better term. There was a great deal of pain in it."

Gray stopped suddenly, and Sophie, holding his arm, perforce stopped with him. "Joanna," he said.

Torn between amusement and alarm—*This is taking the unworldly scholar rather too far*—Sophie elbowed him gently and said, "I am Sophie."

"No." Gray dropped her arm, not ungently, in order to run both gloved hands through his hair. As this was reliably a sign of frantic thought, Sophie waited patiently for the process to unfold; at length he said, "Joanna told you, did she not, that some here believe the blight and the sheep and cattle disease to be of magickal origin?"

"She did," said Sophie. "But, Gray, she did not mean that it is so in fact; she meant only to warn us to mind where we put our feet."

"But what if it *is* so in fact?" Gray persisted.

"Then we should need more than my few heartbeats' worth of confused impressions to discover it," said Sophie. "I cannot imagine flimsier evidence."


She broached the subject in her next tutorial meeting, nevertheless, and was not much surprised when Eithne scoffed at her, and Una said, "What can have given you such an absurd idea?" and Cormac MacWattie listened gravely to her hesitantly marshalled arguments and at last said, with the utmost courtesy and not the least shred of belief, "That is a very interesting theory."

*Even if it were true*, Sophie thought ruefully, *which I do not suppose it is, why should they take my word upon it? As Catriona MacCrimmon says, I am no child of Alba.*

Their excursion into Alban history or legend—whichever the case might be—continued, reaching no conclusion, for the evidence seemed to point all ways at once.

"The scholars whose views are enshrined in our libraries," said Cormac MacWattie, by way of conclusion, "are as human, and as humanly fallible, as any of us; and the converse likewise. When in the course of your lives you are tempted to believe that the world is divided tidily into the known and the unknowable, the good and the wicked, the magickal and the mundane, I hope you shall call to mind our discussions here, and remember that matters are rarely so simple."

By the time Gray had become accustomed to his students, his colleagues, and the rather different expectations of the audiences at his lectures, Sophie's tutor had chivvied his students headfirst into the theory and practice of illusion-spells, and Sophie became so engrossed in her experiments with these that on several occasions, Gray was forced to remind her of the existence of mealtimes. Here was one amongst a considerable number of subjects in whose theory she had acquired a thorough grounding, but whose practice the course of study at Merlin College had not greatly encouraged. As a consequence, Sophie found herself well abreast of her year-mates' reading but hopelessly behind in respect of execution.

"Gray," she said, one evening during this period, pausing with a forkful of boiled mutton in one hand and a bread-roll in the other. "Tell me what you see."

She returned the fork to her dinner-plate, balanced the bread-roll carefully on the palm of her left hand, and began describing circles about it with her right forefinger, muttering the while. *"Noctis umbra tegit te,"* Gray heard; *"te verbo lux revelat . . ."*

A spell of concealment, then—a particular species of illusion-spell, which he had never thought to teach Sophie, past mistress of rendering herself forgettable.

The bread-roll wavered momentarily, then reestablished itself as a sort of ill-made rendering of Sophie's left palm. She prodded at it with the fingers of her right hand, frowning. "The dissonance makes my head ache," she said.

"It shows promise," said Gray, tilting his head to examine the illusion from several angles. "Though if your hand were that colour in truth, I should be summoning a healer at once."

Sophie said firmly, "*Lux*," and the bread-roll resumed its former aspect. She tore off a chunk of it and chewed thoughtfully, turning the remainder about in her hands.

"This is so much more difficult than I feel it ought to be," she said, after a moment. "Like . . . like learning to play the pianoforte with my toes, whilst my hands, which are perfectly capable already, are tied behind my back."

Gray contemplated for a moment whether he ought to take offence at this; at last he said, "I hope you have not tried that analogy on anybody else."

"Certainly not!" Sophie sat up straighter. "I know perfectly well how odious it sounds, and I should not dream of saying such a thing except to you." She sighed. "But it is quite true, for all that."

"Show me what else you have been practising," said Gray, both as a means of changing the subject and because he was genuinely curious; the cross-pollination of the two Schools to which they were attached—of Theoretical and Practical Magick—had excited his lively interest from the first, and led him to consider how different his own life might have been, had a similar atmosphere prevailed at Merlin. Though, of course, had he never been forced to study with Professor Callender, he should never have met Sophie, and such a fate did not bear thinking of.

"There is this," said Sophie, a little doubtfully, and pushing her half-empty dinner-plate aside, she curled her hands loosely on the tablecloth, palms angled very slightly upward, perhaps a foot apart.

She frowned fiercely at Gray's plate and again began muttering under her breath, so low and indistinctly this time that he could not make out the words of her spell.

There appeared in the space between her palms another dinner-plate, hazy and imperfect, but recognisably a copy of his own: here the last half-inch of a slice of mutton, there a sad little mound of boiled cabbage, the fork and knife laid down at odd angles.

The illusion wavered, then stilled; Sophie looked up expectantly.

Gray leaned down to examine the faux dinner-plate more closely. "Is it a visual illusion only?" he asked, then answered his own question by attempting to grasp the handle of the knife; his thumb and fingers passed through it and met in the middle. "Where is the catch?"

In a civilised society, the use of illusion-spells, as Master Alcuin (one of the few Merlin dons willing to teach such spells at all) had drummed into him years ago, must be governed by strict rules, one of which was that an illusion must always be distinguishable from reality by a sufficiently alert observer. A properly worked illusion, therefore, might be deliberately implausible of appearance—as a scarlet peacock, or a chair upholstered in oak-leaves—or, if modelled more closely on reality, contain a *catch*, some small but unmistakable clue as to its illusory nature. Though no very clever worker of illusion-spells himself, Gray had at least absorbed that detail.

"Come now, Magister," said Sophie, grinning broadly; "surely you are capable of detecting it."

Gray moved aside the remains of his real dinner-plate, pushed back his chair, and dropped to his knees, bending to bring his eyes level with the illusory one. He examined it from every possible angle, then climbed to his feet again and circled round to peer at it from Sophie's vantage point, then from each of the other two sides of the oblong table.

"There!" he said at last, triumphantly, pointing with Sophie's fork at the tiny thread of viridian running through a single cabbage-leaf. "That is very cleverly done, *kerra*."

Sophie drew a deep breath and blew it out, dispelling the illusion.

"Do you think so?" she said. "I fear that my detail work is not all it ought to be." Still, however, she looked enormously pleased with herself.

"Perhaps so," said Gray, "but that will come with practice."

Sophie retrieved her fork and addressed herself once more to her dinner. "I do miss Master Alcuin, and Joanna, and all our friends," she said, after a moment. "But I am glad we are come here."

## CHAPTER IX

# In Which Joanna
# Faces the Consequences

*Since their near* quarrel at Her Majesty's ball, Joanna had met Roland nearly as often as formerly, but with none of their former ease; though there had been no direct renewal of his unwelcome attentions, every word that passed between them seemed edged with the knowledge of what he was not saying.

*Perhaps I am only imagining it,* thought Joanna, more than once. Certain it was, however, that the day must be approaching when Roland should discover the depth of her betrayal—that she had known what his father planned for him, and disclaimed that knowledge—and the anticipation sat like a lump of something indigestible in her belly.

Irrespective of Joanna's feelings, however, when His Majesty's Chief Privy Councillor was summoned to his master's presence, go he must; where Lord Kergabet went, Mr. Fowler must follow; and Joanna had no notion of allowing Prince Roland or anyone else to prevent her doing likewise.

Thus it was that she found herself, on this unseasonably warm October morning, following Sieur Germain and Mr. Fowler out of the former's carriage and up the steps of the Palace. They were met as usual by the major-domo and—which was by no means usual—ushered at once into His Majesty's private audience chamber. Joanna pondered, as they paced through the corridors, what this might betoken, and was drearily persuaded that it could be nothing good.

She had not long to fret over the possibilities, however, for they entered the audience chamber to find King Henry deep in conversation with the Alban envoy, Oscar MacConnachie.

"Ah! Kergabet!" he exclaimed, looking up at the sound of their footsteps. "The very man."

"Your Majesty." Sieur Germain inclined his head respectfully. "I hope all is well?"

His Majesty looked at him in perplexity, as though it were slightly absurd of him to have supposed that an urgent summons to the Royal Palace might suggest some cause for alarm. Screened by Sieur Germain, Joanna and Mr. Fowler, their differences temporarily forgotten, exchanged a long-suffering look; they both knew King Henry to be, in most ways, a prudent and competent ruler, and deplored the habit he was presently indulging of affecting light-mindedness or outright foolishness in the presence of visitors from foreign courts.

"You have all the documents, have you not?"

Mr. Fowler hastened to provide Lord Kergabet's dispatch-box, from which the latter extracted several rolls of parchment and a stack of ordinary writing-paper, closely covered in Fowler's clear, elegant script.

"I believe we have everything in order, sir, yes," said Sieur Germain. "I have three copies of each. Which did—"

"Excellent, excellent. Then we shall proceed." His Majesty beckoned the major-domo, and on his approaching said, "Go and fetch Prince Roland."

"Your Majesty." The major-domo bowed and strode away.

It could not have been more than a quarter-hour before the major-domo reappeared, visibly restraining himself from hauling Roland along by the ear, but it was perhaps the longest quarter-hour which Joanna had hitherto endured. Within moments of their arriving, however, she was wishing heartily that they had not.

"Is this Your Majesty's idea of a jest?" Roland demanded, pink with outrage, when the news had been broken to him. "I am to be—to be *queen* of a kingdom of—"

Joanna coughed quietly; when Roland's wild gaze swung half towards her, she tilted her head very slightly in the direction of Oscar MacConnachie, and Roland swallowed whatever slight had been meant to follow.

"Your pardon, sir," he said. "I spoke out of turn."

There was a long, tense silence.

"Prince-consort," said Sieur Germain at last, quietly.

"Sir?" Roland had evidently remembered his manners with a vengeance; Joanna winced inwardly at the chill in his tone.

"The husband of a reigning queen, Your Highness," Sieur Germain said, "is styled Prince-consort. A position of more influence, respect, and responsibility, in fact, than that afforded by any other marriage alliance previously entertained for you."

Roland visibly considered this.

"And how is it," he said at last, "that this Lucia MacNeill inherits from her father? She has no brother, I suppose?"

"She has a younger brother, in fact, Your Highness," said Oscar MacConnachie, "but he is not the heir."

"We call Donald MacNeill *king*, because *king* is an idea we understand," Sieur Germain explained, "but he is not a king as your father is; he is a chieftain of chieftains. There is no law in Alba, as there is in Britain, that the eldest son must inherit, or even the eldest child. As Oscar MacConnachie explained it to me, Donald MacNeill might have chosen any young man—or young woman—of his clan as his heir, subject to the will of the clan chieftains; he chose his daughter, Lucia, for the trust he reposes in her heart and in her wits, and his choice was confirmed by the clan chieftains in council."

Roland's chin lost none of its stubborn set, but his eyes betrayed a glimmer of interest.

"And Lucia MacNeill," Sieur Germain said, "has considered the alternatives her father set before her, and has chosen you."

Joanna prayed to the Lady Venus that Roland would accept the implied compliment and allow the conversation to progress towards the subject of Lucia MacNeill's many virtues, perhaps to the portrait that reposed in the box at Joanna's feet.

For a moment it seemed as though he might indeed fulfil her hopes; instead, however—after a long, speculative silence—he tilted his head to one side, frowning, and said, "Why?"

Jenny, thought Joanna irritably, would have known what to say to steer Roland—writer of love-sonnets to unsuitable young women, would-be adventurer, protector of sisters embarking on long journeys—in the correct direction. But Jenny was in Carrington-street, receiving morning callers whose husbands wished to curry favour with Kergabet or the King, and Joanna was here only because the King chose to indulge Sieur Germain's eccentric taste in assistants; and Sieur Germain himself—

"Because, Your Highness," said that gentleman, "she and her father share His Majesty's desire for a strong and stable alliance between their kingdom and ours."

Roland's expression congealed. Joanna managed—just—to refrain from groaning aloud.

Though Sieur Germain clearly recognised that he had taken the wrong tack, and seemed to be trying to come about, it was equally clear that he did not understand the nature of his mistake. Leaving the subject of alliances, he expended some effort in praise of Lucia MacNeill's political acumen; when this failed to crack Roland's air of grim endurance, he shifted rather abruptly into an admiring disquisition on her achievements as a scholar.

Joanna bent to retrieve the box at her feet. Mr. Fowler saw what she was about—though it appeared that no one else did; she caught his eye and scowled meaningly at him until he stepped forward and touched Sieur Germain's elbow. Sieur Germain paused at once, turning his head in Fowler's direction with the intent, Joanna supposed, of glaring him into better-bred behaviour.

Joanna gripped the sides of the box and stepped forward, neatly sidestepping the distracted Sieur Germain.

"Your Royal Highness," she said, holding Roland's startled gaze.

"Lucia MacNeill of Alba presents her respectful compliments, and asks that you accept this token of—" For a moment Joanna's imagination failed her. Sieur Germain had ceased muttering to Mr. Fowler, and she could feel two sets of eyes focused on the back of her head. "Of her earnest wish to learn your heart as she hopes you will come to know hers."

She proffered the box and held her breath, watching Roland's face.

His eyes softened minutely, though his lips remained set in a tense line. After a painful moment's consideration, however, he took the box from Joanna's outstretched hands and said, "My respectful compliments to the Lady Lucia, and I must hope the same."

Joanna heaved a vast, silent, inward sigh of relief as the box left her hands.

Roland resumed his seat, which the rest of the assembled company chose to regard as a concession of sorts, to judge by the perceptible lessening of tension in the room. Settling the box upon his knees, he carefully removed the lid and set it aside, then unfolded the layers of linen and lifted out the portrait.

Joanna watched him closely as he examined it. She had herself studied the face of the heiress of Alba at some length, when the portrait had first come into Sieur Germain's possession, and had concluded that if the portraitist did not greatly exaggerate, Lucia MacNeill was a very beautiful young woman. The artist had contrived to capture, too, a certain challenging light in his subject's blue eyes, which led Joanna to suspect that Roland's life might soon become rather interesting. Roland's brows drew together in thought; one finger gently traced a curve along the canvas, and at last one corner of his mouth tugged reluctantly upward.

"She looks . . . rather clever," he said, as though he had not very lately heard copious evidence to this effect.

"I believe she is accounted so," Sieur Germain agreed, cautiously; it seemed he had decided to pretend likewise.

"I am glad of that," said Roland decidedly. "I could not bear to be married to a stupid woman."

This was very probably a dig at poor Lady Delphine, Prince Edward's betrothed, of whose intellect Roland (not unjustly) held a very low opinion. Fortunately Oscar MacConnachie did not recognise this—or, at any rate, did not choose to acknowledge it—and accepted Roland's compliment to Lucia MacNeill at its face value, with an accommodating bow.

Whilst the eyes of the company were on Oscar MacConnachie, Roland fixed Joanna with a speaking look. Joanna, after the first startled meeting of glances, gave her very fullest attention to the Alban ambassador.

Roland restrained himself, in the ensuing discussion, from offering further comment on the laws and customs of Alba. Joanna thanked the goddess Minerva for this evidence of wisdom, small as it was, until the moment when, daring another glance at Roland, she found him studying her, his mouth set in a grim straight line, and recognised his motive: As his father, Lord Kergabet, and Oscar MacConnachie laid out their plans for Lucia MacNeill and himself, he was watching Joanna—so clearly in the secret where he himself was not—and remembering her assurances that she knew nothing of any such plans.

She met his gaze squarely now, with no effort at apology. She had brought that expression of hard-eyed betrayal upon herself, and she should not be such a coward as to flinch from it.

It was Roland, in the end, who looked away, though it might only be that he felt he had too long neglected the appearance of attending to his elders. When next he seemed about to turn in Joanna's direction, he interrupted the motion and bent his gaze instead upon the portrait in his hands.

*What trials one brings upon oneself,* thought Joanna, *when one makes the mistake of growing romantical!*

## CHAPTER X

# In Which Sophie Encounters
# a Collector of Butterflies

*Sophie carefully speared* a morsel of trout on her fork and lifted it to her lips. It had been poached in wine and was meltingly tender; she wondered whether she might cadge the recipe from the Chancellor's cook, to send to Jenny and Joanna.

"So, Mrs. Marshall," said Professor Maghrebin, who was seated to her left, "I understand that you come from Britain—from the province of Breizh, is that not so?"

Sophie swallowed, smiled politely, and nodded. Who had furnished him that detail? Mór MacRury, very likely; she seemed to take a proprietary interest in all things foreign, and had also, in advance of this dinner party given by the Chancellor and his wife for the University's visiting lecturers and professors, their spouses and their sponsors, provided Sophie and Gray with lively descriptions of many of their fellow guests.

"I have never visited there, but I have been given to understand that it is very beautiful." At the Chancellor's table, as in his lectures, Professor Maghrebin spoke Latin with a musical cadence quite unlike the Albans', the syntax archaic but perfectly clear.

"That is certainly true," said Sophie. The smile felt more genuine now. "And yourself, Professor? You are come from the great city of Alexandria, I am told; is it true that the library there is the largest in the world?"

"I cannot pretend to have seen every library in the world," Professor Maghrebin replied, his dark face creasing in a pleased smile, "but it is certainly the largest I know of, and the oldest. It contains many works of scholarship which, to my knowledge, exist nowhere else."

Libraries were a subject on which Sophie could converse both easily and with enthusiasm, and without straying into awkward territory. She listened, fascinated, as Professor Maghrebin described how a cataloguing system developed by an enterprising librarian during the rule of Ptolemy III had, nearly two centuries later, allowed the librarians to replace many of the scrolls and codices lost in a fire when Julius Caesar besieged the city. With some effort, she controlled her instinctive shudder; she had no wish to explain to a stranger how she had come by so vivid a sense-memory of burning pages fluttering through smoky air.

The library had suffered such destruction more than once, it seemed, but, thanks to the work of selfless librarians and underlibrarians, it had succeeded always in preserving the greater portion of the works housed there, and in replacing those destroyed.

"Though there have been books lost forever, I am sorry to say," said Professor Maghrebin.

"You speak of the library almost as though it were a person in its own right," said Sophie, smiling.

"That is so, I suppose," the Professor replied. "Has not every library its own character? For example, the University Library here in Din Edin puts me in mind of a matriarch in the prime of life, beautiful and stately, of great girth and immense dignity . . ."

Sophie nearly giggled, and at once pictured the library at Merlin College as a crabbed old man who glared menacingly at all comers as a matter of course, but could be relied upon to recognise seekers after wisdom and welcome them in. Her companion caught the small grin which she could not quite suppress, and returned it upon hearing her fanciful description.

The first remove thus passed so pleasantly that Sophie was astonished to find it over, and the next bringing in.

The gentleman to her right was the Chancellor's brother-in-law, who (so Sophie understood from Rory MacCrimmon) was known throughout Din Edin for his collection of rare butterflies, and for the enormous house with which he shared it. Eithne MacLachlan, whose family belonged to a less illustrious branch of the same clan, had contributed the information that visitors were continually being invited to Conall MacLachlan's town house but seldom returned a second time.

"I have been there myself, with my mother and my elder brother," she had told Sophie, with a little shiver, "and you cannot imagine how unpleasant! It is a very army of the poor creatures, ten or twenty or half a hundred to a case, and the cases on every wall; wherever you turn, you may be sure of seeing a poor dead butterfly pinned to a board. He intends his house to be a museum, when he is dead."

Sophie turned to Conall MacLachlan, therefore, with some trepidation but considerable curiosity. What might a man be like to converse with, who chose to share his house with thousands of decorative dead insects?

He was quite ordinary in appearance, a man of about her own height—at any rate whilst seated—who wore his sandy hair long, tied at his nape with a length of black silk, and a close-trimmed beard.

"Sophie Marshall, you hail from Breizh, I believe?" he said, smiling brightly at her. He spoke in Gaelic, but a little slowly, in consideration of her stranger's ear, and she could follow him well enough.

Sophie acknowledged the fact. Had he had it from Mór MacRury also? Or from some other source? Gossip evidently travelled as quickly in great Din Edin as in little Oxford.

"I travelled there once; not so long ago, not more than ten years past," said Conall MacLachlan, "though I suppose that will seem long indeed to a child such as yourself, my dear!"

This statement was accompanied by a cheerful guffaw, in response to which Sophie managed a tight little smile. It would not do to offend the Chancellor's brother-in-law, and though she resented being thought a child, she was certainly much younger than Conall MacLachlan.

"I have a particularly fine *Cupido osiris* in my collection," he continued, "which I acquired on that expedition . . ."

He told her how he had acquired it, in the tone of one recounting a thrilling adventure tale—how he had been seeking quite a different specimen, had been misdirected by a local man and found himself quite lost, had emerged from a coppice-wood into a meadow where dairy cattle were pastured, and come face-to-face with a stand of wildflowers populated by brilliantly blue butterflies.

Sophie listened with half an ear, eating steadily—the Chancellor's haunch of venison was excellent, and she was rather sorry that Joanna should not have been present to enjoy it—until Conall MacLachlan caught her full attention by saying, all unexpectedly, "I do not suppose you might be familiar with the temple of the Lady Dahut at Kerandraon?"

For a moment Sophie said nothing at all, frozen in shock and dire remembrance: Her stepfather had meant Gray to die in that temple, and Joanna certainly should have done, if not for Gray's quick work with a finding-spell and a strong arm to pull her back from the brink.

At last she said, "I was there once, indeed; though I might mistake, for the temple I visited was dedicated to Neptune, with a shrine of more recent date to Lady Dahut."

Conall MacLachlan waved a dismissive hand. "It is a matter of perspective only," he said. Then, with a little frown: "You do not give preference to the gods of your country's conquerors, I hope?"

Sophie regretted her unconsidered words; she had remarked before this that the gods of Rome had almost no following here, and that, indeed—particularly outside the University—many seemed to consider them a topic unfit for polite conversation.

"I hope I give all the gods their due," she said carefully.

"One can ask no more, I suppose," Conall MacLachlan conceded, though with an expression of mild distaste. After a moment he continued, "I acquired another very interesting specimen in the neighbourhood of that shrine—a swallowtail, *Papilio machaon*, with most unusual colouring—and with it an intriguing legend."

"Indeed?" Sophie managed, concealing her apprehension in a perhaps inadvisably large swallow of the Chancellor's claret.

"I suppose, being from that country yourself, you must be familiar with some of the tales told of the Breton queen?"

Sophie admitted that she was, in order to be spared hearing any of them.

"I stopped for several days at an inn in Kerandraon—well, I say *an* inn; it was *the* inn, in truth, for the town was too small to have more than one."

"The Serpent and Master," Sophie said, without thinking.

"Ah, you know it!"

"As you say, it is the town's only inn."

"Indeed. I stopped there, as I mentioned, for several days, for the proprietor had a most promising garden—for the *Lepidoptera*, you know; and his wife was a surprisingly good cook." He paused for a bite of roast fowl, and Sophie, fortifying herself with another swallow of wine, took the opportunity of inquiring about the garden, and describing, in such detail as she was capable of recalling, the butterflies she could remember seeing in the gardens at Merlin College.

It was soon clear, however, that she could not provide sufficiently exact information to hold her companion's interest.

"I was telling you, my dear," he said, gently interrupting her stumbling description of the enormous blue dragonflies that frequented the banks of the Thames where it flowed through Oxford, "what an intriguing tale I had from the keeper of the Serpent and Master. It seems there is a local tradition that the Lady Laora ar Breizh, she who was afterward the wife of your King Henry, came to the shrine at Kerandraon—though not that one only—with promises and offerings, to beseech the Lady Dahut to spare her from the illustrious marriage to which her father had promised her."

"D-do they say so?" Sophie managed, belatedly remarking that Conall MacLachlan was waiting for her to speak. "That tale is one I never heard at home." This was, in the strictest sense, quite true; she had in fact heard it much afterwards, from Gray, who had had it from her stepfather's coachman on the occasion of that disastrous pilgrimage.

Conall MacLachlan eyed her shrewdly. "They do say so, in fact," he said. "They say it still, I am told; and I have heard, too, that though the Lady Dahut denied her petition, it was to Kerandraon that Queen Laora returned when she fled her gilded prison in London, and in Kerandraon, or its environs, that she died, leaving her daughter to the care of a neglectful stepfather."

Sophie schooled her features—without magick—into an expression of polite interest; beneath the tablecloth, she clenched her fingers in the folds of her gown.

"Of course, being so lately in London, you must have heard the newest rumours from Henry Tudor's court?"

Sophie lifted a forkful of venison to her lips and chewed it, thinking hard. Was the use of her father's name in place of his title Alban custom or calculated disrespect? And what rumours could he mean? Not her own tale, at any rate; even so far away as Alba, events two years in the past could not possibly be considered *new*—and clearly Conall MacLachlan knew exactly who she was, or thought he did. What, then? If there had been any interesting rumours flying about London at Midsummer, they had flown quite over Sophie's head.

"I fear that I have nothing of that nature to relate," she said, when she had finished chewing.

"Indeed?" Conall MacLachlan raised his eyebrows in honest surprise, or a very good counterfeit thereof. "There is no talk, for instance, of a betrothal for one of the King's sons?"

"Oh!" said Sophie. "Yes, as to that, the Crown Prince is to marry Lady Delphine d'Evreux—next autumn, I believe. But that is not rumour; it is settled fact."

"But Edward Tudor has two brothers, has he not?"

"His Majesty has two younger sons, yes." Sophie laid a subtle stress on the Latin title, from a perverse desire to defend the very dignities which she so much disdained on her own behalf. "I have heard nothing of the kind with respect to either of them, however."

Conall MacLachlan's expression suggested that he did not altogether believe her but could not think how to accuse her of dissembling without provoking a scene. As Sophie had been perfectly truthful, however, she had no difficulty in meeting his gaze, and after a moment he turned back to his venison and winter squash.

Her curiosity getting the better of her, Sophie said, "May I ask, sir, what prompted your question?"

"I think you know, Domina Marshall." The slight emphasis on her name and title—her own tactic turned upon her—might be her imagination; the knowing half smile that accompanied it was not.

"You must have heard many such curious tales in your travels," said Sophie, for after all she was not eager to give offence to her hostess. "I have travelled very little myself as yet, but I confess I have a great fondness for it. I suppose you must have seen a vast number of strange and interesting places?"

Conall MacLachlan looked sidewise at her.

To Sophie's relief, however, he took up the offered change of subject with no further comment, recounting with some spirit—though with more than occasional pauses to redact elements which, he said, were not for a lady's ears—his adventures in various parts of the Iberian Empire, until the table turned again with the final remove.

She suspected him of choosing the locale for the purpose of provoking some reaction from her, and unwilling to concede him this victory, she smiled and laughed at his outrageous tales, and sipped at her wineglass—which seemed perpetually full—and turned over in her mind the question which she had asked and Conall MacLachlan had declined to answer.

It was not the custom here as it was at home, for the ladies to rise and withdraw at the end of the meal whilst the gentlemen remained in possession of the dining-room. Instead, a signal from their hostess produced a general shift from table to music-room, where inevitably, in Din Edin as in London, smaller groups began to coalesce as the guests, no longer constrained by their placement at the dinner-table, sought out those others of the party with whom they genuinely wished to converse.

The music room was large and well furnished with a gleaming pianoforte, large and small harps, a little group of music-stands, and sensible racks for sheet-music discreetly concealed behind a tall folding screen painted with twining roses. Sophie did not recognise that she was drifting towards the pianoforte until she found herself standing before the closed keyboard with the fingers of her right hand resting upon the hinged lid; she was just snatching her hand away, hoping that no one had remarked it, when from behind her a hearty voice said, in heavily accented Latin, "Oh! Domina Marshall, are you a musician as well as a scholar?"

Sophie whirled, flushing, and found herself face-to-face with the Erse lecturer whom she had seen at dinner talking with Rory Mac-Crimmon. She produced a panicked smile and held out her hand, Alban-fashion, then at once wished that she had not. The older woman clasped it, however, with a warm smile of her own, and with a rush of relief Sophie at last succeeded in recalling her name. "Meadhbh Ní Sabháin," she said. "Yes, I am, in a small way; and yourself?"

"Sophie Marshall is too modest," said Mór MacRury, looming up behind Meadhbh Ní Sabháin. Her arm was looped familiarly through Rory MacCrimmon's, as though they had been two women, or two men; as they were nearly of a height, however, it did not look so odd as it might have done. "She is a very fine musician, and well she knows it."

"Mór," said Sophie, half in greeting, half in protest. The heat that had begun to fade from her cheeks rushed back redoubled. "Rory."

Mór MacRury drew away and spoke quietly to Meadhbh Ní Sabháin—not so quietly, however, that Sophie could not hear her. "If you wish to persuade Sophie Marshall to play and sing for you," she said, with a smile just this side of wicked glee, "the way to go about it is to offer her a song for her collection."

Sophie smiled at this portrait of herself, collecting songs as Conall MacLachlan collected butterflies. The giggle that next escaped her, despite her best efforts to maintain the dignity appropriate to a scholar, brought home to her just how much wine she had drunk with her dinner.

*I ought to know better than that. I do know better. Imagine the things I might have said, after two more glasses!*

She took a deep breath.

"I should very much like to learn a new Erse song or two, Meadhbh Ní Sabháin," she said, "if you do not dislike the idea." It occurred to her that this was not her own house, and she added hastily, "And if our hostess has no objection."

The Chancellor's lady was at this moment crossing the room towards them, and—before Sophie had quite come to terms with the situation—gathering her guests before her like a mother duck chivvying her ducklings.

"Now, Sophie Marshall," she said, "Mór MacRury has been telling me great things of you. You will not deny us a song, I hope?"

Ceana MacLachlan—Sophie still found it difficult not to think of her as Mrs. Arthur Breck—was much younger than her husband, though not so young as Sophie; the Chancellor and his wife put her in mind, in fact, of her father and stepmother, though she had no reason to suppose their partnership equally fraught. Ceana MacLachlan's elegantly dressed hair was the colour of sunrise in winter, a soft gold just touched with rose, and she had her brother's cornflower-blue eyes and his trick of narrowing them at the object of her scrutiny; but if she shared his desire to extract information from Sophie, she concealed it to much better effect.

"I—" Sophie faltered. "I thank you, very much—I fear that Mór MacRury greatly flatters me—"

"Oh, Sophie, sing 'Ailein Duinn,'" said Mór.

"Later, perhaps," said Ceana MacLachlan. "I should like first to hear a song of *your* home, Sophie Marshall, as we are honouring our visitors this evening. And then perhaps Meadhbh Ní Sabháin may favour us with a song of Eire?"

"Oh! Yes, please," cried Sophie, only just managing to refrain from clapping her hands.

Meadhbh Ní Sabháin smiled at her. "Certainly," she said.

At their urging, Sophie sat down to the pianoforte. Her hands arranged themselves upon the keys, almost without her conscious intention, as she considered: A song of Breizh? Of London? Of Oxfordshire? The melodies that presented themselves to her mind were those she had been learning from Donella MacHutcheon, from Mór and Rory and even Catriona, and she chuckled again, ruefully; had she indeed become a collector of songs?

*Well, it is a more sensible occupation than collecting butterflies, at any rate.*

Behind her, a sudden gust of wind rattled against a window-pane.

"Oh!" said Sophie abruptly, straightening her spine.

She resettled her hands in the necessary positions, and began to play.

> *The trees they grow so high, and the leaves*
> *they do grow green,*

she sang.

> *And many a cold winter night my love and I have seen.*
> *Of a cold winter night, my love, you and I alone have been;*
> *Whilst my bonny boy is young, he's a-growing.*

This song of Somersetshire was one she had loved from a child, one which her stepfather had forbidden—for reasons obscure to her until much later—and which she had reclaimed, in some sense, as a badge of her freedom from him.

When, at the end of the burden, she struck into the interlude, Sophie became aware that the hum of conversation had grown quieter, and eyes were turning towards her. She knew, of course, that her playing and singing were not altogether easy, and not only because Ceana MacLachlan's pianoforte was stiffer than her own well-worn instrument in Quarry Close. Amongst her close acquaintance, it might be no great matter if her singing should transmit her mood to her listeners; here, however, it would not do, being just the sort of uninvited, unacknowledged influence which Dougal MacAngus, the lecturer in magickal ethics, called *an unjustifiable violation of the subject's will*. So far as she was able, therefore, she exerted herself to convey nothing in her singing but the songs themselves.

It was astonishingly difficult.

She reached the final verse at last and slid into the refrain:

> *I'll sit and I'll mourn his fate until the day I die,*
> *And I'll watch all o'er his child while he's growing . . .*

Then, slumping a little and briefly closing her eyes, she lifted her hands from the keyboard and folded them in her lap.

She had just time to notice that the room was very quiet—quieter than she could at all account for—before the company erupted into applause.

When pressed for another song, she ceded to Mór MacRury's reiterated request for "Ailein Duinn," and then in turn petitioned those listeners who had gathered round the pianoforte to contribute a song to her collection—having decided that if she were to be known here in any case as a collector of popular songs, no great harm could come of embracing the title.

Meadhbh Ní Sabháin obliged with an unaccompanied song which she called a *caoineadh*. The music-room fell silent, little by little, as she sang; Sophie, coming back to herself at last to find tears drying on her cheeks, was not in the least astonished to be told that the *caoineadh* was a mourning-song. The one she had sung, Meadhbh Ní Sabháin explained, had been made by her own grandmother, upon the death of her first husband, and sung in the family ever since.

"We have had a song of mine, Mór MacRury," said Meadhbh Ní Sabháin, smiling across the pianoforte despite the almost sombre mood of the room; "will you give us a song of yours?"

"Oh, yes, Mór, do," said Sophie eagerly. "'Fear a' Bhàta,' perhaps? That is Gray's favourite, you know." Sophie did not sing it for him often; though Mór called it hopeful, it seemed to her almost as boundlessly sad as "Ailein Duinn."

Mór, having surely anticipated some such request, accepted it gracefully, though there was a shadow of something in her bright blue eyes that looked very like anxiety. "You will play for me?" she said, moving to stand at Sophie's right, and Sophie nodded.

Mór MacRury, by her own admission, was an indifferent player upon the pianoforte, and only a little more skilled upon the harp, having had no opportunity to learn either as a girl. She had a sharp ear, however, and had learnt to show her voice to best advantage. It was a rich contralto, warm and deep, the colour of burnt sugar; and she invested the words of her song—composed, she had explained to Sophie, by a young woman whose betrothed had been feared lost at sea—with a yearning beauty that made Sophie wonder whether Mór had herself lost a husband or lover. Sophie could scarcely imagine asking such a question of anyone, however, and of the formidable, self-contained Mór MacRury still less.

The final verse of the song flowed into its refrain, and Sophie could not help adding a soft descant above the melody. Mór's vocal range was so much lower than her own that it was very like singing in harmony with Gray, though entirely without the characteristic shiver of magick passing between them.

*Fhir a' Bhàta, na hóro eile,*
*Fhir a' Bhàta, na hóro eile,*
*Fhir a' Bhàta, na hóro eile,*
*Mo shoraidh slàn leat 's gach àit' an téid thu!*

Their listeners applauded, and Mór retired from the field, wearing an expression of quiet satisfaction.

The impromptu concert seemed then at an end, and the gathering round the pianoforte dispersed. Before the end of the evening, however, Ceana MacLachlan sought Sophie out in her husband's library—where she was pleasantly engaged with Gray, Rory, and Professor Maghrebin in comparing two versions of an ancient atlas of the Mediterranean coast—to request another song.

Sophie, still fearful of giving offence, acquiesced with her most pleasant smile, though she had begun to feel rather like a performing bear.

"Perhaps a duet?" she suggested, catching at Gray's hand as they passed out of the room.

"Oh!" Ceana MacLachlan turned to him with a delighted and slightly acquisitive smile. "You are a musician, also, Magister?"

*Perhaps Ceana MacLachlan is a collector, like her brother,* thought Sophie, *but of useful dinner-guests rather than* Lepidoptera.

When they regained the music-room, a debate was going forward between the Chancellor and several of his local guests—for the benefit of their Erse colleagues—as to whether the best views of the city were to be obtained from Castle Hill or from the peak of Arthur's Seat.

Sophie resumed her former seat at the pianoforte, and Gray stood at her back, his left hand resting on her right shoulder.

To assuage her nerves, Sophie fell back on their first and favourite duet, the song of the Border Country which they had sung together long before either had any suspicion of what they should one day be to one another.

Gray's resonant baritone carried the melody, steady and clear; the chord progression was so familiar that Sophie's fingers could execute it almost without conscious thought, leaving the most of her attention to the more interesting question of devising an obbligato. Though she had devoted many hours and a great deal of paper and ink to the annotation of melodies acquired from other sources, Sophie had never tried to pin her improvised descants to the page; it was part of the joy of singing with Gray—unshakable in any melody, once learnt—that she need never sing a descant the same way twice.

Gray's hand on her shoulder warmed her skin, a tangible connexion mirroring the ephemeral link that hummed between them. Sophie forgot their audience entirely, forgot that she was surrounded by near strangers, and surrendered to the joy of the song.

When the final chord died away, she came full awake once more to a deep, unnerving silence.

Gray's fingers tightened along her collar-bone, in warning or in reassurance; she blinked, with a small reflexive shake of her head, and raised her eyes to look about her.

Apprehension seized her at the sight of a dozen faces staring wide-eyed back at her. Had she set her magick loose, even briefly, without intending it? Or unknowingly committed some breach of custom, some insult to the Chancellor's hospitality?

At last Arthur Breck himself cleared his throat and said gruffly, "That was well sung; I congratulate you."

Sophie bowed her head again in pleased relief, and Gray relaxed his hold upon her shoulder.

The silence having been broken, conversations again struck up around the room. Sophie rose from her seat, flashed a brief, tense smile at Gray, and took shelter in the corner behind the standing harp—which was taller than herself and thus offered the best possibility of concealment—to regain her composure. Her back against the oak panelling, she pressed the heels of her hands to her eyes and took a deep breath.

Hearing footsteps, she raised her head, expecting to see Gray—but instead beheld Mór MacRury, approaching with her slim hands clasped about her elbows and a tense, troubled expression on her face.

"Mór—" Sophie faltered. "Are . . . are you quite well?"

Mór's blue eyes studied her, uncomfortably sharp. "I do not understand you, Sophie Marshall," she said at last.

Sophie could think of no reply.

"Your husband told me," Mór continued, "that you and he *are much in the habit of working spells in concert.* Is this what you meant?"

Sophie's shoulders tensed, even as the more rational part of her mind pointed out that she had survived far worse things than an awkward conversation about the nature and idiosyncrasies of her magick.

"I am not altogether sure what you mean," she said—carefully, but with perfect truth.

Mór's russet brows crimped briefly, a flash of impatience that vanished almost as soon as it appeared. "You forget that I see what most cannot."

"Well, then," began Sophie, "perhaps—"

"Do tell us, Mór MacRury." Mór started at the sound of Gray's voice as he stepped up behind her. "What is it that you see?"

With the pianoforte at his back, Gray listened with only half an ear to the conversation around him, keeping an eye firmly on Sophie. She had (as Gray had more than half expected, after having been so much stared at) withdrawn to a secluded corner, where she might feel less like a specimen under glass. At present she was half concealed behind a large harp, her dark head bowed and her hands pressed to her eyes: both trying not to weep and reading herself a stern lecture on the foolishness of her feelings—a habit which he earnestly hoped that she might soon leave behind—and trying, too, to resist the lure of her native magick. If only she were not so determined upon this point . . . ! Her self-imposed restrictions were already wearing upon her, perhaps more than she knew; though of course it was her secret to keep if she chose, he could not think such secrecy needful, in a place where the heiress to the throne could dine in the University Refectory quite without remark.

Mór MacRury hovered at the edge of the little crowd about the pianoforte, her narrowed eyes darting from Gray to Sophie and back again. She could see magick, Gray knew; what had she seen just now, and what had it told her?

He was prepared to consider Mór MacRury a problem for another day, however, until she broke away from the group and stalked purposefully towards Sophie's place of refuge. Then he made polite excuses—though scarcely knowing what he said—to the Chancellor and his lady, and followed her, coming within earshot just in time to hear Mór MacRury say, "You forget that I see what most cannot."

"Do tell us, Mór MacRury," he said, and was gratified by her start of surprise and a little disgusted with himself for it. "What is it that you see?"

Sophie was pale but resolute, her eyes overbright and her slim hands clenched tightly in the folds of her skirts. Stepping warily around Mór MacRury, Gray stood at Sophie's left hand, and drawing her close against his side with one arm, he held fast until she straightened away, squaring her shoulders.

Mór MacRury had all this time stood silently watching them, or rather watching some indeterminate point in their vicinity. Now she spoke at last, her voice low and hesitant: "I see . . . I see magick running *between* you, ebbing and flowing like the tide. I see your magick, and *your* magick, separate from one another, but also . . . twining, joining. Almost . . . *growing*." Her hands sketched these puzzling phenomena in the air before her face, and she spoke faster and faster. "This is entirely beyond a joint working—it is almost a *shared* magick—shared in both directions, which ought to be impossible. And what is stranger still is that your magicks appear to replenish one another: not as a vessel is filled from a stream, but as two streams commingle to form a river."

Gray looked down at Sophie. From this angle he could see her face only obliquely; it was pale and set, but when he took her hand, he found it steady.

"Will you," said Mór MacRury, "will you tell me how you do it?"

Gray gave Sophie's fingers a gentle squeeze; she raised her face to his and nodded minutely.

"We can tell you only what we know ourselves," said Gray, "which is very little: only that since we were married, our magicks have worked together in a way they did not before."

"It is not a thing we *do*," Sophie added, "but a thing that *is*."

Gray nodded. He could still see in his mind's eye—as he had seen them on the morning after their wedding—the faded flowers from Sophie's hair, discarded upon the dressing-table, transformed into living blooms rooted in the wood.

Though such effects had fortunately not proved permanent, the bone-deep thrum of *rightness* which he felt whenever so much as their hands touched, of magick finding magick and returning strength for strength, had never faded. However poorly understood, it was a chapter of their shared tale—as much a part of his present self as the small sufferings and joys of his childhood in Kernow, as his long journey from cowed, stammering boy to Master Marshall of Merlin. As much a part of both of them, in fact, as they now were of one another.

"And . . . has this effect any limits, to your knowledge?" said Mór MacRury.

Gray and Sophie looked at one another, and Sophie shrugged.

Mór MacRury's eyes widened. "Men dream of such power," she said, a little unsteadily.

"I do not doubt it," said Gray.

Mór MacRury cast a brief glance over her shoulder, past the harp-frame at her back, and said, "We cannot stand much longer whispering in corners before someone comes to fetch us out. I should advise you to keep your own counsel on this matter; the world is more full of unscrupulous persons than you may imagine."

It was on the tip of Gray's tongue to say that Sophie and he possessed extensive experience with unscrupulous persons, and needed no such warning. "Of course," he said instead.

The three of them returned to the rest of the party arm in arm, discussing the works of Robert Burns, poet of the Border Country, and amiably debating whether his poetry were more Alban or more English in character. Gray fancied that the Chancellor's brother-in-law—he who had been conversing so animatedly (one might almost have said forcefully) with Sophie throughout the second remove—cast a suspicious glance or two in their direction; but neither he nor anybody else made any remark which could not be construed as entirely innocent, and the company parted for the evening without further incident.

## CHAPTER XI

# In Which Jenny Entertains
# Unexpected Visitors

*Roland's behaviour towards* Joanna had undergone an abrupt revolution, from dogging her every step with love-poetry and even less subtle declarations to avoiding her presence insofar as he was able and addressing her with chill formality when he could not. Joanna's initial relief at the withdrawal of his importunate attentions—though undiminished in itself—retreated into the background as it became clear to her that no return to their former uncomplicated friendship was to be forthcoming.

As Roland was drawn more closely into the ongoing negotiation of the arrangement, moreover, the two of them were increasingly thrown together, and Roland's drastically altered manners drew the notice of more than herself.

"Miss Callender," said Mr. Fowler one afternoon in early November, raising his eyes from the document he was copying to regard her diffidently across their paired desks. "I wonder—it is none of my affair, I am sure—"

Joanna bit back a sharp retort.

"I have remarked," he went on, perhaps encouraged by her lack of sarcasm, "that you are always the most successful at reasoning with Prince Roland. Were it not—that is—"

She watched, unamused, as he struggled to evolve an inoffensive circumlocution for the words *if you were not a girl.*

"I might almost have said," Mr. Fowler at last said, "that you and His Royal Highness were . . . friends."

Joanna returned his gaze steadily, expressionlessly, and said nothing; she knew where he was going, or was seeking to go, and refused to help him on his way.

Mr. Fowler looked down at the pen he was twisting in his fingers, then up at Joanna again; finally, fixing his gaze on a point above her right shoulder, he said, "It seems to me, Miss Callender, that if this was so once, it is so no longer. You understand, I am sure, the importance of this arrangement with Alba, and the absolute necessity of its going forward unhindered; if the disagreement between yourself and the Prince, or any other . . . aspect . . . of your private life should in any way impede—"

Almost without conscious volition, Joanna found herself on her feet, both hands flat on the polished surface of her desk, glaring down at Fowler. Some part of her mind, fierce and deeply buried, snarled in malicious triumph to see him rear back wide-eyed in alarm.

"I have Lord Kergabet's trust," she said coldly, snapping off each word as though she might thus make of it a keen-edged weapon aimed at Fowler's heart. "And I have sworn the same oath of fealty to His Majesty as you have yourself. I hope you do not suppose that it means less to me, because I am not a man?"

Mr. Fowler blinked at her in stunned silence.

"I have stood Prince Roland's friend longer than you have been at all acquainted with him," Joanna continued—though it was not so very long for all that—"and shall continue to do so, whether or not he chooses to acknowledge it." She leant forward a little, to press her advantage of height—which Fowler (being nearly a foot taller than herself) might have obviated at any moment by rising from his chair, and yet had not.

"If you cannot persuade yourself to trust in my loyalty to my kingdom, my patron, or my friend," she said, "you might at the very least consider what a mutton-headed fool I should be to throw away the work of a year and more for the sake of a petty quarrel."

Joanna gathered her fair copies into a tidy stack, squared the corners with aggressive precision, slotted them into a folder, and tied up the red tapes. "Good afternoon, Mr. Fowler," she said icily, and marched away with her head high and her files clasped firmly to her breast to quell the angry roiling in her belly.

Some days later Joanna returned from a damp and chilly morning ride about the park—escorted by Gaël, for Gwendolen had slept badly and declined to accompany her—to find the household in uproar, and a pair of strangers in Jenny's morning-room.

She paused in the doorway, her soggy gloves in her hand, to stare at them in surprise. On the sofa facing the door sat a dark, narrow-faced, whipcord-lean man of middle age, wearing sober country dress and a deeply unhappy expression. A plump fair-haired young woman perched beside him, clinging limpet-like to his elbow; though her attire was that of a matronly gentlewoman, she looked no older than Jenny—young enough, indeed, to be the man's daughter, but it was not with a daughter's eyes that she gazed up at him.

There was something familiar about the man's face. Joanna could not place it, however, until her eye fell upon Jenny, poised and calm but with the glint of battle in her hazel eyes, and beside her on the opposite sofa, Gwendolen. Glancing from one narrow, dark-eyed face to the other, Joanna concluded at once that she was at last about to be introduced to Mr. and the infamous Mrs. Pryce.

"Had you a pleasant ride, my dear?" Jenny inquired.

"I am sorry, Jenny," said Joanna, thrusting the dripping riding-gloves out of sight behind her skirts. "I did not mean to interrupt—"

"Oh, do please come in, Jo—Miss Callender!" said Gwendolen, too quickly; and at once she rose, crossed the room, and clasped Joanna's free hand to tow her back towards the sofas.

"Papa, Stepmama," she said, "may I present my friend Miss Callender? Miss Callender, my father and stepmother."

No sooner was everyone seated again than Mrs. Pryce, with the air of one continuing an interrupted dispute, burst out, "But it is too bad of you, Gwendolen, to give your papa and me such a deal of worry!"

Gwendolen drew herself up, her hands clenched in her lap, and said frostily, "If indeed you have been worried for my sake, ma'am, I am sorry for it."

Jenny's lips twitched minutely. "I regret very much that you should have been alarmed about your stepdaughter's welfare, Mrs. Pryce," she said. "Had I known that her letters were not reaching you—"

"Let us have no pretence, Lady Kergabet," said Mr. Pryce. "We are grateful for the kind hospitality you have extended towards Gwendolen. I must object very strongly, however, to your abetting her in abandoning the situation which my wife was at such pains to arrange for her, and to your harbouring her for such a period, without until lately informing me of her whereabouts." He drew breath, clearly working up a fine head of steam, and turned to Gwendolen. "Did you never consider what agonies of apprehension we should be subjected to, upon the Griffith-Rowlands' returning to Clwyd without you?"

Gwendolen lifted her chin. "If Mrs. Griffith-Rowland did not choose to tell you where I had gone," she said, "or why I left her employ, that is no fault of mine."

Her voice shook a little; her hands were clenched together in her lap.

Jenny laid one slim, pale hand over Gwendolen's darker ones. "I should of course have written to you myself at once to reassure you," she told Mr. Pryce, "had it for a moment occurred to me that Gwendolen's letters to you might *all* have gone astray."

Mr. Pryce did not look as though he believed in those letters any more than Joanna did, in which disbelief Joanna saw the first sign that he at all understood his daughter's character. It irked her a little that Gwendolen did not at once confess to not having written any;

what was she about, to be letting Jenny take the blame for her own irresponsible behaviour?

"In any event," said Jenny, her tone still silky-calm, "here you are, Mr. Pryce, and here is Gwendolen, safe and sound, and, I am persuaded, none the worse for her sojourn in my house; and it now remains to discuss how we ought to proceed from here."

"What can there be to *discuss*?" said Mrs. Pryce. "We have come more than two hundred miles from Clwyd, on the roughest and dirtiest roads imaginable, to fetch Gwendolen home with us; we have all that distance to travel again, and we must be on our way tomorrow morning." Belatedly she added, "Is that not so, my dear?"

"Yes," said Mr. Pryce, with a decisive nod.

"*No,*" said Gwendolen.

There was a long, shocked silence. Gwendolen trembled, but stood her ground.

"So, you see," said Jenny, "we have indeed a great deal to discuss."


The Pryces, cowed by Jenny's calm unwavering smile, allowed themselves to be formally welcomed to her house and spoke the words of acceptance almost, it appeared, in a sort of daze. Treveur and Daisy appeared with refreshments, which everyone but Joanna ignored; whilst she sampled Mrs. Treveur's tea-cakes and *petits fours*, and tried to induce Gwendolen to do the same, Jenny said, "It seems to me, Mr. Pryce, that we have both the same end in view."

Mr. Pryce frowned at her. "And what is that?"

"You, I presume," said Jenny, "wish Gwendolen happily settled?"

He nodded warily.

"And I am sure you had rather that she did not disrupt your household, and your new family?"

"Lady Kergabet, I must object—"

"The difficulty being, of course," Jenny continued, "that Gwendolen is still very young, with little experience of the world, and your wife, Mr. Pryce, not much less so. I can think of no other explanation for her appalling lack of good judgement in placing a girl of Gwendolen's youth and inexperience at the mercy of Juliana Griffith-Rowland."

"How can you say such a thing?" Mrs. Pryce demanded; then, evidently remembering to whom she spoke, she said, "I beg your pardon, Lady Kergabet! It is only that—to be accused of poor judgement, and of making one's own child unhappy—"

"I am *not* your child!" Gwendolen cried, leaping furiously to her feet. "You are not my mother! How dare you speak to me as though—"

By now Mrs. Pryce was also on her feet, sputtering in outrage.

"My dear," said Mr. Pryce.

"Mrs. Pryce, you forget yourself," said Jenny.

At a glance from Jenny, Joanna rose from her seat and drew Gwendolen away from the incipient altercation. "If you will only sit still and be quiet," she said, low, "Jenny will sort it all out."

It was not advice which Joanna would have welcomed herself, in like circumstances, and Gwendolen's expression said very clearly that she liked it no better. Joanna caught both her hands, looked earnestly up into her face (wishing again that Gwen were not quite so tall, or that she herself were a little taller), and said, "Jenny knows what she is about—you have never met her mother, but I have—and they will hear what she says, as they never could persuade themselves to hear you. Do come and sit with me, Gwen."

Gwendolen looked from her father's face to Jenny's, and sat.

Joanna thought back to her first January in London—when the incipient arrival of Agatha had brought Jenny's mother to Carrington-street, affording Joanna the opportunity to observe at close quarters a person whom, on the evidence of many conversations overheard and meaningful looks exchanged between those of her acquaintance who knew Mrs. Edmond Marshall best, she firmly expected to detest. And, indeed, their acquaintance did not begin on a promising note: Mrs. Marshall sailed into Jenny's sitting-room one bitterly cold morning, resplendent in aubergine silk, and beholding Jenny reclining upon the sofa, devoted no more than three sentences to congratulating her on her husband's recent elevation and commiserating with her uncomfortable state, before launching into an eloquent and impassioned diatribe on the appalling behaviour of her own second son. Joanna and Lady Maëlle had watched in astonishment as Jenny, ordinarily so adept at turning an unfortunate conversational current, failed utterly to swim against the tide of her mother's ire, and had waded in to her rescue in a manner not at all to Mrs. Marshall's liking.

But though Jenny might be discomposed, even sometimes cowed, by her own mother, faced with the parents of anybody else, she became a paragon of calm, implacable persuasion.

And it seemed that she had decided—very much to Joanna's surprise, and also to Gwendolen's, if her wide eyes and open mouth were any indication—to persuade Mr. and Mrs. Pryce to lend her, for some indefinite period, their eldest unmarried daughter.

"We should of course expect you to continue whatever allowance you were accustomed to grant Gwendolen for her clothing and pin-money, before her removal to the Griffith-Rowlands'," she said pleasantly, between sips of tea from a delicate porcelain cup painted with laurel-leaves, "and to contribute as necessary to any extraordinary expenses; otherwise, however, we should treat her as a member of the family, with the same privileges and opportunities as are afforded to my sister-in-law Joanna." She smiled. "Through such an arrangement, you should be offering her the best possible opportunity of establishing herself in the world, at comparatively little trouble and expense to yourselves."

Mr. Pryce's expression conveyed suspicion as well as considerable relief; his wife, on the other hand, had altogether ceased to pretend that she was not delighted at the prospect of going home without her stepdaughter, rather than with her.

"This is a very generous offer, Lady Kergabet," said Mr. Pryce, slowly, warily. "Extraordinarily generous, for Gwendolen has not been brought up to such high aspirations, and though Mrs. Griffith-Rowland was kind enough to take her on as a favour to my wife, she seems not even to have made a success of such a little thing as teaching a few children their letters. I am curious, I confess, as to what benefit you can be expecting to gain in return."

Joanna controlled an instinctive wince and felt Gwendolen, close beside her, fail to do so; such a question, from a guest to his hostess, dangerously approached outright insult, and to hear her beloved Jenny, generous and patient almost to a fault, so nearly accused of some base ulterior motive, made her long to disregard her own counsel to keep silence.

At the same time, however, she could not be sorry that Gwendolen's father hesitated even thus much before seizing the opportunity to be rid of his troublesome child.

Jenny chose to ignore the implied insult entirely. "You do not give Gwendolen sufficient credit, I think," she said. "And if she did not succeed with the Griffith-Rowlands, she is in excellent company; did not you know that those children have had six governesses in the past three years?"

There was another long silence, during which Gwendolen's nervous fidgeting with the fabric of her skirts grew so obtrusive that Joanna put her own hands over Gwendolen's to still them. Gwendolen glanced aside at her and produced a tense, miserable smile, which Joanna could not altogether manage to return.

Mr. Pryce turned to his daughter at last and said, "Gwendolen, why did you never tell me that you were unhappy?"

Gwendolen stiffened, and turned her hands the better to clutch at Joanna's.

"I told you so often and in so many ways that I could not begin to count them," she said, her voice shaking with suppressed emotion. "Before you sent me away, and certainly thereafter. Once, when you were gone to Cardiff—perhaps *she* has never told you?—I put up my hair and dressed in a suit of Owein's old clothes, and saddled my pony, and ran away to seek my fortune; I had ridden near forty miles by the time young Hugh Penrys caught up with me to bring me back. It is no fault of mine that you would never hear me."

At this moment, though Joanna would never have dared mention it to either of them, her resemblance to Sophie was astonishing—which perhaps explained the surge of protective ire that quickened Joanna's pulse as she spoke.

"Gwen—" Mr. Pryce began.

"Do you know, Father," said Gwendolen, "why I clapped hold of Lady Kergabet's offer with both hands?" Her grip on Joanna's hands was excruciatingly tight. "I wrote to you that I was lonely and miserable—that if I did not bribe the boot-boy to post my letters for me, Mrs. Griffith-Rowland would open them and read them—that I was to have had a day out every fortnight, and after three months had had none at all—all of those things, and worse ones—I did what I had sworn I should never do, and begged you to rescue me, or to send me sufficient coin to come home myself by the mail-coach—and all of your replies ran the same way: *You are only homesick, and feeling sorry for yourself*; or, *I am sure you must have misunderstood*; or, *You shall learn to like it.*"

Joanna's fingers had gone numb.

"And so you did," said Mrs. Pryce, "or so we concluded you must have done, when your letters ceased being full of grievances."

"I had no more coin to bribe the boot-boy," Gwendolen said, low, "and so then I had to write what would please Mrs. Griffith-Rowland. You suppose me a liar, I know, and you suppose correctly; but it was in *those* letters that I lied, not in the others."

"You were always such a fanciful child, Gwen!" her father exclaimed. "How were we to know that—"

"Mr. Pryce, some things are better left unsaid," said Jenny quietly.

Mr. Pryce subsided, his face taut, one eyelid twitching.

"As your daughter has told you," Jenny continued, "she left the Griffith-Rowlands' house with me, in broad daylight, and with no attempt at concealment. It seems to me that if, as you say, you knew nothing of this, and have had no letters from her these several months, your inquiry into her whereabouts has been strangely delayed."

"Why, my husband began making inquiries the moment we learnt that the Griffith-Rowlands had returned without her!" Mrs.

Pryce exclaimed, indignant. "They seemed quite as astonished to find she was not with us. But such things must be done discreetly—one cannot simply write to all one's acquaintance to ask whether they have seen one's child—imagine how everyone would talk—"

"And what brings you now?" Abruptly letting go Joanna's hands, Gwendolen leapt to her feet again and began pacing back and forth, as though physically incapable of keeping still for another moment. Joanna flexed her numb fingers. "Why now, and not at once? What was in Lady Kergabet's letter that brings you down from Clwyd pell-mell at this late date?"

"Your mama believed—"

Gwendolen whirled and pointed a shaking finger at him. "She is *not my mama*," she hissed. "Mama would never have left me with people who—she would never—"

Her voice cut off abruptly, swallowed into a choking sob, and, dropping her arm, she turned on her heel and ran out of the room.

Mr. Pryce gaped after her; his wife looked affronted.

"She only wanted you to believe her when she told you the truth," said Joanna, rising. She had not puzzled it out before, but now, having seen them all together, she could draw no other conclusion. "To show her that you valued her as much as your wife's children, and to take her part for once. Not to wait until you had something else to gain."

And without staying to witness Mr. Pryce's reaction to her words, or even to apologise to Jenny for having insulted her guests, she stalked out of the morning-room.

As soon as she was out of view of its occupants, she picked up her skirts and ran.

## CHAPTER XII

# In Which Joanna Reveals
# More Than She Intended, and
# Sophie Asks Unwelcome Questions

*Joanna halted outside* the door of Gwendolen's bedroom, abruptly unsure of what to do. The door was very firmly closed, and from behind it came blurred sounds that seemed very like furious sobbing; her welcome seemed uncertain at best.

She could see no particular benefit to be gained from caution, however, and accordingly rapped smartly at the door and said, not loudly but loudly enough to be heard, "Gwen! May I come in?"

Listening hard, she heard a ragged in-drawing of breath, and the scuffing knock of stout country boots against the footboard of a bed.

"Go away," said Gwendolen's voice, thick with tears.

"No," said Joanna.

Beyond the door, the air went very still. Joanna held her breath.

After a long moment, Gwendolen said, "I have nothing to say to anyone." Another ragged breath. "Least of all *you*."

There was defiance in her voice, and a deliberate attempt at cruelty, but beneath it lurked something Joanna knew very well. She drew a deep breath and shut her eyes, laying one hand flat against the door.

"Shall I tell you about my mother and father?" she said, in a conversational tone.

Gwendolen said nothing, and Joanna carried on as she had in any case intended. It was not so very difficult, so long as she was speaking to a faceless, voiceless door, which could neither mock nor pity her.

"My mother married my father in an effort to purchase safety for herself and my sister Sophie," she said, "and greatly regretted it before long. He would not . . . he . . . she knew that he would continue his, his demands upon her, which she found . . . unpleasant, until she had given him a son. She hoped that I should be her deliverance, but her hope was thwarted. She gave me a name meaning 'gift of God'—the god of the Judæi, it appears—in a spirit of bitter irony, and looked at me always as though she could scarcely bear the fact of my existence.

"Though I must concede," Joanna added, in belated justice to her mother, "that she was always patient with me, and never cruel."

*Or cruel only in the smiles and caresses she gave so generously to Sophie, and never to me.*

Never before had she said any of this to anyone but Sophie—not even Lady Maëlle, who had always stood in place of a mother to her, could have any notion how much of this history she had pieced together in the course of the past several years.

"Jo—"

"And my father's history I am sure you know," Joanna said, sorry now that she had begun this tale but possessed of a reckless determination to finish it. "It was in all the broadsheets, after all. As for me, he fed and clothed me, and sent me to something resembling a school, for which I suppose I must be grateful to him; and when I was eight years old, he bought me a pony, because my sisters would not leave off badgering him until he agreed. I loved him then, I think, for Gwenn-ha-du's sake—that was the pony's name, because he was black and white—and I wish I had not, for it made everything worse, later.

"When I was thirteen, he set a trap for my brother-in-law that nearly killed me by mistake; and when Sophie and I ran away from home, he—"

The polished wood of the door parted from Joanna's spread hand.

Startled, she opened her eyes and beheld Gwendolen's blotched, swollen face, half hidden behind the handkerchief with which she was blotting her nose and cheeks.

"You have made your point, Jo," said Gwendolen. Her voice was blurred and muffled.

The words might be callous, but above the handkerchief her dark eyes were soft with compassion. Joanna—who had meant only to show Gwendolen how fortunate she was to have had, once, a mother who loved her—turned her face away and gripped the door-jamb. *Gentle Brighid, noble Aesculapius, spare me from being sick here in the corridor.*

Gwendolen's hand smoothed circles against her bowed back.

"I told him," Joanna said, low-voiced, through gritted teeth. "Your father. He understands, now, I believe, so far as he ever will."

She swallowed once, again; the sharp nausea was passing, but she felt trampled and wrung out.

"What, Jo?" said Gwendolen. "What did you tell him?"

Joanna repeated her words, as best she could remember them, and watched Gwendolen's face set in lines of bitter satisfaction.

She wound an arm diffidently about Joanna's shoulders. Joanna returned her embrace with equal caution, and allowed herself to be shepherded by degrees through the door and into Gwendolen's bedroom.

They perched side by side on the edge of the bed, which was mussed and rumpled, the pillow squashed and tear-stained.

Their arms stole wordlessly about one another's waists, and they leaned their shoulders together.

"My father came to London in search of Sophie," Joanna said, speaking indistinctly into Gwendolen's shoulder, "because she was necessary to his scheme. By that time I do not suppose I still believed him fond of me, and the gods know that I had no great love for him; but I confess I should have liked to believe that he had at least remarked my absence."

Most people, Joanna reflected, would have leapt to reassure her that of course she had been missed. Gwendolen, wisely, held her tightly and said nothing.

\*   \*   \*

They sat in companionable silence for so long that the hesitant rapping at the door startled them out of all proportion to its volume.

The door opened to reveal Daisy, her freckled face pinched with worry. "Miss Pryce," she said, bobbing a little curtsey. "Miss Joanna. M'lady wished me to say that dinner will be served in 'alf an hour's time, if you like to come down, and that there will not be any guests to dinner."

"Thank you, Daisy," said Joanna. She cast a sidelong look at Gwendolen, who was staring at the laurel-leaf pattern of the carpet as though her life depended on learning it by heart, and nudged her shoulder gently.

Gwendolen nodded, though she did not look up.

"You may tell Lady Kergabet that we shall both be down to dinner," said Joanna to Daisy.


And down to dinner they were, as composed as half an hour's determined application of cold water and towels, hair-pins, and fresh gowns could make them. Jenny kissed them both, one on each cheek, and smiled kindly, and a little sadly; otherwise no reference was made by anyone to the events of the morning, unless it were in their unaccustomed quiet. Joanna was certain that Jenny had taken the opportunity of Gwendolen's absence and her own to apprise her husband of developments, for though Kergabet was too well bred, and too kind, to knowingly raise an awkward subject at the dinner-table, his manner towards Gwendolen—otherwise perfectly natural—was just solicitous enough to give him away.

Mr. Fowler, by contrast, apparently labouring under some compulsion to fill the void left by the pensive near-silence of everybody else, subjected the company to a lengthy disquisition on the subject of peculiarities in the tax rolls of Maine.

"Prince Roland inquired after you," Sieur Germain told Joanna, when the family had gathered in the drawing-room after dinner, "and hopes you are quite well."

"Does he?" Joanna pretended to be watching Gwendolen and Jenny opening the pianoforte and paging desultorily through the music in the rack, though in the absence of Sophie and her magick, such an activity could hold no charm for her.

When she again felt able to look at Sieur Germain, she found him studying her with disconcerting interest. As he seemed about to speak, she forestalled him by saying, "I hope Jenny is not terribly cross with me over my behaviour to Gwendolen's father."

He regarded her in honest perplexity. "I do not know why you should think so," he said.

"He was—that is, they were—Jenny's guests," said Joanna doubtfully. "And I was *very* uncivil to him."

"I am assured—" Kergabet began. Gwendolen glanced briefly in their direction, and he sank his voice still further: "I am assured that he heartily deserved it."

This remark—considering its source—so astonished Joanna that she nearly laughed aloud.

"I wonder that Mór and Rory do not make a match of it," said Sophie, looking after them as they strode away, the last of her small supper-party to depart into the damp November night, bickering amicably with Mór's friend Sorcha MacAngus over the results of some experiment of Mór's. "They seem certainly to be in one another's confidence, and very fond of each other; and it seems to me . . ."

Her voice trailed off. Had she been thinking, as Gray had found himself doing of late, that Rory MacCrimmon seemed likely to benefit from spending less time in his sister's company? Catriona had of course left the house with her brother, but she seemed somehow apart from the rest of the laughing, animated group. She had in fact, it occurred to Gray now, behaved rather peculiarly all evening—laughing at things he said which had not been particularly amusing, and leaping in abruptly to turn the conversation, for no apparent reason, when the others began to talk of crop failures and the opening of the clan storehouses in their own clan-lands. And not for the first time.

Gray hesitated for a moment, his gaze levelled at Catriona's retreating back, but at last said, "I do not think such a marriage would suit either of them."

"No?" Sophie turned, catching something perhaps in the tone of his voice, and frowned at him in puzzlement. "Why not? That is, I do not say they are in love; but, but nor was Jenny with Kergabet, and yet—"

"Because . . . because Rory is a Greek," said Gray. "And Mór MacRury likewise."

Sophie's frown deepened. "You do not mean that they were born in . . . in Athens or Sparta," she said slowly. "Or Crete."

"No," he acknowledged, when she had run through her sadly limited knowledge of Greek city-states, and paused (even as one small corner of his mind made a list of improving books upon the subject) to choose his words with care. "I mean . . . I mean that the gods do not make everyone alike, where the desires of the heart are concerned. Marriage is a joy for some, but only a necessary expedient for others; some would gladly marry but can find no partner, whilst some choose not to marry despite perfectly eligible offers; some seek companionship amongst those of their own sex in preference to others, and some may find it in any. You have read the verses of Sappho, I am sure?"

It was not, he felt compelled to acknowledge, the most transparent of explanations, but Sophie seemed to find it adequate, for her frown was smoothing out into an expression of enlightenment.

After a moment's thought she astonished him by saying, "My cousin Maëlle is one such, I think. A Greek."

Gray stared.

"I may be quite wrong, of course," said Sophie hastily, perhaps supposing that his gobsmacked expression was the result of what she had said, and not of her having said it. "Only, when . . . when Mama was dying . . ."

She turned as though to look out of the window, and her voice trailed away into a little hitching breath. Gray understood it; since her cousin's dramatic injury in the course of their misadventures in London, not three years since, had restored the remembrance of her mother's death so abruptly and brutally to her mind, Sophie had been unable to think of it without pain. But the sound reminded him, too, of Lady Maëlle's starkly white face and wide, shocked eyes, her terrifying stillness and silence, when confronted with a portrait of the young Lady Laora, the companion of her youth. Her distress—swiftly mastered, yet no less keen for that—might have been only a woman's grief for the distant cousin whom she had loved almost as a sister; but might it have been more—regret for sentiments never spoken, a mourning of what now could never be?

Gray vividly remembered feeling, at the time, that he was witnessing the inadvertent expression of feelings which their owner had much rather have kept strictly private.

"You mistake me, *cariad*," he said. "I should not be at all surprised to discover that your reasoning is sound."

Sophie's delicate eyebrows flew up. "Indeed?"

"Do you remember—you might not notice at the time, for you were . . . confused, yourself—at that inn in Breizh, when we saw the portrait of your mother—"

Sophie closed her eyes, as though the thought pained her. "I remember," she said, low.

Her hand reached blindly for Gray's; he caught it and drew her into his arms. She leaned her ear against his heart.

"I almost wish that Mama had known of it," she said, "had known how she was loved; though perhaps it might only have made them both the more unhappy. It seems cruel of the gods, to fashion some men and women so that they must marry and be miserable, or not at all."

Gray could scarcely dispute this. "To be a god," he said instead, "is to have great power over mortals; there is no law of nature which requires that such power be yoked to benevolence, as the laws of men may from time to time attempt to impose upon kings and princes. If history teaches us anything, it is that the gods are as likely to act for their own amusement, as for any benefit of ours."

"That is so," said Sophie. She scrubbed one hand surreptitiously across her eyes and affected a tone of detached scholarly interest. "Consider the existence of nettles, and of thistles; and for that matter, of horseflies and stinging gnats."

"And marriages are miserable for many other reasons also," said Gray; mimicking her tone, he continued, "Consider my parents. Consider George and Catharine."

Sophie's little snort of uneasy laughter made her shoulders quiver briefly in his embrace.

"In any case," he said, "you do not suppose that companionship is only to be found in marriage? You know of course that Mór keeps house together with Sorcha MacAngus?"

"Ye-es." Sophie pulled away a little, within the circle of his arms, and looked up at him with narrowed eyes. "Of course I know it. Do you mean—you do not mean—"

"I cannot say certainly one way or the other," said Gray carefully; "I am not so much in Mór's counsels."

"Nor I," said Sophie, "but I do hope for their sake that it is so, and that it makes them happy." She pressed closer, her breath hitching, and he knew she must be thinking of her mother.

Gray bent his head and kissed her silk-soft hair. "Your mama was happy in you," he said. *Who could not be?* "I am certain of it."

Sophie's arms tightened about his ribs. Though she said nothing, her silence thundered in Gray's ears.


Sophie sought out Rory on the following afternoon, in the interval between Professor Maghrebin's lecture on astronomical notation in the Egyptian Middle Kingdom and her meeting with Cormac MacWattie, and threw caution to the four winds by saying bluntly, "Why does Catriona not wish you to speak to me about the crop failures, or the sick sheep and cattle, or the clan storehouses?"

Rory flushed an unbecoming scarlet and looked away.

If Sophie had learnt one lesson from her sister-in-law Jenny, it was that silence could be more effective than any persuasion; accordingly, she clasped her hands about her elbows and stood patiently waiting for Rory to succumb.

"She thinks of it as hanging up our dirty linen before the neighbours' eyes," he said at last, his gaze still fixed firmly on the corner of his desk. "Alba's trials are Alba's to face, she says, without interference from strangers."

It made a sort of sense, Sophie supposed, if one thought of the kingdom as a young woman who did not wish to be rescued from a humiliating scrape by her elder brother.

"But Gray and I are not strangers," she pointed out. "Not any longer. And it seems . . ." She paused, seeking an adjective that might convey her meaning without giving offence. "It seems short-sighted to be always twitching the curtains over the windows when behind them, there may be thousands of children starving to death."

Rory's head snapped up. "The clans and the Cailleach will not let people starve," he said, in a scandalised tone. "That is the whole purpose of the Law of the Storehouses: to make sure that every clan and grove maintains—"

"And next winter?" Sophie interrupted him, and brushed away the guilt she felt at having done so. "Where shall we all be, if the storehouses are emptied this winter, and we cannot turn to our neighbours for help?"

"We?" He lifted an eyebrow.

Sophie looked away, caught out in the daydream she had not yet revealed even to Gray, of finishing her degree in Din Edin and, just possibly, making a home here.

"I am curious to know," said Rory, "what provision is made in Britain for like circumstances. You do not have clans as we do, I know, but you have . . . lords, have you not? Men of property, who must take responsibility for the tenants who work their lands? And the servants of your gods?"

"Yes," said Sophie slowly. "That is so. But we have no formal law that I know of, to force any man to make adequate provision for his tenants; only customary law, I suppose, and knowledge of the consequences of failure—which some men, I regret to say, appear to regard not at all."

"That seems a very poorly conceived system indeed," said Rory, wrinkling his freckled nose.

"I dare say it is," said Sophie, "but if what I have heard of the doings of His Majesty the King and his Privy Council is in any degree true, there are great lords who had sooner take up arms against the throne than submit to be told how they must husband their estates and care for their tenants."

She was sufficiently astonished at this speech—or, rather, at the evidence it represented, that she recalled far more from Joanna's sometimes excessively political correspondence than she had previously imagined—as to be caught off guard by Rory's asking her, in tones of equal surprise, "Have you acquaintance at King Henry's Court, then?"

"Well, yes," Sophie conceded. "I have."

His eyebrows rose again, but—to Sophie's relief, for she did not wish to distract him from the matter of the clan storehouses—he did not pursue the question. Instead he said, thoughtfully, "So it was in Alba, before the time of Ailpín Drostan."

Ailpín Drostan had been King of Alba long ago, Sophie recalled, and his was the imposing statue of a wild-haired man in a kilted plaid, thrusting a sword aloft from his seat atop a rearing horse, which dominated Teviot Square, near the main gates of the University. "Before his time, but not since?" she said.

"As well as being more or less the founder of the kingdom," said Rory, "Ailpín Drostan was also the originator of the Storehouse Laws, for which he is justly celebrated. The one point on which all the historians, living and dead, agree, is that had it not been for Ailpín Drostan's great dream-vision—a gift of Brìghde and the Cailleach, so he claimed, and given its sequel, it is a difficult claim to refute!—which forewarned him of a year of terrible plague and famine in his clanlands, and spurred him to preparations which both his allies and his enemies thought absurd—"

Rory paused, his burnished-copper eyebrows drawing together, and Sophie carefully did not smile; he had become so entangled in his own Latin syntax, it appeared, that he could find no way out. "Ailpín Drostan had a vision, you say," she prompted, switching into Gaelic in the hope of easing his way.

"Yes," Rory said, and—accepting the cue—went on: "The Cailleach spoke to him in a dream, and gave him this warning, after which the other clan chieftains—and many of his own clansmen, it appears—thought him mad, to be stockpiling grain and preserved foodstuffs in such quantities that surely they could only end as rotted waste. Mad, or very devious, in service of some end which none of them could see. But Ailpín Drostan insisted that his stores should be needed, and so indeed it proved; and thus he gained a reputation for prescience which served him well when later he set his sights on building himself a kingdom."

Somewhere in the back of her mind, Sophie was translating all of this into tidy Latin periods for conveyance to Joanna, whom it must certainly interest. Who could have predicted, in the days when Joanna was making mischief as a schoolgirl in Kemper, that she might one day be more enthralled by histories than by fantastickal minstrel-tales, or that hanging about the edges of Court politics might be the catalyst of such a change? Certainly not Sophie, who had loved her younger sister to distraction while at the same time sympathising wholeheartedly with the exasperations of the headmistress whose reports on Joanna's conduct (directed to the Professor, and read stealthily over Amelia's shoulder) had tended towards the despairing.

"Do you suppose," she said, "that the gods spoke to him in truth? Or was he only very fortunate and very clever?"

Rory grinned down at her and said, "I have not the least idea. It is a fascinating tale, however, and"—he glanced out of the window of his study, gauging the angle of the sun, and then began poking about in one of the bookcases—"one which we have not time for at present, if you are not to be late for Cormac MacWattie."

Sophie started, and heard the great University bells begin to chime the hour. She made to depart, stammering apologies, but Rory halted her on the threshold of his study to hand her a small stack of codices, the topmost of which was titled in Latin, in faded gold leaf stamped upon russet leather, *The Rise and Fall of Clan MacAilpín.*

"There you are," he said, smiling the smile of the tutor well pleased with the efforts of his student.

"Thank you," said Sophie, and hastened away to her own tutor. Not until much later did she recognise the manner in which her questions about Catriona had been deflected, or think to ask herself whether Rory had done it with intent.

## CHAPTER XIII

# In Which Sophie Learns
# Lessons of More Than One Variety

*The history of Alba is to a considerable degree the history of Clan MacAlpine, and more particularly that of the great mage-king Ailpín Drostan, for whom it came to be named. The origin of this great kingdom—for a great kingdom it is, whatever claims to superiority may be adduced by my countrymen—*

Sophie turned back to the frontispiece of *The Rise and Fall of Clan MacAlpine,* and noted that the author was one Edward L'Arbalestier. An Englishman of Normand descent, then, very likely. It was dated at London, in the first decade of her own father's reign.

*—is bound up in the exploits of this remarkable man, to whose inspired dream of uniting the warring clans to the benefit of their people and establishing an unbreakable line of defence against their acquisitive neighbours to the south, the shape and structure of the modern Kingdom of Alba are principally owing.*

*Ailpín Drostan was born on the island Ioua, which the Albans name Eilean Idhe, a pebble on the shores of An t-Eilean Muileach, which we call the Isle of Mull, and though not the eldest son or even the eldest child, was chosen as his father's heir (in a tradition which Alba's rulers continue to this day) by reason, first, of his great magickal talent, and, second, of the skill and prowess he is said to have early shown, not in pitched battle against the rivals of his clan, but in devising strategies to prevail against such rivals with cunning rather than brute force.*

*Though the precise details of Ailpín Drostan's early life are lost to us, we may safely assume that he received the best formation in both practical magick and practical warrior-craft which his father—that great Drost Maon of Ioua who, as legend has it, set forth as a boy from Ioua insula to seek his fortune, and became a great leader of men—was able to provide for him. Certain it is, in any event, that the young Ailpín was mage first, and warrior second; some accounts, indeed, paint a compelling picture of a man both reluctant to join battle and relentless in pursuing victory by any means necessary. Some scholars have gone so far as to argue that the tactics of Britain's own mage-officers owe as much to the tactics and strategy of Ailpín Drostan as to those of the Roman Legion's vaunted sorcerer-centuries. Yet for all the lore that has come down to our day, there remain aspects of Ailpín Drostan's reign which resist explanation.*

*Like his father, Ailpín Drostan cherished aims far outside the sphere in which his birth had placed him. Unlike his father, however, he inherited on the distaff side a prodigious magickal talent which—*

Sophie started violently as a large, warm hand clasped her shoulder, and the book fell to her desk with a leathery slap.

"I am sorry, *kerra!*" Gray said. He looked down at her with consternation writ all over his guileless face. "I thought you must have heard me calling for you."

"I was reading," said Sophie, blinking. "Are you just now arrived?"

Gray grinned. "Very nearly," he said. "I have been upstairs, putting myself back to rights."

Sophie examined him more closely, and saw that his hair was damp and *en bataille*, his hazel eyes gone faintly tawny, and the remainder of him wrapped in an elderly dressing-gown—all sure signs that he had returned from the University Library not on foot but on the wing.

"Oh," she said, still blinking stupidly. How had she become so deeply engrossed, so quickly, as not to have heard him descending from the first floor? Ordinarily, the sound of his tread on the steep, uncarpeted staircase—even without boots—was enough to wake the dead.

Gray perched on the corner of her desk and smiled at her again—quite a different smile, this time, of the sort which was never bestowed upon any person else. "Can I persuade you," he said, reaching out a hand, "to—"

Sophie did not wait to discover what arch or absurd circumlocution her husband had been meaning to employ to invite her upstairs to their bedroom; instead she clasped his hand, returned his warm and secret smile, and said, "Yes, I should imagine you can."

There was a letter from Joanna in the following morning's post, and though Joanna's letters had lately tended to the uncommunicative, Sophie nevertheless pounced eagerly upon it and tore it open without pausing to dust the crumbs from her fingers.

Alas, it proved to be more of the same. Joanna's mare Kelvez had thrown a shoe, in consequence of which Joanna had missed her day's ride in the park. Jenny had taken Joanna and Gwendolen to several more balls since Joanna's last letter, and Sophie was subjected to a detailed description of each of these entertainments, which she rather wondered at Joanna's having had the patience to set down.

She was near to losing patience with it herself when she came to the penultimate paragraph, in which Joanna's tone shifted abruptly from cheerful gossip to earnest lecturing.

> *Sophie, His Majesty's ambassador in Din Edin has written to Kergabet to ask why you have not yet been to call upon him; I must say that it is beyond me why you should not have done so long before now.*

The word *long* had been underscored twice, which Sophie felt was unfair; it was not as though Joanna—Joanna who gossiped with kitchen-maids and grooms, who spent her days taking notes at meetings of the Privy Council and her nights (to all appearances) deciphering coded messages—were in any position to criticise Sophie's manners.

On the other hand, of course, this was not the first time that Sophie had received similar instructions, nor was Joanna the first to issue them to her.

> *Do go and pay your respects, Sophie, please; Lord de Courcy is not a man to take insult over nothing, but should you be in any difficulty and require his help, a prior acquaintance would be of material service. You must see that it looks very odd for a gentleman and his wife from Oxford to have been in Din Edin three months, without calling upon the representative of the Crown in Alba?*

"'Should you be in any difficulty, and require his help'?" Sophie said aloud.

"I beg your pardon?" said Gray, looking up from his own stack of letters.

"Joanna," said Sophie. She frowned. "She is seeking to rescue us in advance from the consequences of our own incompetence." She read out the offending paragraph, and added, "You see? One would think we were children, not fit to be let out alone."

"I confess, love, I cannot see anything so very dreadful in the idea of calling upon Lord de Courcy." Gray looked honestly perplexed. "It is natural enough, surely? Anyone inclined to see such a visit as suspicious, it seems to me, must be so generally inclined to suspicion that it could not possibly matter what we do."

Try as she might, Sophie could not deny that this was a perfectly reasonable argument.

"Very well," she said, after a long, obstinate silence. "Let us go this morning, then, as we have nothing else pressing in train, and have it over."

Sophie was prickly and generally unlike herself all that morning, and it was in a mood of grim resignation that Gray escorted her across Din Edin, to the very fashionable street which housed the official residence of Aurélien, Lord de Courcy, Ambassador from Henry of Britain to the court of Donald MacNeill. Goff and Tredinnick trailed them at a discreet distance, so familiar by now that even Gray almost forgot their presence.

The house was stone-built, looming grey and forbidding behind a high wrought-iron fence screened by prim yew-trees. "The better to poison unwelcome visitors," Gray muttered, under his breath.

A pair of liveried pikemen stood guard on either side of the heavy gate and frowned at Gray and Sophie whilst Gray explained their errand. Sophie at length produced a letter of introduction—directed to Lord de Courcy, in Sieur Germain de Kergabet's hand—of which Gray had until this moment been perfectly ignorant, and said, "We are to give this letter into my lord of Courcy's hand."

The left-hand guard—a gangling fellow whose speech held a strong flavour of the Borders, and whose elaborate moustache was, Gray strongly suspected, an attempt to camouflage the fact that he was not much older than Sophie—ducked his head into the tiny gate-house and barked an order, at which there emerged a little page-boy in matching livery and incongruously muddy boots. The other guardsman (older by at least a decade, nearly as tall as Gray and much bulkier) opened his half of the gate just enough to let a child slip through; and, without so much as a glance at the visitors, the page-boy turned tail and ran in the direction of the house.

"Sophie," Gray hissed, seizing the first moment of guardsmanly inattention that offered, "where had you that letter? You have not been carrying it with you all this time?"

She gave him a reproving look, jerking her head at the guardsmen, and wordlessly tucked the letter away in her reticule.

Not a quarter-hour later—though it was a very long quarter-hour indeed, for Sophie would not discuss the mysterious letter in the guardsmen's hearing, and Gray was discouraged from conversing with the guardsmen themselves by their rigid posture and forbidding expressions—the page-boy returned to the gate and, from the other side of it, made Sophie and Gray a deep, if not notably elegant, bow.

"His lordship's compliments, Monsieur Marshall, Madame Marshall," he recited, panting a little as he straightened up, "and he invites you to take some refreshment, and apologises for your being detained at the gate."

The guardsmen's gobsmacked expressions, thought Gray, did not much look as though it were indeed a natural and unremarkable thing for every British subject passing through Din Edin to call in upon the Ambassador. As he and Sophie passed through the gate on the page's heels, however, he heard the Border-country guardsman mutter to the other, "He intends to *feed* them apparently! He never feeds the uninvited ones."

Gray was not sure whether this fact ought to worry him more, or less.

The page-boy conducted them through the small but elegant garden that hid behind the yew-trees, up the steps to an imposing front door, and stood on tiptoe to rap energetically with a brass knocker in the shape of a gloved hand holding a sphere.

"That knocker is an Iberian design," Gray murmured, and Sophie looked up at it suspiciously. He had seen and admired one like it in a shop in Oxford, and contemplated its merits as a gift for her, but at last determined that its origins would outweigh any enjoyment she might derive from its whimsical design.

The door was swiftly opened by an elderly manservant of the sort whom one could easily imagine growing up and growing old in the service of a great house. He bowed them through with excruciating correctness, but out of the corner of one eye Gray caught him affectionately ruffling the page-boy's dark curls before sending him briskly back to his post.

They were now escorted through the house to a spacious library looking out into another garden, again small but artfully arrayed. The Ambassador's gardens did not call to Gray as the garden of his childhood home had always done (and did yet, if he were honest), with its exuberantly asymmetric stands of bright flowers and fragrant herbs, its darting butterflies and humming bees; but he could see that they were beautiful.

Lord de Courcy rose behind his desk to greet them, smiling politely. He was a tall man, dark, with a face like a hatchet. On the near side of the desk, another man also rose—younger, stiff-starched and purse-lipped at the interruption—twisting as he did so to present his face rather than his back to the door. It was a face that niggled at the corner of Gray's memory.

"Ah," said Courcy, with the shade of a smile. "Monsieur Marshall, Madame Marshall, we meet at last." Then, turning to the other man, "Powell, the wards, if you please."

The younger man—Powell, then—raised his eyebrows briefly. Then he closed his eyes, settled his shoulders, and spoke a brief, decided spell that sent a perceptible shiver of magick out to the circumference of the room.

"You were at Merlin," said Gray, remembering at last where he had seen Powell's face before. "You were a student of Professor Maurice, and you took a Double First in the year when I matriculated. Everyone was astonished that you did not go on to study for Mastery."

"Marshall," said Powell, thoughtfully. As Gray's (perhaps ill-considered) speech proceeded, Powell's eyes had gradually narrowed in concentrated study of Gray's face and of his person. Now they widened almost comically as Powell said, "Oh! You are *that* Marshall, the one who was sent down and then reinstated, the one who— *Oh!*"

He turned abruptly to Sophie and gave her a bow which (thought Gray) nicely skirted the servility which Sophie so detested. "Your Royal Highness," he said. "It is a great honour to make your acquaintance."

★   ★   ★

"To what do we owe the pleasure of your company this morning, Your Royal Highness?" Lord de Courcy inquired, when Gray and Sophie had been welcomed to the small slice of sovereign Britain represented by the Ambassador's house, and all four of them were seated about the small table at the study window, drinking tea. "I hope you do not find yourself in some unfortunate circumstance?"

Gray darted a nervous glance at Sophie, but finding her perfectly composed, he relaxed again and reached for his teacup.

There was a long silence before Sophie said, "I was reminded to-day that we have been remiss in paying our respects since our arrival in Din Edin, and naturally sought to remedy this omission." She fished once more in her reticule and extracted Sieur Germain's letter, which she presented to Lord de Courcy with a gracious incline of her head, clearly modelled after a gesture of Jenny's. "This is a letter for you, from Sieur Germain de Kergabet, which I was charged to give into your hand."

Gray frowned at it. He could not for the world have humiliated Sophie by demanding to know its history in front of these virtual strangers; but he could not account for it, and the mystery nagged at him. Had she been concealing it since their departure from London? If so, to what purpose? Or had it arrived more lately, and if it had done, why in Hades should Kergabet use Sophie to convey a missive, which he might more easily—and more properly—have sent through diplomatic channels? If Sophie had not delivered it at once, it surely could not be a matter of urgency, might in fact be nothing but the simple letter of introduction it pretended; but in that case why the insistence on its being delivered directly from her hand to Courcy's?

Meanwhile Sophie was calmly sipping her tea and Lord de Courcy calmly slitting open Kergabet's letter. Whilst he perused it, with the occasional frown and the occasional thoughtful *hmm*, Sophie drank tea and nibbled at a gooseberry tart, and Powell pretended—poorly—that he was not staring at her in a sort of befuddled fascination.

Gray, after briefly glaring at him (though Powell took no notice), helped himself to shortbread and sat back in his chair to observe.

It was not difficult to deduce the source of Powell's bafflement.

Supposing that his employment with Courcy dated to the year in which he had left Merlin, it was entirely likely that he had been present at the Samhain Ball two years since, and he might well have been a witness to much of what followed from the attempt on King Henry's life; even if his knowledge of the Princess Royal came at second hand (perhaps all the more in that case, given the tendency of rumour to exaggerate for effect), he must now be experiencing some difficulty in reconciling the desperate, frantic, breathtaking Sophie of that hideous night with the composed and decidedly ordinary-looking young woman presently seated opposite him.

*Outwardly composed*, Gray amended, taking in the minuscule tremor of Sophie's hand as she returned her teacup to its saucer.

Courcy reached the end of Kergabet's letter and folded it up again.

"This letter was written more than four months ago," he said mildly. "An eventful journey, was it?"

A thunderous expression crossed Sophie's face, lingering for the duration of a breath and then—perhaps fortunately—vanishing into smooth unconcern before either Courcy or Powell could remark it.

"Sieur Germain did not specify that its contents were of especial urgency," she said, in a colourless tone that, had they only known it, boded ill for anyone who continued to mock her.

"My lord Ambassador," Gray interceded, before the sardonic curl of Courcy's lip could set fire to the smouldering resentment in Sophie's eyes. "May we know what is in the letter?"

"Certainly," said Lord de Courcy. "It merely requests that I make welcome Lord Kergabet's brother-in-law and his wife, and render them any assistance which they may require, as I am bound to do for any British subject who finds himself in difficulties in Din Edin." He paused, then added almost carelessly, "And that I on no account reveal to anyone at all, except at Her Royal Highness's express request, Madame Marshall's true identity."

"It is *not* my true identity," Sophie insisted. "*I* am Sophie Marshall, a student at the University in Din Edin. The Princess Royal is only the . . . the cloak I must wear when I visit my father."

"Nonetheless," said Courcy dryly, "I am expressly forbidden to reveal the secret. Now, why should Kergabet consider that necessary, do you suppose . . . ?"

Gray drew himself up to his full height—as best he could, sitting—and said, "Is it not reason enough, that she has asked it?"

Courcy, to his surprise, said mildly, "You misunderstand me. Madame Marshall, your secret is safe, though I confess myself baffled by the importance which you appear to attach to it. The question is why your brother-in-law should believe me in need of such counsel. It has perhaps not escaped your notice that I serve His Majesty as ambassador at the court of Donald MacNeill, which post requires a not inconsiderable degree of discretion."

Sophie flushed, and Gray began to apologise, but Courcy waved him away.

"The discrepancy interests me," he said. "One is tempted to ask whether Kergabet intended his words for other eyes than mine." He glanced at Sophie. "But no matter. I trust that you will call upon me again, should you at any time have need of assistance?"

"Certainly, my lord," said Gray, and Sophie nodded.

"Very well. And, if no such difficulty should arise, I believe I may undertake to leave you to your studies."

"I thank you, sir," said Sophie earnestly. After a moment she added, the words tumbling out like apples from a barrel overturned, "You think it eccentric of me, I am sure; but only suppose yourself in my position, and perhaps you may imagine what a relief it is to have even the illusion of making one's own choices."

Powell looked baffled—it was not the first time Gray had observed this reaction to Sophie's insisting on her status as an ordinary undergraduate student—but Lord de Courcy regarded Sophie gravely, his long index fingers pressed to his lower lip, and said merely, "Indeed."

They spoke for a time of matters less inflammatory—mutual acquaintance at Merlin College whom Gray or Sophie had seen more recently than Powell; the sights of Din Edin, and the climb which the Marshalls had made on Arthur's Seat early in the autumn, before the turn of the weather; and the winter weather in Din Edin—which latter topic, however, led them inevitably to crop failures and the Law of the Storehouses, and ultimately to Sophie's inquiring almost plaintively, "My lord, is there nothing that Britain might do to assist Alba? Have we not food enough, to lend a little to our neighbour?"

Courcy's face—already the smooth and unrevealing countenance of a diplomat—shifted just that infinitesimal distance into icy inscrutability. "It is my business to keep His Majesty and Lord Kergabet informed of circumstances and events in Alba," he said, "and to advise as I may see fit, in light of my closer acquaintance with the terrain. The government of kingdoms, Madame Marshall, is more delicate and complex than you appear to imagine."

This was so conspicuously not an answer to Sophie's question that Gray was not much surprised when, rather than make any reply, she only blinked in confusion.

"What my lord de Courcy means to say," said Powell—who looked far more alarmed than the circumstances appeared to warrant, though he nonetheless spoke with near perfect aplomb—"is that while, to the uneducated eye, His Majesty's government may appear to be standing idle—"

At this Courcy cut him off with a quiet word and a sharp look, and he fell unhappily silent.

"My lord Ambassador," said Gray, casting about for a change of subject, "what can you tell us of a man called Conall MacLachlan? He is brother-in-law to the Chancellor of the University, and is said to be a collector of *Lepidoptera*."

Sophie went very still beside him, and Courcy gave him a long, considering look.

"I have only a passing acquaintance with the gentleman to whom you refer," he said at last, "though Arthur Breck himself I know well. I may say, however, that I know no great ill of him."

"He knows who I am," said Sophie abruptly.

Gray glanced aside at her. Her face wore an expression compounded of chagrin—as though she had not meant to speak those words, and knew not what to do now that she had done so—and resignation.

Courcy's gaze on Sophie sharpened a little. "What makes you say so?" he inquired.

Sophie described in meticulous detail her conversation with Conall MacLachlan. If her tone tended sometimes towards the defensive, it was perhaps not without reason, for everything Conall MacLachlan had said was, it seemed to Gray, capable of an entirely innocent interpretation. The difficulty was that some of his remarks were equally capable of a malevolent one.

Courcy heard her out in attentive silence, his face as impassive as ever.

"This dinner at which you met Conall MacLachlan," he said, when Sophie had come to the end of her recital. "When did it take place?"

"Nearly a month since," said Sophie.

"And yet there has been no rumour of your presence in Din Edin—the presence of your alter ego, I should say," he amended, with a slightly condescending smile. "Not to my knowledge—and my knowledge in this particular sphere is considerable. If Conall MacLachlan is indeed intending to expose you, he is taking a deal of time about it."

"My stepfather," said Sophie tightly, "waited fourteen years. The consequences were not therefore the less . . . significant."

Gray wondered what less politic adjective she had swallowed back.

Lord de Courcy inclined his head very slightly—acknowledging a hit, Gray supposed. "Nevertheless," he said, "I cannot see what benefit could accrue to Conall MacLachlan from such a course of action, which suggests to me that he represents no great risk to your incognito." He paused for a moment, studying Sophie's expression, and then continued: "Whereas your stepfather, I believe, stood to gain a great deal by his betrayal."

The words were well chosen; watching Sophie side-on, Gray saw the taut lines of her face and posture soften.

"You may be assured," said Courcy, "that should any such rumour come to our ears, you should be informed of it at once. I reiterate, however, that I do not believe any danger to attach to the Princess Royal at present."

Sophie thanked him graciously enough, and gave Powell their direction; lest they outstay their welcome, Gray said, "I believe we must be on our way."

He paused for a moment, awkwardly undecided between rising and keeping his seat, and unreasonably resenting their host for the remembrance of youthful ineptitudes which the present circumstances called to his mind.

The three other occupants of Courcy's study regarded him in silence: Courcy coolly, Powell still a little anxiously, Sophie with a baffled frown. Ignoring the others, Gray met her gaze calmly and attempted to convey without speaking the words, *We shall discuss all of this later, in privacy.*

"Quite so," she said at last, deciding presumably that she had made her point—or that she had taken his. She rose from her seat, and the men hastened to follow her; or, rather, Gray and Powell hastened, whilst Courcy rose languid and graceful from the curve of his desk-chair.

He held out his right hand to Sophie, and when, with a bemused half smile, she extended hers towards him, he took it in his and raised it to his lips.

Gray bristled, and resolutely refrained from showing it. Sophie's expression of astonishment was almost comical—a clear reminder, had anyone present required it, that she was altogether unaccustomed to the manners of her father's court.

"I trust," Courcy said again, "that you will call upon me should you have need of assistance during your stay in Din Edin, for any reason."

And again Gray said, "Certainly, my lord Ambassador."

Courcy nodded. "Well, then," he said. "Good morning to you, Monsieur Marshall, Madame Marshall. It has been most interesting to make your acquaintance. Powell will see you out."

And indeed Powell—after only the briefest moment's startled hesitation—did so, escorting them not only out of the front door but, by a meandering path through the garden, to the gate itself. Along the way he engaged Sophie in a discussion of her studies—in particular, the differences between Merlin's course of study in magickal theory and her present one—which led her by degrees to lay down her armour of wary civility and speak with real interest and enthusiasm. Gray paced behind them, listening, and was smiling to himself, until the moment when Sophie (who had just been enumerating in a rueful tone the books in Gaelic which she had still to read, and could read only slowly) exclaimed, "Oh! If only we need never go back!"—and then clapped one gloved hand over her mouth and looked back at him with dismay writ all over her face.

Powell was perhaps not quite so perceptive as Gray had been beginning to suppose him; for he appeared not to remark that anything was amiss, and, worse, said in a rallying tone, "I dare say you do feel so, now; but I wager in six months' time you shall be very ready to be at home again!"

As Sophie was no more inclined than anyone else Gray had ever met to be told how she ought to feel—indeed, rather less—he was not surprised to see her straighten away from her new acquaintance, her defensive reserve at once fully restored, or to hear her say frostily, "Your opinion is noted, Mr. Powell."

They took their leave of Powell very formally, under the curious eyes of the guardsmen at the gate, and Goff and Tredinnick loitering outside it. As they emerged again onto the pavement—out of Britain again, and in Alba—Gray offered Sophie his arm as usual; she took it, but hesitatingly, and when he covered her hand with his, she looked up at him with something very like apprehension in her dark eyes.

Gray cast a brief glance around them, to be sure they had no near witnesses. Then he halted on the pavement and turned to take both Sophie's hands in his.

"Sophie," he said, and waited for her to meet his eyes again. "You surely do not believe me angry with you for—for wishing to remain in a place where you have been happy?"

Sophie looked away again. "Merlin is your home," she said at last, softly.

"*Sophie.*" Her gaze snapped back to his face, her eyes wide in startlement at his vehement tone. "*Ubi tu Gaia, ego Gaius,*" he said. "Have you so quickly forgot what we promised to one another?"

She flushed a little but did not look away this time. "I have not," she said, low. "Of course I have not."

"Well, then," said Gray, and he allowed himself the indulgence of bending to kiss her upturned brow, though in so public a place. He let go her hands, with a last little press of her slender fingers, and tucked the left one up under his right elbow again, and they turned once more for home.

"I have not felt certain enough of the prospect to speak of it," he said, after a long moment's companionable silence, "but now I think I ought: The Dean of the School of Practical Magick is pleased with the progress of my students, and has hinted that I may be offered a more permanent post, should matters so continue."

"Oh," said Sophie, sounding a little breathless. "*Oh.* Then—then we might truly stay here!"

"Well, for a few years more, at any rate," said Gray. "If you like to do so, that is. I have been thinking . . . well, to say true, I have been thinking that it might be a relief to you to be at home again, where you need not hide."

But at this Sophie tugged away from him and, flinging up her hands, exclaimed, "But you have got it all wrong, just as Lord de Courcy did! *I* am not hiding; I am only concealing an accident of my birth, which ought not to matter to anyone. And at home, I . . . it . . . *it* conceals *me.* Do you see?"

To Courcy and Powell, she had called the Princess Royal a cloak she must don when visiting her father; he had once heard her tell her father himself, *You are mistaken; my name is Sophie Marshall.* And what had she said—wondering at it, her eyes alight with joy—as their carriage rolled into Din Edin? *There are so many people, and not one of them knows or cares who I am, or who my father is!*

"Yes," he said slowly. "Yes, I do see. I am sorry, Sophie."

Sophie ducked her head, stepped closer, and took his arm again, and they resumed their journey.

## CHAPTER XIV

# In Which His Majesty
# Issues a Proclamation

*Prince Roland's betrothal* to the heiress of Alba was announced at last at the height of the Yule season, after a day like a gift from Apollo, a day which had burned bright with sunshine on new snow for a few brief hours before the midwinter twilight swallowed it whole. Roland bore up admirably under the onslaught of well-wishes from his father's guests, who were many and seemed, to Joanna's eye, to be divided between those who welcomed the match for reasons strategical or sentimental, and those who were eager to court His Majesty's good opinion by pretending to do so.

The reaction of the rest of His Majesty's Privy Council, upon the betrothal's being announced to that august body in the course of the previous month, had been very much as Joanna might have predicted. Sir Aled ap Gwyn and young Karaez pronounced it shrewd strategy; Lord Craven, whose lands were nearest the Roman Wall, took sober thought on the matter and cautiously agreed. Essex and Angers wished to know why Roland's bride should have been sought outside the kingdom; and Bayeux and the Vicomte de Cotentin were instantly persuaded that the King had been taken in by some manner of Alban plot, aimed at gaining a political foothold in Britain. It was at least, Joanna reflected, a change from their insistent beating upon the single drum of Breizhek sedition.

There was a sort of bitter comedy in it, too, in light of Lord de Courcy's reports from Din Edin that a vocal faction in Donald Mac-Neill's court considered the entire affair an attempt by King Henry to place his son on the throne of Alba. *What should we want with their ridiculous kingdom,* Joanna found herself thinking, in a moment of black self-mockery, *with its sick sheep and its withered grain and its men who do not wear trousers? And what should they want with ours, when it seems we can think of nothing but each other's capacity for treachery?*

But Lord Craven's approval had been a victory of sorts, and by Yuletide it was only the Comte de Bayeux and his particular cronies who continued to nurse dark theories of Alba's designs on King Henry's throne.

"Will they make trouble, do you think, my lord?" Jenny asked her husband over dinner, on the day following the public announcement. Bayeux and Angers had been seen at Court the previous evening, pointedly omitting to wish Roland joy of his marriage and casting dark looks at Kergabet and any of his allies whom they chanced to encounter.

Sieur Germain sighed, and thoughtfully sipped his wine. "I hope very much," he said, "that they may have the sense the gods gave a goose, and refrain from stretching out their necks to do mischief."

They had both, it appeared, quite lost the caution they had once exercised before Gwendolen, who now said, "I wonder whether there are crabbed old men in Alba who dislike their heiress's betrothal as much."

"The Comte d'Angers is not a crabbed old man," said Jenny.

Gwendolen tossed her head. "Perhaps not on the *outside*," she said, and Joanna, in spite of everything, snickered. It was odd, she thought, how often she laughed at Gwendolen's absurd remarks instead of disparaging them as they almost certainly deserved.

Jenny and Sieur Germain looked as though they should have liked to snicker, also, but they contrived matching looks of mild reproof instead, one from each end of the table.

"As for the news from Alba," said the latter, "I cannot pretend that there is not some cause for concern; I do not say *alarm*," he added, a shade too quickly for Joanna's liking, "but approbation of the match is by no means unanimous. The timing has proved unfortunate. I do not think, however, that any advantage was to be gained by putting off the announcement here, and a public announcement by Donald MacNeill will at any rate put paid to the wilder rumours presently circulating in Din Edin."

"How, unfortunate?" Gwendolen asked. "And what sort of rumours?"

Sieur Germain sighed again and ran one long finger slowly along the foot of his wineglass; Joanna rather fancied that he was now regretting his lack of circumspection. She wondered whether Mr. Fowler, had he been present, might have thought to avert it in some way, and whether she ought to have made the same attempt. Yet she could not pretend to regret this interesting turn of the conversation.

"Unfortunate because there is danger of famine in Alba," he said at last, "which has lent credence to the preposterous idea that Donald MacNeill has sold his daughter and her throne to Britain in exchange for the waggon-loads of grain and other provisions which are travelling north to Alba at this moment, as part of His Majesty's bride-gift."

"Oh!" said Joanna, sitting up. So this plan was going forward already! "Sophie will be pleased to hear of such a gift."

Indeed, Sophie's letters of late never failed to mention the hardship in this or that district in which some acquaintance of hers had left friends or relations to come to the University in Din Edin, and by Lord de Courcy's report, her belated visit to him had been much the same.

He had also reported that Mrs. Marshall seemed *unduly anxious* at the possibility of her identity's being discovered.

What, Joanna asked herself, had Sophie been leaving out of her letters? The reports of ill tidings from her acquaintances' families aside, the most recent had consisted largely in exactly the sort of news to which Sophie's letters had always been liable—accounts of lectures she

had attended, of which Joanna understood perhaps half; amusing anecdotes (or anecdotes intended to be amusing) in which various friends
and acquaintances played the principal roles; when weather permitted,
descriptions (and occasional sketches) of sight-seeing excursions—and
in inquiries after the health of everyone in London with whom Sophie
had any acquaintance whatever. There had been nothing in any of
them to cause alarm; they had in fact been, on the whole, more cheerful than those which Joanna had been accustomed to receive from
Oxford towards the end of her sister's sojourn there, and Sophie had
more than once gone so far as to say outright that she was finding the
University at Din Edin more congenial than Merlin College.

She could not have done so, surely, if she were genuinely afraid?

"But if their folk are starving," said Gwendolen, "they will be glad
of any help, surely, though they disdain the giver?"

Sieur Germain sighed. "That is the rational and the humane
course, certainly," he said, "and Donald MacNeill is, I believe, a rational and a humane man. I am less certain of his counsellors, and of
public opinion in Alba. The people of Alba have a long memory, and
it is not so very long ago, as these matters are accounted, that a British
king sought to conquer them entirely. It is not so strange that some
should hesitate to offer us wholehearted trust."

"Ye-es," said Gwendolen doubtfully, "but—"

"And there is also the Law of the Storehouses," said Joanna. "I
have been studying the history of it," she explained, when this remark was greeted with looks of mild surprise and of incomprehen-
sion, "because when Roland is married to Lucia MacNeill, it will be
part of his charge. The storehouses are meant to preserve the people
from famine, of course, as we know; but it seems that the law was
also intended to preserve the kingdom itself from relying too heavily
on goods imported from elsewhere. To prevent the Crown's sinking
into ruinous debt, originally; but might a gift of food in time of famine be similarly perceived?"

Sieur Germain looked at her thoughtfully. "In the proper hands,"
he said, "any act, no matter how noble its intentions or how beneficial
its effects, can be so explained as to look like malice."

★   ★   ★

It was on a bright afternoon in January, no more than a fortnight after Solstice-time, that Sophie and Mór MacRury emerged from the University Library into an astonishing cacophony of sound.

"Whatever can all that shouting be?" Sophie said, resisting a childish urge to press her palms over her ears as they descended the broad steps. "It sounds like a drunken brawl in Tartarus."

Mór raised her emphatic eyebrows in surprise. "Have you not heard?" she said. "The Senior Common Room could talk of nothing else today. You were at Professor Maghrebin's lecture this afternoon, were you not? Did you not find the attendance shockingly thin?"

"It was that," Sophie admitted. "I thought perhaps this sunny weather might account for it. Where was everyone, then?"

The noise was growing louder.

"There," said Mór, pointing, as they came into sight of Teviot Square, through which Sophie and Gray habitually passed on their way home.

Sophie halted abruptly, her mouth falling open. She shut it again, hard.

The square was filled from edge to edge with people—men and women and even a few children; students and labourers; and here and there men in grey robes, with long hair and longer beards, whom Sophie recognised as priests of the Cailleach—and all of them were shouting and chanting, together or severally, to the limits of their lungs.

At the northeast corner of the square, on what appeared to be an overturned waggon, stood two tall, broad-shouldered men whose kilted plaids, from this distance discernible only as two kindred shades of green, set off their vividly red hair and beards. One held a broadsword nearly as tall as himself. Their gestures suggested they were speaking, or singing, or possibly shouting, but nothing could be heard above the noise of the crowd.

Sophie stretched her neck to bellow into Mór's ear: "What are they doing? What are they *saying*?"

Mór was listening intently, a small frown creasing her ivory forehead. "A moment, Sophie," she said absently.

Sophie stood beside her, quivering.

After some moments, Mór caught Sophie's elbow and inclined her head. "Come away," she said, her breath warm against Sophie's ear.

"Why?" said Sophie.

Mór's grip on her elbow tightened. *"Come away,"* she repeated. "Now, this moment."

Sophie had heard that tone before, though not from Mór Mac-Rury; it meant certain danger, and she obeyed it almost without meaning to do so.

They retreated to the University's back gate and paused there, in the lee of the fieldstone wall, watching the flow of passersby in both directions: many towards the square, some eager and some hesitating, and some few hastening away from it with looks of trepidation.

"Mór," said Sophie, "tell me."

Mór looked at her in troubled silence.

"I have heard worse things, I expect," said Sophie, before she thought.

"Have you so?" Mór quirked a russet eyebrow.

Under her breath, Sophie called herself every sort of fool. "I only meant—"

"You have heard, I suppose, the rumour that Donald MacNeill has made a marriage for Lucia?"

Sophie nodded, puzzled though relieved at the change of subject. It was not a question that interested her particularly, except insofar as she liked Lucia MacNeill and wished her happy; but many of the Alban students in her year had strong views on which of the various clan chieftains' sons—there seemed to Sophie to be dozens of chieftains with hundreds of sons—was most likely to be chosen.

"The news today—or the rumour, rather, for there is no more reason than usual to suppose it true," said Mór, "is that the consort Lucia MacNeill has chosen, when she might have had nearly any chieftain's son in Alba, is a Sasunnach prince."

Sophie gaped at her. *Roland? Or Ned?—no, Ned is spoken for, now. Surely not Harry, for that must mean a very long delay.* Only by clapping one hand across her mouth did she prevent the words from spilling out aloud. *And, in any case, it is only a rumour. Joanna should certainly have told me, if such a thing were afoot.*

Unless, of course, this were the explanation for the sudden and mysterious absence of news in Joanna's letters.

Silent gaping, it appeared, was nearly as bad as ill-judged words, for Mór's gaze upon her sharpened in the way that meant nothing should stand in the way of her discovering the answers to her questions.

"That is very unlikely, surely?" Sophie said hastily. "All the talk I have heard was of chieftains' sons, as you say—Mór, the crowds, that man with the sword, they—"

"Are expressing their opposition to Lucia MacNeill's choice, yes," said Mór. "I cannot say that I should altogether understand such a decision myself; though if I were Donald MacNeill I certainly should not object to have a firm ally in the British King, which we must suppose to be the object of any such marriage."

Even Sophie could follow this line of reasoning. "Yes," she said. "Yes, I expect we must."

Mór's eyebrows drew together, a graceful accolade above her narrowed eyes. "And how should you expect this news to be received at home?" she inquired. Her tone was light, but her bright eyes sharp and implacable. "Assuming for the moment, that is, that it were true."

"I . . . I hardly know," said Sophie, with perfect truth.

Mór gave her a long look but said nothing.


They made their way to the Marshalls' lodgings by a route that swung wide around the square. When they reached what Sophie recognised as the turning to Mór's lodgings in MacDuff-street, she made to pause and take leave, but Mór only took a firmer hold of her arm.

"You are not going home?" said Sophie, puzzled.

Mór looked at her disbelievingly. "Sophie, you surely cannot imagine it wise for a young Sasunnach woman to wander the streets of Din Edin alone, when no more than a mile away a mob is calling for—"

Then she shut her mouth abruptly and quickened her pace.

"I trust," said Sophie—a little breathless, and therefore less scathing than she had intended—"I trust that you are not attempting to protect me by keeping me in ignorance? I am not a child, Mór, *Sasunnach* though I may be."

Mór halted abruptly, dropped Sophie's arm, and turned to face her. "You are my friend," she said, "and I hoped to spare you distress. And . . ." She glanced aside, as though she could not quite meet Sophie's eyes. "I thought we had been a more hospitable people."

"Mór—"

A passing trio of men regarded them curiously.

"Come," said Mór, low and urgent. She caught Sophie's hand and set off again, walking now with what seemed a deliberate lack of haste.


They reached the little house in Quarry Close with no further incident, and—despite Sophie's best efforts—no further conversation. Sophie was fitting her door-key into the lock when the door was wrenched violently inward.

"Sophie!" Gray exclaimed. He caught her outstretched hand, key-ring and all, and pulled her across the threshold and into his arms. His big hands patted at her back, her arms, her shoulders, as though expecting to find some sort of injury.

Behind her, there was a delicate little cough, and Sophie's face heated with embarrassment as she recalled Mór's presence. What must she be thinking of such an unseemly display? And, really, it was *too* ridiculous: What did Gray imagine to have happened to her?

She extricated herself with some difficulty and looked up at her husband, keeping her hands on her hips so as not to shake him. At once however she forgot her annoyance; a livid bruise was rising on Gray's cheek, his face was pale, his eyes a little wild, and there was mud streaked along his trouser-leg and on the sleeve of his coat. "Gray, what on *earth*—"

He ran a hand through his hair, which was already in more than usual disarray. "There is some sort of riot in Teviot Square," he said. "Rory and I ran straight into it and were nearly trampled. We have only just arrived, and when I found you were not here—"

"I was at the Library," Sophie said, nonplussed; it was not like Gray to panic. "I sent a message by one of your students—the Erse boy with the stammer, you know—" She silently apologised to the student in question, whose name she knew perfectly well.

"Eoghan Ó Tuathail," Gray said. He sighed. "I shall find it pinned to the door of my study tomorrow morning, I expect; I have not seen him since yesterday afternoon."

Uneven footsteps approached from the kitchen. Sophie peered around Gray's shoulder and gasped. Rory MacCrimmon had halted in the doorway, leaning one shoulder against the jamb; his coat-sleeve was torn, his boots and trousers caked in mud, his lower lip split and swollen, and with one hand he held a folded linen towel against his left eye.

Before Sophie could even summon the wit to ask what had befallen him—or to demand why he and Gray had not, apparently, defended themselves—Mór was rushing past her, exclaiming in Gaelic so rapid and furious that Sophie could catch only one word in three, and propelling Rory back into the kitchen. Sophie and Gray exchanged bemused glances and followed. As they went, Gray curled one arm about Sophie's shoulders and drew her close against his side.

Mór had pushed Rory into a wheelback chair and was leaning down to examine his face, long fingers prodding tenderly at the darkening skin around his eye. She was still berating him, but slowly enough now that Sophie could easily follow her tirade.

"Brawling in the streets, Rory! What can you possibly have been thinking? How do you expect to explain yourself to Catriona? You—"

"We were not *brawling*," Rory said. The words were blurred by his swollen lip. "We were only trying to cross Teviot Square."

"It was my fault entirely," said Gray. Mór straightened, turned, and frowned at him. "As you said yourself when we first met," he elaborated, with a sheepish and almost apprehensive glance aside at Sophie, "I am English. Too English, apparently, to escape notice in a crowd."

Sophie gently detached herself from Gray and set about making a pot of tea. Donella MacHutcheon had left the kettle filled, as was her habit, and Sophie poked up the kitchen fire, hung the kettle on its hook, measured tea leaves into the pot, set out cups and saucers. The domestic routine had grown familiar over the years of her new life as a student, and she slipped gratefully into it, soothed by the sense that she was accomplishing something useful with her own hands, and listened to the others' conversation with only half an ear.

Gray and Rory, it transpired, had learnt more from their sojourn amidst the disgruntled crowd than Mór had done—or, at any rate, were more inclined to discuss what they had discovered: There were gatherings elsewhere in the city, as well as in Teviot Square, and some said even in Glaschu; the priests of the Cailleach were rumoured to believe that their mistress opposed any marriage alliance outside the clans; and the offence which had so exercised the people of Din Edin was not only the choice of a foreign prince over the heads of dozens of eligible Alban chieftains' sons, but the notion that the marriage would give the British king undue influence in the affairs of Alba. Mór and Rory debated at some length whether this idea had any merit, but reached no firm conclusion.


"What do you know of these Princes, Marshall?" Rory inquired. He sipped his tea gingerly, wincing at the pressure of the teacup's rim against his split lip.

"Edward is betrothed to a Normande," Gray said evenly, "the daughter of the Comte d'Evreux, I believe. Either Roland or Henry, I suppose, must be the prince in question. Roland is the elder, and second in line to the throne at present; but of course that is expected to change once Prince Edward marries. He does seem much the likeliest, as Prince Henry is only twelve."

"This Roland must also be very young, then?" said Mór.

"Quite young, yes," said Gray.

"Prince Roland is accounted an excellent horseman," Sophie offered, and, rather less truthfully, "I do not know anything to his detriment."

"I hope he is reasonably sensible," said Mór, with an odd sort of smirk; "Lucia MacNeill will have no patience with him else."

Sophie, to Gray's surprise, gave a little half laugh. "*That* is certainly true," she said.

"I do not know her well," Rory said, "but Adalbert de la Haye is her tutor, and Cormac MacWattie before him, and both think very highly of her as a scholar."

Gray was not at all certain that this boded well for the success of a marriage between Lucia MacNeill and his brother-in-law Roland, who—though undoubtedly clever—was one of the least scholarly young men Gray had ever met.

"I was very much astonished," said Sophie, in a reminiscing tone, "when I discovered that I had been arguing about light-spells with the heiress of Alba."

Mór and Rory looked at one another, and then at Sophie, with identical expressions of bafflement. "Why?" said Mór.

"Well—because—because she—"

"In Britain," Gray put in, when Sophie's attempt at explanation sputtered to a halt, "it is usual for the royal children to be educated privately—even those not expected to inherit the throne."

Though it had not always been so; the Princess Edith Augusta—Sophie's namesake and co-Regent, with her elder sister, the Princess Julia, for the young King Edward the Sixth during his minority—had famously studied at Lady Morgan College in Oxford, very shortly before its doors were permanently closed.

Rory looked politely astonished.

Mór was less polite. "I understand that your king cannot choose his heirs, as our rulers do," she said, "and so perhaps thinks it less important to see how his children conduct themselves in the world before making his choice; but such isolation seems to me very foolish."

"Mór," said Rory, in gentle reproach.

"*I* think Mór is perfectly right," Sophie declared. "And if Lucia MacNeill is indeed to marry Prince Roland, perhaps her example will encourage him to further his studies here at the University, after they are wed! I expect—"

She stopped abruptly and, making some excuse about the tea things, rose from her seat beside Mór and fled past Gray into the kitchen.

Rory looked anxiously after her. "Is Sophie quite well?" he asked. "Mór, are you quite sure she was not hurt in the crowd, or . . . or frightened?"

"You may be sure that Sophie went nowhere near the crowd," said Mór, low and rather grimly, "and I do not think she was nearly as much frightened as she ought to be."

"What do you mean by that?" Gray kept his tone neutral with some effort. Sophie, it was plain, had nearly said something revealing just now, and had taken herself away to fret over it in privacy; had she also, at some earlier point in this unnerving day, been too frank with Mór? Were they, in fact, about to be discovered?

For the first time since their arrival in Din Edin, the prospect filled him with trepidation rather than relief.

Mór gave him a long, speculative look. "Do you tell me, Gray Marshall," she said at last, "that you can look at yourself at this moment, and ask me what I mean?"

*Ah. I see.* Ruefully, Gray touched the bruise on his cheek. "Sophie is not so conspicuous as I am," he said, by way of explanation. "And I am sure she believed no harm would come to her whilst she was in your company, Mór MacRury."

"And yet," said Mór, with a little quirk of her lips, "it is you who might easily have flown from the danger."

"I have never known Gray to fly from danger." Sophie's voice, behind him, was calm and even, but beneath there lurked a hint of steel. "Literally or otherwise. I should scarcely expect him to begin by abandoning a friend to the mercies of a mob."

Gray turned to look up at her, standing in the doorway with a plate of Donella MacHutcheon's butter shortbreads in her hands and the glint of challenge in her eyes.

"And Sophie has always thought better of me than I deserve," he said lightly, hoping that neither of their guests would think to inquire whence came this knowledge of his response to danger. "But if you have determined that I deserve a second helping of Donella Mac-Hutcheon's shortbread, *cariad*, I shall certainly not dispute your judgement."

To his great relief, Sophie took the hint and managed a moderately convincing grin.

"I ought to have told them," said Sophie, flinging herself full-length upon the sofa. "I wish I had done; it is only a matter of time, and I had rather they heard the truth from me."

Mór and Rory had gone away at last. She had been eager for them to go, and expected to feel their absence as a relief; but in fact, she now began to feel that she had wasted an ideal opportunity for confession and explanation, and rather wished that she might call them back.

Gray emerged from the kitchen, whither he had vanished with the tea-tray, and said, "Until today, I should have agreed with you entirely."

Sophie raised her head, the better to stare at him in bafflement.

"Our friends will forgive us this small deception," he said, crossing the room to sit on the sofa, "and I should have said that we need not care for the opinions of anybody else, but given what we have seen today—"

"What would you have me do, then?" cried Sophie, exasperated. And then, a further thought occurring, she exclaimed, "Oh, gods and priestesses! Lucia MacNeill!"

Gray's lips twisted. "She may not be best pleased with you," he said, "if the rumour be true."

Two days later, the afternoon's post brought—in the form of letters for Sophie from her father and Joanna, and one for Gray from Jenny— the rather startling intelligence that the rumour was indeed perfectly true.

Her father's letter was again very formal—more King to Princess than father to daughter—and very brief, almost identical to that which had announced Ned's betrothal to the Lady Delphine:

> *His Majesty, Henry, twelfth of the name, King of*
> *Britain, &c., is pleased to announce that a betrothal has*
> *been contracted between His Royal Highness, Roland Edric*
> *Augustus, Duke of York, and Lucia MacNeill, daughter of*
> *Donald MacNeill and heiress to the chieftain's seat of Alba,*
> *for the furthering of peaceable trade and alliance between*
> *our two Kingdoms, to the benefit of both.*

This, however, unlike the other, closed with the stern instruction to say nothing of the matter until a public announcement should be made.

Joanna's was much longer and more voluble, and was filled both with apologies for her earlier silence on the subject and with anxious speculations as to Roland's state of mind. It was also, Sophie felt, oddly filled with Gwendolen Pryce—though perhaps no more so than had been usual of late.

> *I am truly sorry to have kept you in the dark all this*
> *while, Sophie,* the letter concluded, *but I am sure you*
> *understand that having given my word to Lord Kergabet, to*

*say nothing of this matter to anyone whatsoever, I could not
make exceptions even for you. I did come very near to
breaking my promise on the day when you and Gray
departed for Din Edin. I trust that my warning will prove
unnecessary, but, however, I could not be easy about your
going, had I not given it.*

"I am very curious to know," said Gray, looking up from Jenny's
letter, "how Roland is taking this news, and to what sort of histrion-
ics he may be subjecting your father."

Sophie chuckled wanly. "Indeed," she said, "if my father and Sieur
Germain surprised him with it, I should imagine that he is not over
pleased. And he cannot have known of it, I think—or not for long—
for he has said nothing to me in any of his letters. Certainly he did not
mention it, when last we met in London; and this matter must have
been in train even before that."

"Brothers do not always tell their sisters everything, you know,"
said Gray. He reached towards her; his left hand smoothed comfortingly up and down her spine.

"I do not doubt it," said Sophie. "But Roland has made a special
project of befriending his unexpected sister, and often tells me things
that really he ought not. I do hope . . . I hope he is not truly distressed."

Gray did not ask, as many might have done, why she should
suppose that Roland might be distressed by the prospect of marrying a clever and very handsome young woman who stood to inherit
a kingdom.

"I am sure," he said, "that your father will not hold Roland to any
arrangement which causes him genuine distress." He hesitated, then
went on: "Have you . . . have you any particular reason to suspect . . ."

"He is . . . he has a preference for some other woman," Sophie
admitted, reluctantly. "I have not the least idea who she is, but from
the hints in his letters I believe his regard is not reciprocated."

The warm hand on her back faltered momentarily, then resumed
its steady rhythm.

"I do not much like this manner of arranging things," Sophie sighed, "but Roland is old enough and certainly impertinent enough to make his position clear, if he should object to marrying Lucia Mac-Neill; and if the news of the match is made public at home, and is shortly to be announced here also, it would appear that he has not done so. Only . . . I hope they may find some way to be happy together."

Gray, wisely, attempted no reply.

Sophie turned over the last page of Joanna's letter, which had formed the envelope, and found on the bottom third of it a postscript, hastily scrawled, which she had not remarked before:

> P.S. I have opened this up again, Sophie, to give you a piece of news that will please you: H.M. is sending a great convoy of waggons loaded with grain and salted meat and such to Alba—for the storehouses, you know—as part of the bride-gift, and they are on their way already! J.

"Oh!" she exclaimed. "Gray, listen—"

The betrothal was formally announced in Din Edin in the middle of January, and was received with heated discussions in drawing-rooms and public-houses—opinions seemingly divided between approbation and disapproval—as well as further public demonstrations both for and (in the great majority) against. To Sophie's astonishment and dismay, the news of the bride-gifts described in Joanna's letter, far from changing the minds of the doubters, seemed to fan the flames of their objections; the charge that Donald MacNeill had sold his daughter—or even Alba itself—in return for the right to glean from the fields of Britain, stooping like a beggar for the leavings of her harvest, seemed to be on the tip of every tongue, to shout from the pages of every broadsheet.

Sophie began to wonder that Donald MacNeill and his daughter should not be having serious second thoughts.

For Gray and herself, the month that followed was a constant trial. Formerly more or less unremarkable members of the University community, of no especial interest once their novelty had worn off, both of them—in common with every other British subject presently resident in Din Edin—had abruptly become notorious.

Reflecting on what her own feelings must have been had she found herself in Lucia MacNeill's position, Sophie had taken the earliest opportunity of approaching her future sister-in-law with felicitations and a request to speak with her in private.

"Of course," said Lucia MacNeill, graciously enough, though evidently puzzled.

There being no other immediate demands upon her time, she led the way to her own carrel in the Library and borrowed a second chair in which she invited Sophie to sit.

"If you will permit," said Sophie, still on her feet, "I should like to set a ward."

Lucia MacNeill did not trouble to hide her astonishment. "Certainly," she said, "if you think it needful."

She watched Sophie's spellcasting with a shrewd interest, which Sophie found rather unnerving.

"I have a confession to make to you," said Sophie at last, sinking into the proffered chair.

"To me?" Lucia MacNeill said, frowning. *Does she suspect? Surely she must suspect.*

"To you," said Sophie. She had thought carefully about what to say but found the words skittering away from her, and instead stammered, "As . . . as my brother's betrothed."

Lucia MacNeill's frown evaporated into undisguised shock.

Sophie, feeling miserably guilty, looked down at her hands, clasped tightly in her lap.

"So it is true," said Lucia MacNeill, after a long moment. Sophie raised her head abruptly. "You *are* the Lost Princess."

Sophie nodded.

"And Prince Roland's sister."

"Yes," said Sophie. She swallowed around the dry lump in her throat and added, in the spirit of honesty, "His half sister, at any rate."

Lucia MacNeill leaned forward a little, and Sophie squared her chin and looked the heiress of Alba in the eyes. They were beautiful eyes, of a calm clear blue, and fringed with long russet-gold lashes; and in them Sophie read both challenge and entreaty.

But for their colour, in fact—and the fine-drawn heart-shaped face from which they regarded her—they were Joanna's eyes to the life.

"You are not much alike," Lucia MacNeill remarked. "Unless the portrait I was sent is very unfaithful indeed."

"No," Sophie agreed, a little wrong-footed by this sudden turn of the conversation. "Roland favours his mother, and . . . I suppose I must favour mine."

Lucia MacNeill sat back in her chair, squaring her shoulders. "I could wish that you might have told me sooner who you are," she said. "In the circumstances."

"I knew no more of the circumstances than rumour could tell me," said Sophie, "until my father's letter reached me not a se'nnight ago, and I did not like to proceed on the strength of rumour alone."

This explanation was received with a slow, thoughtful nod, after which Lucia MacNeill tilted her head on one side, Joanna-like, and said, "I can see that with the priests of the Cailleach encouraging riots in the streets, this might not seem the best moment for such a revelation. But what I cannot see is—well—why hide to begin with?"

Sophie sighed. "If you knew what my life was, at Oxford," she said, "you could not ask me that question."

"Tell me, then," Lucia MacNeill suggested, with a wry smile.

Sophie smiled hesitantly back at her, and did.


Catriona MacCrimmon called upon Sophie in Quarry Close for the express purpose of discussing the news; not (so far as Sophie was able to observe) because she suspected Sophie of being in the secret, but because she knew no other Sasunnach visitors to interrogate. Catriona's manner was overbright and brittle—very like the evening of the Marshalls' supper-party, when she had interrupted Sophie's conversation with Rory on the subject of clan storehouses. Earlier in their acquaintance, Sophie might have taken it at its face value and concluded that Catriona favoured the Alban heiress's marriage with a British prince and was eager to know all about him; now, as so often of late, she was baffled and wrong-footed, unable to deduce what Catriona might be at.

"I fear the match is not well looked upon everywhere in Alba," Sophie ventured, testing the waters, "though Lucia MacNeill herself is so highly thought of. It seems to me a good thing—the cementing of a friendship, so that each kingdom may have less fear of the other— but perhaps you do not agree?"

Catriona smiled broadly with her lips, and not at all with her eyes.

"Can any true friendship subsist between such unequal parties?" she said. "Between a great kingdom such as yours, with its standing army and its vast lands and great treasuries, and little Alba?"

"I . . . I had not thought of the question in quite that way," said Sophie, wishing now that she had not asked.

Catriona's smile took on a pitying edge. "I did not suppose you had. It is the privilege of the powerful never to consider such questions from the perspective of the powerless."

Sophie blinked.

Catriona patted her hand, and Sophie fought to control her instinctive recoil. "The stones are cast, now," she said, not unkindly, "and what is there for the likes of us to do, but learn to live with the consequences?"

But she did not look as if she meant what she said.


The heiress of Alba might be perfectly able to keep a secret; but having told Lucia MacNeill the truth, Sophie found herself increasingly unable to justify hiding it from her closest acquaintance.

Eithne and Una were full of questions for their one Sasunnach friend, almost none of which Sophie could answer: *How long has this match been in the offing? Is it true that London is sending waggon-loads of food to Alba? What does your King intend by it, and by the match itself? What can you tell us of this Prince Roland?*

"As for the marriage arrangements, I do not believe I know much more about the matter than you do," she said at last, helplessly. "Except that I can certainly vouch for the bride-gifts of stores against famine, for I had that news from my sister. This match must have been under discussion for some time—such things are not decided overnight, I know—but I cannot recall that any such thing was talked of when last I was in London—"

Her next words fled her mind temporarily as she took in the astonishment on her friends' faces. She gathered her wits about her again, and went on: "I can tell you something of Prince Roland, however, because—and I am sorry not to have told you before—because—because he is my half-brother."

Una and Eithne gaped at her.

At last Eithne said, "Then . . . it is true that you are the Lost Princess? And not Sophie Marshall at all?"

"It is *not* true that I am not Sophie Marshall," said Sophie, rather more vehemently than she had intended. "I have been Sophie Marshall since the day I was married, and I cannot help what else I am besides." She scowled, looking down at the scuffed toes of her sturdy boots. "But . . . but I was born Princess Edith Augusta; that much is certainly true."

For another long moment, no one spoke.

Sophie raised her head at last—half wondering whether Eithne and Una had somehow vanished whilst her attention was elsewhere—and found them both staring at her as though antlers had sprouted from her head.

"You," said Eithne, shaking her head. "I cannot credit it."

"And why on the gods' green earth, Eithne MacLachlan," Sophie said, with some asperity, "should I tell you such a tale, if it were *not* true?"

"I wish you will not take offence, Sophie," said Eithne, half apologetic, half defensive. "You must allow that this is entirely unexpected. And," she added, "if it *is* true, then, for the gods' sake, why have you never said so before?"

Sophie restrained herself from rolling her eyes. "Lucia MacNeill asked me the same question," she said. "If my fellow students at Merlin College had been anything like hers, I daresay I should have felt differently."

Una, meanwhile, had been studying Sophie intently, her head on one side.

"It's said the Sasunnachs' Lost Princess is very beautiful," she remarked. "And that she can sing the birds out of the trees, and the rocks from the river-bed, like—"

Sophie's snort of laughter at this romantical notion brought Una up short, frowning.

"You may believe whatever you like," said Sophie cheerfully. She was rather surprised to find that this was, in most respects, true. "It makes no difference to me."

She was entirely surprised when Una, after another long, considering look, said firmly, "I believe you."

Eithne—ordinarily so much more credulous—still looked doubtful. "The thing is, you see," she began, "my mother told our cousin Conall MacLachlan—the butterfly collector, you know—she mentioned to him that—"

"Eithne," said Una, "whatever it is you have to say, will you for the gods' sake cease *trying* to say it and *say* it."

Eithne swallowed visibly, and nodded. "Conall MacLachlan spoke to you at the Chancellor's dinner, he said, and concluded that he had been wrong to think you must be the Lost Princess, because you were too plain and too dull, and your singing had no magick in it."

"Ah," said Sophie. So Conall MacLachlan had indeed known who she was—and this must explain why he had said nothing about it thereafter. "But that is because Conall MacLachlan has forgot the other magick for which the Lost Princess is renowned."

"What is that?" said Eithne, frowning.

"This," said Sophie.

She closed her eyes briefly, imagined herself in her own sitting-room—seated at her pianoforte, alone with Gray—and, for the first time since leaving London, stood in a public corridor and let her native magick have its way. She could not have said precisely what she now looked like, but Gray had shown her, once (or, rather, had made her show herself), how her face grew brighter, livelier, and more colourful when she was happy, when her worries receded, when she was surrounded by the people she loved.

"*Oh,*" said Eithne.

"Brighde's tears!" said Una.

When she felt they had looked their fill, Sophie carefully resumed her plainer, soberer self—which produced another astonished *Oh!* from Eithne—and regarded them both solemnly.

"Eithne MacLachlan," she said, "Una MacSherry, we are friends, are we not?"

"Of course, Sophie," said Eithne.

Una nodded warily.

"Then I may rely on you both, I hope," said Sophie, "to stand my friends still? *I* have not changed, you know; I am Princess Edith Augusta only when I must be, and am Sophie Marshall always, deep down."

She would not plead—would not say, *Please believe me, I have never lied to you about anything that truly matters*—but she did wish, again, that she had never taken it into her head to keep this secret. Only, it had been so pleasant to be Sophie Marshall and nothing more, so uncomplicated and easy . . .

"Did you," Una began. She paused, then began again: "Did you know—"

"No," said Sophie at once. "Or only a very little before the news was made public here, in a letter from my father; and at the same time he insisted upon silence, so of course I could not say anything about it to anyone."

Una's gaze was steady upon Sophie's face, solemn and considering. "Good," she said at last, with a sharp nod.

Sophie felt oddly as though she had just passed some sort of test, without at all knowing in what the ordeal consisted.

"And now," said Una, her solemn face breaking into a grin, "you must tell us all about Lucia MacNeill's betrothed!"

In the lively discussion that followed, Eithne was oddly silent, but Sophie was so much encouraged by Una's reaction that she scarcely remarked it.

*Gray was quite right,* she thought wonderingly. *It is a relief not to be hiding any longer.*

## CHAPTER XV

# In Which Sophie Loses
# One Friend and Gains Another

*Sophie was playing* something unusually mournful on the piano-forte, and Gray listening whilst reading and drinking tea, when Mór MacRury called in Quarry Close very early one January morning.

Apart from Sophie's choice of music, none of these circumstances was at all out of the common way. It had become a settled habit for many of their University acquaintance to call upon them at all hours, for the scholars of Din Edin shared with those of Oxford a general tendency to disregard those social conventions which they found inconvenient; and such visits had become more frequent in the past fortnight, as their friends chose this means amongst others to show that, manifestations against Lucia MacNeill's marriage notwithstanding, the Marshalls had been welcomed by the University and remained so. Goff and Tredinnick, and the various relief sentries lent to them by Lord de Courcy since the announcement of the betrothal, by now knew all of Gray's and Sophie's friends by sight, and so they were never hindered in their progress up Quarry Close by any inconvenient encounter with an apparent shipping-clerk or itinerant knife-mender. And Gray often asked Sophie to play for him when there was a particularly trying student essay to be read.

This one was very trying indeed, and Sophie's melancholic humour was becoming infectious. It was with some relief, therefore, that Gray rose from his armchair in reply to a more than usually insistent knocking at the front door.

His relief was short-lived, however, for upon opening it, he beheld Mór MacRury standing on the step, wearing a heavy woollen cloak and an anxious expression.

"Is Sophie here?" she said, in lieu of a greeting. "I must speak to her—is she—"

"She is here," said Gray, cautiously. "Mór, are you quite well?" A thought occurred to him, and he added, "There has not been some new disturbance? You are not hurt?"

He stood aside to let her in and to shut out the heavy rain.

The melancholy music ceased, and footsteps succeeded it.

"Mór!" said Sophie, with uncomplicated welcome in her voice. "Come in and sit down! Oh, you are wet through—"

Mór only stared at her, a small frown creasing her brow; she seemed not to hear Gray's offer to hang up her damp cloak to dry, or Sophie's of a fresh pot of tea, and Sophie at last faltered into silence.

"Sophie," said Mór, when the silence had gone on so long as to be nearly unbearable. "Why did you never tell me?"

Gray sighed; Sophie flushed an unbecoming crimson, and looked at her toes.

"I suppose you have been speaking to Eithne MacLachlan," she said. "I am sorry; of course I meant to tell you myself, but you were ill in bed all the past se'nnight, and it did not seem—"

"So it *is* true, then." Mór MacRury's vivid eyes were large with the aftermath of fever. "You are truly the daughter of King Henry— the Lost Princess—the sister of Lucia MacNeill's Prince Roland. Everyone is talking of it, Sorcha says."

"Yes," said Sophie, almost inaudibly. "And Eithne MacLachlan, it seems, cannot forgive me for it. That, I suppose, is the source of the rumours, for Lucia MacNeill I am sure has said nothing to anyone."

*Ah. That explains the melancholy music.* Sophie had told him very cheerfully that Lucia MacNeill and Una MacSherry had taken the news in good part; why had he not remarked her (in retrospect, obvious) omission of her other close comrade?

Gray crossed the small sitting-room to stand behind her, laying a protective hand on each of her rounded shoulders. "Sophie is the Princess Edith Augusta through an accident of birth," he said, frowning down at Mór MacRury, "and lost because her mother loved her too well to give her up to be raised by the Iberian Empress."

His left thumb stroked the soft curve of Sophie's neck, skin against warm skin to draw strength and to give it. "She is Sophie Marshall through her own choice and promises, and a member of this University—if only a temporary one—on her merits as a scholar. I should hope, Mór MacRury, that you are a woman of sufficient sense, and stand enough our friend, to judge rightly which of these titles best reflect her character."

As Gray's speech proceeded—his voice, despite his best efforts, growing rather edged—Sophie's left hand had come up to her shoulder to grip his fingers, and Mór's astonished gaze had transferred itself from Sophie's bent head to his face.

"I am sorry," she said, low. "I meant no insult, Sophie. Only—"

Sophie straightened her spine and raised her head. "I beg you will think no more of it," she said, with fragile dignity. "It is my own fault, for being so stupid as to attempt concealment."

"Sophie—"

"Please, Mór." Sophie's fingers tightened painfully around Gray's; he gently pressed her other shoulder, and at once she loosened her grip, glancing up in mute apology.

Mór dropped into Gray's chair and sat very still, studying her clasped hands. Gray nudged Sophie gently in the direction of her own chair, which faced his; when she had taken the hint and sunk down into it, he came round one side and, keeping one hand on Sophie's shoulder, perched on the upholstered chair-arm, both feet flat on the threadbare carpet beneath. Sophie leant briefly against his side.

"What do you mean to do now?" Mór asked, raising her eyes at last.

Sophie sat up straight. "I beg your pardon?" she said. "What should I mean to do, but what I came to Din Edin for?"

Mór MacRury frowned at Gray as though to say, *Surely you understand what I am driving at?* "If I were your father," she said, turning her gaze back to Sophie, "I should not be at all easy in my mind as to your safety in Din Edin at present."

"She is not unguarded," said Gray, bristling a little. "His Majesty is not so careless, and nor am I."

"Ah." Mór MacRury's expression cleared a little; she looked speculatively at Sophie, who looked away. "They must be very discreet, these guards."

"They are," said Gray; "I daresay you have seen them dozens of times, without recognising them as such. Sophie does not like to feel . . . hemmed in."

"In any case, Mór MacRury," said Sophie, "I hope you do not think we shall be chased out of Din Edin by a few malcontents chanting slogans!"

"Sophie, if Mór thinks it truly dangerous—"

"If you have guards always by, that does put a different complexion on the matter," said Mór MacRury. "It may well be that this present unrest is only a maelstrom in a millpond. I will say, on that head, that I have lived in Din Edin nearly half my life, and seen many public scandals come and go—I should not be greatly surprised if this one were no different."

"There, Gray," said Sophie, looking up at him.

Gray was not altogether persuaded; he did not choose to continue the dispute before an audience, however, and therefore shut his mouth until Mór MacRury had gone away.


"Eithne MacLachlan?" said Gray, when the front door had closed behind their visitor.

"Do you remember the Chancellor's dinner party?" said Sophie, à propos of nothing which Gray could divine.

"Ye-es," he said.

"Then you will recall Eithne's cousin Conall MacLachlan," said Sophie, "the collector of *Lepidoptera* who asked me so many questions about Breizh?"

"Oh," said Gray vaguely, attempting to dismiss from his mind the arresting image of Sophie's fingers spread across the keys of a pianoforte. "Yes"—and then, making the connexion at last, "You thought he suspected you. Did he so, indeed?"

"So Eithne told me." Sophie sighed, putting her face in her hands for a moment; on raising her head again she said, "After speaking to me at length, he concluded that he had erred—though by now I suppose he has discovered his mistake. Eithne had heard his verdict from her mother, and so she would not believe me until I showed her Mama's magick. And now I wish I had not done it."

Sophie sprang up from her chair and began pacing in tight circles about the sitting-room.

Gray watched her for the length of three circuits, pondering his approach. Sophie in furious motion was, as always, a sight both daunting and alluring. He could, he suspected, stop this crisis in its tracks by distracting her with kisses—but only for the moment, and (though the temptation was strong, for many reasons) that of course would not do.

"Should you," he began, cautiously, "have any strong objection to my consulting Lord de Courcy? Though I am sure that if he believed us to be in danger, we should have heard from him before now; he certainly was not laggard in—how did he put it?—*strengthening your security detail* after the announcement was made."

"I have no intention of fleeing back to London with my tail between my legs," said Sophie, folding her arms. "If Lucia MacNeill can walk the streets of Din Edin in safety, surely we can do so also? She is not better guarded than we are, with Courcy's men as well as our own, and she is far more directly concerned in the case."

"But she is on her home ground," said Gray, "and we are not." He was also reasonably certain that Lucia MacNeill was indeed rather better guarded than Sophie; he and his colleagues had remarked, if Sophie had not, the half-dozen new students, strapping young men (and one young woman) with the alert and serious look of those trained in arms and sworn to service, at least three of whom were now seen to inhabit whatever corner of the University Lucia Mac-Neill happened to be in. Lord de Courcy could not possibly spare so many; his household had no more than a dozen guards all told—the better, as Powell had explained, to reinforce his status as peaceful emissary rather than reconnaissance force—though the look of the Courcys' coachman and footmen suggested to Gray that they too might be good men in a fight.

He sighed. "If it were possible, I should wish you shielded from all possible harm," he said, "though I am perfectly well aware how little you like my saying so; and I confess that I should think you safer in London, or in Oxford, or anywhere south of the Wall. You could pay a visit to Breizh, you know, if you do not like to go to London without me—"

Sophie huffed an exasperated sigh. "It is not *London* that I object to," she said; and, softening her tone, added, *"Ubi tu Gaius, ego Gaia.* You remember, Gray."

She crossed the sitting-room to stand before him, so close that the fall of her skirts hid the toes of his boots, and taking his hands in hers, she looked up at him with her heart in her dark eyes.

"Yes," said Gray, who had never held out much hope of winning this argument, and now had none. "I remember."

Sophie let go his hands and for a moment leant her head against the buttons of his waistcoat, sliding her arms about his waist as he curved his around her shoulders. When she looked up again, she was smiling, and he was lost.

In the absence of Eithne MacLachlan's company, Sophie began to spend more of her time with Lucia MacNeill, who—though she was on good terms with everyone, and her circle of friends appeared to embrace half the population of the University—had, Sophie discovered, very few trusted and intimate acquaintance.

Lucia MacNeill inquired, with a surprising diffidence, whether Sophie might teach her a little Français, and some English. Less surprisingly, she also wished Sophie to tell her all about Roland—not of his appearance (for she had seen a portrait) or his pedigree or his magickal talent, all of which must already have been discussed at some length, but of the man himself. Was he clever? Had he a head for politics, or did he prefer his books? What were his favourite poets, his favourite songs, his preferred recreations? Had he (and here Lucia MacNeill's voice faltered a little, and a flush spread across her delicate cheekbones) any particular favourites amongst the young women at his father's Court?

It was easier for Sophie to keep her countenance now that she felt free to use her concealing magick at need. "He is not sixteen," she temporised. "I love my brother very much, Lucia, but do remember that he is only a boy."

"You were married at seventeen," said Lucia MacNeill. "Or so I am told."

Sophie could not deny it. "It is not a course of action which I should necessarily recommend," she said.

Lucia MacNeill's fine-drawn brows drew together in worry. "Sophie, surely if you were unhappy, your father—"

"No, no!" cried Sophie in some alarm. "That is not what I meant, at all. And I shall tell you, though I should not own it to anybody else, that my father *did* try to persuade me—to persuade both of us—to renounce our promises, knowing that they had been made in haste, and that I have never regretted refusing him. I only meant that had it been in my power to choose, I should have wished for a longer engagement. Though certainly we were well enough acquainted."

"Longer than . . . ?"

Sophie blushed and ducked her head; it sounded so much more

absurd when spoken aloud to one who had not been there. "Than three days."

Lucia MacNeill clapped one hand over her mouth to stifle a burst of startled laughter. Above her long fingers, her blue eyes danced.

"In that case," she said, after a moment, "I believe I may undertake not to follow your example. But"—and here her voice grew hesitant, and her expression unexpectedly shy—"I hope I may rely on you for advice, as I have no mother or elder sister to guide me?"

"Of course you may." Sophie smiled at her in a rush of real affection. "I have not said it before, but I shall be very glad to call you sister."

Then, pointing to herself: "In Latin, *soror*; in English, *sister*."

"*Sister*," Lucia MacNeill repeated.


As January progressed into February, Sophie came to consider that, generally speaking, their circumstances might have been enormously worse. Eithne MacLachlan's retreat from their friendship still rankled, and there was a certain amount of staring and whispering to be endured as she went about her business at the University; still, the latter was no more onerous than it had been at Merlin, and to counterbalance the former, she felt more confident in the regard of those friends who had not turned their backs upon learning who her father was. It was not always pleasant to walk home through streets in which, two or three times in a se'nnight, she must pass by groups of Albans shouting abuse at her father, her brother, or her kingdom in general; but she told herself that it was only shouting and took comfort in the presence of the guardsmen dogging her steps, whom she had sometimes resented before. Perhaps best of all, she had Joanna's visit to look forward to—though she could not help feeling that perhaps she ought not to be so eager to involve her sister in the present mess.

*On the other hand, it seems rather as though Joanna has been involved in it longer than I have.*

Sophie's nights, however, had become something of a trial; it seemed her unconscious mind could not be entirely persuaded by her reason, and after a respite of many months, it began again—her prayers to Morpheus notwithstanding—to plague her with bad dreams.

In one such, one February night, she woke in chill, starlit darkness to find herself quite alone in the bedchamber of their Oxford digs. "Gray?" she whispered. Then louder: "Gray! Gray, where are you?"

There came no reply—no sound, no whisper of turning pages—no glow of magelight, no line of fire- or candlelight beneath the door. She threw back the bedclothes, padded barefoot across a floor as cold and slick as ice, on which her bare feet slipped treacherously; searched everywhere, panic rising, calling aloud with no thought for the comfort of others in the house. And at last she stood before the study window, through whose shattered panes the chill wind blew, each jagged point of glass tipped bright with blood.

Her howling sobs, as is the way of dreams, seemed like to choke her; she wailed and wailed, and made no sound, and could not catch her breath. Her bare feet slipped and slid on the floor; when she looked down, she found them cut about and bloodied, and the pain she had not hitherto felt rushed in swift and fire-bright, and she fell to her hands and knees amidst gleaming shards of window-glass.

She jolted into true wakefulness in the dark before dawn, her face wet with tears, and lay shivering and gasping as she tried to slow her rapid, panicked breathing. The details of the nightmare had already fled, but the panic and terror lingered, almost more distressing for the vagueness of their source.

On waking she had turned away from Gray, so as not to disturb him; behind her, still asleep, he reached for her, curling one arm about her. "Sophie?" he muttered sleepily. "'wake?"

Sophie drew a long, shaky breath. "No," she said. "Go back to sleep, love."

Gray's arm tightened a little, drawing her in close. The beating of his heart soothed her, as it always had before; but dawn had begun to light the sky when at last Sophie drifted back into sleep.

When they both woke in the morning, it was to the sound of Donella MacHutcheon indignantly demanding to know what coward had piled horse droppings on the step before their door and written *Go home, Sasunnach Princess, and take your brother with you*—and other sentiments far less polite—all over the frontage of their house.

## CHAPTER XVI

# In Which Sophie Receives an Unwelcome Summons, and Gray Is Read a Lecture

*On the heels* of this distressing, if not actually dangerous, instance of vandalism, Gray and Sophie were summoned to the residence of His Majesty's ambassador. The invitation—if such it could be called—arrived not in the post, nor by a messenger, but in the person of Lord de Courcy's confidential secretary, Mr. Powell; and so early in the morning that Sophie (who had tumbled into bed long after midnight, red-eyed from hours of translation and transcription which Gray could not persuade her to abandon) was yet abed. Donella MacHutcheon admitted him to the house and conducted him into the dining-room, where Gray was eating his breakfast.

Gray—deep in contemplation of Sophie's translation, which yesterday he had blearily promised her that he should read over for errors, as soon as he might—did not at once register the intrusion upon his solitude. Donella MacHutcheon cleared her throat and knocked on the door-jamb without success, and at last resorted to saying, very loudly, "Maighistir!"

Gray raised his head, blinking. "Yes, Donella MacHutcheon?" he said.

His gaze found her, and only then remarked the presence of Powell looming at her shoulder. On the heels of this observation came the remembrance of his having dispatched a rather heated note to Lord de Courcy, following the unpleasant discovery. Was this Courcy's reply?

"Mr. Powell!" he exclaimed. "Er . . . have you breakfasted? May I offer you—"

"I am not come to pay a morning call, Mr. Marshall," said Powell, stepping forward around Donella MacHutcheon, "only to convey a message."

Gray raised his eyebrows in invitation; Powell looked pointedly at Donella MacHutcheon.

"Thank you, Donella MacHutcheon," said Gray. She gave Powell a look of pointed disapproval as she left the room, having first briefly altered her trajectory in order to bestow a motherly pat upon Gray's shoulder.

Powell looked after her, frowning in bafflement. Perhaps the Ambassador's household had all come with him from Britain, and he had had no opportunity to become acclimated to the customs of Alban servants? Or perhaps Donella MacHutcheon was in fact particularly egregious in her familiarity, which Sophie (it must be conceded) never made the least effort to curb.

"The Lord Ambassador's compliments," Powell said after a moment, seeming to recover his sense of purpose, "and he invites you to call upon him today at the first hour after noon."

Gray blinked.

"The word *invite*," he said, "ordinarily implies the possibility of refusal."

"Ordinarily, yes," said Powell, steadily meeting Gray's gaze.

"I see." Gray took refuge in a large swallow of tea, unfortunately now rather tepid. "This . . . invitation . . . has I suppose some connexion with the . . . *offering* which we found on our doorstep three days ago?"

In addition to Gray's note, Courcy must have had a report of the incident, either directly from one of his own men or through some back channel.

Powell inclined his head.

Gray was coming more fully awake now, under the influence of strong tea and the need to think rationally and carefully about present circumstances. "I have a bone to pick with your master," he said. *And not in front of Sophie.* "As I am sure you know. How was such a thing permitted to occur? Must we now fear being attacked the moment we step foot outside our front door—or worse?"

Powell had the grace to look—if not so guilty as Gray felt he ought—at least discomfited. "The persons responsible have been detained," he said, "and, I believe I may promise, shall be suitably punished—"

"I should not care if they were not punished at all," said Gray, waving this away, "so long as nobody else follows their example. I am only concerned for my wife's welfare—though of course I wish His Majesty's guardsmen no ill, either. Her younger sister is to come to us for a visit in March, and I shall write at once to my brother-in-law to stop her departing London, if I cannot be assured that they shall both be safe."

"Mr. Marshall—"

Footfalls on the staircase, the creak of the last step from the bottom, silenced Powell and heralded the arrival of Sophie, soberly attired and still blinking sleepily.

"Good morning, Mrs. Marshall," said Powell, with a little bow.

Sophie gaped at him. "Mr. Powell," she said. Gray could almost see her suppressing the words *Whatever do you here?*

"I must be going," said Powell. He offered Sophie a brittle smile. "I shall see you both at the first hour after noon."

"I expect you shall," said Gray, grimly, and rose to see him out.


They presented themselves once again at the gate of the Ambassador's house, a little before the appointed hour, and this time were admitted at once, with a deferential alacrity quite unlike their previous reception. Mr. Powell met them at the front door and ushered them within, where they found Lord de Courcy just rising from behind his desk to greet them.

Tea and *petits fours* appeared as though by magick; indeed, Sophie was not at all certain that Mr. Powell had not summoned them before setting his wards upon the room, for surely she had not been so deeply absorbed in Lord de Courcy's greeting as to fail to remark the arrival of sufficient servants to convey refreshments for four people. Sophie accepted a cup of tea and a plate of cakes—despite a rather childish wish to owe nothing to her father's emissary, even so much as a bite of cake or a swallow of tea—because she was in fact very hungry, Mr. Powell's untimely visit having rendered her too anxious to eat much breakfast. The tea was, she grudgingly conceded, very good, in the English way, and the *petits fours* a not unwelcome change from the ubiquitous oatcakes and butter shortbread.

"You must be eager to know the reason for my invitation," Lord de Courcy began, tracing a long forefinger along the edge of his saucer.

Gray snorted softly at the word *invitation*.

"I hope," said Sophie, "that it is to beg our pardon for having failed to prevent the recent incident, and to assure us that such a thing will not occur again."

Lord de Courcy raised his eyebrows at her. "I regret very much that you should have been subjected to such an indignity," he said. "In fact, however—"

He set aside his teacup and reached for a letter that lay open upon his desk. As he picked it up, Sophie saw at the top edge of it, upside down, the lower half of her father's seal, and her heart clenched.

"Is my father ill?" she demanded. "Has something befallen one of my brothers? Or my sister? Or—"

"Calm yourself, Madame Marshall, I beg," said Lord de Courcy. Sophie drew in a deep, trembling breath, only now registering the warm pressure of Gray's hands enfolding hers.

"I beg your pardon, my lord Ambassador," she said, when she felt able to speak again without shouting.

"Your father and your brothers are all perfectly well," he said, "and your sister also. I assure you that, had there been any news of the kind, I should not have required you to wait upon me to receive it."

Sophie nodded, unspeakably relieved. But if not that, then—

"Your father, however," Lord de Courcy continued, "in light of recent developments, supposes that you and your husband must wish to return to London, if not at once, then certainly at the end of the present University term; for which purpose, he has dispatched one Edwin Cooper, who apparently is known to you, to convey you thither. Regrettably this also requires that your sister's visit be abandoned; but, however, I trust this will be no hardship to either party, as you shall after all meet in London so soon."

To look at Sophie now, Gray thought, one could not possibly guess how lately she had been fretting over the very question of Joanna's safety, and asking him whether he thought they ought not to advise her against coming to Din Edin.

"We shall do no such thing!" she exclaimed, sitting up straight as a pikestaff, and clenching her hands into ivory-knuckled fists. "I am sorry for Cooper's trouble, in coming so far for nothing, but what my father asks is quite impossible."

Courcy raised his eyebrows. "You understand, Madame Marshall, that this is not a *suggestion* on His Majesty's part. Not only is he your father, and thus within his right to command you—"

"I beg your pardon, my lord," Sophie interrupted him. "You forget that I am a married woman." She turned to Gray and said evenly, "Gray, do you wish me to return to London?"

Gray sat straighter, conscious of the role which Sophie apparently needed him to play. "I should be loath to forbid you, if you truly desired it," he said carefully, "but no."

Sophie turned back to Lord de Courcy. "I am a married woman," she repeated. "You surely cannot wish me to dishonour my husband by obeying my father's wishes in preference to his."

Had Lord de Courcy (or, for that matter, had Sophie's father) sought Gray's advice beforehand, Gray might have explained that Sophie's peculiar upbringing had given her a pronounced contrarian streak; that though she might sometimes seem a biddable young woman, this was only the effect of the dramatic contrast provided by her younger sister; that, in fact, perhaps the most effective means of persuading her to do a thing was to set oneself up in authority over her and command her to do its opposite. Though of course he should not have given anyone any such advice, absent a strong conviction of its being necessary to Sophie's well-being.

Courcy, however, did not seem cowed either by Sophie's reasonable tone or by her logic. "*You* forget, Madame Marshall," he said, "that His Majesty does not speak only as your father."

There was a silence as all present contemplated his implication.

"Do you tell me," said Sophie at last, speaking carefully and quietly, "that in remaining in Din Edin to continue our studies, my husband and I should be expressly disobeying a royal command?"

"No," Courcy conceded, after another long silence. His expression suggested that he should have liked very much to return a different answer. "His Majesty's letter is not so phrased as to give you no choices but obedience or treason. But, Madame Marshall, I beg you will consider—"

Sophie held up a hand—the Princess Royal, now, as suddenly as the sun breaking through storm-clouds—and he fell silent.

"We have considered the question at length already," she said, "and have determined that unless circumstances should change materially for the worse, we had rather remain where we are. And you may tell him, too, that I am considering his reputation. Lucia Mac-Neill is my friend, and we are very nearly the only British subjects of her acquaintance; what must she think of us, and of my father and Roland, if we turn tail and flee at the least sign of trouble?"

Gray looked at her in some surprise. It was a sound argument, in its way, and one far more sensitive to the political circumstances than he should have expected Sophie to make.

Courcy, for his part, looked very thoughtful, and as he made no move to argue with her, Sophie unbent so far as to say, "I shall write to my father myself, of course, and make certain that no blame for my recalcitrance attaches to you, my lord."

Courcy's mouth quirked briefly. "I thank you for that favour, Your Royal Highness."

"I shall undertake to inform you, my lord," said Gray, before Sophie could react to this mockery (if mockery it was), "should any circumstance arise to alter our decision."

"Yes," said Sophie; more bluntly, she added, "If we wish to depart, in haste or otherwise, you shall be the first to know it."

"Very good, madame," said the Ambassador, offering Sophie a little bow. "And now perhaps you will permit Monsieur Powell to provide pen and ink, so that your letter may be conveyed to His Majesty with all possible speed?"

Sophie visibly set her teeth for a moment, then smiled politely at Lord de Courcy and said, "Certainly. I thank you."

Sophie held her peace the length of the return journey to Quarry Close, for which Lord de Courcy had insisted on providing his carriage-and-pair, together with the quite unnecessary company of Mr. Powell. The latter made one or two efforts to engage her in conversation, but upon her saying, civilly enough but with great determination, "Mr. Powell, I beg you will excuse me; I am very tired," instead favoured Gray with a disquisition upon the subject of University politics—one which Gray had hitherto steered wide around, as likely to be hazardous to his health.

"You are very well informed about the University," said Gray, "for a man who has never so much as attended a lecture there."

"It is part of my purview," said Powell, who seemed to have taken no offence, "as milord's secretary, to keep an eye on the University, which is more my milieu than his."

He eyed Gray speculatively. "I do not suppose . . ."

"I hope," said Gray, "that you do not mean to ask me to spy upon my colleagues."

Powell looked genuinely startled, and Gray at once regretted his readiness to jump to unpleasant conclusions. "I beg your pardon," he said.

"No, no," said Powell, waving a dismissive hand. "I am a diplomat, and you are perfectly placed to engage in covert observations; it was a natural enough conclusion, I suppose. But I think you do not understand the unusual status of the University. You will of course have remarked that it was your letter of invitation from the head of your School which gave you passage into Alba?"

"Yes," said Gray, who had not; they had carried so many letters northward with them—including his brother-in-law's missive to Courcy, which Sophie had so long concealed from him—that it had not occurred to him to wonder which of them might be most persuasive in the eyes of the guard captain on duty at the time of their arrival.

Out of the corner of his eye he saw that Sophie had ceased staring out of the window, and turned minutely towards the conversation; there was a listening quality to her silence now, which had not been there before.

"The University," said Powell, slowly, "is under the personal patronage of Donald MacNeill, and of Clan MacNeill as present holder of the chieftain's seat in Alba, but it also functions as a sort of quasi-independent clan-land—you do understand clans and clan-lands?"

"Yes," Gray repeated, more truthfully this time.

Powell nodded. "So: The University is in many respects its own clan, and its own clan-land, with the Chancellor as its chieftain, if you like; and thanks to the patronage of Clan MacNeill, and to the circumstances of its founding by Ailpín Drostan, in the first days of the Kingdom of Alba, it can act on its own behalf to grant admission to lecturers, fellows, and students from abroad—subject always to the will of Donald MacNeill, of course," he added conscientiously. "In this it is very different from, say, Merlin College, which may accept applicants, or invite guest lecturers, from outside the Kingdom of Britain but has no power to secure or even influence their admission to the kingdom itself."

Gray frowned. "I do not perfectly understand the distinction," he said. Nor did he understand what had led Powell to broach this subject to begin with, but it had caught his interest now, in spite of himself. "If Donald MacNeill can override the decision of the Chancellor . . ."

"Ah." Powell held up an admonitory finger, looking for a moment exactly like the teaching fellow whom all of Merlin had expected him to become. "Any of the Colleges at Oxford, in such a case, must seek permission from the Crown, and obtain letters of passage in the prospective visitor's name." Gray nodded his understanding, and Powell went on: "The University in Din Edin, on the other hand, may—as you have seen—issue such letters on its own behalf, without reference to what I shall for convenience call the Crown of Alba. The Crown may order the expulsion of a person to whom the University has granted entry, provided that it can show just cause for so doing— that is to say, some grounds such as a history of criminality, which render him undesirable."

There must be some reason for this very decided turn of the conversation, but Gray could not for the life of him make it out.

"This also means," said Powell, "that the University has more power than Merlin College, to protect its own, but that power is nonetheless finite. For example, should a visitor's own sovereign demand his extradition, the University may refuse it—as Merlin, of course, could not—but such refusal may be overruled by the Crown."

*Ah.* "Yes," said Gray, firmly. "I understand perfectly."

Had Courcy dispatched Powell with instructions to read them this lecture along the way? Or had Powell conceived the idea himself? In any event he now seemed satisfied, and allowed a pensive silence to reign for the brief remainder of the journey.


The supply-waggons of which Joanna had written had duly crossed into Alba, and their arrival raised the gratitude of some, and the ire of others, as anticipated. Donald MacNeill issued a very gracious public proclamation on the subject, which thanked King Henry (or, as Donald MacNeill styled him, with more poetry than precision, Henry Tudor the Twelfth) for his generosity to a brother in arms, and confidently promised a like generosity should Britain ever find herself in similar difficulty. Sophie felt it had been very well done, and could not herself regard her father's bride-gift with anything but uncomplicated gladness; that there were men, women, and children in the hinterlands of Alba who should not starve before the end of the winter, or in the course of the next, seemed to her a benefit worth any amount of wounded pride.

She remained acutely aware, however, of the resentment which so many in Din Edin seemed to feel, and thus was not altogether surprised, though very much dismayed, when on a chill and fiercely bright afternoon late in February, her journey home from the University was interrupted by a river of people marching along the eastern edge of Ogilvy Square, up Stewart-street, and in the general direction of Castle Hill, chanting variations on the general theme of *Keep the Britons out!* She retreated into the dubious shelter of an oak-tree at the edge of the square—black and leafless, but for a sad brown curl here and there amongst its branches—and watched the marchers pass by.

They were a very mingled lot—every age from babes in arms to their grizzled great-grandparents, to all appearances; men and women; clerks and labourers and students—and in the midst of them, unmistakably, the grey-robed priests of the Cailleach.

Some of the marchers, inexplicably, carried tree-limbs over their shoulders as one might carry a pitchfork or a spade; a few bore lumpy bundles which looked distressingly likely to be filled with stones. Floating above the heads of the crowd—no, not floating, Sophie saw, but carried atop long poles like pikestaffs—were roughly human figures clad in a peculiar assortment of clothes. Peering up Stewart-street and down the edge of the square, Sophie counted four of them. A strangely attenuated figure, faceless and vaguely feminine in outline, attired entirely in what appeared to be ribbons and streamers: rowan-berry red, white and black and grey like winter-bare branches, dun and gold and the crimson of autumn dogwood. A barrel-chested man-thing—its torso was in fact, she saw as it drew near her, an age-darkened barrel missing several staves—dressed in a kilted plaid whose pattern seemed to be woven mostly of greens and blues. A slighter figure dressed in breeches and coat, whose rough, faceless head was surmounted by a bright shock of straw—

*Mother Goddess! It is meant for Roland.*

And the last figure, also clad in coat and breeches, its head a mop of grey wool: *My father.*

Where were all of these people going? Where—this was perhaps the better question—were the priests leading them, and for what purpose? And what, after more than a month's relative peace, had prompted what looked very like an escalation from peaceful manifestation to mob violence? There was anger simmering very close to the surface—there were men with weapons to hand, or at any rate objects which might be put to use as weapons. *Or as fuel for a fire?* Actual violence might or might not be intended; but in either event there seemed a very strong likelihood of the gathering's ending in grief.

The prudent, the sensible, the *obvious* course of action, then, was to await its passing and then, in the company of her father's guardsmen, to continue with all possible dispatch her interrupted journey to Quarry Close, where she should be safe.

Sophie swallowed, straightened away from her oak-tree, and, wrapping herself in her mother's magick, stepped out into the crowd.


The torrent flowed up Stewart-street, through Teviot Square, up Candle-makers' Row to the Grassmarket, where it surged and eddied around the priests in a manner that suggested they had reached their intended destination. Sophie hung back, wary, until the rising murmurs of the crowd and the efforts of those closest to her to peer over the heads of those ahead of them persuaded her that there must be something of significance afoot in that direction. She wove her way slowly towards the centre of the crowd, dodging elbows, and found herself at last almost within arm's reach of four grey-robed priests—and the effigy of her brother.

Close to, it was more crudely made even than it had appeared from a distance, but for the avoidance of doubt, it wore about its neck a placard on which had been painted—with more skill than was evident elsewhere in its construction—what were recognisably the golden lions of England and the dragon of Cymru. (Some part of Sophie's mind wondered dimly why those two symbols and not any of the rest, but they were certainly sufficient for identification.)

The branches and the makeshift sacks of stones—they were indeed stones, Sophie saw, as their bearers laid their bundles down and opened them, and some quite large enough to do significant damage, should anyone be so moved—had also migrated to the centre of the crowd. A sort of clearing had opened up, and the priests moved about it almost in the manner of players on a stage, directing the men who carried the four figures on their poles and the men, women, and children who bore branches and stones as they disposed themselves about the edges of the space.

One of the priests raised his arms, and a hush fell over the crowd.

Then another of them—a man of perhaps five-and-thirty, with a long plait of red-gold hair and a long beard a shade darker—stepped into the centre of the cleared space, then raised his head and began to speak.

Sophie's facility with Gaelic had grown by leaps and bounds over the course of her months in Din Edin, but she was by no means so easy or fluent as in her other languages, some of them familiar to her from childhood. Her own acquaintance, when not making use of her to practise their scholarly Latin, were accustomed to slow their speech very slightly, and acceded graciously to her requests for repetition or explanation—less frequent now than formerly; even the shopkeepers of the University district, resigned as they were to the perpetual presence of foreigners, made a habit of speaking slowly and clearly.

Of the rapid, dramatically inflected speech of the priest, therefore, she at first caught no more than one word in a dozen, and those not very enlightening: *Donald MacNeill, heiress, Sasunnach, betrayal, en-*

*emy*. Nothing, in other words, which she had not heard stated or implied a dozen times before. Gradually, however, her ear grew more attuned, and she began to pick out whole phrases, and at last to understand at least the purport of everything she heard.

The more she understood, the colder seemed the raw February air, and the farther removed from the strangers pressed close about her.

At last the other priests appeared to have arranged everyone and everything to their satisfaction, and an anticipatory ripple ran through the onlookers as the four of them stood together in the centre of the cleared space, shoulder to shoulder, each facing one of the cardinal points. This must be some signal, though Sophie could not divine what its meaning might be.

The effigies, it transpired, were to be puppets of a sort; the priests were staging a play, in which the principals were the Kings of Britain and Alba, the hapless Sasunnach Prince, and the Cailleach herself, Queen of Winter. From this much reduced distance, Sophie could see that the figure representing this last had been carefully and lovingly made; its proportions were strange, its face almost featureless, but its head and limbs had been carved from some pale wood and sanded smooth, and its arms were jointed at shoulder and elbow, so that the two men whose charge it was (and for whom it was evidently not a new one, so smoothly did they work together) could produce graceful, almost natural movements. By contrast, the other three figures were rough, crude, hastily jury-rigged things, but their wielders made the best of their lot and contrived to endow them with some—entirely fabricated—personality.

The players did not speak; rather, their dumb-show illustrated the tale told by the four priests.

"In the Castle at Din Edin sits Donald MacNeill in the chieftain's seat of Alba. He seeks among his children and his sisters' children for an heir to his powers and his charge, and settles upon his daughter Lucia MacNeill. He seeks a husband for his daughter and heir, and passes over one chieftain's son after another . . ."

The plaid-wrapped figure of Donald MacNeill passed from man to man along the edge of the crowd.

"In a palace in London sits the Sasunnach King, and he casts his greedy eyes north and north to the fair hills of Alba. His father and grandfather tried and failed to march over our wall or to land their armies on our coasts, but he is a crafty King, and sees a means to succeed where his forebears failed—not with the arrows of Mars but with the arrows of Cupid will he conquer us."

Sophie was so startled to hear the gods of Rome invoked—even so flippantly—by the priests of Alba's presiding goddess that she was a beat behind the rest of the crowd in grasping precisely what he had said. *Surely not,* she thought at once; and then, uneasily, *but . . .*

"The Sasunnach King woos Donald MacNeill and his daughter with sweet words and promises, and he prays to his conqueror-gods, to his Ceres and his Robigus, to blight our crops and our beasts, to make his offers more difficult to refuse. *Now,* he thinks, *now Donald MacNeill will sell me his daughter and his kingdom in exchange for a few sacks of corn.*"

Sophie's feelings for her father were complicated and ambivalent, but this base accusation was so absurd that she could scarcely contain an indignant protest. *But is it? Has my father depths of cruelty, of subtlety, which I have not imagined?*

"The gods of Rome are greedy for new conquests, and Alba has felt the sting of their lash ever since. The British King and his heir rejoice in Alba's suffering"—here the effigies of King Henry and Prince Roland did a crude, horrible sort of jig together, and Sophie gritted her teeth against a new access of indignation—"and Donald MacNeill wrings his hands and orders the storehouses opened, and like the men of Troy, welcomes in his enemy's self-serving gifts."

Mutters of confusion amongst Sophie's immediate neighbours suggested that this barbed reference to *Danaos dona ferentes* had perhaps not found its intended target; but certainly the priests' attempt to portray Donald MacNeill as the hapless dupe of the scheming King Henry had done so. What might these people say, if Sophie should tell them that—if Joanna spoke true, and in this matter, why should she not?—the impetus for Lucia MacNeill's marriage had come from her father and herself, and not from Henry of Britain at all? But surely they had heard Donald MacNeill say as much, just as she had, and his words had made no difference.

"Hear therefore, people of Alba, what awaits us all, if this ill-starred marriage should take place. Hear the speaking of the Cailleach."

The crowd fell silent, now—so silent that Sophie fancied she began to hear the beating of hearts about her, though she knew that it must be only her own pulse hammering in her ears.

The slender figure of the Cailleach rose high above the crowd on its long pole, arms outstretched, ribbons and streamers fluttering in the chill breeze, and for the first time the four priests spoke all together, in a manner that recalled to Sophie's mind her single and terrifyingly memorable encounter with the priests of Apollo Coelispex—though there seemed to be no coercive magicks at work in this case.

*At any rate, none that I can feel. But what workings might these men be capable of, which I should not perceive?*

"Alba's gods will not be supplanted," they intoned. "Alba's lands will not be tilled by Sasunnach hands. Alba's people will not be subdued. As it was in the time of the Roman invaders, as it was in the days of the longship raiders, as it has been since the days of the great Ailpín Drostan: Alba shall not be conquered."

Sophie shivered. False though she knew their accusations to be, she was within a hair's breadth of being caught up in what was unmistakably a call to arms—and if even she could only just resist it . . .

Bodies pressed in around her, behind her; on the far side of the central clearing, she saw, the crowd had grown denser as more and more passersby adhered themselves to its edges, and drew closer to better see and hear the goings-on at its heart.

The figure of the Cailleach raised its arms.

"Come, lands and waters of Alba!" cried the priests. "Come, fields and streams! Come, trees and stones! Rise up against the enemies of Alba—enemies without and enemies within—and do the will of your gods!"

*The magick of the land,* thought Sophie. *The priests and all these people believe in it, whatever anyone else may say.*

And then all at once the still air was thick with sound and fury, and Sophie clapped both hands over her mouth to stifle a howl of irrational terror as the crude, ill-made effigies of her father and brother disintegrated under a hail of stones and an onslaught of bludgeoning tree-branches.

"The Cailleach has spoken," the priests intoned, in the fraught aftermath. The figure of the goddess faced the figure of Donald Mac-Neill, which tilted forward as though hanging its head.

The crowd dispersed, conversing in subdued mutterings and whispers, and Sophie, shivering for reasons entirely unconnected to the February chill, made her way silently back to Quarry Close.

"You must write to Kergabet," said Gray at once, when Sophie had related the afternoon's unsettling events. "This is no vague rumour of discontent or unrest; it is a serious threat. Whether these priests are indeed doing the will of their goddess, or whether they have decided for her what her will is to be, it seems clear they intend genuine harm to Roland, and perhaps to Lucia MacNeill as well. And Lord de Courcy I am sure will also wish to hear what you have witnessed, in case he should have had no one upon the spot."

Sophie's fine dark brows drew together, and for a long moment she stared down into her half-drunk tea.

At last she set the teacup down very carefully in its saucer, sat up straight, and squared her shoulders. "I shall write to Kergabet," she said, "and perhaps you will write to Lord de Courcy? We shall save time by writing both letters at once."

*If she has not yet forgiven Courcy his attempt to persuade her to flee, then there is certainly nothing to be gained from my pressing the same argument.*

Gray spoke none of these thoughts aloud. "Certainly," he said instead, and giving her knee a little pat, he rose to fetch writing-paper and pens and an ink-pot.

The sequel of the mummers' play staged by the priests of the Cailleach—as Sophie and Gray soon learnt, it had been repeated up and down the kingdom before its appearance in Din Edin—was a formal meeting between Donald MacNeill and the most senior members of the priesthood. Within the University (which was, with a few outspoken exceptions, generally in favour of Lucia MacNeill's British marriage, as tending to produce stability and peace between the kingdoms, and thus conducive to scholarship), the latter event produced no less astonished talk than the former, which greatly puzzled the Marshalls, until their enlightenment by Mór MacRury's patient explanation that the priesthood of the Cailleach were by inclination and by oath abstainers from political matters.

"It is very shocking that they should have taken any public position in such a dispute," said Rory, shaking his head, "and more shocking still that they should give it against the ruling chieftain. And that Donald MacNeill should give countenance to that position by proposing to meet with them is . . . well! I scarcely know how to tell you how astonishing."

"No wonder, then, that the people were so quiet!" Sophie exclaimed. "I did wonder at it, you know, at the time; I quite expected a riot, or at any rate a great deal of shouting, but nearly all of them went away whispering and muttering to one another—*slunk* away, almost—and there was no shouting at all."

Mór exchanged a look with Rory and Sorcha MacAngus, whose meaning Gray could not divine.

"*I* wonder that they were not arrested," said Gray, turning one of Mór's blue-green glazed teacups round and round in his hands. "I suppose it is no treason to threaten a foreign King, but surely the threat to Donald MacNeill and his daughter was perfectly clear, if not quite so . . . direct."

"I do not suppose that Donald MacNeill imagines it a serious threat," said Mór, in what was evidently meant for a soothing tone. "It is all theatre, you see—a means of swaying public opinion, and thus swaying Donald MacNeill himself, and so long as they do no real injury, there is no advantage to him in attempting to silence them. And as for the priests and their goddess . . . it is not the rocks and trees of Alba that threaten harm to your brother, Sophie; it is sticks and stones in the hands of people who know no better."

"If that is your notion of comfort," said Sophie, rather tartly, "I should counsel you to take up some other line of work."

Mór looked away, her cheeks colouring; Gray cast Sophie a gently reproachful look and inquired of the company at large, "What has become of Professor Maghrebin? Rob MacGregor told me this morning that he had been called away home to attend on his dying brother—which I hope may not be so—but two days since Duncan MacKerron was perfectly persuaded that the cause was some sort of turmoil at his own university in Alexandria . . ."

The conversation turned to their absent colleague, and both Sophie and Mór rejoined it by slow degrees.

For some time thereafter, Gray lived in a state of perpetual tension, awaiting some escalation of the threats against the Kingdom of Britain, King Henry, or Sophie herself. But whether because Lord de Courcy or some one of his minions had dropped a judicious word in someone's ear, or simply because—as Mór MacRury had conceded—no scandal could hold the attention of Din Edin society longer than a month, no further insult was offered to the Marshalls' house, and no direct insult to Sophie's person.

Her letters to her father and Lord Kergabet had produced a flurry of replies from Ned and Roland, as well as from Kergabet and the King, such as Gray thought might have tempted her to reconsider—particularly in respect of Joanna's visit—and certainly had the situation deteriorated. Though opinions of Lucia MacNeill's betrothal, and of British subjects resident in Din Edin generally, continued deeply divided, however, the unpleasant distinction briefly accorded to Sophie was already fading, and whilst Gray did not entirely share her apparent confidence, each day that passed without some worse incident made him less anxious for her safety.

Still he made sure that she went nowhere unescorted; and Sophie, for her part, made a very handsome job of pretending not to have remarked his solicitude.

## CHAPTER XVII

# In Which Joanna
# Amends Her Plans

*Joanna was contemplating* the contents of her wardrobe, from which within the next se'nnight she should be packing her trunk for the journey to Din Edin, and was weighing the trials of a four-hundred-mile journey in the company of Oscar MacConnachie's tedious wife against the promise of a month with Sophie, when there came a knock on her bedroom door, startlingly loud.

"*Quo vadis?*" she called.

From outside the door—still firmly closed—Gwendolen's voice said, "Jo, may I come in?"

Joanna surveyed the chaos of her bedroom, then laughed derisively at herself for supposing that Gwendolen Pryce, of all people, should think herself qualified to read her a lecture upon that subject.

"Yes," she said.

The door opened just wide enough to admit Gwendolen, who wore a figured muslin gown of (in Joanna's opinion) surpassing ugliness, together with a troubled frown. Joanna gestured carelessly at the armchair by the hearth; Gwendolen perched on it willingly enough, but said nothing, and frowned into the fire with such ferocity that Joanna rather regretted not having barred the door.

She took out her fawn-coloured riding-habit to examine it for rents, and had succeeded almost in forgetting Gwendolen's presence when the latter abruptly said, "I wish I might come with you."

Joanna turned, startled. "But I thought," she said, "I thought you had been pleased with the prospect of staying here."

"Oh!" Gwendolen flushed becomingly and ducked her head. "It is not that I have any wish to leave Lady Kergabet—not in the least!— only, I . . . I am not so very fond of London. And . . . and I should like to go with you, Jo."

She looked up at last, and her expression was one which Joanna had seen often and often, but never before on Gwendolen's face: soft and wistful, with an edge of anxious trepidation, as though she had said or done something which she did not regret, but for which she expected a vicious scolding.

"I should like that, also," said Joanna.

She had not meant to say this, but it was perfectly true. Her eagerness to see Sophie again had not abated—they had never been so far from one another for so long—but as the longed-for visit approached, she had also begun to realise that she should miss her London family nearly as much as she now missed her sister; and, to her dismay, that she might possibly miss Gwendolen in particular. When had she come to depend so much upon Gwendolen's presence—her sharp tongue and sharper eyes, her silent sympathy, and their tacit agreement never to speak further of the confessions they had exchanged in the wake of the Pryces' visit? Never before had Joanna had such an intimate confidante, apart from Sophie; friends she had had at school, certainly, but none with whom she should have dreamed of discussing, for example, the history of her parents' marriage.

Not that she had had any intention of confiding that sorry tale to Gwendolen, either, until the moment of doing so.

"And," said Gwendolen, looking down again at the toes of her boots, "I do not much like your going, either, for you have been out of sorts this past month and more, and I am sure the reason for it must be in Din Edin."

"No," said Joanna curtly; and then—before she could stop herself—she added, "the reason for it is here."

"Prince Roland, you mean," said Gwendolen.

Joanna looked up sharply at her tone. "You cannot possibly be *jealous*," she said, incredulous. "And if you were, you ought to be jealous of Lucia MacNeill of Alba, and not of me."

Gwendolen laughed aloud. "That is the most absurd thing I have ever heard you say, Joanna Callender," she declared.

Joanna turned back to the wardrobe in some confusion and extracted her blue woollen gown.

There was certainly something to be said for the notion of travelling with Gwendolen, rather than alone; she should have someone to talk to, apart from the irritating Lady MacConnachie, during the journey, and once there, a companion who was a friend of her own and not of Gray's or Sophie's. She imagined herself and Gwendolen trading barbed remarks on the subject of Lady MacConnachie's unedifying conversation and unfortunate taste in hats, and smiled.

To impose an unexpected and uninvited guest upon Sophie, however—and a near stranger, at that—was a less appealing idea. The Marshalls' lodgings in Din Edin were small, she knew, if not so cramped as their Oxford rooms; even with some warning, could Sophie accommodate a second visitor?

Besides all of that, there was her work to consider, and the question—still unanswered, for all the breezy reassurances in Sophie's letters—of what circumstances presently prevailed in Din Edin, and whether they should any of them be safe.

Gwendolen had begun to wander about the room, taking up objects seemingly at random and putting them down again. "You, I suppose, are very fond of London," she said casually.

"I?" said Joanna, half laughing in surprise. "No, indeed. That is," she amended, "I am interested in the work of government, which Kergabet has kindly allowed me some small share in; and I am fond of him and of Jenny and the children; and London is where all of them are. But as for the noise and the formal dinners and the rout-parties and the interminable morning-visits, I had a thousand times rather a country house with a stream and a wood and a frog-pond, and a good stable and enough open country for a good gallop."

Gwendolen's long face lit with a delighted grin. "I knew it!" she said.

"But one cannot have everything at once," said Joanna primly, "and I had rather be in London, with something interesting to do, than in Breizh with only my sister Amelia for company. Or at school again, learning embroidery and dancing."

"But you love to dance," said Gwendolen. "And"—she reached for the gown still in Joanna's hands, and pointed out a split seam—"you cannot tell me that there is no use in learning to sew. Where is your work-basket, Jo?"

"In the morning-room?" said Joanna vaguely. "No: There, under the dressing-table."

Gwendolen bent to retrieve the work-basket, and before Joanna could reply, was threading a needle.

"I do not say so," Joanna managed at last. "But you shall never convince me that my skill in crewel-work—if I had any—is of any use to anyone, or that I might not have spent that time more fruitfully."

"That, I grant you," said Gwendolen. She stitched in silence whilst Joanna watched her—dark head bent, long fingers flying—and wondered why it should be so difficult to look away.

She rolled stockings and folded linens in silence until at last Gwendolen said, "There!" and Joanna heard the soft *snick* of her scissors snipping off a thread.

"I am more grateful for Lady Kergabet's kindness than I can say," Gwendolen went on, which made Joanna wonder where her thoughts had been whilst her fingers were busy with her needle. "But—you must have remarked it—the gods did not fashion me for morning-visits and fancy-work, any more than you."

"You know of course, Gwen," said Joanna cautiously, kneeling beside the bed to retrieve a bandbox from beneath it, "that Din Edin is a city like London? Well—perhaps not quite like London—"

"But what an adventure we should have, Jo!" Gwendolen exclaimed.

Startled by this sudden enthusiasm, Joanna twisted to look up at her and got a face full of blue woollen skirts for her trouble. She brushed them away impatiently.

Though Gwendolen's smile was rather hesitant, it did not look feigned or forced.

"Din Edin may not be altogether safe," said Joanna.

"If Lord Kergabet thought it truly dangerous," Gwendolen countered, "he should not be sending you, even with half a dozen guardsmen."

Joanna had in fact been at some pains to persuade her patron to limit the number to six, but it was certainly true that Kergabet was more than capable of putting his foot down—diplomatic opportunity or no—if the necessity arose, and yet had not done so. Moreover, His Majesty might at any time have ordered Lord de Courcy to send Gray and Sophie back to London, and though she knew (from Sophie's indignant letter on the subject, recently arrived in Carrington-street) that they had been urged to depart, he had stopped short of an outright royal decree.

Though, of course, it was also true that Sophie's father was a very poor hand at denying her anything once she had set her heart upon it.

"I suppose," said Joanna, "if Jenny can spare you, and if Lady MacConnachie does not object to a second passenger . . ." She looked about for pen and ink. "I must write ahead to Sophie, to—well, it is too late to ask permission, I suppose, but I shall at any rate have warned her; she is not overfond of surprises. And I think we must tell Jenny that Sophie has invited you—"

"I do not much like lying to Lady Kergabet," said Gwendolen doubtfully.

She stiffened a little in offence at Joanna's bark of incredulous laughter.

"How can you say so?" Joanna demanded. "You told her for *months* that you were writing letters to your father, when it was no such thing!"

Gwendolen's mouth tucked down at the corners, an odd admixture of amusement and wounded dignity. "It was perfectly true," she said, "about writing the letters. I wrote a great many of them, though some are too much blotched to read and contain language not fit for a lady's ears. I do not believe Lady Kergabet has ever asked what was in my letters, or whether they were put into the post."

It was so exactly what she herself might have done in like circumstances, that for a long moment Joanna could do nothing but gape at Gwendolen, true, delighted laughter bubbling up under her ribs. At last it surfaced—she could not help it—and in an entirely uncharacteristic moment of abandon, she flung her arms about Gwendolen, as if Gwendolen had been Sophie, and still shaking with laughter, hugged her tight.

Gwendolen's longer arms came up about her back, tentative and gentle, and she laid her cheek against Joanna's hair.

This did not feel like embracing Sophie, not at all.

Joanna broke away and stepped back, shaking her head to clear it. "Pen and ink," she said, and Gwendolen grinned at her, and plucked a pen from the chaos of Joanna's dressing-table and a fresh sheet of paper from the neat stack on her desk.

At last the provisioning and mending were finished, the trunks packed—Joanna's concealing a dispatch-case full of letters for Lord de Courcy, for Sophie, and for Lucia MacNeill—and the day of departure arrived. As arranged months since on Joanna's behalf, they were to travel with the Alban envoy's wife (known in London as Lady MacConnachie, and in Alba, as she had explained at some length to Jenny and Joanna, as Sìleas Barra MacNeill), who was returning to Din Edin to relieve her mother from the care of her children. In her company—for she was a cousin of Donald MacNeill and his daughter, as well as the wife of Oscar MacConnachie—they should be adequately vouched for and require no additional letters of entry from the Alban court.

Jenny embraced Joanna, **kissed her** on both cheeks, and peered down into her face with a **familiar mixture** of affection and anxiety. "You will be on your best behaviour with Lady MacConnachie, Jo?" she said quietly, not for the first time. "I know that she is very trying, but remember that she is doing you a great service, and—"

"*Yes*, Jenny," said Joanna. Then she counted ten in Greek—a trick she had learnt from Gray—and held her tongue, whilst Jenny adjured her to be careful, to keep a tight rein on Gwendolen, and, should any danger threaten ("which Lady Juno forbid"), to take shelter with Lord de Courcy, and to drag Gwendolen and Sophie and Gray with her, "by the hair if need be."

All decorum vanished when Rozena brought Agatha out to see them off. Joanna had meant to say her nursery farewells earlier in the day, before Lady MacConnachie's arrival, but Agatha and Yvon had been both asleep, and she knew better than to wake them. Yvon she had merely kissed, inhaling the warm milky smell of his fine hair, but Agatha was not so young that Joanna could forgo a proper leave-taking; here she was, therefore, weeping buckets on the muddy pavement before the Kergabets' front door because Aunty Jo and Gwennie were going away.

"We shall be back soon, Agatha, I promise," said Joanna, crouching on the pavement with her skirts rucked up awkwardly in a (probably futile) effort to keep them out of the mud, and smoothing hot tears from Agatha's face with her thumb. "Not tomorrow, or the next day; it may seem a long time, but we shall come back, and it will be as though we had never gone away. You shall have all sorts of new things to show to me, you know, and perhaps Yvon may have learnt something new also, and you shall be the first to tell me of it."

Agatha screwed up her face and howled.

"Agatha," said Joanna, "look at me." She inflected her voice with just a hint of the tone which Jenny used when she wished to gain her daughter's immediate compliance, and Agatha instinctively swallowed a sob and opened her swimming eyes.

Joanna caught her small hand and, looking at her very seriously, said in a low tone, "You must be very brave, and look after Yvon and Mama, as I should do if I were here. I am sure you may be trusted for that; is it not so?"

Agatha nodded. Two last tears tracked down her cheeks, accompanied by a loud, determined sniff. "Yeth," she said firmly.

Joanna smiled at her. It was odd, she thought, how quickly and how thoroughly Agatha and Yvon (and Jenny and Kergabet, and Gray, and lately perhaps even Gwendolen) had insinuated themselves into the space in her heart formerly reserved for Sophie alone. "I knew that I could," she said; and, holding out her arms, she continued, "Now Gwendolen and I must be getting into the carriage, in truth, for else Lady MacConnachie will be so very cross!"

She swung Agatha up into the air as she said this, whispering loudly, and Agatha giggled, and kissed her, and allowed herself to be handed over to Rozena.

As Gwendolen was climbing the steps into Lady MacConnachie's carriage, Joanna ran back for a last embrace of Jenny, who held her very tight for just a moment, and whispered in her ear, "Remember your manners, Jo!" in a tone which clearly said, *I shall miss you very much.*

Their northward journey was plagued by badly maintained roads, sleet, mud, and even, on one very unpleasant day—though it was March—by snow so heavy that Lady MacConnachie's coachman could not see the heads of his wheelers, and insisted on leaving the road to take shelter until the storm should have passed. Despite these hardships, both Joanna and Gwendolen remained on their best behaviour, reserving their less charitable remarks—of which there were many, for Lady MacConnachie seemed unable to muster more than three sentences on any subject apart from the weather, London fashions, and her children—for the privacy of their bedchamber after dinner. To Joanna's secret relief, Gwendolen was an entirely unobjectionable travelling companion: She was tidy in her habits, was content to be silent when there was nothing interesting to be said, and, when it so fell out that a particular night's lodgings had only one bed for the two of them (it went without saying that Lady MacConnachie could always command a private chamber for herself ), kept herself considerately to her own side of the bed. She was not so cheerful at night as she was in daylight, but Joanna, in whose mind the problem of Roland was receding, and the happy anticipation of a reunion with Sophie looming larger, the farther they came away from London, did not give this observation much thought.

## CHAPTER XVIII

# In Which Gray Receives Ill Tidings, and Sophie Receives a Gift

*On a bright,* chill morning early in March, shortly before the end of the University's second term, Catriona MacCrimmon called for Sophie in Quarry Close for a visit to her seamstress: Catriona meant to depart within the next se'nnight to visit her parents on Leodhas, and had been commissioned to have new gowns made for her mother and younger sister; and she and Gray between them had contrived to persuade Sophie that the latter was also due a new gown or two. Gray was still finishing his breakfast when Catriona's knock sounded upon the front door, and upon Sophie's jumping up to answer it, he allowed his attention to drift to the journal at his elbow, open to a paper arguing for the existence of aetheric currents which could be diverted to carry thoughts from one mind to another and setting out an experimental protocol for demonstrating this phenomenon. By the time Sophie returned to the table to drop a farewell kiss on the top of his bent head, he was so deeply absorbed in the authors' arguments that he could muster only the most perfunctory response; he vaguely heard Sophie's cheerful farewell to Donella MacHutcheon, who was engaged in scrubbing the kitchen floor, and Catriona's to himself.

The sound of the front door closing behind them, however, called him back to the world of matter long enough to shoot the bolt, then to go to the sitting-room window and peer out of it, until he saw Lord de Courcy's men Menez and Williams (the one dressed as a crossing-sweeper, and the other loitering at the turning into Grove-street with a broadsheet spread open in his hands) fall in a discreet distance behind.

Then he sat down at the table again, refilled his teacup, and propped the *Transactions of the Royal Society of Natural Philosophers* against the teapot, so that he should not get a crick in his neck.

It was midmorning, and the earlier bustle on Quarry Close had died away, by the time he finished the paper and laid aside the journal, already mentally composing a letter to the editor. He was just standing up from the table, stretching limbs which had grown stiff without his remarking it, when there came another, more assertive knock at the door.

Two of Lord de Courcy's three guardsmen having gone with Sophie, Gray was cautious in opening the door, first peering sidewise out of the sitting-room window to determine who might be standing on the step; he was at first relieved to see that the caller, though a stranger to him, wore the royal arms upon his coat, and then mildly alarmed at what news such a courier might be bringing.

He drew back the bolt, threw open the door, and said, "What news?"

The stranger gave him a perfunctory bow and a sealed letter. "For you, sir, by way of the Ambassador." He spoke in Latin, rather than English or Français, and his accent was not altogether familiar.

Under other circumstances Gray might have remarked this more strongly, but by now he had broken the seal on his letter and begun to read it, and all else had gone entirely out of his head.

"I must go and see Lord de Courcy at once," he said, keeping his voice even with some difficulty; the letter had infected him with so strong a feeling of urgency that it was almost a physical ache.

"Of course, sir," said Lord de Courcy's man; "I have a carriage waiting in Grove-street."

"I must . . . I must pack a valise, and—oh, horns of Herne! Where has Sophie gone?"

"Maighistir?" Donella MacHutcheon emerged from the kitchen, drying her hands on her apron. "Is all well?"

Gray blinked at her to bring her kindly, frowning face into focus. "No," he said, shifting into Gaelic. "It is—my father is—will you fetch my valise from the stair-cupboard, if you please, and put . . . and put some of my linens into it?"

"Of course," said Donella MacHutcheon, and hurried away.

Within the quarter-hour Gray, valise in hand, was striding up Quarry Close, a headache collecting behind his eyes at the prospect that lay before him.

Both grateful for and exhausted by a day in the company of Catriona MacCrimmon, her seamstress, and the helpful clerks of Din Edin's wool- and linen-merchants, and carrying wrapped parcels of new handkerchiefs, gloves, and stockings which one or all of the former had insisted she needed, Sophie unlocked the door of the house in Quarry Close and set down the parcels with a sigh of relief.

"Gray?" she called, first into the sitting-room and then up the stairs. "Gray, are you there?"

A brief prowl about the house established that he was not. Sophie tried to recall whether he had mentioned a plan to dine elsewhere, and could not—which might mean, she reflected rather irritably, that he had said nothing, or that she had forgot it, or that his plans had altered in her absence, or all three. It was a pity, for she had been looking forward to amusing him by an account of the more absurd details of her shopping expedition, and to learning what it was which had so absorbed him at breakfast-time. But perhaps, she thought, poking up the banked sitting-room fire and sinking dispiritedly into her armchair, she was after all too tired to speak to anyone, even Gray.

It was not until she had dozed off before the fire, and awakened chilled and stiff in the dark because the fire had gone out, and rebuilt it and called fire to light it again, and wandered into the kitchen to see what Donella MacHutcheon might have left for their supper, that she discovered the folded sheet of writing-paper propped up amongst the tea things, unsealed, with her name written upon the outside in Gray's most careless, haphazard scrawl.

She sat down at the table and unfolded it. There was a plate of oatcakes beside the tea-tray; she reached for one (for by now she was very hungry) but let it fall again, scattering crumbs upon the scrubbed table-top, almost as soon as she had begun to read.

*Cariad*, the letter read,

> *I have just had word by way of Courcy that my father is very ill and has asked for me, and that if I do not go at once, it may be too late. I am loath to leave you alone, but Joanna and her friend will be here presently to bear you company; and of course I hope to travel very swiftly, and shall return as soon as I may. You will understand I hope that if my father is at all minded to attempt a reconciliation, I cannot let the opportunity pass.*
>
> *I shall write again to let you know of my safe arrival, and how the land lies. As for yourself, be careful! Do not wander about Din Edin alone.*
>
> *Yrs with all love,*
> *G*

Sophie had met Gray's father—had spent a fortnight in his household—and try as she might, could not picture him as other than hale, hearty, and coldly indifferent to the presence or absence of his second son. But she knew, too, that whatever might have passed between them since, Gray had craved his father's respect and approval all through his childhood, and she could not be altogether surprised at his grasping after this chance to receive them. *I only hope that you are not to be bitterly disappointed, love.*

Sophie sighed. The single oatcake she had consumed sat heavily in her middle, and the thought of eating the cold ham and pickles she had glimpsed upon lifting the tea-cloth briefly from the supper-tray made her faintly queasy. Instead of sitting down to her supper, therefore, she retrieved her parcels and climbed the stairs to the bedroom to begin putting her purchases away.

She paused on the threshold, staring. The room was not precisely a shambles—her own things had scarcely been disturbed, and Gray's were not, objectively speaking, in a significantly greater state of chaos than was usual—but it was clear that the latter had been rifled through by someone unfamiliar with Gray's methods of organising his possessions. A careful inventory of both bedroom and desk, however, revealed nothing missing but what Sophie might have expected: brushes, strop, and razors; a selection of shirts, drawers, and neckcloths; the notes for a lecture which Gray had been preparing for the spring term; a pair of trousers in addition to those he had been wearing at breakfast.

"Well," said Sophie, speaking aloud to herself, as there was no one else here to call her crackbrained for doing so. "At any rate, I shall have Joanna here very soon."

The following morning Rory MacCrimmon appeared in Quarry Close just as Sophie was wrestling with the question of how to honour both Gray's plea not to go about alone and her obligation to appear in her tutor's rooms at the appointed hour.

"I had a note from Marshall," he explained, when she opened the door. "A dreadful business, indeed! He seems to have left in a tearing hurry; we must hope the news did not reach him too late to do any good."

"Yes," said Sophie, torn between affectionate gratitude and exasperation. How like Gray to have made arrangements for her safety, even whilst frantically preparing for an unexpected journey; how like him, too, to forget to inform her what those arrangements might be.

The term ended two days later; Catriona MacCrimmon departed

for her parents' home on Leodhas, and Mór MacRury and Sorcha MacAngus on an excursion to the sea-coast, where Sorcha's aunt and uncle kept an inn; and Sophie—missing Gray, but buoyed by the prospect of Joanna, even a Joanna inexplicably accompanied by a near stranger whom Sophie had not invited—tidied her books and her notes and set about making her small house ready for visitors.

Lucia MacNeill was nowhere to be found between terms, her time and attention being all claimed by her father and his court, but Una MacSherry called upon her several times, and Rory—evidently taking to heart Gray's request that he keep an eye on her—nearly every day.

Sophie was glad of it, for after Donella MacHutcheon had departed for the day, the house was far too quiet. Even the pianoforte was not the panacea it had once been, for it was difficult to find anything to play or to sing that did not somehow remind her of Gray and sharpen her sense of solitude.

It was worst on rainy days, on which for the most part no one called at all, and Sophie felt shut up in a box like one of Conall MacLachlan's butterflies. She was more than ordinarily pleased, therefore, on one such day, to perceive through the haze of settled rain a person approaching her front door—swathed in a heavy cloak and an exceedingly unflattering fisherman's hat, but recognisable at last, by his gait and the determined manner of his approach, as Rory MacCrimmon—and almost ran to open the door at his knock.

When she had settled Rory into her own armchair by the sitting-room fire, steaming gently, and hung his coat and hat to dry (or, at least, to drip in relative comfort) in the kitchen, Sophie busied herself with the makings of tea, feeling almost herself again.

She perched in Gray's chair, nursing her cup of tea to warm her hands, which seemed always to be chilled now, and said, "Have you heard yet from Catriona? I hope your parents and your sister and brothers are well?"

"They are, I thank you, as of my mother's last letter," said Rory, almost absently. He sipped his tea. Despite the hat, his bright hair was dark and draggled; he put down his cup and saucer, shook his head like a wet sheep-dog, then gave Sophie an apologetic grimace and ran a hand through his hair in a doomed attempt to tame it.

The gesture was so like Gray's that Sophie was forced to turn away for a moment to hide her face.

"And have you heard yet from Gray?" said Rory.

"I have not," Sophie admitted; it was true, but felt like disloyalty.

"I suppose one cannot blame him, when his father is so ill."

"Yes," said Sophie.

"I must confess," Rory was saying, "that I wondered at his leaving you all alone here, in the circumstances—though of course I know that the, er, that your father's envoy is keeping an eye, and I shall do the same. And"—seeing perhaps that Sophie had begun to bristle—"I do understand that you are far from helpless, Sophie!" He sat up straighter, and his face creased in an unexpected grin. "Which reminds me: I did not come out in this dreadful weather only to drip upon your carpets and drink your tea; I have something for you from Catriona."

He drew it from an inner pocket of his coat and passed it across to her: a slender octavo volume bound in cream-coloured leather. Upon the front board was stamped a title in Gaelic, which Sophie's eye took longer than it ought to interpret as *Love Songs from the Outer Isles*. She opened it at random; on the page before her she beheld the words of Mór MacRury's song about the boatman, and her heart seemed to turn over.

"I . . . I thank Catriona, very much," she said. "She is too kind."

Sophie sat before the fire while Rory drank two cups of tea, and they spoke of Joanna, and of Roland, and of Rory's childhood on Leodhas and her own in Breizh. When at last he rose to take his leave, she fetched his coat (still unpleasantly damp) from the kitchen, and smiled up at him when he awkwardly patted her shoulder and bade her call upon him for whatever she might need.

When he had gone, she curled up again in Gray's armchair with a book of odes to Minerva and read determinedly, though to very little purpose, until she fell asleep.

## CHAPTER XIX

# In Which Joanna Is Surprised, and Gwendolen Is Disappointed

*Joanna and Gwendolen* arrived at Sophie and Gray's lodgings as afternoon was just beginning to shift towards twilight and the sinking sun to gild the westward-facing planes of the city. Joanna's smart rap upon the door of the little row-house went so long unanswered that she had begun to think that Gray and Sophie must be elsewhere, and to ponder what they ought to do instead; she ought to have reckoned, but had not, with the lack of resident servants. At the least, she thought irritably, Lord de Courcy's guardsmen might have been moved to lend a hand—there was one of the men she had seen with Sophie and Gray in London washing the windows of the house over the road, or pretending to do so.

At last there came a scuffle and a thud from overhead, followed swiftly by the sounds of rapid footsteps descending an uncarpeted staircase, and of a heavy bolt's being drawn back; and then the door swung inward and there was Sophie herself, clutching a patterned shawl about her slender shoulders and grinning at Joanna.

"Jo!" she cried. "I had begun to think you had been set upon by bandits."

Joanna flung her arms about her sister, and was gratified to be embraced with equal enthusiasm. Acutely conscious of Gwendolen standing behind her amongst the trunks and valises, however, she drew back much sooner than she might otherwise have done, and said, "Sophie, I am sure you remember Miss Pryce? And, Gwen, this is my sister, Mrs. Marshall."

This last because, as one look at Gwendolen's baffled face confirmed, Sophie at present did not look at all as she had in London at Midsummer.

They were ushered past a tiny sitting-room half-filled by a pianoforte and up a narrow flight of stairs. As there was no one but their three selves to carry the trunks, carry them they did, but it was an anxious business, and Joanna felt she could hear everything which Gwendolen was not saying on the subject of proper accommodations for the Princess Royal.

"This house has only one guest bedroom," Sophie explained, opening the door thereof. "I had meant to put you here, Jo, and the bed is certainly large enough for two, if you do not object to share; but as Gray is not here, you may prefer—"

"Not here?" Joanna exclaimed. "Why not? Where is he?"

Sophie halted, one hand on a bedpost and the other against her cheek. "Oh!" she said. Joanna did not know what to make of her tone. "Have you not—Jo, when did you leave London?"

Joanna told her, and Sophie's face took on the inward look it always wore when she was attempting mental arithmetic. "No," she said after a moment, rather vaguely; "no, I suppose if it came by express . . ."

"Sophie," said Joanna, impatient. "Sophie, *tell me.*"

"He had a message from Jenny," said Sophie. "That is, I suppose it must have been from Jenny; I did not see it myself. Eight days ago it was, and he went off to Kernow that very day."

"To Kernow?" Joanna repeated. "Why on earth?"

"To see his father," said Sophie, as though this were perfectly evident, and not perfectly absurd.

"His *father.*"

"Perhaps," said Gwendolen—visibly startling Sophie, who had

perhaps forgot her presence—"we might all sit downstairs, and have a cup of tea, and begin at the beginning."

They trooped down the stairs, perforce in single file, through the sitting-room, and into the kitchen, where Gwendolen turned once about, examining her surroundings, and having located the kettle, at once set about making tea. Sophie, on the other hand, sank into a battered wheelback chair and stared pensively at the large green-glazed teapot which Gwendolen had shifted from the dresser to the table.

The sight, or perhaps the sound, of the water pouring from kettle into pot seemed to bring Sophie back to herself; at any rate, she blinked and jumped up from her seat, and whilst Gwendolen and Joanna were carrying the tea-things into the sitting-room, they heard her rummaging about in the kitchen.

Joanna was therefore unsurprised when Sophie reemerged carefully bearing a small, plain, highly polished cup which Joanna had last seen in a similarly book-cluttered sitting-room in Oxford.

"My welcome to this house," Sophie said, holding out the cup to Joanna.

"We thank you for this welcome," Joanna replied, as she rose and accepted it. "May the gods smile on you, and on this house and"—she altered the supplication on the hoof, to include Gray—"all who belong to it."

She drank a little of the wine in the cup, then passed it to Gwendolen, who set her cup and saucer down beside Sophie's, took the cup from Joanna's hands, and drained it.

"That is much better," said Joanna, resuming her seat and her cup of tea.

By the time the tea was drunk, they had succeeded in decanting the full story—not that, in the end, Sophie had so very much to tell—and Joanna had begun to be suspicious. Though she was prepared to concede the possibility that Edmond Marshall might have fallen ill between the date of Lady MacConnachie's departure from London, just over a fortnight since, and the date on which Jenny should have had to dispatch a letter to Lord de Courcy, either by express or via the diplomatic courier, in order for it to be delivered to Quarry Close eight days ago—and it was no more than a possibility—Sophie did not seem to have taken account of the additional distance between Glascoombe and Carrington-street, or of the myriad small delays which might afflict a message between Carlisle and Din Edin, or of the necessity of its being enciphered before sending, and deciphered before delivery. It was frankly implausible, to Joanna's mind, that, if Edmond Marshall were gravely ill, she should not have heard of it from Jenny before coming away; there simply was not enough time.

And if the illness itself were implausible, the notion of Gray's being sent for as a consequence of it seemed even more so—though here Joanna was forced to concede that Sophie's understanding of the circumstances must be far superior to her own.

But if not a genuine message from Jenny via Lord de Courcy, then . . . what?

Possibilities chased one another through her mind, each worse than the last. Suppose Gray really had set out for Kernow; there were good roads between Din Edin and London, and between London and points south, but aside from the changeable weather at this season, many misfortunes might befall a carriage making that journey, from bolting horses to overturning to highway robbery and even murder—less common in these peaceable days than formerly, to be sure, but Joanna could with very little effort call to mind several recent instances of which news had come to London. And besides the everyday mishaps that might befall anyone, there existed all manner of dangers particular to mages, and others specific to hangers-on of the House of Tudor in foreign and intermittently hostile lands.

And Sophie had not even seen the letter, or the messenger who brought it . . .

"Sophie," said Joanna, "are you . . . are you quite sure there is nothing odd about Gray's going away so suddenly?"

Sophie looked acutely uncomfortable; she frowned at Joanna and darted her eyes at Gwendolen.

Joanna sighed. Sophie's scruples were inconvenient and irritating, but it was after all her house, and Gwendolen and herself guests in it. "Gwen," she said quietly, "perhaps you might be very kind, and clear away the tea-things?"

Gwendolen shot her a darkly amused look over Sophie's head, but nonetheless straightened and reached for her cup and saucer.

"Well?" Joanna said, as soon as Gwendolen had gathered the tea things and gone (to listen from the kitchen, she had no doubt; it was what she should have done herself). She was tempted to speak in Brezhoneg, to thwart said listening, but Gwendolen had left the room only to oblige her, and in any case she should only have to explain everything later on. "You *do* think it odd—I can see you do, and so do I. Had anything unusual happened, just before? Had you . . . quarrelled?"

"No," said Sophie instantly. "That is—"

She embarked on a long and confused explanation of a dispute between herself and Gray, in which he had attempted to persuade her to leave Din Edin for her own safety, and she had refused even to entertain the idea of a separation. Joanna—moving about the room with a candle to light the lamps, for night had fallen without—listened patiently, and carefully refrained from rolling her eyes. It was even odds, she reflected as she took her seat again, which of them was the most exasperating; but certainly this did not seem the sort of quarrel which might lead to a husband's departing in a huff, even had the husband in question not been Gray Marshall.

Sophie went on to describe the attempts of her father, by way of Lord de Courcy, to drag her and Gray back to London, and with shining eyes related Gray's staunch support of her refusal.

"But suppose," she said at last, her slender fingers clenching in the fringes of her shawl, "suppose he has thought better of that decision?"

"Nonsense," Joanna said, more sharply than she had intended; had Sophie lost her wits along with her husband? "Gray, run away to Kernow—or anywhere at all—and leave you here alone? You must be raving, Sophie, to conceive such an idea."

A thought occurred to her; frowning, she stood up from her chair, crossed to stand in front of Sophie, and laid one hand across her brow. It was cool and dry. Not the delirium of fever, then . . . but there were other sorts.

There was a faint sound of clinking crockery from the kitchen, suggesting that Gwendolen was washing up the tea-things—and doing so as slowly and as quietly as possible, the better to hear all that was said in the next room.

"Gray left a letter, you said?" Joanna prompted.

Sophie nodded. "I suppose he was too much distracted to think of using a finding-spell," she said; "and certainly I could not have been quickly found by any other means, for I am sure Catriona and I were in more than a dozen shops and merchants' warehouses in the course of the day."

Yet this too seemed entirely uncharacteristic: Gray might be heedless and forgetful of days and hours, but never of Sophie or her sensibilities. Joanna debated whether she might ask to see the letter without giving offence. Before she could make the request, however, Sophie rose from her seat and went to the other end of the small room, where two writing-desks were wedged into a corner at right angles to each other. She rummaged briefly in a pigeonhole, extracted something, and returned to place a folded paper in Joanna's lap.

"Read it," she said, when Joanna hesitated. "There is nothing in it that will offend your delicate maiden eyes, I assure you."

Joanna gave her a small, wry grin—concealing the faint ache occasioned by Sophie's affectionate mockery, which she had not heard for so long—and unfolded the first letter.

Having read it, she frowned thoughtfully. She had received very few letters from her brother-in-law, and had certainly never before seen one directed to his wife, but apart from its being very brief, there was nothing in it which did not seem entirely characteristic of Gray— and, after all, its brevity might be only the effect of haste. *Am I too suspicious? Perhaps; very likely. But it is all so very odd.*

In the kitchen, something quietly splashed.

"The words seem to me like Gray's," Sophie said, after another long silence. Again she stood and crossed to the desks, then lifted the topmost pages from a neat stack nearly half a foot high. "And it is certainly his hand; look."

Joanna rose to join her.

The page in Sophie's hands was a list of some sort—books, it appeared, for here and there amongst the strings of unintelligible words in what must be Gaelic was the name of an author Joanna recognised, or an erudite-sounding title in Latin. Even these, however, seemed to have no words in common with the brief letters.

"Have you anything with more Latin in it?" Joanna said.

Sophie riffled through the pages she held, then deeper into the stack on the desktop. "Here," she said at last, extracting a single sheet and holding it out.

*On the history of shape-shifting in the Roman world,* it read, in blessedly clear Latin. *Lecture the First. Read by G. V. Marshall at the University of Din Edin on . . .*

"Yes, much better," said Joanna.

For some time they studied the two samples, eyes darting back and forth from the known to the suspect. At last Joanna was forced to agree that the letter was indeed in Gray's own hand, or (though she did not mention this notion to Sophie) very skilfully forged indeed.

"Have you any scry-mages amongst your learned acquaintance, by any chance?" she said.

That night, one so chilly that it might have belonged to midwinter rather than mid-March, Sophie woke with a bitten-off sob and sat bolt upright, staring about her with wide eyes and pounding heart.

At first the solid ordinariness of the bedchamber reassured her. The little oak dressing-table whose oval looking-glass was obscured by stacks of codices, the moonlight-silvered folds of a dressing-gown hanging untidily from the half-closed door of the wardrobe, the curtain blowing in the half-open window: all was entirely as usual—except, of course, that Gray had gone.

But, if this was the case, what was it that had woken her?

She had, she recognised at once, been hoping—half expecting—to open her eyes and find him home again, caught in the act of removing his boots, perhaps, or settling his wings on the window-sill preparatory to shifting back into his own shape. But stare she never so long into the moonlit darkness, no creature besides herself could she discern.

Instead, she began to remember her dreams.

Sophie had suffered from nightmares much of her life, and she had long thought that nothing could torment her more than the dream-memory of her mother's death; but whatever deity or baleful shade had sent this latest manifestation was proving her badly wrong. The more she lay awake in the darkness, the more she feared to sink back into sleep, for every eye-blink cast her back into her torment, or—worse, and more exactly—into Gray's.

*They are only dreams,* she told herself, over and over. No matter how many times she repeated the words, however, they grew no easier to believe.

At last she did succumb—only to dream again and again, in the long hours before dawn, the same distressing scenes. Just before dawn she woke again, heavy-eyed and weary, and knelt for some time with her elbows on the window-sill, waiting for daylight to disperse the fears of night.

The sun was well above the horizon when at length she gave it up; her dreams had lost none of their immediacy, surrendered none of their power over her imagination, and she was frightened for Gray, and for herself, as she had not been (had not allowed herself to be?) until today.

They had been separated before, of course, and on each such occasion she had felt vaguely discomfited, slightly askew, as though nothing were quite as it ought to be. But the grim, sickening dread of these speaking dreams . . .

*Joanna is right; this cannot be what it seems. What ails me, that I did not see it at once?*

\* \* \*

"What should you like to see today?" Sophie asked her guests the next morning, with a sort of determined cheerfulness. "The weather is fine, but I expect it is still a great deal too muddy for climbing Arthur's Seat; perhaps you may like to go down and look at the Firth, however, and the ships coming in—or to see the University Library?"

"Sophie," said Joanna, frowning, "I think we had much better call upon Lord de Courcy."

"What? Why? Oh—do you mean that you have letters for him?"

"No—that is, yes, I have, but they are not such as might not be handed to his secretary. I meant that you ought to tell him about Gray."

"Jo, what am I to tell him? Indeed, if the news came via Courcy, as Gray's letter says, what can I tell him that he does not know already?" Inexplicably restless, she pushed back her chair from the dining-room table—where Donella MacHutcheon had insisted upon laying the breakfast things, in honour of Sophie's having guests—and stood up to prowl about the sitting-room.

Joanna and Miss Pryce continued to spread crab-apple jam on Donella MacHutcheon's scones, of which they had between them consumed a round half dozen thus far.

"It is all perfectly plain," Sophie burst out, after a long moment's pacing. "Gray's father is ill; he was summoned to Kernow; he has gone thither, and I shall hear from him when he is safe arrived. I shall be happy to go with you to deliver your letters, Jo, but I shall not go crying to Lord de Courcy like a child who has lost her doll!"

Joanna swallowed the last of her scone and jam, stood up from the table, and crossed the sitting-room to stand by Sophie at the window. "Sophie," she said quietly, "have you never met Edmond Marshall?"

"Of course I have," said Sophie, "and I take your point, Jo; but a dire illness may greatly alter a man's sensibilities, and make him think better of decisions made in anger."

Joanna sighed. "A bargain, then," she said. Sophie tilted her head in tentative acquiescence. "If you have heard nothing from Gray before Joveday next—that is to say, within a fortnight of his leaving Din Edin—we shall go and speak to Lord de Courcy."

Joveday next! Surely she should have a letter by that time, which should put Joanna's mind at rest as well as her own. "Very well," Sophie said, contentedly enough, and put out her hand. "A bargain."

The hoped-for letter did not wait for Joveday, but was delivered to Quarry Close on Marday morning; its arrival, however, did not bring Sophie the peace of mind which she had been expecting. By this time Joanna had called at Lord de Courcy's residence, found him from home, and handed her letters from Lord Kergabet in to Mr. Powell; and Sophie had escorted Joanna and Miss Pryce to half a dozen bookshops, the University Library, the Grassmarket, and the harbour, and felt as though she should have liked to sleep for a week.

The letter was very short, its exterior very grubby and battered (which was in no way remarkable, for the Marshalls' post from Britain frequently arrived in a like state), and the postmark so badly smudged that Sophie could not at all make out where it had originated. The wax seal bore the unmistakable imprint of one of Gray's cufflinks, the ones she had given him—an owl, an oak-tree, a rhododendron leaf—but there was, to her enormous frustration, no return address.

She broke the seal.

> *My dear Sophie,* she read,
>
> *I regret to say that my dear papa is very ill indeed, and I cannot say how much longer I shall be needed here. I hope that you will give my best regards to all our friends in Din Edin, and particularly to our friends Aurélien and Einion. Mama sends her best love.*
>
> *I shall write again as soon as I may.*
>
> *Fondly,*
> *G.V.M.*

Sophie's hands shook so that she was forced to lay the letter down upon her desk before she dropped it.

"Jo," she said, in a voice that did not sound at all like her own. "Jo, go to the front door and fetch in Mr. Menez or Mr. Williams. I must go and see Lord de Courcy at once."

## CHAPTER XX

# In Which a Cat Is
# Set Amongst the Pigeons

*Joanna and Sophie* were escorted to Lord de Courcy's residence by the broad-shouldered Breizhek guardsman called Menez, while Williams took up a station within sight of Sophie's front door, the better to keep his eye on Gwendolen. Sophie was pale and silent, speaking only when necessity obliged it; she overrode Menez's attempt to insist upon Lord de Courcy's carriage, and strode along at so rapid a pace that Joanna, walking beside her, was forced into a sort of trot.

The guards at the gate had plainly met Sophie before, for she was admitted both without question and without delay. A page-boy ran ahead of them to the front door, and by the time they reached it, he had summoned forth the envoy's secretary, Mr. Powell—a young man so like Sieur Germain's secretary, Fowler, in so many respects that Joanna half wondered whether they might be brothers, though she knew Fowler to be an only son with five sisters.

"Mrs. Marshall," he said blankly. "Miss Callender. To what do we—"

"We are come to see Lord de Courcy," said Sophie, cutting off his question. "At once, if you please."

*Or if you do not please,* said her uncompromising tone and the set of her chin. *The Princess Royal has come to call,* thought Joanna wryly.

"O-of course," said Mr. Powell, and with a gesture he invited them to precede him into the hall.

"My Lord de Courcy," said Sophie, when they were shown into the Ambassador's study. Mr. Powell retreated into the corridor and shut the door behind him.

"Madame Marshall," said Lord de Courcy. "And . . . ?"

"My sister," said Sophie. "Miss Joanna Callender."

"Ah!" said Lord de Courcy. "The protégée of the estimable Lady Kergabet, I believe?"

This, Joanna supposed, was not inaccurate. "I am also by way of being an apprentice to Sieur Germain de Kergabet," she said, "in which capacity I have been deciphering your letters for at least the past twelvemonth, and the letters you had from Kergabet on Joveday last came here by my hand."

Briefly Lord de Courcy's face wore an expression of utter astonishment; then his lips smiled at Joanna (though his eyes did not) and he said, "A pleasure, Mademoiselle Callender."

Still smiling, he gestured them to a seat and retreated behind his desk, which was piled high with books, papers, and dossiers tied up in red tape.

Sophie and Joanna perched on the edges of a pair of wing chairs upholstered in an unpleasant shade of puce, clasping their reticules in their laps.

"Madame Marshall," said Courcy, after some moments of awkward silence, "may I know to what I owe the pleasure of this unexpected visit? I hope you are not in some manner of difficulty?"

Joanna considered him. He was not at all as she had imagined him—neither staid, nor middle-aged, nor portly, nor particularly affable, but a dark-haired, sharp-eyed blade of a man some years younger than Sieur Germain, with a formidable nose, and long fingers faintly stained with ink.

"My husband has disappeared," said Sophie baldly. "He left Din Edin nearly a fortnight ago, apparently acting on information about an illness of his father's, conveyed to him by some member of your household—"

Abruptly all trace of the polite diplomat vanished from Lord de Courcy's face, and Joanna fought an instinct to shrink away from his fierce, narrow-eyed gaze. "I assure you, Madame Marshall," he said, "no such information has crossed my desk, or Powell's."

"So I have concluded," said Sophie. Her tone was bleak. "He left a letter for me, and promised to write again when he should have arrived in Kernow. I have had another letter this morning which gives me strong reason to suppose that he is neither in Kernow nor free to return to Din Edin."

She fished in her reticule, extracted the two letters, and laid them one by one upon Lord de Courcy's desk. Lord de Courcy frowned at the first—looked baffled at the second—frowned again.

"'Aurélien and Einion,'" he said; "that is a clear enough message."

"It is not clear to me," Joanna muttered. Sophie cast a surprised glance at her, as though she had forgotten her presence, and whispered, "Aurélien, Lord de Courcy; and Mr. Einion Powell."

"*Oh,*" said Joanna. "I *see.*"

"But the rest of it seems perfectly unremarkable," Courcy continued, ignoring their whispered exchange; "I do not see—"

Joanna leant forward to peer at the second letter. She could not read so quickly upside down, but by the time Sophie's emphatic finger descended she had seen enough: *my dear papa,* and *Mama sends her love,* and *Fondly, G.V.M.*

"Gray's father cast him off five years ago," she said, forestalling Sophie; "if you do not like to take my word upon it, you may consult Lady Kergabet, who was witness to the whole sorry affair. His mother refers to Sophie as *that girl* and has as much as accused her of bespelling him. And do you not see the difference in the valedictions?"

Lord de Courcy looked very thoughtful and increasingly grim.

"Your husband is a mage, I know," he said, turning to Sophie. "Should you call him a powerful one?"

"Certainly," said Sophie, "very powerful indeed. What has that to do with . . ."

Her voice trailed off uncertainly.

Courcy looked as though he were suppressing language he thought unsuited to ladies' ears; Joanna and Sophie did not disabuse him of his inaccurate ideas, but watched in silence as he rose from his chair and crossed the room to search for something in a cabinet drawer.

"Mademoiselle Callender!" he called over his shoulder. "May I trouble you to ring for my secretary?"

Joanna looked about her for a bell-pull. None was apparent, but a polished brass bell slightly larger than her fist sat prominently atop a locked dispatch-case upon the desk. Joanna picked it up and shook it, then quickly damped its surprisingly loud peal with her other hand.

As she was surreptitiously polishing away her fingerprints with the hem of her petticoat, she heard rapid footsteps in the corridor; the door burst open, and Mr. Powell erupted into the room.

He looked at its occupants in some confusion.

"Ah, Powell!" Courcy said, straightening up from the drawer. "Set the wards and find me our notes on all the missing mages, if you please."

"Missing *mages*?" echoed Joanna, horrified. "Do you mean that there have been others before?"


There were four dossiers, neatly labelled: four mages who had come to Din Edin and, in the past twelvemonth, had left it again—the first, exactly as planned; the next two, some days before their scheduled departures; the last, nearly a month early—but had failed to reappear at home as expected. Two were British subjects, one hailing from Karaez in Breizh, the other from Cymru; one was an Erseman, and the fourth a visiting scholar from Castilia in Iberia, who had vanished without trace somewhere between Din Edin and Madrid.

Sophie looked at them, one by one, and grew so pale that Joanna rose from her chair to stand beside her sister's, a hand on her shoulder, so as to be nearby in case she should faint.

Joanna did not ask, though she was very curious to know, how

Lord de Courcy had laid hands on such detailed information respecting subjects of foreign and not notably friendly realms.

"They were none of them known to one another," said Mr. Powell, helpfully spreading the dossiers across his desk for Sophie and Joanna's perusal, "so far as we have been able to ascertain; the only points of similarity amongst them are that all were foreigners to Alba, and all mages of notable talent."

"And they have none of them turned up again?" Joanna asked. "Alive, or . . . otherwise?"

"No," said Courcy. "Not one has been seen again, whether alive or otherwise. Which seems to me to suggest that these men were not simply killed for their purses, or bested in a violent quarrel, or the like; in a city of this size, where so many live in such close quarters, it is not so very easy to conceal an unexplained corpse."

Joanna grimaced; under her hand, Sophie's shoulder trembled.

"Believe me, Madame Marshall," said Mr. Powell, earnestly, "we have been at considerable trouble and expense to seek information on our vanished countrymen, from any source that might offer; but there seems none to be had, and we have no jurisdiction here to do more. Nor have we any proof that the crime—if crime there be— occurred in Alba; only that no trace of the missing men has yet been found in Britain."

Joanna thought through the implications of all of this and at last said slowly, "You believe all these disappearances to be connected, do you not? And connected with that of my brother-in-law."

Courcy nodded, his dark eyes sharply attentive; if he had been humouring Sophie to begin with, he was in dead earnest now. "I am no believer in coincidence," he said.

There was a long, grim silence, broken only by four persons' tense breathing and by the rhythmic tapping of Sophie's fingers upon the upholstered seat of her chair.

"You cannot act, you say, for want of proof," Sophie said at last. Her voice was firm and even, though under Joanna's hand her pulse fluttered as rapid as a bird's. "I take it, then, that should I bring you that proof—"

"Your Royal High—I beg pardon, Madame Marshall—that is entirely out of the question," said Lord de Courcy. "You must understand that in the circumstances—"

"I understand nothing of the kind," Sophie said, cutting him off in her turn. In a flash she was out of her seat and facing down her father's ambassador across his own desk, her slim hands flat upon its polished surface. "What *you* must understand, my lord Ambassador, is that the Princess Royal returns to Britain with her husband or not at all."

"Madame Marshall—"

Lord de Courcy looked rather alarmed, and when Sophie turned from him, saying crisply, "Come, Joanna," and sweeping towards the door, Joanna did not wonder at it; Sophie's eyes were wide and night-black in her ashen face, and the air around her fairly crackled with suppressed fury.

Joanna cast an apologetic glance at Lord de Courcy and Mr. Powell, and followed her out.

Sophie's cold, furious determination carried her half across Din Edin, into Quarry Close, and through her own front door and up the stairs to her bedroom. Then her eyes lit on Gray's copy of the *Metamorphoses*, abandoned on the window-sill with an owl's tail-feather marking his progress through the poems, and all her tight-wound composure unravelled into tears.

A damp and wretched half-hour later, she smoothed the signs of weeping from her face, descended the stairs, and emerged into the sitting-room, where she found Joanna and Miss Pryce perched in her own armchair and Gray's respectively, their dark heads bent close together—talking over the morning's excursion in great detail, Sophie had no doubt.

They straightened guiltily at the sound of her footsteps crossing the floor. Sophie gazed steadily at Miss Pryce until the latter took the hint and vacated Gray's chair, then curled into it herself and addressed her sister.

"My friend Mór MacRury is a scry-mage," she said. "A particularly gifted one, I am given to understand, and certainly an authority on the subject. She is on holiday at present, but is expected to return in two days' time; and then perhaps we shall have our proof."

"That is well thought of, Sophie," said Joanna, warmly approving, as though she had not herself made the same suggestion within moments of discovering Gray's absence. *If only I had listened then! . . . but Mór was not here, and there is no other scry-mage in Din Edin to whom I should entrust this matter.*

"Mrs. Marshall."

Sophie looked up, startled, at Miss Pryce's hesitant address.

"I— I feel I ought to apologise," Miss Pryce continued, stiffly formal. Not, Sophie noted, *I apologise*; this was a sense of social duty speaking, rather than any genuine regret. "For intruding at such a time, uninvited—"

"You are not uninvited, Gwen," said Joanna stoutly; "I invited you. Sophie cannot possibly blame *you* for my presumption."

Sophie repressed an exasperated sigh. "You are both here now," she said. *And I ought to have stopped them coming; evidently there is more danger here than any of us imagined.* She pressed the heels of her hands to her smarting eyes—drew a deep breath—opened her eyes again and settled her hands in her lap. "And now I think you must both go back to London. I—"

"*Edith Augusta Sophia Marshall.*" From the look on Joanna's face, she had startled herself as much as Sophie by this unusual mode of address; she had also sounded, for just a moment, so much like Lady Maëlle that Sophie's throat closed up and her eyes stung anew. "If you suppose that I mean to leave you alone in a foreign kingdom, just as I discover that someone has *kidnapped your husband—*"

Sophie's attempt to overrule this argument was curtailed by a knock at the door, loud and forthright and so unexpected that all three of them started in surprise.

Joanna was the first to recover, and before Sophie could prevent her, she ran to the front door and stood on tiptoe to peer through the transom. "It is a tall freckled fellow, with ginger curls," she reported, "carrying a great many books."

*Rory MacCrimmon.* Sophie reflexively wished him away, but then another thought occurred: Rory, too, had had a letter from Gray, which perhaps she might make use of.

"Stand aside a moment, Jo," she said, and opened the door to let Rory in.

The faltering of his habitual cheerful grin told her, too late, that she had failed to conceal her own disquiet.

"Sophie," he said, hurriedly setting aside his stack of codices in order to clasp her hands. "What is the matter?"

Sophie heard Joanna's indrawn breath at his familiar address. "A moment, Rory," she said, and turned to her sister. "Jo, this is Rory MacCrimmon—he is a lecturer at the University, and Gray's nearest friend in Din Edin. Rory, my sister Joanna Callender, of London."

Joanna essayed a very London sort of bow, but upon Rory's putting out his hand in the Alban manner, she rallied sufficiently to return the gesture.

Miss Pryce having followed them out into the corridor—now very cramped indeed—the introductions were repeated; she then said, "I shall make tea," and abruptly vanished into the kitchen. A further attempt at apology? No matter.

Sophie ushered Rory to her own armchair, and herself perched on the edge of Gray's. He peered at her in baffled worry. "Rory," she said, "if Gray were in some sort of trouble, should you be minded to help him?"

Rory sat up straighter. "Of course I should," he said. "How can you doubt it?"

"I am glad of it," said Sophie, "and glad to see you here, for I believe Gray needs my help, and I need yours."

"Of course," Rory repeated. "Has—is it—I hope his father is not—"

"Gray is not gone to Kernow," Sophie interrupted, before he could further entangle himself. "His father is not ill, so far as I know; my father's envoy, from whom I supposed the summons to have come, knows nothing of it, nor did Gray's sister when Joanna last saw her in London. And I have had another letter from him which clinches the matter."

As she was speaking, Rory's green eyes had gone wide and dark, and he appeared to be holding his tongue with some difficulty. To her surprise, however, he did not inquire after the contents of the letter or demand tiresome explanations.

"How," he said instead, "how can I be of help?"

Sophie swallowed and, determinedly pretending not to see Joanna's disapproving frown and gestures of negation, offered a brief and bald précis of her meeting with Lord de Courcy.

Miss Pryce returned with the tea-tray; the others absently accepted cups of tea, all of which but Joanna's cooled untouched.

Rory blanched at being informed that Gray was not the first foreign mage to go missing from Alba and muttered under his breath, "Professor Maghrebin."

Sophie halted midsyllable. "Oh," she breathed. "I had not thought."

"Of course I may be quite wrong," said Rory hastily. "But you cannot deny that the circumstances fit."

And indeed Sophie could not.

"Being reliably informed that Lord de Courcy can do nothing in the matter without some sort of proof," she concluded at last, "I am determined to provide it, insofar as I am able. When Mór and Sorcha are come back, I intend to take both letters to Mór and ask her—beg her, if need be—to scry them for me. I hoped that you might do the same."

"Of course," Rory repeated. He gazed earnestly at Sophie. "And—and if there is any other way in which I may be of service—"

"We shall not hesitate to call upon you," said Joanna briskly. Again Sophie started; absorbed in her narrative and overwhelmed with relief at Rory's accepting, she had half forgot that their conversation had an audience.

"Indeed," said Sophie. Joanna's briskly cheerful tone rang utterly false to her ear, though Rory—who after all had known Joanna scarcely an hour—seemed oblivious. She pressed Rory's hand and tried to smile at him, though his stricken expression suggested the effort had not been very successful. "I thank you."

Joanna ushered him out, and Miss Pryce began to gather up the tea-things, waving away Sophie's attempt to assist her. Balked of these opportunities for useful endeavour, she drifted towards the pianoforte and trailed her fingers along the keys.

The door closed, the bolt slid home; footsteps approached, halted. "That was very foolish, Sophie," said Joanna.

Sophie turned, frowning. "Foolish, how?" she demanded.

"*Think*, Sophie," said Joanna, her tone shifting from stern reproof into exasperation. "Have you forgot that there is another mage in this household more powerful than Gray? Someone in Din Edin is making away with powerful foreign mages—luring them here for the purpose, it may be—and what should you do but throw yourself upon the mercy of the very man at whose behest you came here to begin with!"

*Oh*. Sophie pondered this, the ebony keys warming under her fingers: A, F, G. Her fourth finger strayed to B-flat, cool ivory.

"I cannot believe such a thing of Rory," she said; her conviction bolstered by their recent exchange, she added, "And if it were anything to do with him—which I do not for a moment concede—why should he so readily agree to my having Gray's letters scried, when he must have known he should be implicated by whatever Mór MacRury can discover from them?"

She folded her arms triumphantly, but she had reckoned without Joanna's determined suspicion.

"This Mór MacRury—have I reasoned rightly, that they are known to one another?"

"They have been friends for many years," Sophie conceded. "But Mór would not—"

"How can you be sure?" Joanna's voice was rising; Sophie retreated, trapped against the keyboard. "You have known none of these people more than half a year! How is it that you so cavalierly trust them with Gray's life, and with yours?"

Miss Pryce had come quietly up beside Joanna during this out-burst and laid a calming hand upon her arm; Joanna shook it off.

"You are too trusting altogether, Sophie," she continued. "For all you know, they—"

Sophie found her voice at last, though it was rough and scraped her throat. "If all of Alba is so little to be trusted," she said, "how is it that *you* have been conspiring with Sieur Germain and my father these past six months and more, to offer my brother to them as a hostage?"

Joanna's breath left her in a sharp huff. They glared at each other, flushed and furious, until at length Miss Pryce caught at Joanna's arm again and bent to murmur in her ear. Sophie could not hear what she said, but whatever it was made Joanna close her eyes and turn her face away, and suffer herself to be shepherded into the kitchen.

Sophie kept hold of her quivering rage for a moment more; then reaction overcame her, and she sank to the floor, leaning one shoulder against the leg of the pianoforte. She clasped her arms about her shins and pressed her face against her bent-up knees. *What ails me, that I should speak so to Joanna, of all people?*


Gwendolen grasped Joanna by the elbow, her long fingers pressing; her warm breath brushed Joanna's ear. "Jo," she murmured, "she cannot strike at her enemies, and you are seeking to take away her only means of discovering who they are. Can you wonder that she is angry with you?"

Joanna closed her eyes, but Sophie's face—consumed with a furious anger which Joanna had seen before, but never directed towards herself—hovered before her nonetheless. When Gwendolen put an arm about her and urged her towards the door, she went unresistingly.

Sophie did not follow; indeed, the next sound Joanna heard from the sitting-room was that of stumbling footsteps making for the stairs. Above their heads, a door closed—not with a bang, but with great finality—and Joanna fancied that she heard a key turn in a lock.

"When I said we should be going off on an adventure," said Gwendolen at last, with a wry little smile, "I confess this is not quite what I imagined."

Joanna, looking at her across the scrubbed pinewood table, could not help feeling that she had badly miscalculated. "I ought never to have brought you here," she said. "Sophie is quite right about that, at any rate; you had much better be in London, where you should be safe. I am sure that Lord de Courcy—"

"No," said Gwendolen, quietly but very firmly.

"Gwen—"

"You may save all the rest of your arguments, Jo. I have no doubt they are excellent ones, but if they had no effect upon your sister or yourself, surely you do not imagine that I am likely to be persuaded by them."

Joanna could think of nothing to say.

They sat in silence for a long moment; then Gwendolen jumped up, dusted her hands on her skirts, and said briskly, "Now, come and help me with the washing-up."

Joanna laid aside her shawl and stood, glad of something to do with her hands.

"Do you think the ginger fellow has made away with your brother-in-law, truly?" Gwendolen asked, passing Joanna a teacup to be wiped.

Joanna sighed. "Rory MacCrimmon? Yes," she said. "No. I have not the least idea, Gwen. But do the circumstances not suggest it?"

"Perhaps they may," said Gwendolen thoughtfully. "Though he did not strike me as a particularly able liar."

Joanna considered Rory MacCrimmon. Tall, much freckled of face; some few years older than Gray, and perhaps about Kergabet's height. Hair that curled and shone like a new copper coin. He had arrived in Quarry Close wearing a voluminous great-coat which entirely obscured the shape of him, and a woollen muffler in a shade which some lady of his acquaintance must have chosen to bring out the startling new-grass green of his eyes; when last seen, he had also worn an expression of confused dismay with which, at present, Joanna could very readily sympathise.

"Perhaps not," she said, stretching up to return the teacup to its proper place. "But I should never forgive myself if I let him—or any of them—do harm to Sophie."

Gwendolen rinsed four saucers in thoughtful silence. Then she said, very low, "Take care you do not do the same yourself."

Sophie did not reemerge from her bedroom until late the following morning, and it was immediately clear that she had not spent a restful night: her eyes were red-rimmed, her face pale, and she moved about the house with an air of slow, resigned misery which Joanna found very difficult to bear. She would not eat any breakfast, though she consented at last to drink a cup of tea.

"I have been thinking," she said, à propos of nothing, halfway through a very long afternoon. Joanna raised her head from her knitting—it was Sophie's knitting, in point of fact, but she had plainly lost all interest in it, and it provided employment for Joanna's restless fingers—and offered an encouraging *Hmm?* but Sophie was staring once more into the middle distance, and said no more. Her eyes were damp and her face grown ashen; as Joanna watched, a tear leaked from the corner of one eye and tracked down her cheek, apparently unremarked.

Joanna and Gwendolen, tucked up into one corner of the sofa with her *broderie anglaise*, exchanged a worried look.

It struck Joanna then what it was that so alarmed her: What was Sophie about—Sophie who concealed everything remarkable about herself as easily as breathing—to allow not only Joanna but *Gwendolen* to see her misery so plainly?

## CHAPTER XXI

# In Which Mór MacRury
# Makes Herself Useful, and
# Joanna and Gwendolen Pay a Call

*The following day* was to bring the return of Mór MacRury from her seaside excursion, which event Joanna had confidently expected to spur Sophie into action. In this, however, she was disappointed: though two days since Sophie had appeared to have every intention of calling upon her friend as soon as she might, when Rory MacCrimmon returned to Quarry Close with a request that Sophie should come with him to Mór MacRury's lodgings, she was so ill—or so deeply sunk in melancholy—that Joanna could not persuade her to leave her room.

Short of carrying her sister bodily down the narrow staircase and out into the street, there was nothing for Joanna to do but take the letters from Sophie's dressing-table and go away. She paused in her way, however, to speak to Gwendolen, and to dispatch her to sit with Sophie—a precaution not likely to be much to the taste of either but necessary to Joanna's peace of mind.

Rory MacCrimmon frowned at her explanations but duly escorted her to Mór MacRury's lodgings in MacDuff-street. The plump, fair-haired woman who opened the door in answer to his knock—she was no taller than Joanna, and was wrapped in a grey cloak and an elegant little grey hat—greeted Rory MacCrimmon familiarly and gave Joanna a pleasant smile.

This was not Mór MacRury herself, as Joanna had first supposed, but her fellow lodger, one Sorcha MacAngus, on her way to call upon her own brother and sister. Joanna followed Rory MacCrimmon into a bright, untidy sitting-room, where she found him speaking quietly with another woman, of entirely different appearance—tall, angular, and altogether rather severe—but about the same age: perhaps six- or seven-and-twenty.

"Miss Callender," said he, "allow me to present my colleague, Banmhaighistir Mór MacRury; Mór, this is Joanna Callender, of London—she is Sophie Marshall's sister."

"I am very pleased to make your acquaintance, Joanna Callender." Like her colleague before her, Mór MacRury put out her right hand in a businesslike manner, and Joanna, less ill-prepared this time, took it.

She swallowed back a yelp of surprise; the scry-mage had a grip like a farrier's. "I am grateful for your help"—she groped for a title she was able to pronounce—"Magistra MacRury."

To her secret relief, the imposing lady lecturer seemed not to take offence at this. "Do call me Mór," she said. "And there is no question of gratitude. Your sister and brother-in-law are friends of mine, as well as very promising scholars, and I feel—were it not for—" She stopped abruptly, pressing her lips together, and after a moment went on, "Any small assistance I may render them in this . . . difficult circumstance, I am very glad to offer. But Sophie is not come with you?"

"She . . . is not feeling quite herself today," Joanna said, acutely uncomfortable, "and has asked me to act for her in showing you these letters."

She passed them to Mór MacRury, who laid them flat upon one of the two desks—the one piled with stacks of books and papers, as against what appeared to be astronomical equipment—arranging them so as to catch the best light from the bow window.

"Now, Rory," said Mór, "where is yours?"

Rory MacCrimmon extracted another letter from an inner pocket and laid it beside the others; Mór MacRury hummed thoughtfully, and settled herself at the desk.

Despite her acute concern for the results of the scrying, Joanna could not help being interested in the process itself, which—to her untalented and untutored, though experienced, eye—appeared very different from Jenny's. Instead of shutting her eyes and repeating a scrying-spell under her breath, Mór MacRury sat very still and silent for a long moment, with one hand spread flat on the first of Sophie's letters; then, so softly at first that Joanna was not certain she had not imagined it, she began to hum.

Whether the humming was a melody or only a drone, Joanna had no means of knowing; it was evident, however, that this was a quite different song-magick from those Sophie habitually used, for it had no effect whatever on Joanna.

The bright blue eyes gradually closed, and the humming grew louder and developed something almost like words, though Joanna could not catch hold of any that she recognised. At length the sound died away, finally ceasing altogether, and Mór opened her eyes, shook out her fingers, and laid her other hand upon the next letter.

Having repeated this process twice more, she looked up at the others, frowning deeply.

"There is nothing out of the ordinary about either of these first two letters," she said, nodding at those which Gray had written be-fore leaving Din Edin, "apart from its being entirely out of character for Marshall to abandon Sophie in such a way, and except as subse-quent events suggest. When he wrote them, whatever may have be-fallen later on, he believed himself to be going to Kernow, and was hopeful of a reconciliation with his father. But *this* one—"

Joanna leant forward, peering over Mór MacRury's shoulder, as though she might somehow see for herself.

"There is something in the way of my seeing," said Mór MacRury, "some other spell or working, whose source I cannot fathom. It clouds everything I attempt to see. I ought to be able to glean a great deal from something so personal as a letter, and so recently made, but

I cannot. I can only tell you that though Marshall *did* write this letter himself, just as he wrote the others . . ." She paused, casting a troubled look at Joanna.

"What is it?" the latter demanded, as calmly as she could manage. With some effort she refrained from howling, *Do not speak to me as though I were a temperamental child!*

"There was compulsion," said Mór MacRury. Her voice was low and grim; Joanna clearly heard Rory MacCrimmon's startled intake of breath. "The words are in some measure his own—else, as you say, he could not have planted so many clues—but he was under some form of compulsion when he wrote them, whether magick or trickery or main force. The whole of this letter is full of his outrage against it."

"That is . . . that is very much what I feared," said Joanna. Her heart thumped in her throat, and her brain seemed to grow too large for her skull. "I wanted so much to be mistaken . . ."

She had been hoping desperately, all this time, that her conclusions were quite wrong, that Gray was safe and well at Glascoombe and she and Sophie were making a mountain of a molehill. The appalling reality, which had been gradually seeping into her mind and heart, now finally drenched her in an icy flood. "Mother Goddess," she whispered. "How am I to tell Sophie?"

Abruptly and unexpectedly, scarcely hearing the others' exclamations of solicitous alarm, she dropped into a chair, put her face in her hands, and burst into tears.

Joanna pushed open the front door of Sophie's house with a dull, dragging feeling of inevitability. The Joanna of a few years ago might have felt some degree of triumph—or at any rate some satisfaction—at the double confirmation of her suspicions. She almost wished that she could do so; she felt hollowed out by the afternoon's revelations, sick with vaguely reasoned guilt at the thought of Gray's coming to harm and with dread at the prospect of the news which she must shortly give to Sophie. It could not be put off—all else aside, she had faithfully promised Sophie's friends that Sophie should be immediately and fully informed of their discoveries—but oh, how she wished that someone else might do it for her!

Gwendolen, having evidently heard the door opening, came swiftly but quietly down the stairs. "She is sleeping," she said. "What had the scry-mage to tell us?"

Joanna tossed her bonnet and cloak over the stair-rail and dropped into Sophie's armchair with a sigh, putting her head in her hands. She was sorely tempted to pour the whole tale out at once, to plead with Gwendolen to take on the unenviable task of relaying it to Sophie. But she owed it to her sister not to seek such a coward's path—though she could not be sorry for this brief reprieve.

"Gray is being held prisoner somewhere," she said bluntly. Gwendolen winced. "And Mór MacRury could not tell us where, or by whom, because she could not see clearly, for all that she is so *particularly gifted.*"

"I do not know very much about scrying," said Gwendolen, "but I do know that it is no more invincible than any other branch of magick."

She briefly clasped Joanna's shoulder; Joanna sighed, and allowed herself the small luxury of closing her eyes and curling up in Sophie's chair. *For a moment only,* she told herself.

"*Jo,*" said Gwendolen's voice, some indeterminate time later. From the sound of it, this was not her first attempt at attracting Joanna's attention.

Joanna opened her eyes blearily; there was Gwendolen herself, holding something—which, when she put it into Joanna's hand, proved to be a cup of tea, very hot and, if the colour were any guide, much stronger than necessary.

"I know you don't want it," said Gwendolen, in what Joanna privately called her governessing voice, "but I can see perfectly well that you need it."

Joanna raised the cup to her lips. The first sip confirmed that the tea was not only too strong but also much too sweet; Gwendolen looked at her expectantly, however, until she had finished drinking it, and she was forced to admit—at least to herself—that she felt rather better as a result.

"You mean to go back to see Lord de Courcy again, yes?" said

Gwendolen, taking the cup and saucer away from her and bestowing them upon the mantel-shelf. "You had better go at once, I suppose, though I do think your sister ought to go with you—"

"I had a thousand times rather speak to Lord de Courcy than to Sophie," Joanna confessed, "but I cannot in conscience tell him anything before I have told her." She sighed again, and was at once disgusted with her own cowardice. "I shall just go upstairs and see whether—"

But she did not go at once, for at that moment there came a loud, determined knocking at the door.


There was a soft tap at the door of Sophie's bedroom. She considered feigning sleep, but as she had been sitting at her dressing-table, leaning her head on her hand and attempting (without much success) to read a manuscript which Rory had lent her, this seemed altogether too much effort—and it could only be Joanna, after all. "Come in," she called, not looking up from the page before her.

The door creaked open, and Joanna's voice said, "Sophie, I have brought Mór MacRury to see you."

Sophie sat up straight, so suddenly that her head swam. Had she not said *very clearly* that she did not wish to see anyone, anyone at all, for any reason?

Before she had gathered herself to tell them to go away, she heard the door close again, and Joanna appeared at her elbow.

"Jo—"

"I know," said Joanna, "and I shall apologise later if I must, but I do think you ought to see her, Sophie." Head on one side, she surveyed her elder sister critically. "You look a little better than you did this morning, I believe. Come and sit by the fire; Gwendolen has made a pot of tea."


Joanna poured out tea for Sophie and for her guest; then she retreated to hover with Gwendolen in the doorway, for there was not room for two more chairs within.

"I saw almost nothing," Mór explained gravely, "which is very suggestive, but does not help us. But we do know one thing now, which you only suspected before, and that is, that wherever he has gone, it was not of his own will. It was clever of him; the clues in the text were for you alone, but no one could possibly scry that letter, no matter how little they knew him, and fail to see that it was written under duress."

Sophie's face had gone the colour of tallow; Joanna started forward, and Mór MacRury half rose from her seat, ready to support her if she should faint. She did not, however, and though her teacup rattled in its saucer, it stilled after a moment without shattering or even cracking.

Joanna told herself firmly that this might as easily indicate improved self-control as depleted magick.

"Sophie," said Mór MacRury, giving her a quizzical look, "I do think you might have told me that your husband had vanished without trace. Or, if not me, *someone*. Surely you cannot have thought—"

"I have told you," said Sophie, "and my father's ambassador, also, the moment I had reason to do so. You saw the first letter, as well as the other; I could not have known, then, that anything was amiss, and if I had run about Din Edin like a lost sheep, bleating, because my husband had packed a valise and gone home to see his dying father, I should only have been laughed at. Or, worse, packed off back to London myself."

She was not altogether wrong, Joanna conceded—though it was also true that had she gone at once to Lord de Courcy, and thus discovered the message to be a false one, there might perhaps have been some opportunity of intercepting the culprits before they left the city.

Mór MacRury, it appeared, did not see things in the same light. "I should have advised you to sound the alarm at once," she said; "the letter was plausible enough, I grant you—scrying it could tell no one anything but that he believed every word he wrote at the time of writing it—but the whole tale, taken together: that, no."

"That is exactly what I said," said Joanna.

Her sister's consequent glare, though halfhearted, lifted Joanna's spirits a little, as showing some return of Sophie's.

"But that was guesswork; this is evidence enough to take to Lord de Courcy," said Sophie. Turning to Mór MacRury, she added, "That is . . ."

"Enough to convict a man in the law-courts, certainly not," said Mór MacRury. "But more than sufficient to justify an investigation. On the one hand, of course, I should have wished to see more clearly; but on the other hand, the fact that I was prevented from doing so is as good as a signpost reading *Here be foul play*."

"Foul play of what sort, exactly?" said Gwendolen. Joanna glanced up at her in pleased surprise. "A powerful ward might be responsible, might it not? Or a sufficiently potent spell of concealment? And either might be used for a benign purpose, as easily as for a malevolent one."

"That is so," said Mór MacRury. "But a man whose circumstances demand wards and concealment-spells, and who also writes a letter which has one meaning to its intended recipient and another to those who do not know him well, is a man in difficulties, whether the wards and concealments are his enemies' or his own."

"Yes, I see," said Gwendolen.

"I tried a finding-spell this morning," Sophie said glumly. "You can guess its outcome, I am sure. Either he is outside my range, or the same mechanism—whatever it may be—is interfering."

Mór MacRury leant across the space between their chairs to squeeze Sophie's hand.

"In any event," said Joanna, "we must go back to Lord de Courcy as soon as may be, with this news."

"Yes," said Sophie, raising her chin. For a moment she looked almost herself again; but then she said, "Yes, Jo, you must go at once."

Joanna had feared that they might have difficulty in explaining to Lord de Courcy—who was not a mage any more than she was herself—the process by which they had come by their evidence. Fortunately, however, Mr. Powell appeared to understand all of it easily, and nodded briskly at things which Joanna herself found baffling.

"I know nothing to speak of about this Rory MacCrimmon," he said, "though if he is a friend of Marshall's, my lord, you may be sure he is at least no fool. But Mór MacRury I do know, at any rate by reputation; she is one of the University's foremost experts on the craft of scrying. Whatever she has told you, Miss Callender, Miss Pryce, I believe we may rely on absolutely."

*Unless Mór MacRury considers herself an enemy of Britain,* Joanna thought. But she recalled Mór's tone of voice, her unconcealed anxiety for Sophie, for the missing Gray, and could not believe that even such a cause could have persuaded her to deception in a matter touching their safety.

"What we know, then," said Lord de Courcy, folding his hands on the desk before him, "is this. First, that Monsieur Marshall was alive and well at breakfast on the morning of his disappearance, and said nothing to his wife at that time of any intention to leave Din Edin. Second, that at some point after his wife's leaving the house with a friend and before her return thither late in the afternoon, he received a message purporting to come from this house, and as a consequence allowed himself to be driven . . . somewhere.

"Third, that he certainly wrote the letters received from him by his wife and by his colleague Rory MacCrimmon—which may indicate that the latter had no involvement in the business, but may only mean that Marshall was not aware of his doing so—but, fourth, that one of them was written under duress, and its surface import dictated by some other person or persons unknown to us."

His gaze flicked first to Mr. Powell, industriously taking notes, then to Joanna, who swallowed, licked dry lips, and said, "Yes, sir."

"Fifth," he continued, "that Monsieur Marshall has two points in common with four other men who have disappeared within the last twelvemonth, without satisfactory explanation: He is a stranger to Din Edin, and a powerful mage. Sixth"—and here his decided recital of facts took on a more hesitating quality—"that some . . . spell, or . . . other barrier, is preventing his being located by means of scrying."

Mr. Powell raised his head. "Surely someone has tried a finding-spell?" he demanded.

Joanna regarded him levelly. "So I am told," she said. "My sister has made several such attempts, she tells me, and I understand that both Rory MacCrimmon and Mór MacRury have also done so, without success."

Again doubt flickered in her mind—how was she to know the difference between a mage who had attempted a finding-spell and a mage who only claimed to have done so?—and again she firmly quashed it.

"Duly noted, Miss Callender," said Mr. Powell. He looked chastened and bent his head to his notes once more. "Which tells us only that Mr. Marshall is no longer here in Din Edin, or within the operative range of the said mages—which may be very considerable," he added, with a nod to Joanna, "but cannot possibly extend beyond, say, a radius of fifty miles."

"Now," Lord de Courcy said, "having established these facts of the matter, we may draw some logical inferences." His tone—precise, even, almost didactic—so closely recalled what Sophie called Gray's lecturing voice that Joanna was abruptly, painfully glad of Sophie's absence. "First, that given the clear parallels in these cases—two such might be coincidence, but five?—we must consider the disappearances as linked. Second, that whatever Monsieur Marshall's present whereabouts, he did not come there of his own volition."

"And, third," said Joanna, "that he is not in Kernow. Because," she added, as Mr. Powell seemed about to object, "if he *were* in Kernow, they—whoever *they* are—should have made him tell Sophie that he is somewhere else."

"If I were to attempt to hide a man," said Mr. Powell, "I should go to London; surely there can be no better bolt-hole for persons who wish not to be found."

"Have you ever lived in London, Mr. Powell?" Joanna inquired.

"Not . . . lived, as such," he admitted. "But I have been staying there quite often—"

"If *I* wished not to be found," said Joanna, "I should not attempt to hide in London, for a kingdom. You are thinking, I am sure, that concealment must be very easy in so large a city, so full of people who cannot possibly all know one another. But what I have discovered is that London is not so much a great city as a vast collection of villages, which are as quick to note the arrival of a stranger as any village anywhere; and that, where so many people live in such close proximity, nothing can long go unremarked—and almost any tongue can be loosened by the judicious application of coin. Surely Din Edin is not so very different? I have heard Lord de Courcy say as much, unless I am much mistaken."

Mr. Powell—who had bristled a little, to begin with—was now nodding thoughtfully. It was fortunate, thought Joanna, that he had been long enough in Din Edin to lose the habit of treating women's opinions as surplus to requirements; though he was of Cymric birth, by his surname and his speech, which was perhaps not unimportant. What was it about Normandins and Englishmen (and here she thought irritably of her own father, as well as of Sieur Carel de Bay-eux and his faction of the Privy Council) that made them so obtuse and so intransigent upon this point?

"And let us not forget," said Lord de Courcy, "that if our second supposition is correct, they have had not one captive to conceal, but five."

"Indeed," she said.

"If not London or Din Edin, then," said Mr. Powell, "where should you conceal yourself, should you require concealment?"

"In the country," said Joanna at once, and Gwendolen nodded agreement. Joanna herself had never attempted to run away from home, until the night when Sophie had announced herself to be do-ing so; unlike Sophie, however, she had spent many a resentful hour in plotting how she might successfully abscond, either from her fa-ther's house or from her school in Kemper. "In my own country, where every croft and hayrick and fox-hole is known to me—where I am no stranger, and may therefore go unremarked, and perhaps command the loyalty of others—where there are places so isolated as to permit of true secrecy. Where"—she paused to swallow back a wave of revulsion—"where a man might scream as loud as he liked, with no one to hear him."

There was a long, fraught silence.

Joanna waited to be told that this was no fit subject of conversation for a young lady, or that she was overwrought and would be the better for a glass of watered wine and a good night's rest. Instead, however, Lord de Courcy said, "Your theory, then, is that once we have discovered who is responsible for these disappearances, we shall also have discovered—broadly speaking—where to look for them."

"Yes," said Joanna; "and also, I must suppose, what led them to do . . . whatever it is they have done, or are presently doing. But," she added dejectedly, "as the *who* of the matter remains as much a mystery as ever, I do not see that it gets us any forwarder."

The Ambassador's study fell silent again as all present contemplated this dispiriting conclusion.

"Might this," said Mr. Powell, hesitating a little, "might it have any connexion to the Prince's betrothal to Lucia MacNeill?"

Joanna considered it. "I do not see how," she said, "if it is true that mages were vanishing long before anyone outside Donald Mac-Neill's inner circle was let into the secret. And then, too, the mages who have vanished are all foreigners to Alba, but not all are British subjects . . ."

"It seems to me, moreover," said Lord de Courcy dryly, "that if I were minded to kidnap subjects of a foreign kingdom for the purpose of revenge, or in order to hold them hostage against the carrying out of some scheme to which I objected, I should be foolish to do so in secret."

"That is so," Mr. Powell conceded. "Nevertheless, sir, you cannot deny that there *are* objections to this scheme, and very strong ones, in certain quarters, and it is only reasonable to suppose that—"

"Einion," said Courcy sharply, startling Joanna with the vehemence of his tone and Mr. Powell, evidently, by the use of his given name. "I should advise you to take careful thought before making such an accusation against the priests of the Cailleach, from your position as a guest of the Alban Court. You should not, I hope and trust, be so foolish as to stand on the mustering-ground of a battalion of His Majesty's army, and offer insult to the priests of Mithras?"

"If the boot fits—"

"But if the priests of the Cailleach were indeed responsible," said Joanna, keeping her voice even with some effort, "then surely, as the Ambassador says, they should have made their actions, and the reasons for those actions, public knowledge. You suspect them of holding British subjects captive in an effort to stop Lucia Mac-Neill's marriage; but any such scheme must depend entirely on our knowledge—on the *Ambassador's* knowledge, and through him, the attention of His Majesty—of what they intend, of what they *want*."

Mr. Powell pressed his thin lips together tightly, stared over Jo-anna's shoulder, and said nothing.

His employer, on the other hand, now looked at her with all his attention. "I take it, Miss Callender," he said evenly, "that Sieur Germain de Kergabet still supposes you to be making an innocent visit to your sister, saving your mandate to scrape an acquaintance with Lucia MacNeill?"

To anyone else, it might have seemed a *non sequitur*, but Joanna—with Courcy's steady, speculative gaze now focused entirely upon her—parsed the chain of unstated connexions without difficulty, and was forced to concede that even a Normandin may be capable of learning from experience.

"You are correct, my lord," she said. "In this matter, I am at present an envoy for no one but myself."

Mr. Powell raised his eyebrows.

"You are here alone, are you not?" Lord de Courcy inquired.

"She is not alone, my lord," said Gwendolen, sitting up—if it were possible—even taller.

"Your pardon, Mademoiselle Pryce." He inclined his head politely; then, turning again to Joanna, he said, "You are not, however, in any sense part of an official delegation?"

"No," said Joanna. "I came here by prior arrangement, in the company of Lady MacConnachie—that is, of Sìleas Barra MacNeill—on an *entirely* innocent visit to my sister, without the least inkling of what I should find when I arrived. Though I dare say," she added, somewhat against her better judgement, "that if Kergabet had had any idea, Gwendolen and I should never have been permitted to leave London."

"And yet, knowing this," Mr. Powell said indignantly, "you insisted upon staying here—"

"My sister will not leave Alba without her husband, and I have certainly no notion of leaving Alba without my sister," said Joanna.

"—and thought nothing of taking matters into your own hands, in a foreign city, hundreds of miles from London, essentially alone—"

"That will do, Einion." Courcy's voice was low, even, and impossible to be disobeyed, and Mr. Powell shut his mouth with an almost audible snap. Joanna's heart sank.

Lord de Courcy turned back to her. "Both you and your sister appear to be in the habit of taking foolish risks for the sake of those who have earned your loyalty," he said, "and I suspect that I have not yet seen the last of yours." One corner of his mouth quirked up minutely. "I do hope that your guardians will refrain from punishing you for it; the kingdom needs young people with your species of talent as much as it needs mages."

Joanna blinked at him, too gobsmacked even to flush at the unexpected compliment. "You . . . you do not intend to send us back to London? . . . sir?"

"Certainly not!" said Lord de Courcy. "On the contrary: I intend to take you—and your sister, if she can be persuaded—to see Donald MacNeill."

"Sir!" Mr. Powell protested, but weakly.

"And as soon as the thing can be managed. For the first time we are in possession of genuine evidence of wrongdoing, and as the matter now so nearly concerns the Princess Royal, Donald MacNeill would not thank us for keeping him in the dark."

## CHAPTER XXII

# In Which Joanna and Rory Draw an Unsettling Conclusion

*Even for the* envoy of King Henry of Britain, to arrange an audience with Donald MacNeill of Alba was not the work of a moment. The next several days, therefore, Joanna, Sophie, and Gwendolen spent quietly—or unquietly, as their several humours dictated—at home in Quarry Close, awaiting a summons from Lord de Courcy.

On the afternoon of the third day, and for at least the fifth time since Mór MacRury's unexpected visit, Joanna came out of the kitchen to find Sophie curled on the sofa with her arms about her drawn-up knees, staring sightlessly at a faint tea-stain upon the sitting-room carpet. Joanna put a hand on her shoulder; Sophie acknowledged neither the gesture nor, indeed, her sister's presence. Joanna set her teeth and counted to ten in Greek; then she said quietly, "Sophie, Donella MacHutcheon has left a ragout and an apple tart for our dinner."

Sophie deigned to acknowledge this, but only by turning away into the back of the sofa.

Joanna stared for a moment at the wings of Sophie's shoulder-blades, sharply visible through nightdress and dressing-gown as they had not been whilst she retained the habit of dressing for the day and the season.

"Sophie," she said, "I beg you will exert yourself! I do not blame you for worrying over Gray—I am very much worried myself—but you must see that you are not helping matters by— by—"

Sophie raised her head. To Joanna's dismay, her sister's dark eyes filled with tears, which overflowed unnoticed and ran in shining tracks down her face. "I cannot help it, Jo," she said softly. "I have tried—I am trying—but I cannot help it."

Joanna sank down on the sofa and drew her sister into her arms. Sophie's head sank onto her shoulder, but she did not return the embrace.

"Sophie," Joanna whispered. "Sophie, *please*." She was near to weeping herself, in terror and exasperation. "I cannot bear to see you wasting away. Promise me you will eat a little dinner, at the least!"

Sophie drew a great breath and sat up, extricating herself from Joanna's embrace. "I am not hungry," she said distantly. Her face was pale and damp, her eyes reddened, and she made no effort either to wipe the tears away or to conceal them by magick; Joanna, hiding her own alarm as best she could, got out her own handkerchief and gently blotted her sister's face.

"Please?" she said. "To oblige me?"

Sophie sighed. "To oblige you, Jo," she agreed.

She allowed herself to be led away to the dinner-table, and—to her credit, and Joanna's relief—made a visible effort to consume the delicately flavoured *ragoût de veau* which Donella MacHutcheon had concocted for the express purpose of tempting her palate. More than half of her portion still remained, however, when she laid down her fork and declared, in a voice wrung thin with exhaustion, that she could eat no more.

Joanna suppressed a sigh and forbore to comment.

Her conversation with Gwendolen after Sophie had gone upstairs to bed, however, was less restrained.

She had never doubted that Sophie and Gray loved one another—had herself, with Jenny, schemed and manoeuvred to force them into confessing their feelings—but that this was the truth of love, this desperate dependence, had not before occurred to her. Sophie, single-handed saviour of her king and kingdom, reduced to moping by day and sobbing into her pillow by night, by the absence of her husband: It did not bear thinking of.

"Is it this that young girls dream of and sigh over, truly?" she demanded at last. Gwendolen's eyebrows flew up at her savage tone. "If I was ever so foolish as to harbour such dreams myself, I shall certainly not do so again."

"It seems to me," said Gwendolen mildly, "that you may be drawing too strong a conclusion from too small a set of observations."

Joanna gave her a long, repressive stare, and they went up to bed in silence.

When Rory MacCrimmon called late in the following afternoon, on his way home from the University, with yet another stack of books, to ask after Sophie—who had not so much as left her room today, and had consumed nothing but half a bowl of oatmeal porridge and a cup of tea—Joanna could not help answering him candidly, that Sophie was very ill, and she herself at the end of her tether.

Rory MacCrimmon gave her a long, considering look and invited her to walk with him for half an hour.

"Walk with you, where?" Joanna said, suspicion for the moment overruling gratitude.

Rory MacCrimmon waved a careless hand. "Nowhere in particular," he said. "It appears to me that you should be the better for some fresh air, and perhaps when you have had your outing, I may escort your friend likewise, whilst you take your turn at dancing attendance upon your sister."

Gwendolen, somewhat to Joanna's surprise (though it was true that Gwendolen was no great respecter of proprieties), encouraged this plan, and so she found herself walking along Grove-street with her gloved hand tucked into Rory MacCrimmon's arm, and talking at great length of her anxiety over Sophie.

"Is your sister often subject to such despondency?" Rory Mac-Crimmon inquired. "Some people are, I know."

Joanna considered this question. "I . . . do not think so," she said slowly. "Of course I have seen her unhappy"—desperately unhappy, indeed, and with cause enough, the gods knew!—"and it is a very trying situation, but this is beyond everything. What alarms me most is that . . . I am not sure how best to explain . . . that she is concealing nothing from me."

"But surely you should not wish her to conceal—"

"You misunderstand me," said Joanna, clenching her free hand to keep her voice even. "Sophie, you see, practises concealment as naturally as breathing. But I am explaining myself very ill! I do not mean that she lies or misleads—indeed, she is tiresomely truthful!—I am speaking only of her magick. She has done nothing to conceal how wretched she is, from me or from anybody else; I must conclude, then, either that she does not care who sees it, or that she does wish to hide it, and cannot. If you knew Sophie as I do—"

"*Cannot?*" Rory MacCrimmon said sharply. "Do you mean that you believe her magick to be affected?"

"I am the last person to consult on such a question," said Joanna, rather bitterly. *If only Master Alcuin were here! Even Lady Maëlle would know better than I what to do.* "I have no more magickal talent than that lamppost, and I dare say you should do better to ask the oak-tree we passed in the little square a few moments ago."

"But you know your sister," he persisted.

"I knew my sister once," said Joanna. Ought she to tell this very new acquaintance what she was thinking about? But he was a mage, and thus likely to understand things magickal; and he was a friend of Gray's, and thus unlikely to be either a bounder or a fool. *And it is not as though I am spoilt for choice.*

"When we were children," she said at last, very quietly, "she threw stones at a pair of grown men, to try to stop them hurting our mother." That tale carried many a bitter memory, and she swallowed back a furious half sob. "For years she stole out of her bedroom at night, in the dark, to study in my father's library, because she was *only a girl* and he would not let her learn magickal theory, and when at last he caught her at it and set out to stop her, she smashed the drawing-room to flinders—well, she did not *mean* to do exactly that, of course—and ran away from home, and married Gray. It is not *like* Sophie to sit moping at home like—like a fair damosel in a minstrel-tale, when someone she loves may be in danger. I do not at all know what to make of it."

They walked on some way without speaking; glancing up, Joanna saw that her companion was frowning, apparently lost in thought.

"Joanna Callender," he said at last, "you were at your sister's wedding?"

"Of course," said Joanna, turning to frown at this *non sequitur*. "Why do you ask?"

"I collect," he said, "that it was rather a hasty affair?"

"Well . . . yes," she conceded. *How much does he know already?* "Very hasty, in fact. We— There were reasons to proceed without delay."

"I suppose it was not a Roman rite, then."

"Oh! No, it was terribly Roman," said Joanna, and was astonished when her companion abruptly stopped walking, dropped her arm, and seized both of her hands in an urgent grip. "Because . . . because if they were only handfasted, Lady Maëlle said, then—"

"Will you describe the rite for me?" Rory MacCrimmon interrupted urgently. "As exactly as you can?"

He tucked her left hand into the crook of his arm once more, and they resumed their interrupted trajectory.

Still frowning, she marshalled the details in her mind and told the tale as clearly as she could manage: the irritable and slightly furtive-looking priest of Tamesis, the declarations and the vows, the wedding-cord and the offerings . . .

"A cake of spelt?" he demanded. "They shared a cake of spelt?"

"Yes," said Joanna, baffled; "and then Sophie said, *Ubi tu Gaius, ego Gaia*, and Gray said the same—only the other way about, you know—and then the thunderstorm stopped."

Rory MacCrimmon looked down at her, his face very grim and a little pale beneath its dusting of freckles. "A marriage *confarreatio*," he said softly, as though to himself. "It would have to be that." And then, in almost a shout, "Brìghde's tears! What did that priest think he was playing at?"

As this outburst only increased Joanna's bewilderment, she had no answer to give, and they walked on for a little time without speaking; they were no longer walking leisurely and aimlessly, but going somewhere with all reasonable speed. Joanna wondered which of Sophie's guardsmen was following her now, and she made a mental note to apologise to him later for leading him such a merry chase to no purpose.

At last Rory MacCrimmon said, "Marriage *confarreatio* is a form of marriage that the gods make—the conqueror-gods, the gods of Rome—and only they can unmake it."

"Well . . . yes," Joanna conceded. "That was the general idea." Throwing caution to the winds, she added, "It was the most important idea, in fact—that Sophie should not be free to marry anyone else."

He gave her an odd look. "Perhaps," he said, "but—in old Rome it was only the patrician class who married in that way, and then *very carefully*, with due attention to lineages and talents, because if both parties to such a marriage are mages, the rite does not only bind *them* but also binds their magicks."

"Binds their magicks . . . to what?" Joanna said.

Rory MacCrimmon looked surprised. "Why, to one another," he said. "I—somewhere I have got a book which explains the matter properly—"

They stopped before a small, neat house in Drummond-street, and Rory MacCrimmon opened the front door—it was not locked—and ushered Joanna inside. He called a greeting in Gaelic to someone within, and a woman's voice answered him; but whoever it belonged to, Joanna was evidently not to discover, for Rory MacCrimmon waved her to a seat in a formal and evidently little used sitting-room and disappeared.

When at length he returned, he carried in his left hand a thick octavo codex, whose spine was faded to a watery pale blue.

"Here," he said, and handed it to Joanna. The leather binding which was so badly faded on the spine remained deep green on the front board, across which was stamped in gold the title *On the Laws of Matrimonium and Familia from the Days of the Caesars to Our Own*, and below it a name—*Charles Augustus Beauharnais, Mag.D.*—and a date which showed the book to be nearly a hundred years old.

Rory MacCrimmon opened the book to the place he had marked with what appeared to be a length of fingering wool and tapped a forefinger halfway down the recto folio, saying, "There."

The text, to Joanna's relief, was printed clearly in perfectly ordinary Latin, and thus was not difficult to decipher:

> *Marriage* confarreatio. See also coemptio, usus; *marriage* sine manu; *handfasting and lesser forms of marriage.*
>
> *Whereas the law of Rome originally dictated that only the offspring of marriage* confarreatio *could marry by this rite, no such requirement now exists, to the author's knowledge, in the territories of the former Empire, which nevertheless maintain a form of the rite* confarreatio. *In their original forms, the rite* confarreatio *and the rite* coemptio *were more sharply delineated than the rites known by these names today, the modern rite* confarreatio *having absorbed, for instance, the vow* "ubi tu Gaius, ego Gaia" *from the rite* coemptio, *and the rite* coemptio *the requirement of witnesses and offerings from the rite* confarreatio—

Rory MacCrimmon turned the page impatiently and ran a long forefinger down the following verso folio, then the succeeding recto.

"Aha!" he said, tapping his finger on a paragraph halfway down the latter. "Here we are."

Joanna bent her head again and read:

> *The chief distinction of the rite* confarreatio—*and, concomitantly, the reason for which it is now so seldom employed—is the strong legal link which it forges between husband and wife. In the time of the Empire as today, a marriage* confarreatio, *once consummated, could not*

*be dissolved by mutual agreement of the families party to the betrothal, but required in addition a countervailing rite of dissolution or divorcement, conducted by a priest of the same order (cf. Flamen Dialis). It is for this reason considered, in practical terms, a binding form of marriage (cf. marriage usus; marriage coemptio; handfasting).*

*Roman records suggest that one use of the rite confarreatio, in its original form, was the preservation of bloodlines possessed of strong or unusual magickal talents, to prevent their dilution, and its use for this purpose has continued, albeit sporadically, to the present day. There is a legend, hinted at in several sources but nowhere verifiably documented, that, perhaps in service of this purpose, the original rite confarreatio, when used to join two persons both possessing magickal talent, created a species of aetheric channel between the partners' sources of magick, along which ran thereafter a sympathetic link.*

*This link was said to permit the magick of each to magnify and replenish that of the other, so that the powers of both were increased by virtue of propinquity, and the risk of injury to either, by the overuse of magick, materially decreased. The same contemporary sources, however, also refer obliquely to a corollary effect, namely, the link's being attenuated by distance, such that the parties when separated ceased over time to feel its beneficial effects; and, if the separation were of too long continuance, might be materially weakened by its absence. One source (though it must be emphasised again, that its veracity cannot be relied upon) explicitly describes an instance in which a prolonged separation led to the death of both parties to a marriage confarreatio.*

Joanna looked up, shocked into silence. Rory MacCrimmon gazed earnestly into her eyes—his, she remarked in a sort of daze, were at present the clear green of willow-leaves—and said, "Do you see?"

"I . . . I think I do see," Joanna managed to say. "But you must remember that I have neither studied magickal theory nor ever so much as called light for myself. This Dr. Beauharnais appears to be positing that—to apply his conclusions to our own case—Sophie is ill, *truly* ill, only because Gray is missing. Do you—you do not think . . . ?"

Rory MacCrimmon looked momentarily nonplussed. "I should not ordinarily counsel you to believe everything you read in books, especially books whose authors concede that their sources are suspect. But, given the evidence of our own eyes: Yes. I fear that I do think so."

Joanna felt suddenly very cold.

"Sophie used too much of her magick once," she said, remembering, "when she was so furious with my father—that is what I meant, you know, when I spoke of her smashing the drawing-room—and Gray was angry with her, she told me, and said she must never do so again, because it was only good fortune that she had not died of it. Magick shock, you know; I have seen them both suffer it, because they *will* do idiotic things. Is this . . . might this be anything like?"

Rory MacCrimmon nodded soberly. "In respect of its effects," he said, "I should expect it to be very much like. But magick shock, as you must know, can be cured by rest and sleep and good food, while this . . ."

"This . . . what?" Joanna demanded.

"If I am right, then there is no cure for what ails your sister," he said, "except for someone to find her husband and bring him back to her."

"Well!" said Joanna, with a great deal more confidence than she felt; "if that is so, then that is what we must do."

She began, immediately upon her return to Quarry Close, by penning a brief, bald note to Lord de Courcy, outlining Sophie's symptoms, Rory MacCrimmon's premises, and their mutual conclusions.

By way of postscript, she added,

> *I have yet to discover any concrete evidence to tie Rory*
> *MacCrimmon to the vanished mages in general, or to my*

> brother-in-law's disappearance in particular, and am, on
> the whole, disposed to believe him guiltless. But as I am sure
> you will agree, my lord, an absence of evidence is not
> evidence of absence.

This she sent to him—together with Dr. Beauharnais's book, now marked at the relevant pages with strips of writing-paper—by way of Menez, catching him as he and Williams were turning over their duties to another pair of guardsmen and returning to their quarters at the Ambassador's residence.

"You must give it directly into his hand, or Mr. Powell's," she said, reverting to their shared mother tongue, the better to make her point.

Menez gave her a reproachful look and answered her in Gaelic.

Joanna's face warmed in embarrassment as she recollected, far too late, his incognito as an ordinary Alban labouring-man. She had no Gaelic to offer, beyond the few words she had contrived to learn from Donella MacHutcheon; but she could at any rate say *Please*, and did so. Menez tucked the parcel under his elbow, touched his cap to her, and trotted away.

## CHAPTER XXIII

# In Which Lord de Courcy Makes a Petition

*"Sophie Marshall!" Lucia* MacNeill, so elaborately attired for her role as heiress of Alba as to be almost unrecognisable, ran to Sophie with open arms. They embraced briefly; Lucia MacNeill stood back a little, her hands on Sophie's shoulders, and a frown of dismay gathered on her face as she studied Sophie's.

"I am only a little fatigued," Sophie tried to say.

She swayed a little on her feet, and could not even summon the energy to resent it; she was unutterably weary, oppressed with fear for Gray, and wanted nothing so much at present as to sit down quietly somewhere and weep.

"Sophie!" Joanna's voice, sharp with anxiety, cut through her lethargy like a stiff breeze sweeping away fog. "Sophie, come and sit down at once, before you do yourself an injury."

"I am perfectly well," Sophie tried to say, for she could not sit down when the King of Alba might at any moment descend upon her. In the end, however, she let herself be steered towards a chaise longue and sank down upon it gratefully enough.

When she opened her eyes, some unguessable time later, Joanna, Rory, Mr. Powell, and Lucia MacNeill were engaged in some low-voiced, energetic conversation, and there was still no sign of Lord de Courcy and Donald MacNeill.

"She would come with us," she heard Joanna say, in a sort of exasperated mutter. "I could not prevent her—because Courcy asked it—though anyone can see that she ought never to have left her bed."

"Hush, she will hear you!" This from Rory, with a furtive glance over his shoulder at Sophie. She attempted to glare at him and failed.

At a faint noise of footfalls in the corridor, the disputants fell silent; a moment later, the great doors banged open, and the King of Alba strode into the room, with Lord de Courcy dogging his heels.

Sophie struggled to her feet, one hand white-knuckled on the high arm of the chaise, and shoved herself upright in time to make her curtsey to Donald MacNeill. She managed it creditably enough, or so she was telling herself when a hot black wave of nausea struck her and she clutched at the furniture again.

At once Joanna was at her side, and Rory at the other, each curving one arm about her, at waist and shoulders, to keep her upright.

"Sit *down*," Joanna hissed. "Rory MacCrimmon, please—"

"Sophie, I do think you ought to rest," said Rory, in a gentling manner even more infuriating to Sophie than Joanna's peremptory tone. "You are not—"

With Herculean effort she stiffened her spine, willed strength into her shaking limbs, and shook off solicitous hands on either side, ignoring the resulting sotto voce expostulation. She managed the necessary three steps without assistance, though it cost her every last iota of strength and concentration, and seated herself with what dignity she could muster, her back as straight as she could make it against the back of the chaise and her trembling hands folded in her lap.

"I am well enough, I thank you," she said. "And we are not come here for the purpose of discussing my health."

There were dark spots dancing before her eyes, but they did not prevent her seeing the exchange of glances—furtive, frightened—between Joanna and Rory. She closed her eyes and drew a deep breath, fighting down nausea. People were speaking, but she could not parse their words.

*I could bear all of this, and more, if there were some purpose in it—but it is all so pointless and stupid, and Gray is gone, and what purpose is there in anything, if—*

There was a hand on her shoulder again. Not Gray's hand, which had so often rested there; it was too small and insufficiently warm. She opened her eyes again just as Joanna settled close beside her on the chaise longue and, raising her chin to speak to someone, said defiantly, "As we are speaking of the disappearance of *my sister's husband*, I cannot conceive of any reason why she ought not to be present."

This was surprising; had not Joanna been trying to persuade her to stop quietly at home, not an hour since?

"I have at least one excellent reason to offer." The voice was deep and gruff and entirely unfamiliar, and Sophie forced her head up and around to see who was speaking.

"And that is," Donald MacNeill continued, approaching the chaise longue the better to pin Sophie with his intent blue gaze, "that, if Your Royal Highness will forgive my blunt speaking, you have the look of one who has already made friends with death."

Sophie managed a glare, but even she knew it for a very poor one. Her head ached; in fact, there seemed no part of her body that did not ache. Her heart, perhaps, worst of all.

Donald MacNeill's face blurred and swam.

"Do not cry, Sophie," said Joanna, reverting to Brezhoneg as they both tended to do when in distress. She flung both arms about Sophie and drew Sophie's head down to rest upon her shoulder. "We shall find him, I promise you—only, do not cry, love, please. I cannot bear it."

Joanna sounded near to tears herself, and this was so unusual a circumstance as to jolt Sophie back to full awareness of her surroundings, if only for the moment. At once she wished herself anywhere but at the centre of the circle of faces—faces bearing expressions of worry, of impatience, of unsettled speculation, but every eye focused on her own—that hemmed her in. *Stop it,* she thought, desperately, *stop looking at me, go* away—

The magick welled up, thready and uncertain—a shade of its former self—but still too much, too quickly, to be so long sustained.

In Sophie's mind, Gray's voice said, *Have a care!*

But it was Joanna's voice, crying "Sophie!"—high and raw and sharp—that she heard last of all, before the darkness crowded in and swallowed the anxious faces one and all.

Joanna had never been nearer to fainting herself than at this moment, staring down at her sister's limp form and pallid face, at the blood smeared bright across her skin. Her own throat was raw—had she been shouting?—and her eyes felt huge and hot.

If only Gray were here, or Jenny, or Lady Maëlle! Any of them must have been better suited than herself to cope with this disaster.

*But they are none of them here,* she reminded herself sternly, drawing as deep and slow a breath as she could manage, *and you are. You wished to help Sophie, and now you must do what she requires of you.*

By the end of this bracing little speech, Joanna had—at least outwardly—regained her equilibrium.

The babble of voices all about her—questioning, exclaiming, recommending, deploring—faded gradually back into her awareness. She dismissed those which she could not understand, and sorted the rest according to their likely usefulness to Sophie.

"Mr. Powell," she said, pitching her voice to carry through the noise and proud of its relative lack of wobble. "Your assistance, if you please."

Mr. Powell, though startled to be so addressed, fairly leapt to attend upon her, and willingly provided both his handkerchief and his help in stretching Sophie out upon the chaise longue, her head pillowed in Joanna's lap and one knee slightly bent to prevent her rolling forwards onto the polished stone floor.

From Lucia MacNeill she demanded a basin of warm water, a towel, and a bottle of smelling-salts, if such a thing were to be had; and from Rory MacCrimmon, advice on how best to treat a severe case of magick shock, for she had never done so without instruction from some more knowledgeable party and did not wish to forget some critical point.

By his greenish face and wide eyes, Rory MacCrimmon was operating more from theoretical than from practical knowledge, and at first he produced a torrent of stammering Gaelic which was of no use whatever.

"In Latin, please!" said Joanna sharply; he shut his mouth abruptly, swallowed, and began again with more confidence.

The result was a flurry of orders from Lucia MacNeill to her father's major-domo, which brought servants bearing blankets, a pot of tea, hot toddy, and trays of cheese and bread and fruit, as well as the smelling-salts and wash-water—all of which confirmed Joanna's somewhat hazy recollection that the treatment for magick shock was very like that which healers recommended for persons suffering from loss of blood, or from a sudden shock of surprise or grief.

Joanna supervised the arranging of blankets and sponged the blood from her sister's face, murmuring prayers and pleas and imprecations under her breath. Sophie had lain insensible, now, far longer than on that previous, deeply alarming occasion when she had tumbled off her horse on the road to Douarnenez—longer, surely, than could be at all good for her—and smelling-salts and every other ministration seemed altogether unavailing.

Every eye was on them both, now, and Joanna no longer wondered at Sophie's often wishing to disappear, for at present she heartily wished the same herself.

"What can she have been attempting, to bring this on?"

Lucia MacNeill's sotto voce question had perhaps not been meant for Joanna's ears, but Joanna answered it nevertheless: "You were all of you staring at her, as though she had been a pickled specimen laid out for dissection. No doubt she was attempting to turn your attention elsewhere." She had seen that cornered-fox expression of Sophie's more than once, and it generally preceded some daunting feat of magickal misdirection, invisible to ordinary eyes. "It is a sort of instinct with her. She—"

Joanna broke off abruptly as Sophie's hand stirred under hers. "Sophie!" she said.

Sophie's one visible eyelid lifted minutely. *"Pelec'h emaon?"* she whispered hoarsely.

"You are in Donald MacNeill's castle in Din Edin," Joanna replied, also in Brezhoneg. "You remember, Sophie; we are here to speak with Lord de Courcy and Donald MacNeill about finding Gray. Do you feel well enough to sit up?"

"I . . . yes," said Sophie, but her tone was justifiably dubious.

Joanna glared at the others until they retreated.

"Come, then," she said encouragingly.

It was a long business, complicated by the tangle of blankets and by Sophie's small huffs of pain, but at last Sophie was sufficiently upright and in command of herself to sip at the cup Joanna held up for her, and eventually to eat a little bread and cheese.

"I cannot think what is the matter with me," she said some time later, pressing a slim hand to her temple. Her colour, Joanna noted, was still very bad, though her face was not quite so much the colour of a green cheese as it had been, and she moved carefully, as though every small motion hurt her.

"Rory MacCrimmon has a theory," Joanna offered, cautiously. She did not think Sophie in any fit state for this conversation, but as, on the other hand, there did not seem any great likelihood of improvement in the immediate future, it was perhaps best to have the thing over.

"Have you, Rory?" Sophie looked up at her friend. Joanna was watching him, and saw his eyes widen at whatever he saw in Sophie's face.

"Yes," he said.


"And all of you agree that this is possible," said Sophie, staring around at them.

They looked back at her with solemn eyes—Lucia MacNeill and her father, Lord de Courcy and his secretary, Joanna and Rory, all seated in a sort of haphazard arc before her—and try as she might, she could detect no sign of prevarication in any of them.

"It is of course impossible to be sure," said the Ambassador's secretary (Mr. Powell, that was his name), "without extensive empirical testing, which is equally impossible. But it does seem to me not only *possible*, but much the most likely explanation; the one, that is, which most parsimoniously accounts for all of the facts."

Sophie looked from Mr. Powell to Rory and found him nodding earnest agreement.

"I have never heard of such a thing," she protested, though even she could hear the weak, capitulating tone of her voice.

"Nevertheless," said Lord de Courcy, "and whether or not this theory is in fact correct, surely our best course of action is to proceed as though it were. The costs of ignoring the possibility are simply too high."

Sophie frowned, attempting to parse this—it seemed to her—unnecessarily cryptic declaration. If only her head were not so woolly! It was preposterous, was it not, to suggest that Gray's mere absence should be making her ill? The strain of not knowing where he was, or why, or what might be happening to him, certainly—the terrifying knowledge that his last letter had been written under duress—but—

"But," she demanded breathlessly, as the corollary at last came clear, "but what about Gray?"

"The magick runs both ways, Sophie," said Rory gently.

"Then—then we must *do* something." Sophie's grip on Joanna's hands tightened involuntarily; at Joanna's muffled squeak, she forced her fingers to relax, but the tension stringing her tight was not eased in the least. "There must be something, some better way to seek him—"

"That was, in fact, our purpose in coming here, Your—Madame Marshall," said Lord de Courcy mildly. "As you may remember."

Sophie flushed.

Courcy turned to Donald MacNeill. "I have no jurisdiction here, my lord," he said, "except insofar as this matter concerns subjects of my King, and I should not wish to appear to be overstepping my authority. I should however be remiss in my duty as liaison between my kingdom and your own, did I not offer you this counsel. You, I trust, will not take it amiss."

He paused; every eye in the room was upon him now. Donald MacNeill cocked a sardonic eyebrow.

"His Majesty, Henry of Britain," said Lord de Courcy, "is in all things temperate, moderate, and deliberate; he is slow to anger and pragmatic in his choice of adversaries. There is, however, one exception to this general rule, which is that whosoever threatens harm to his children, and his daughter most particularly, may expect swift retribution."

Sophie blinked in astonishment, and no little alarm; unless she much mistook, her father's ambassador had come very near to issuing a direct threat to the King of Alba.

"My lord Ambassador," she said, "I beg you will not—"

"As I hope I have made clear," said Donald MacNeill, narrowing his eyes at Lord de Courcy, "any assistance which we may reasonably offer in this matter, you may be sure of receiving."

"And we do thank you, my lord," said the Ambassador, with a little bow.

"What assistance?" said Sophie.

"I beg your pardon, ma'am?" said Donald MacNeill.

Joanna narrowed her eyes; Sophie's voice might be low and husky with exhaustion, but her query had been perfectly clear.

"What assistance," Sophie repeated, a little more loudly, "had you intended to offer us, sir?"

Mr. Powell looked appalled.

"Mrs. Marshall," he said, in a tone of gentle remonstrance which made Joanna long to bite him, "may I suggest—"

But Donald MacNeill held up a hand, and Powell fell silent.

Donald MacNeill paced slowly across the distance that separated Lord de Courcy from Sophie and stopped once more before the chaise longue.

"This affair concerns me as closely—that is, very nearly as closely as yourself, Sophia of Britain," he said quietly. "The University in Din Edin operates under my personal patronage as well as by the charter of the clan which holds the chieftain's seat of Alba; any harm perpetrated within my borders upon such visitors as these is a direct threat to the continued flourishing of that ancient institution, which exists for the advancement of knowledge and to welcome all those who seek it, no matter their origins—and thus an offence to Alba and to myself. It is a matter of great personal regret to me, and no little frustration, that our investigations thus far should have discovered nothing of substance which might lead us to an explanation of the facts."

He had by now seated himself beside Sophie on the chaise, perhaps tiring of the painful-looking curve of her neck as she looked up at him.

"What we now possess, thanks to you and your friends," he went on, "and had not before, is direct evidence of foul play. Whether or not, as Lord de Courcy has posited, these several disappearances are all the work of the same person or persons unknown, the similarity of the persons concerned, and of the circumstances of their vanishing, would seem to preclude mere coincidence."

"Indeed," said Sophie, a little stiffly.

"My serjeant-at-arms will be fully briefed by Lord de Courcy and his assistant," Donald MacNeill continued, glancing up at them with an expression which Joanna could not read, "as they appear to have collected considerable intelligence on this matter. All of which I presume they are very ready to share, for everyone's benefit."

Lord de Courcy bowed, and Donald MacNeill nodded in satisfaction.

Just as he turned away, Joanna caught Courcy's face in a just perceptible smirk of satisfaction; he had got exactly what he wanted out of this meeting, then.

*Good.*

★　★　★

Joanna was enormously relieved that neither Courcy nor Donald MacNeill seemed inclined to waste time in organising their search for Gray and the other vanished mages, and had circumstances been otherwise, she must herself have leapt in to help in whatever capacity might be permitted her. But this was not London, where she could expect to be indulged, and Sophie's need for her was plainly much the greater.

She kept her seat on the chaise longue with Sophie, therefore, whilst Donald MacNeill summoned his serjeant-at-arms—a stocky, grey-headed man of serious mien and very few words, by the name of Ciaran Barra MacNeill—and the latter departed with Lord de Courcy and Mr. Powell; whilst Rory MacCrimmon and Lucia Mac-Neill conferred in low, worried voices; whilst the latter took her father aside for a whispered conference, which resulted in the arrival of yet another pair of servants bearing tea and scones and half a dozen varieties of preserves.

The refreshments were plentiful and smelled delicious, and Joanna was not a woman to turn down the offer of an excellent meal. But she had a great deal of difficulty in enjoying this one, and her companions likewise; the sight of Sophie picking at her share with trembling fingers, struggling to swallow a morsel of buttery scone spread with an exquisitely balanced greengage jam as though it had been a mouthful of gravel, thought Joanna, might have put even Gwendolen off her feed.

At last Joanna had had enough. "I am grateful for your hospitality, sir, ma'am," she said, addressing Donald MacNeill and his daughter in turn, "and extremely grateful for the promise of assistance in finding my brother-in-law, but my sister is very ill, and I must take her home."

There was a chorus of protest and apology. Lucia MacNeill earnestly pressed them both to consider themselves her guests, and had she been speaking only to Sophie, she might have succeeded—though it was plain from Sophie's stiff shoulders and frozen half smile that she had no liking for the scheme. Joanna's temperament was woven from less pliable and more abrasive fibres than her sister's, however, and she met each new overture with a perfectly civil but implacable refusal. Though not blind to the obvious advantages of such an arrangement, she could not feel that they outweighed the loss of privacy and independence which must inevitably result.

"We are immensely grateful," she repeated at last, in what she hoped was a tone of finality, "and honoured by your invitation, but it is impossible for me to accept it." She gently extricated herself from Sophie, who curled away into the curved back of the chaise like a wet kitten seeking the warmth of its mother's fur, and rose to her feet. "Lucia MacNeill," she said, more quietly, "a word in your ear?"

From the corner of her eye she saw Rory MacCrimmon move, as though casually, towards the chaise longue and perch on the end of it—within reach of Sophie, though he made no move to touch her. She turned away, satisfied that an eye should be kept, to address Roland's betrothed, whose air of polite inquiry, it seemed to Joanna, hid a deeper curiosity.

"I hope I have not offended you or your father," she said.

Lucia MacNeill raised her elegantly arched eyebrows, at once rendering Joanna acutely self-conscious of her own straighter, heavier ones. "Not at all," she said neutrally.

"I am glad of it," said Joanna, "for I should not have changed my mind even if I had."

She opened her reticule—Gwendolen's, in fact, for her own was too small for today's purposes—and from it extracted a letter, sealed and tied up with bright blue cord. "I am charged by Prince Roland to give this into your hand," she said, and did so—trying to forget how Roland had looked, the stiff words and determinedly neutral countenance.

Lucia MacNeill said softly, "Oh."

"Sophie," Joanna said, after a moment, "is not at her best with strangers. And crowds of people. And . . . and pomp and circumstance." She gestured vaguely at their surroundings. "We were neither of us brought up to all of this, and Sophie finds it . . . difficult."

Lucia MacNeill accepted this with a provisional nod. "You must not suppose that I attend lectures at the University dressed as I am now," she said. "I have not Sophie's gift of hiding in plain sight, but it does not follow that I cannot understand the impulse to be known for myself, and not for my rank and title."

This was something, to be sure, but was it enough? Joanna saw in her mind's eye Sophie's shy, eager, face-transforming smile; saw her slender hands curved over the keys of Mama's pianoforte, coaxing from them some melody to whose tones Joanna might be quite deaf, but whose magick soothed her dark or fretful humours; and, reaching still farther back in memory, saw her dark eyes gleaming with delight as she crouched at the edge of a pond, watching a grey heron stalk through the shallows.

"You may well be correct in supposing that Sophie should be safer here," she said at last, "but it would make her miserable, and she is miserable enough already."

"If Sophie will indeed be happier at home," said Lucia MacNeill, casting a worried sidewise glance at her, "then I shall certainly not press her to remain here."

"I thank you, ma'am," said Joanna. She dropped a respectful curtsey as a means of concealing the relief that must otherwise show on her face, already preparing to turn away from this conversation and back to Sophie. *When Kergabet charged me to befriend Roland's betrothed, I do not suppose this was what he meant.*

"I wish you would not call me *ma'am*," said Lucia MacNeill; Joanna looked up sharply at her suddenly less formal (not to say irritable) tone. "It makes me feel like the dowager duchess of somewhere-or-other."

Joanna regarded her consideringly, attempting to picture Roland at her side. It was a pity, she thought, that Roland was not taller, though of course he might not yet have reached his full growth. But at any rate he should not find his bride insipid and dull. And at least she was not actually *taller* than himself.

"You do not look it," Joanna said, and turned away.


"I have been thinking," said Rory MacCrimmon, without preamble, the moment Joanna opened the front door.

She stood back to admit him into the house, and he strode forward determinedly, shucking off gloves and overcoat.

Joanna watched him in some bemusement. "May I ask," she said at last, "what it is that you have been thinking?"

Rory MacCrimmon turned on one heel and regarded her with wide eyes and raised eyebrows, as though the question baffled him. "A relay," he said. "What we need is a relay."

"A relay of . . . what, exactly?"

He strode towards her, looming rather, and gripped her shoulders; she controlled an instinctive yelp.

"Jo?" Gwendolen called softly from the top of the stairs. "Is all well?"

"Of finding-spells, of course," said Rory MacCrimmon. "What else should we want, when we have lost someone, but to find him?"

"Ye-es," said Joanna, doubtfully. She had not the least idea what a relay of finding-spells might look like when it was at home; still, if anyone might be supposed to understand such things, a lecturer in practical magick was surely the man. "But you have tried such spells already, have you not? And Sophie and Mór MacRury also—"

"Ah! But a *relay*—"

"A relay, yes. What is that? And what should we need, then, for a *relay of finding-spells*?"

Rory MacCrimmon was pacing about the Marshalls' tiny sitting-room now, scrubbing one hand through his fire-bright curls in a manner so strongly reminiscent of Gray when deep in thought that Joanna was very grateful for Sophie's being laid down upon her bed upstairs, and not here to see it. He stopped abruptly, looked at Joanna, and produced a startling grin. "Mages," he said. "A great many mages."

"Ah," said Joanna, feeling no wiser than before.

He was putting his overcoat on again, and his gloves—why had he put them off, then?—and sweeping out of the room. "I shall be back directly," he called over his shoulder, just before the front door slammed behind him.

*Mages.* Joanna rolled her eyes, shot the bolt on the door, and started up the stairs to look in on Sophie.

She found Gwendolen placidly reading Cymric poetry, and Sophie sleeping—by the kindness of Morpheus, sleeping peacefully, the tight unhappy lines of her face relaxed in slumber. Joanna kissed her softly, brushing the dark hair back from her pale brow; exchanged a weary smile with Gwendolen; and when the latter had gone downstairs, leaving her in sole possession, circled the small bedchamber, subsuming her anxiety in the useless tidying away of Sophie's things.

A storm of knocking at the front door startled Sophie into wakefulness; she sat up straight, and for a moment hope dawned in her eyes—the more painful for the almost immediate clouding over of her face. "No," she said dully, "it cannot be Gray, for I should have felt it."

Joanna wished very much to know what this might mean; but she wished even more to discover who was knocking so importunately below, and the one question would keep, whilst the other must be investigated at once. She nudged the window-curtain aside to peer down into the street. Could this be Rory MacCrimmon and his *great many mages*, back again already?

Rory MacCrimmon it was, though he had brought with him only four people that Joanna could see; did that suit the definition of *many*?

"Sophie," she said, "Rory MacCrimmon has come to see us, and has brought some friends of his—I see Mór MacRury, and some others whom I do not know. Should you like to see them? Or had you rather not?"

She turned from the window to look at Sophie, who grimaced at her and said, "I had very much rather not."

Joanna suppressed the exasperated sigh that rose to her lips and said carefully, "I shall go and let them in, then, and tell Rory that you are resting."

Sophie produced something that she presumably meant for a smile—though if that were so, it was a miserable failure. "I thank you, Jo," she said. Her eyes drifted closed, then opened again. "Jo, I am sorry. But—" She paused, her pale lips twisting in frustration, and at last went on, low, "It is not only a lack of will, Jo, I promise you. Truly I am doing my best."

Joanna did not trust herself to make any reply to this. Instead she kissed Sophie, gently gripped her shoulder for a moment, and drew the door closed behind her with a gentle *snick* of the latch as she passed out of the room.

Sophie's sitting-room was full of mages—Rory MacCrimmon, Mór MacRury, and, as it transpired, three more young men and two more women, one of an age with the men, the other at least two decades older—as well as Sorcha MacAngus, whom Joanna had met briefly at Mór MacRury's lodgings, and who seemed to have come along to provide moral support, or perhaps simply to watch the mages at work. They had brought with them a long cylindrical leather case which had proved to contain maps—of Alba and of various regions thereof, and of the cities of Din Edin, Glaschu, and Obar Dheathain—and were arguing over them in a disorienting mix of languages.

Joanna escaped into the kitchen to cajole Donella MacHutcheon (assuming that she had not already gone home for the day) to produce tea for all of them; there she found not only Donella MacHutcheon but also Gwendolen, wrapped in a vast, floury apron and apparently learning the art of shortbread cakes.

"Tea, *ma 'se ur toil e*?" said Joanna, producing a winning smile and one of her few Gaelic phrases: *if you please?* "For ten?"

Donella MacHutcheon clucked disapprovingly but set about making tea nevertheless.

"What sort of party is it you are holding in the sitting-room, Jo?" Gwendolen inquired. "Must they make so much noise, when your sister is ill?"

"It is not my party; it is Rory MacCrimmon's," said Joanna. "University mages—seven of them—who seem to think that they can do something to find Gray by working together somehow. But being scholar-mages, they must first debate what, exactly, they ought to do; hence the noise."

She collected a wedge of Gwen's shortbread for herself—coping with Sophie's tears and apologies always made her feel both wrung out and ravenously hungry—and began arranging the rest on a plate.

When she reemerged from the kitchen with the tea-tray, the mages had colonised the dining-room table. Mór MacRury was arguing with a beetle-browed young man who appeared to have dressed himself in a tearing hurry, and possibly in the dark; Sorcha Mac-Angus perched calmly on Sophie's piano-stool, watching in silence, a pair of bone knitting-needles flashing in her fingers.

Joanna, feeling as though she had wandered into some other world which no longer made sense, deposited the tea-tray on the sideboard and retreated to join Sorcha MacAngus in the corner of the sitting-room occupied by the pianoforte.

"What are they doing?" she asked, sotto voce. "Are they about to come to blows, do you think?"

Sorcha MacAngus smiled indulgently. The quiet clicking of her knitting-needles continued uninterrupted, gradually producing what appeared to be a shawl and reminding Joanna irresistibly of Sophie in happier times: playing contredanses upon the pianoforte, her slender fingers never faltering in their rhythm, for an hour or more together; stitching away endlessly at some piece of fancy-work, unnoticed in a corner with her ears pricked.

"Mór is explaining to Teàrlach MacDougall that his suggestion is idiotic," said Sorcha MacAngus, speaking in Latin as Joanna had done, "and he is explaining in return that hers will never work with so few mages to drive it." She paused, tilting her head thoughtfully. "I wonder which of them is correct?"

"You are not talented yourself, I collect?" said Joanna.

"Not to speak of, no," said Sorcha MacAngus. "I can call a little light, or a little spark to light the fire, but no more than that. And you, Joanna Callender? Your sister is a very great mage, I am told, when she is well, but perhaps that does not run in the family?"

"The tale is more complicated than that," said Joanna, a little stiffly. "But in any case, I have not even as much talent as yourself, and I confess that to hear so many persons whom I do not know, arguing so vehemently in a language I do not speak, about matters I do not understand, makes me rather anxious. I trust that they are not preparing to explode my sister's sitting-room?"

Sorcha MacAngus laughed quietly. "No," she said; "you may be easy on that score. If there are any explosions, I expect, they will be of Mór MacRury's temper."

Joanna, who had witnessed more than one quite literal explosion as a result of Sophie's losing her temper, was not in the least reassured.

The construction of a spell relay, from Joanna's point of view, proved to consist largely of sitting in a circle with eyes closed and fingers touching, muttering incomprehensibly turn and turn-about. Gradually, as her ear grew attuned to the sequence of sounds and of voices, it became clear to her that the muttering was a continual repetition of the same few phrases: a spell, then, seven mages endlessly repeating the same brief spell.

On the table, cleared of its habitual stacks of books, someone had spread out the large map of Alba, weighting its four corners and its in-curling edges with a miscellany of small objects: a silver candlestick, a smooth reddish stone, an empty ink-pot, a fish-slice, a pounce-box, a small and battered codex. On the map's representation of Din Edin reposed what appeared to be an ordinary pebble, wound about with scarlet thread to secure to it a draggled and much-mended pen.

"What is that?" she asked Sorcha MacAngus, who might have seen one of the others put it there.

"A pen, to all appearances," said Sorcha MacAngus; "one belonging to your brother-in-law, I must suppose. The pebble I believe is only a counterweight."

Joanna nodded absently and returned her attention to the circle of muttering mages—which appeared to her admittedly uneducated eye to be accomplishing precisely nothing.

"Have you seen this sort of spell before?" she said at last. "What ought we to expect to happen?"

"I believe," her companion said slowly, taking up her knitting-needles again, "and I must stress that this is very much outside my sphere, that the pen is used to represent your brother-in-law, and that, supposing that the spell functions as it is meant to do, and that he is somewhere within their collective range, it ought to show his location by moving there."

Joanna frowned. "That is . . . that is a spelled map, then?" she said. Did such a thing exist, a map which somehow *recognised* the territories represented on its surface?

Sorcha MacAngus shrugged. "I suppose it must be," she said. Her tone suggested that the matter was of no great import.

"The feather has not moved at all," Joanna pointed out.

As though in reply—though Joanna had spoken very quietly, and was scarcely even in the same room with the others—Rory Mac-Crimmon opened his eyes, studied the unmoving feather, and said, "On my count."

Six other pairs of eyes snapped open; Rory MacCrimmon counted slowly, *one—two—three—four*, and seven pairs of hands disengaged from one another. Rory tilted his head as though listening, and after a moment said, "Mór?"

"The relay is holding," she said, sounding pleased.

A collective sigh of relief, and seven mages lunged for the tea-tray on the sideboard.

Joanna waited patiently until the first assault upon the plate of shortbread had abated; then she left her seat by Sorcha MacAngus, approached Rory MacCrimmon, who seemed the least likely to mock her ignorance, and said, "Will you explain to me what your spell does?"

He had just opened his mouth to reply when a commotion from the far side of the sitting-room caused Joanna to bolt for the staircase. Halfway up, Sophie was clinging to the bannister-rail; Joanna sprang forward to intercept her, her mind at once beginning to spin out unhelpful images of Sophie tumbling down the staircase to her death.

"Sophie, you ought not to be wandering about alone," she said reproachfully.

The effect of Sophie's glare was undermined by her inability to stand upright without swaying and clutching the stair-rail. "Someone is working magick in my house," she said. "I have been feeling it this past half-hour."

Joanna slipped her arm about Sophie's waist (slimmer than before—too much so) and drew Sophie's arm about her own shoulders, where it trembled perceptibly. "And I shall tell you all about it," she said, "when we have got you back to your room." How in Hades had Sophie managed the ladder?

Her attempt to steer Sophie back to bed, however, met with unexpectedly effective resistance; Sophie clutched the stair-rail as if she meant never to let it go, and held herself rigid against Joanna's gentle pressure to turn back the way she had come.

Thwarted, Joanna changed her tactics. "You are in your nightdress, Sophie," she pointed out, "and your dining-room is full of strange men."

"And of my friends, by your account," said Sophie.

"Yes," said Joanna, "whom an hour ago you flat refused to see."

Sophie tossed her head, then grimaced as though regretting it—but still refused to be turned back.

Further arguments proving equally futile, Joanna at last conceded defeat and turned her efforts to helping her sister negotiate the staircase without incurring serious injury. When finally they reached the foot of the stairs—both pink with exertion, and breathing hard—she steered Sophie to a chair near the fire, wrapped a shawl about her, and darted into the dining-room, where an entirely different dispute was now in progress, which—being conducted entirely in Gaelic—Joanna could not at all comprehend.

Rory being now entirely absorbed in this debate, Joanna sought out Mór MacRury (who had retreated to her own former seat near Sorcha MacAngus) and bent to murmur in her ear, "I beg you will come with me to the sitting-room and explain things to Sophie."

Mór MacRury looked up at her, startled, but at once rose from her seat to follow.

Sophie was sitting up determinedly in her chair, her spine as straight as she could manage, when Joanna returned with Mór in tow.

"Sophie," said the latter uncertainly, "ought you not to be—"

"What magick are you working?" Sophie demanded, before that supremely irritating sentence could be finished. She was pleased to find that her voice shook only a little.

"A finding," said Mór at once. "Or rather, a circular series of findings—a relay. Spells of protection and concealment are often worked in this way, though I have never seen it done with a finding-spell. It was Rory's notion, to increase the range, and to maintain the spell so that if . . . if there is any change, we shall know at once."

Sophie studied her carefully. She looked tired and harassed, but there was nothing in her expression to suggest any intent to deceive. "How? How shall we know?" Sophie said.

Mór sighed. "That is what they are attempting to decide at present," she said. "The spell is Alasdair Cameron's mapped finding—do you know it?"

Sophie made to shake her head, preemptively regretted it, and instead said, "No."

Mór looked briefly disapproving, and Sophie wondered guiltily whether Cameron's mapped finding had been described in some lecture which she had failed to attend.

"The finding is in two parts," said Mór. "First, the map, which is spelled to link its symbols to the landmarks they represent—only very approximately, you understand; and, second, the focal object, which stands in for the person or thing sought. When the magick spirals back—just as it does in an ordinary finding—it points the way by situating the object on the map, rather than the person, or thing, in the world."

"So, then," said Joanna, "if the feather and the pebble . . . go somewhere, we shall know that Gray is there? If that is so, why has it not told us that already?"

"That is not a question which I or anyone here is capable of answering," said Mór carefully. "He may at present be beyond even our collective range, or the finding may be impeded by strong wards, or shields, or other protective spells, or perhaps—though it is not very likely, unless he should be imprisoned in a literal prison—by an interdiction."

Sophie shuddered. "I hope it may not be that," she said; and, gathering her wits again, continued, "Our hope, then, is that at some point whichever of these conditions presently obtains shall cease to do so? And the feather and the pebble, as Joanna says, shall show us where that lapse in vigilance has occurred?"

"Exactly," said Mór, with a pleased nod.

"But," Joanna objected, "that would mean that we must watch it day and night."

Mór gestured expansively in the direction of the dining-room. "Hence the dispute," she said.

"I will watch it," said Sophie. "I shall watch as long as I must."

## CHAPTER XXIV

# In Which Sophie
# Receives an Illustrious Caller

A *peremptory knock* startled Sophie from her restless doze, curled in Gray's armchair by the sitting-room fire; she opened her eyes just in time to see the swirl of Mór MacRury's skirts disappearing into the hall. Guilt stabbed her; she had been watching the map, watching the spell for some sign, and what had she done but doze off, so that Mór must keep vigil in her stead!

She was struggling to sit up when she heard the door open.

An astonished "Oh!" was all the warning afforded to her before Mór reappeared in the sitting-room, accompanied by, of all people, Lucia MacNeill.

The heiress of Alba was dressed simply and soberly, as though she had just come from attending a lecture, and her bright hair was tucked up under a soft grey capote. With grave, measuring eyes she watched Sophie's valiant attempt to rise and greet her, and when its futility became apparent, she crossed the small room to seat herself in the other armchair. She leant forward and propped her elbows on her knees. "Sophie," she said, and seemed not to know how to go on.

Sophie could at least command herself sufficiently to look her friend in the eye. "Lucia," she said. It was oddly disorienting to see her here: for all their camaraderie, Lucia MacNeill had never before crossed the threshold of Sophie's house.

Fortune smiled upon her in the form of Mór MacRury, who had vanished into the kitchen and now returned bearing the Marshalls' unprepossessing welcome-cup. She offered it wordlessly to Sophie, who prayed to Brighid and Aesculapius to steady her hands and spoke the ritual words she had learnt at her mother's knee: "My welcome to this house, Lucia MacNeill."

Lucia took the cup from her and replied gravely, "My thanks for this welcome, Sophie Marshall, and the peace of your gods and mine be on you and on all who belong to you."

Like Joanna, she had altered the traditional words of the ritual to include the absent Gray, and Sophie summoned a smile to show her gratitude.

The welcome having been drunk, Lucia seized the opportunity of Mór's taking the cup away again to clasp Sophie's hands in hers and, leaning close, to whisper, "I cannot stay so long as I should like; my father and I . . . do not see eye to eye in this matter, and I hope to return before my absence is marked. Sophie, will you trust me?"

"I—" Sophie began.

Mór came quietly in again, however, and Lucia retreated into platitudes; whatever she had intended to say, was plainly not for Mór's ears.

"Mór," Sophie said, seizing the chance of a momentary pause in the conversation, as soon as she had invented what seemed a plausible excuse, "may I ask a great favour of you? I should so much like to see the latest edition of the *Transactions*; one of our Oxford friends has got a paper in it, and he promised to send a copy to me himself, but it appears he has forgot it . . ."

It was an absurd errand to demand of Mór, in the circumstances, but Sophie was counting on Mór's relief at the slightest sign of any ordinary interest in food, conversation, or intellectual engagement to overcome her natural suspicion.

She was not disappointed. Almost before Sophie had reached the end of her artfully unfinished request, Mór was on her feet. "I shall go to Eochaid Balfour's at once," she said.

The front door had scarcely shut behind her than Lucia MacNeill was crouching before Sophie's chair, clasping her hands and gazing earnestly up into her face. "Will you trust me?" she said again. "Please, say you will trust me in this."

In her father's audience chambers, Lucia MacNeill had been cool and regal, where now she most resembled an anxious, exhilarated child, but her eyes were the same as ever, summer sky encircling pools of midnight—the eyes of the young woman she had met in the Central Refectory and argued with over summoning-spells and the nature of younger brothers—at once daring and begging Sophie's trust.

Sophie turned her palms up and returned the hand-clasp. "Yes," she said.


Lucia MacNeill had drawn the window-curtains against the incipient rain and vanished into the kitchen, whence she presently emerged carrying a basin on which was balanced a tray holding a lit candle-stub and a small stack of folded linen towels. She deposited basin and tray on the floor by Sophie's chair, knelt at Sophie's feet, and spread one of the towels over her knees.

"There is a spell," she said, "a spell of my clan, for sharing one's magick with another. Every mage of Clan MacNeill learns it upon coming of age. I believe I may be the first to use it since my great-grandfather's time." She paused. "That is, if you should consent to it."

She extracted from her elegant little reticule (embroidered all over with tiny scarlet lions rampant) a small object which, on closer examination, Sophie discovered to be a tiny knife in a similarly elegant sheath of gilded leather, stitched with more lions rampant. Its haft was of smoothly polished bone, stained a deep red-brown—the colour, Sophie remarked absently, of Catriona MacCrimmon's hair—and its blade, when Lucia MacNeill drew it out of the sheath, gleamed silver.

Intricate, swirling patterns—no, *letters*—were incised along the flat surfaces of the blade. Sophie reached a tentative finger towards it. "What does it say?"

"*Nuair a thig air duine thig air uile,*" said Lucia MacNeill, and repeated the phrase in Latin: "What befalls one, befalls all. It is a reminder of my responsibilities as heir to the chieftain's seat."

She passed the blade through the candle-flame, once, again.

"*Nuair a thig air duine thig air uile,*" Sophie repeated. The words felt heavy in her mouth. "Lucia, why?"

Lucia MacNeill paused, knife in hand, and raised her blue eyes to Sophie's. "Because you have stood my friend," she said. "Because you are Roland's sister, and will be mine. Because if I loved any man or woman as you love your husband, I should stop at nothing to keep them from harm."

She took Sophie's left hand in hers, turned it palm up, and examined each of her fingers in turn. At last she seemed to decide on one of them—the third finger, on which Sophie wore the slender gold band, chased with laurel-leaves, that had been her betrothal-gift from Gray—and again looked earnestly into Sophie's eyes. "May I?"

"Yes," said Sophie, before she thought; and then, "what . . . ?"

By way of reply, Lucia let go Sophie's hand, picked up the knife, and opened a minuscule slice in the pad of her own left thumb.

Sophie swallowed hard and nodded; Lucia MacNeill took her hand again—more firmly now, though her grip was not so tight as to be painful—and raised the blade. The thin film of bright blood that coated the pad of her thumb smeared across Sophie's palm. The bite of the blade was swift and painless; blood welled, scarlet as the lions rampant, and she watched in fascination.

Lucia dropped the knife into her lap, where their mingled blood stained the white linen, and released Sophie's hand—only to press her bleeding thumb to Sophie's bleeding fingertip.

She began to sing her spell—it was certainly sung and not spoken, though more drone than melody—and Sophie tried to follow it but could catch no more than one word in ten. As it was such an old spell, perhaps the language was archaic? Perhaps Lucia—

Sophie dropped the thread of her thought with a sharp gasp as magick flooded through her, sharp as hunger, hot and sudden as desire. Her breath came fast and desperate; her lungs burned; her sitting-room, dimmed by the drawing of the window-curtains, brightened so rapidly that she instinctively squeezed her eyes shut. The light, inexplicably, persisted.

Dimly she heard the ending of the spell trail off to silence—a living, breathing silence filled with the noise of beating heart and rushing blood and, beneath all the rest, the restless thrum of a magick that was not her own.

She opened her eyes, slowly and cautiously, just as Lucia drew her bleeding hand away.

Sophie blinked and tried to focus her gaze on Lucia's face—on the candle-holder—on the fire-screen. Everything she looked at glowed and danced, and when she closed her eyes again, though the objects themselves vanished, the shimmer and glow of them did not. She felt that she could not sit still another moment, but Lucia MacNeill was holding her wrist, and something warm and wet was sliding over her bloodied left hand.

When next she dared open her eyes, her fingertip and Lucia's thumb had been neatly bandaged, and the neat stack of clean towels on the tea-tray had become a damp and bloodstained heap in the bottom of the basin.

The earlier glow had faded, and the dance and shimmer calmed; Sophie's vision was not exactly as usual, but she no longer felt in danger of bursting into flame. For the first time in many days, she reached consciously and deliberately for her magick, slow and careful, as though she were again learning the process as Gray had first taught it her.

The blue-white flower, singing in treble chorus, which was her mind's representation of her magick, burned yet at the still centre of herself—whole, unmarred, though small and weak compared to its former self. But around it, winding like ivy or clematis about that coldly flaming core, a stranger-magick burned, red-golden, fierce; and when she caught hold of one blue-burning petal, it was twined around with the red-gold vine, and neither could be grasped without the other.

"It is well?" Lucia asked anxiously.

Sophie formed in her mind an image of the green-glazed teapot which, when not in use, habitually reposed in the centre of the kitchen dresser, dwelling carefully on the precise curve of its handle and the tiny chip on the lip of its spout, and shaped the magick to bring it to her. *"Accedete,"* she said, holding out her hands.

The teapot emerged from the kitchen—fortunately for this experiment, it appeared that Lucia had left the door open—and floated gracefully into her cupped hands.

It was not altogether like using her own, familiar magick—which, even when reinforced by Gray's, had never felt other than *hers*. The spell left an odd unfamiliar sort of echo in whatever part of her mind perceived such things. But here in her hands was the teapot, real and solid, and she had summoned it from the kitchen entirely unaided— an accomplishment which, not half an hour earlier, had been altogether beyond her. However disconcerting the corollary effects of sharing Lucia MacNeill's magick, she should bear them willingly, for the sake of feeling almost like herself again, and capable of doing something—anything—to help Gray.

"It is well," she whispered.

Lucia lifted the teapot carefully from Sophie's grasp, rose to her feet, and carried it back into the kitchen. When she returned, grave-faced and intent, she seated herself opposite Sophie and folded her hands in her lap.

"It will not last forever," she said. "Perhaps a se'nnight, but certainly no more, and very likely less."

Though clearly meant as a warning, this came as something of a relief to Sophie, who had been too clouded in her wits before to think through the consequences. "Good," she said, rather vaguely. Already most of her conscious mind was focused on the image of Gray's face, familiar and infinitely beloved, on which she meant to build a finding-spell.

She turned to Lucia. "If I were to turn your magick to a finding-spell," she said, "what might be its range?"

"I am my father's heir," said Lucia MacNeill, matter-of-factly; "my talent is not so powerful as yours, but my range is the whole of Alba."

*The whole of Alba!* Sophie grinned fiercely.

There was a finding-spell which Gray had taught her, and which he had named especially powerful. This was not her first attempt upon it—she had run through every finding-spell she knew, since receiving that second letter, and this one most often—but her own range was no more than twenty miles, and surely less when she had scarcely strength to walk. Now, *now* it would be different; now she should succeed where the rest had failed.

"*O amisse reperiaris!*" She spun the words out into the aether. "*Verba oris mei ad te eant. Remitte ea ut me ad te adducant.*"

The words spiralled out, away, drawing the threads of magick with them. Out farther, astonishingly farther, than any previous attempt, till Sophie was dizzy with the distance and the implications thereof.

But the result, in the end, was the same: the magick flowed out, but instead of rushing back to her with the knowledge she sought, it echoed away into silence.

Sophie slumped back into Gray's chair, her ears ringing.

*The whole of Alba.* She had cast her magick—or, to speak more rightly, Lucia MacNeill's—over thirty thousand square miles.

*And Gray in none of them.*

Sophie's head had begun to throb with the buzz of unfamiliar magick. She pressed the heels of her hands against her temples. "He is not in Alba," she said, "or there is something blocking the spell. As we had already surmised."

Lucia, however, looked at her in puzzled reproach. "I have always been taught," she said, "that no conclusion based on a single experimental trial can be regarded as valid."

Sophie's huff of disbelieving laughter edged dangerously close to a sob.

Lucia raised her eyebrows. "Have I said something amusing?" she said.

Sophie swallowed hard. "No," she said. "It is only that . . . for a moment, you sounded so very like Gray."

For just a moment, Lucia's blue eyes were soft and deep with grief. Then she squared her shoulders and said firmly, "A second trial, then."

After the third attempt, however, even Lucia MacNeill was ready to concede defeat.

But Sophie's mind was clearer than it had been for some days (or, at any rate, her attempts to think felt less like swimming in treacle), and she was determined to make the most of it.

What could block a finding-spell so powerful and far-reaching as those she had worked just now? Wards, certainly; she and Gray had done exactly this, though their wards had been meant for another purpose, when her stepfather had come seeking them in the Kergabets' London house. A shielding-spell. An interdiction.

Other mages' wards—even Gray's—she had overcome before now; and a shielding-spell . . . what was it Master Alcuin said of shielding-spells? *What is only strong is also vulnerable, in the end.* Of course, he had been speaking of shielding against projectiles and elemental magicks . . .

A sudden vision—uninvited, unwanted—of flames and smoke and shouting, half-disintegrated books and shards of glass flying, made her catch her breath.

She shook her head irritably, and clenched her clasped hands together until pain drove the visions away. *I have only a little time to think, and this is a waste of it.* Wards. Shields. An interdiction?

*Mother Goddess help me . . .*

It was not by any conscious resolution that Sophie, her mind full of Gray and of her longing to find him, began to hum the familiar melody that first had drawn him to her, a lifetime ago in her stepsister's drawing-room, but even before finishing the first stanza, she had thought through the consequences and made up her mind. This was magick which she had not allowed herself to use since leaving London, and to do so again must have felt strange, even without the disorienting addition of Lucia MacNeill's magick twined about her own; instead of attempting to ignore the strangeness of it, however, Sophie opened wide her metaphysickal arms and flung herself in head-foremost.

Lucia's face conveyed an open and profound bewilderment. She did not interrupt, however, and Sophie had at present no attention to spare for the thoughts or feelings of anyone else. It was not that she had any real hope of a drawing-spell's reaching where a finding-spell could not, and in any case, if Gray were indeed being held against his will, such a spell could not change the fact. Nor could its results—should any eventuate—be immediately apparent, for the target of a drawing-spell did not thereby develop the ability to travel at superhuman speeds; unless Gray had been all this time within a few streets of Quarry Close, success and failure should look exactly alike.

No; what had decided Sophie on this self-evidently futile course of action was that—as there seemed nothing practical to be done—she at least wished Gray to know, if such a thing were possible, that she was seeking him.

She sang, therefore, to the end of one song and, almost without pausing for breath, into the beginning of another; she was singing yet (though badly, in a voice clotted with tears, her forehead resting on Lucia's shoulder) when the front door was shoved violently open and Mór MacRury burst into the sitting-room.

Sophie (still singing, for by now it seemed impossible to stop) raised her head from Lucia's shoulder and looked up at Mór. She had evidently been running, and appeared to have been caught in a shower of rain; she was pink-faced and breathless, her russet hair dishevelled and her eyes wild. Tucked under one arm was a flat, oblong parcel tied up in brown paper and string. This Mór flung onto the sofa, where it landed with a damp, accusing *flump*, before advancing upon Sophie and Lucia, her slim hands rhythmically clenching and unclenching at her sides.

"What are you about?" she demanded.

Sophie straightened her back, hiccoughed, and sang, half under her breath,

> *Fhir a' bhàta, na hóro eile,*
> *Mo shoraidh slàn leat 's gach àit' an téid thu.*

Then she caught a breath and began the next strophe.

She had been a fool to choose this song, for it had moved her to tears even at the best of times. But Gray had—

But Gray loved it, and it was surely no more foolish to think that a song he loved might draw him more swiftly than to suppose for a moment that the spell might succeed at all. Her head ached and her limbs felt as though they had been hollowed out and filled with wet sand, but the magick pulsed bright and steady in her mind's ear.

Deciding perhaps that it was futile to attempt interrogation of Sophie, Mór turned on Lucia MacNeill and demanded, "What have you let her do?"

Lucia shook her head and, to Sophie's dimly felt astonishment, said, "She is only singing."

For a long moment, Mór stared at her, wide-eyed and open-mouthed. *"Only singing,"* she repeated incredulously. "Have I not taught you better than that, Lucia MacNeill? Look at her! There is a very storm of magick erupting from this house, which I could see from more than a mile away, and the gods know who else may have seen it also."

Sophie inhaled sharply, and lost the thread of her song for a moment, but remembering that Gray might possibly be at the other end of it, she took it up again at once.

Mór had turned at the sound, however, and was studying her now with narrowed eyes. "That is not your magick," she said, "or not yours alone."

Her gaze flitted from Sophie to Lucia and back again, and at last she said, appalled, "Lucia MacNeill, *what have you done?*"

The heiress of Alba seemed to take courage from this direct challenge, for she rose gracefully to her feet and (allowing for some difference in their heights) looked Mór directly in the eye. "I have *helped*," she said. Her voice was low and furious. "I had at my disposal the means to do some good for a friend—for a sister—and with her consent, I made use of it. My magick may help Sophie find her husband, or it may not, but in any event she will not die of the separation whilst I can prevent it. And I shall not apologise to you, Mór MacRury of Uist, or to anyone else, for offering help to one who had need of it!"

Sophie faltered to the end of the song Mór had taught her, her breath coming in sobs, and, casting about for another, hit upon a grisly ballad describing a young man's poisoning of himself and his lover for jealousy at her daring to dance with another man. What small part of her mind could be spared from her spell and the confrontation before her was distantly grateful that the song was in English, and thus largely incomprehensible to her companions.

"This is not the help she needs!" Mór returned, equally furious. Gone, entirely gone, was the collegial respect which she had earlier accorded Lucia MacNeill, and very long gone any hint of deference to her rank. "Sophie and Gray are my friends as much as yours," she said, "and to suppose that you know better than I, or than her sister—"

But here the diatribe broke off abruptly, and Mór gazed in shocked silence at something which, evidently, only she could see.

Then, just as abruptly, she turned to Sophie, crouched down to clasp her hands, and said urgently, "You are working a drawing-spell, are you not?"

Sophie nodded, baffled; Lucia said, "Oh!" in a tone of enlightenment.

"Go on singing," Mór commanded, and sprang up again. "As long as you are able."

The light of bright curiosity—more, of *hope*—in Mór's eyes made it difficult to continue, for Sophie had a hundred questions burning to be asked, but impossible to consider stopping.

Mór paced towards the dining-room, her right hand outstretched, as though following . . . something. Arrived at the far wall, she stopped and raised her hand shade to her eyes. Shade them from what?

Sophie tried to clear her mind of every question, every thought except Gray, and went on singing. She stood from her chair, abruptly unable to bear sitting still for another moment, and stumbled towards the dining-room in Mór's wake. Lucia darted after her, curving an arm about her waist in support, and Sophie was too preoccupied to object.

She turned back at the sound of the front door crashing open once more, and Joanna's voice, sharp with anxiety, calling, "Sophie? *Sophie!*"

Joanna in person, with Gwendolen at her heels like an evening-stretched shadow of herself, erupted into the sitting-room, shoving back her dripping bonnet; then both of them stopped short, gaping at Sophie.

Sophie could offer no explanations at present, and looked pleadingly at Lucia; but just as the latter opened her mouth, Mór cried, "There!" and turned back to the dining-room table—to the spelled campaign-map, and the bedraggled owl-feather pen with its scarlet counterweight.

She studied the map with feverish haste, muttering under her breath.

"Bring me . . . bring me some twine or wool or thread, and some pins," she demanded, holding out her right hand. "Quickly, at once."

"Sophie, where is your work-basket?" cried Joanna, but Gwendolen was already rummaging in her own, extracting a bristling pin-cushion and a half-used skein of violet silk. In another moment Joanna was at Mór's side, thrusting the silk into her reaching fingers.

"Go on," said Mór to Sophie, as she bent over the map, plucking pins from the pin-cushion with one hand and catching at the end of the embroidery-silk with the other. "We must not lose this chance."

*"And I have drunk the same, my jewel,"* Sophie sang, her breath coming fast and urgent, now, not from grief but from wild anticipation. She peered round Mór's shoulder, and—yes—the feather was moving! Anxiety clogged her throat, but she sang through it, though her voice was half a croak: *"I soon shall die as well as thee."*

She felt rather than saw Joanna's eyes on her, Gwendolen's and Lucia's.

Mór had driven a pin into the map somewhere amidst the representation of Din Edin; now she stood stock-still, watching the feather as it tilted drunkenly northeastward and began to drag its weighted foot across the surface of the map.

"Horns of Herne!" muttered Joanna, somewhere behind Sophie. "I have seen garden-snails go faster." The reproving *Jo, hush!* that followed was surely Gwendolen.

When at last the feather stopped and stood quivering in place for the length of a verse, she lifted it carefully, straight upwards, and affixed another pin beneath it. Then she tied the two pins together with the violet silk, and stood straight, pressing both hands to her temples.

"I have it," she said, quietly exultant, and Sophie's song-spell stuttered to a halt.

## PART THREE

# The Ross of Mull

## CHAPTER XXV

# In Which Gray
# Confounds Expectations

*Gray was no* more than half conscious when his captor's two lieutenants, whom he had dubbed Steel-Eyes and Ginger, opened the door of his cell and hauled him up off the noisome mattress in the corner. Passing the boundary of the interdiction on his cell revived him sufficiently to get his feet under him; he struggled against the hands gripping his arms, more from habit than from any real hope of escape, and was not surprised when the only result was a sharp upward jerk of his left elbow (it was always the left, when he annoyed them; Ginger had yanked him upright by that arm, very early in their acquaintance, and the pain had waxed and waned in the intervening days but never entirely vanished) and a ringing clip round his right ear.

In retaliation—such as it was—Gray abandoned all attempts at locomotion, and even at bearing his own weight, so that Ginger and Steel-Eyes must drag him bodily along the dim corridor. This tactic was less effective now than when he had first used it, before they had begun to punish his recalcitrance with long periods in that interdicted cell and the resulting nausea and vertigo had sapped his appetite; but even now his long limbs made him an awkward burden, and there was a bitter satisfaction to be gained from forcing his captors to bear it.

He had, he was fairly certain, been a fortnight in this place—whatever place it was. The length of the journey hither from Din Edin, however, remained a vague and timeless jumble: here the rumbling of a farm-waggon, there the pitch and roll (and the smell, great Neptune, the smell!) of a fishing-boat, here a low ceiling and the scents of small beer and burning peats—and always the blindfold and the rough hands herding him, rarely cruel but never kind.

They dragged him round a blind corner, along a dim corridor, up a spiralling flight of narrow stone steps, along a passageway and out through a postern-gate into blue-velvet twilight, and down another staircase, walled and even more narrow. At its foot, Gray fell sprawling on uneven flagstones from whose haphazard cracks arose tiny forests of green shoots.

So long was it since Gray had last opened his eyes in daylight that even this dim approximation of it was startling. Pushing himself up on his elbows, he drew a deep lungful of crisp evening air; it caught in his throat, convulsed his lungs, and reemerged in a heavy, rasping cough.

Ginger made a noise of disgust and kicked him.

This was all to the good, however; any little delay meant prolonging his time outside the castle walls and the wards upon them—and, more importantly, away from the interdiction. He drew breath, past the sharp pain in his ribs, and waited.

Presently heavy-booted footfalls announced the arrival of some fourth person. "Where are you taking him?" someone demanded—a voice Gray did not recognise.

"The grove," said Steel-Eyes shortly. "The chieftain wants him."

The newcomer grunted what must have been agreement, for rough hands caught at Gray's arms again and dragged him to his feet.

"Walk, now," Ginger growled, speaking now in Latin for Gray's ears. "We know you can walk."

Gray stood still, swaying a little.

"*Walk.*" The command was accompanied by a firm shove to the middle of his back, and he stumbled forward involuntarily; one pace, two.

No one was holding him now, and for a brief, mad moment he contemplated running. Two more steps persuaded him that any such attempt must be worse than useless.

Ginger and Steel-Eyes propelled him through a grove of elm and yew trees that grew nearly up to the foot of the curtain wall. The elms were newly in bud; his timekeeping was not badly amiss, then, for it was still early spring. The cool glow of magelight spread its fingers between the tree-trunks, and beneath it, at the centre of an almost perfectly circular clearing, stood the man whom all the others called simply "the chieftain," a copper knife gleaming in his right hand.

He was a tall man—quite as tall as Gray—and wore always the kilted plaid, a pattern unfamiliar to Gray, over a finely made linen shirt; his hair was a deep russet-brown, worn long and tied back from his aristocratic face in the fashion affected by the most traditionalist members of Din Edin society. His eyes, the cold clear blue of Windermere under a cloudless sky, regarded Gray as they always did, with a disconcerting blend of acquisitiveness and contempt.

"May I hope to hear that you have reconsidered, Magister?" he inquired. His Latin was fluent and flawless, but, as always, he spoke the words as though they burnt his mouth and grated on his ears.

"No," said Gray.

What the *great enterprise* might be to which his captors wished him to lend his magick, or how this might be accomplished, he had yet to discover, but, as it apparently required kidnap and even more unsavoury practices, there seemed little likelihood of its being in fact, as they claimed, for the good of Alba.

The chieftain sighed. "A pity," he said. "A free exchange of gifts is of greater worth than a payment exacted; but time runs on, and we must make do with what we can obtain. Bring him," he snapped, shifting abruptly into his native tongue.

His followers hastened to obey, and Gray found himself pinioned in the centre of the clearing, no more than a foot from the chieftain himself.

"You are standing," said the chieftain, reverting to Latin, "in the place where all the paths begin." His hands sketched lines in every direction. *I have heard that phrase before, or something like it . . . where, and when?* He gestured at the largest of the circle of trees—a mighty elm, live but still scarcely in bud, pruned close to a height of ten feet or more and branching gracefully above—and Steel-Eyes caught both Gray's wrists in a grip like a vice and propelled him towards it.

"So," said Gray, putting all the bravado he could muster into his voice, which rasped and creaked from disuse—how long had it been since he last spoke any words but *No?* "You mean to take by force what you could not obtain by persuasion, bribery, or abuse? What do you expect I have left to give you?"

It was half the truth, but half a bluff; his hours in the interdicted cell were always long enough to make him weak and ill, but never so long as to incapacitate him, and already he could feel his magick stuttering back to life.

Ginger was binding him to the tree-trunk at ankles, hips, and chest; the rough-spun shirt and trousers in which they had clothed him were wholly inadequate to muffle the bite of the hempen rope or the scrape of the rough elm-bark against the half-healed weals across his back—relic of an earlier attempt at forcing his cooperation.

The chieftain paced closer, holding Gray's gaze. "Only say the word, Magister," he said softly. "Only say the word and you shall be prisoner no more, but one among the honoured guests of the true chieftain of Alba."

Gray shook his head.

His captor mimicked the gesture, adopting a sorrowful expression, and gestured again at Ginger and Steel-Eyes. The work of binding done, Ginger stepped away from the elm trunk; each seizing one of Gray's wrists, they stretched his arms out towards the yew-trees to either side.

Gray did not struggle, and not only because he recognised the futility of doing so; the truth was that he was desperately curious to know what might come next.

The chieftain took a step towards him, then another and another, until he stood no more than an arm's length away. Gray watched his face, half entranced, until by chance a brief, tiny gleam drew his eye to the copper blade in his captor's hand.

He was testing the edge against his thumb. A thin bright line of blood welled; he drew the pad of his thumb along the flat of the blade, painting first one side and then the other in a thin film of gore. In the cold glow of magelight, the blood shone against the pale wings of his hands.

Moving with slow deliberation, and muttering in Gaelic the while—it was a spell, Gray thought by the cadence, though he could make no sense of it; a spell or a prayer, or both together—he pressed Gray's head back against the tree-trunk with his left hand and, with his right, drew the point of the gleaming blade across Gray's cheek-bone. The knife was sharp, so sharp that the pain scarcely registered, though Gray felt the blood run down his cheek.

*What is happening here?* This much was now clear: The "great magick" of which his captor had spoken, which was to right the great wrong done to his clan and to Alba, was borne in men's blood and fed upon it—a working, and a form of worship, older than any now practised. Gray had felt out of his depth before; now he was drowning.

The chieftain's palm scraped across Gray's cheek, collecting the blood he had spilled; then he drew back, his lips curving in a soft, unfocused smile more chilling than any previous word or gesture, and reached over Gray's head to lay his hand flat against the bark of the great elm.

The hairs on the back of Gray's neck rose so suddenly that his skin seemed to prickle beneath them.

Still smiling, the chieftain stepped aside and took Gray's left hand in his. Gently he turned it palm downward, and the blade flashed across its back. The cut on Gray's cheek was stinging fiercely now, but again he scarcely felt the fresh wound. The blood welled, dripped. Gray heard the soft *spat* as the first droplets struck, and looked down to see his blood soaking—improbably, vanishing—into a twisted root of elm protruding through the leaf-litter of autumns past.

He felt light-headed—far more so than such a small loss of blood could possibly account for. Whatever this man was about, would it—could it—work against Gray's conscious will?

"There!" the chieftain exclaimed, narrowing his eyes at the blood dripping from Gray's hand. "It begins, yes!"

Gray came very near to asking—and, worse, to asking in Gaelic—what it was he was seeing. He hoped he was not squeamish, or more cowardly than necessary, but he could not deny that the sight of his own blood running so eagerly out of his veins and into . . . what? . . . unnerved him.

His captor was cradling his right hand, now, turning it, poising his knife.

The knife bit; after a little, the pain followed it. Gray watched, waiting for the first *spat* of blood on bark.

The first drop fell—spread—vanished.

Gray's knees buckled as magick flowed into him—magick howling, shrieking—magick deep and fierce as the tide in flood.


For one brief, interminable moment, the four men in the yew-grove were all alike struck still in shock. Then three of them exploded into movement and noise, the details of which the fourth could never afterwards remember with any sort of clarity.

There was a great deal of shouting, not all of which Gray understood. The bloodied copper knife, knocked free in the mêlée, somersaulted to the ground and stuck point-first in the soil, upright and quivering. Some other blade, wielded with more haste and less skill, opened a long shallow gash along Gray's ribs as it cut away the last of the cords binding him to the elm-trunk.

Once again he fell forward, sprawling.

To his surprise, however, the terrifying, exhilarating buzz of magick—his own and not his own, familiar-strange—did not immediately lessen. He reached for it, aligning the words of his shape-shifting spell behind his eyes—caught hold—shaped the syllables quickly and silently, and poured the magick in.

There was no time for care or for finesse; already the chieftain had ceased berating his minions and one of them was reaching down to grasp at Gray's right arm. He was just too late, however—outflung arm already bending and shifting into close-folded wing—and the eye-blink moment of astonishment was just sufficient for Gray to effect his scrambling, ungainly escape.

Hope swelled in Gray's breast, buoyed up his newly lightened bones. But so long as he remained earthbound, he was slower by far than his pursuers, with their long-striding legs and reaching arms. Could he go aloft like this, from a running start (and to call it *running* was to be very charitable indeed), with no branch or rail to drop from and no hands to toss him upward?

*I shall have to try.*

He imagined himself leaving behind the leaf-mould and the tangled tree-roots, leaving Ginger and Steel-Eyes and their gods-accursèd chieftain, their spell that fed on the blood of mages to accomplish the gods alone knew what—saw spreading below him the woods and streams and crags of Alba—saw the lamplit window of a tiny house in Quarry Close, and the silhouette of a slim young woman bending over the keys of a pianoforte.

He spread his wings and ran.

The first powerful wing-beat proved the futility of any attempt at flight; the movement set loose a hot overpowering tide of pain from his injured left shoulder, half forgotten in the heady surge of new magick and old terror, that swamped his wing, his back, his leg, and tore an almost human shriek from his strigine throat.

Ginger and Steel-Eyes were upon him in moments, cursing at his feeble attempts to claw and bite them, wrapping him up in his discarded shirt and trousers like a recalcitrant infant in its swaddling-bands. Despair took the place of his earlier wild hope, sitting heavy like iron-stone on his heart.

Then something tugged at him: some faint aetheric thing, unrelated to his physical captivity. A familiar thing, though so distant as to be almost imperceptible; a pull he had felt before, without at first recognising or comprehending it. A sound heard in his mind's ear, like the echo of a half-remembered song.

*Sophie.*

## CHAPTER XXVI

# In Which Sophie
# Seizes the Moment

*They blinked at* one another in the sudden silence: Sophie and Mór at either end of the dining-room table, Lucia and Joanna and Gwendolen crowded along one side.

Lucia rested her forearms on the table and brought her face so close to the map that her nose nearly brushed the pins. "Brìghde's tears," she breathed. When she straightened up again, her expression was grim; she turned to Mór and said flatly, "Explain."

Joanna meanwhile had put her arm about Sophie's shoulders and drawn out another chair from the table. "Come and sit down," she said gently, guiding Sophie into it.

Sophie went without protest, for after the effort of sustaining the spell so long, following upon a period of enforced inactivity, her limbs were trembling despite the infusion of Lucia MacNeill's magick. She folded her arms upon the table and rested her chin upon them, staring uncomprehendingly at the map.

Joanna stood behind her sister's chair; she said nothing, but her hands on Sophie's shoulders, gripping just short of actual discomfort, conveyed her opinion more clearly than any words. Lucia MacNeill took a seat facing Mór across the table, both looking rather shaken.

Sophie could not see where Gwendolen had gone, but suspected her of lurking out of sight behind Joanna.

"Mór," Sophie said. "Mór, that was—was that—"

"Gray was hidden from us when last we sought him," said Mór, perhaps taking pity on her inarticulate anxiety, "and I confess I doubted whether Rory's scheme were worth the effort all of us put into it, but it seems he was quite right."

Sophie raised her head in desperate hope; before she could speak, however, Mór turned to her and said, "Your spell . . . I am somewhat at a loss to describe what I saw, for it is quite out of my experience. But I saw your magick, Sophie, wound all about with Lucia Mac-Neill's; and just now, at the end, I saw . . . I *believe* I saw Gray's magick echoing back, as I have seen your magicks do before—but faint and weak and distant. It did not look quite as it usually does—just as yours, at present, does not—but I do not believe I could mistake it for any other's. And the echo came—"

She drew her forefinger along the line of violet silk, west-northwest from Din Edin to a point along the coastline of one of the great islands.

As she did so, the quivering owl-feather—until now nudging up against the second pin, as though unable to bear being parted from that spot—abruptly stilled, then quietly heeled over.

Sophie clapped one hand across her mouth to stifle a cry of alarm. Her face was hot, her heart battering wildly against her ribs. "What does that mean?" she demanded. "What has happened?"

Her voice emerged as a sort of breathless shriek. From either side they gazed at her, measuring, assessing, till she longed to disappear, to divert their attention elsewhere; she held herself in check, and did not.

"It means that we were right to seize our moment," said Mór, grave and thoughtful. "Whatever has been blocking the finding-spell was temporarily in abeyance—perhaps he was behind a ward, and was briefly outside it?—but that reprieve is now concluded" (she waved a hand at the upended owl-feather) "and we do not know when there may be another."

*If at all*, she did not say, but Sophie heard it nevertheless.

"But we do not need another," she said, as calmly as she could manage. "*I have it*, you said; you know where to look for Gray—on"— she leant forward to peer at the map—"on Mull."

The map, she saw, recorded not only the names of places—towns and fortifications, rivers and lochs and firths—but also the names of people: *Lindsay. Bruce. MacDuff.*

No; not the names of people, but the names of clans. *And what clan name is written along the coast of Mull, that makes Lucia MacNeill look so grim?*

She levered herself upright and peered down the table, trying to see what Lucia MacNeill had seen. *MacLean . . . MacQuarie . . . MacAlpine.*

The name was familiar, why? She had seen it printed, not in the Gaelic manner (as on the map) but in plain Latin—she had heard it spoken, too, and where?

The others were staring at her; she adjured herself not to care. Lucia knew something—perhaps Mór, also—was it the same something which Sophie (perhaps, possibly) knew?

"Clan MacAlpine," she muttered experimentally, and squeezed her eyes shut and tugged at a loose curl of hair. The words tickled at the edges of her memory; she spoke them again; then, "But Clan MacAlpine do not rule Alba now."

Sophie stood bolt upright, her eyes open wide, but seeing nothing of her own surroundings. *Arthur's Seat. Gray and Rory and Catriona MacCrimmon, sitting over the remains of a picnic hamper.* The memories tumbled through her mind, almost too quickly to be caught hold of. Rory's voice: *A crossroads of Ailpín Drostan's spell-net.* Catriona's, reproving. It had been legend to him—idle talk for an idle moment— but not to her. And Gray, afire with curiosity: *No one mage has ever had such power, or such a range. A group of mages, then . . . I should like to know how it was done . . .*

And then . . . and then Catriona had smiled at Gray in that odd, acquisitive way.

Later, a supper-party here in Quarry Close: Sophie had been curious about the opening of the storehouses, and though the other Albans present had been ready—even eager—to exchange the latest news from their own clan-lands, Catriona had again turned the conversation—and not for the first time. Even Rory had sent Sophie away with a book about Alba's past when she attempted to discuss its present circumstances. Though it had been an enlightening volume, and she was grateful to him for the loan of it, hindsight clearly showed it to have been an evasion.

A parade of memories of Catriona MacCrimmon presented themselves to Sophie's mind, each in some way entirely out of character with the last. Here she cast arch, flirtatious glances at Gray; there sat at Sophie's elbow in a lecture theatre, patiently translating from Gaelic into Latin. In January she had asked Sophie, in a tone of distant reproach, what manner of friendship she imagined might subsist between two such unequal parties as their two kingdoms; in March, insisted upon trundling her all round Din Edin, from warehouse to dressmaker to milliner's shop—

"Oh," Sophie said, and sat down hard. She had come home that very afternoon, very late, to find her house chill and empty, and Gray not in it. "Oh, surely not."

Sophie collapsed backwards into her chair as abruptly as though her strings had all been cut.

"Sophie!" cried Joanna in sudden alarm. She quickly folded herself into the next chair to Sophie's, pulling it as close as the shape of the table permitted.

"Lucia," said Sophie urgently, ignoring her sister altogether, "Mór, that place on Mull, where you put in the second pin—where Gray is, if Rory's spell does not mistake—what is at that spot?"

Lucia MacNeill and Mór MacRury exchanged a guarded look.

"Castle MacAlpine," Lucia MacNeill said grimly, after a long moment. "Birthplace of the last MacAlpine to hold the chieftain's seat of Alba, and of none since, for his descendants abandoned it after his death—there are MacAlpines everywhere in Alba, for they ruled for hundreds of years, and they have many a more convenient seat. It has lately been rumoured to be haunted; now I suppose we know why."

Sophie's fingers traced the long curve of the Ross of Mull, wrought in faded green ink upon the parchment of the sea.

"You shall tell your father?" she said, looking up at Lucia MacNeill.

The heiress of Alba grimaced. "As soon as ever I can," she said.

"You did not say that you were here on your father's behalf!" cried Mór MacRury, turning to her eagerly.

"I did not, because I am not," said Lucia MacNeill. "He will deplore my act of deception in coming here, but my father is not a man to neglect a promising avenue only because its origin annoys him. And of course the discovery is Sophie's and not mine, and will be the more welcome therefore, in the circumstances."

Joanna eyed her sidelong, attempting—unsuccessfully—to determine whether this remark indicated resentment.

"There is no need to peer at me in that manner, Sophie," Lucia MacNeill said tartly—frowning at Sophie, who must evidently have succumbed to the same impulse.

Sophie turned to look her in the eye. "I do beg your pardon," she said. "This . . . this business of fathers and daughters is quite outside my experience. I hope I am not to blame for—"

Lucia MacNeill threw up an imperious hand, suddenly every inch the heiress of Alba. "There is a wealth of blame to be shared out in connexion with this mess," she said. "None of it is yours. Let us have no more apologising."

"Yes, ma'am," said Sophie. "There is another point—I had almost rather not—but what if Gray should not be their last victim? I am very much afraid, Lucia, that Rory MacCrimmon's sister Catriona—"

A sharp indrawn breath from Mór MacRury; glancing in her direction, Joanna saw shock and surmise and sorrow chase one another across her face. "Oh, my poor Rory," she said, rubbing her brow as though her head ached.

"I am sorry for it," said Lucia MacNeill, "and I honour your scruples, Sophie, but if I am to tell my father anything of this—and I must—then I must tell him all."

Sophie nodded glumly.

Joanna heard, as though from very far away, the arrhythmic *clop-clop* of carriage-horses in the street, and was vaguely surprised when, instead of fading into the general hum of sound as the carriage passed along Quarry Close, it halted abruptly and was succeeded by a jingle of harness, and then by a sharp rap at her own front door.

"Whoever can that be?" she said, jumping up to peer around the window-curtain.

Lucia MacNeill ran to the window and peered likewise, then turned away again and groaned.

"Who is it?" said Sophie, as Gwendolen ran to open the front door.

"The compliments of Donald MacNeill, Chieftain of the Clans," came a measured, resonant voice from the entry, speaking in a formal and strongly accented Latin, "and will Lucia MacNeill be pleased to take her seat in her father's carriage at once." The voice rose a little in volume: "At once."

"M-my duty to Donald MacNeill," stammered Gwendolen, "and . . . er . . ."

Lucia MacNeill grimaced, muttered something uncomplimentary beneath her breath, and turned to Sophie and Joanna. "I am discovered, evidently," she said. "I shall send to you with news, as soon as I may."

She hesitated, biting her lip; then, darting forward, she clasped Sophie's hands and whispered fiercely, "Do not despair."

Then, giving Sophie no opportunity of reply, she straightened, threw back her head, and assumed an imperious expression—putting on the heiress of Alba, exactly as Sophie herself might have put on the Princess Royal—and paced very deliberately towards the front door.

The tug of Sophie's magick faded over the course of the return journey—to which Gray was blind and nearly deaf, for his wings were pinioned and his small feathered body tucked (not very gently) under someone's elbow—and at last vanished altogether. Not for the first time, Gray wished desperately for some hint to the situation of Castle MacAlpine. How far was he at this moment from Din Edin, from Sophie? The distance must be less than he had supposed, if her spell could reach him, even so faintly as this. Why had they never tested her limits systematically, like the scholars they purported to be? Had he been certain of her range, he might now have calculated his own distance from her, and thus determined . . .

What?

By the position of the sun as it sank below the horizon, just before the mad brangle in the clearing, he could at least be certain that the pull of Sophie's spell had been towards the southeast: he was north and west of Din Edin, then. Though he could hardly have been east of it without falling into the sea, it was something to know that they had travelled north and not south or due west.

The scrape of heavy oak on rough-dressed stone signalled the opening of a door. Abruptly Gray found himself unwrapped and flung carelessly onto the straw pallet in the corner of his cell; the impact, though greatly lessened by his presently weighing less than half a stone, set his shoulder and knee ringing with pain. His bedraggled garments were tossed in after him and the door pulled to with a dull *thunk*.

If the sensation of escaping the interdiction was akin to a wellspring bubbling up through newly thawing earth, returning to it in this form was like being violently turned inside out. Gray's human shape reasserted itself with nauseating suddenness, and quite without volition; every part of him ached and itched at once; sprawled on the stinking straw-tick, he was swallowed by waves of nausea, and retched helplessly, though—perhaps fortunately—there was nothing in his stomach to bring up.

At long last—it might have been a quarter-hour that passed in this manner, or several days, for all that Gray could tell—the sick fitful darkness rolled over him again.

## CHAPTER XXVII

# In Which Joanna Writes
# a Letter and Attends a Council of War

*My dear Jo,* Joanna read, in Jenny's clear, elegant hand,

> *Please write very soon, and tell me that you and Sophie*
> *and Gwendolen are safe and well, as it seems that my*
> *brother has not after all outgrown his tendency to attract*
> *trouble. My lord had a letter from Din Edin this morning, by*
> *the diplomatic express, whose contents I expect you can very*
> *easily imagine—indeed, I should not wonder if the hand*
> *that enciphered them was your own—and you may*
> *therefore imagine, too, my state of mind at present . . .*

Joanna sighed. Lord de Courcy could not, of course, reasonably have kept the MacAlpine débacle from his masters. She had hoped, however, that Kergabet might for the time being refrain from terrifying Jenny with its details.

*My dear Jenny,* she wrote,

> *I am very sorry that you should have learnt of the*
> *circumstances here in such a way. I had hoped to delay in*

*telling you of it, until I should be able to tell you also of Gray's safe return; but that, I suppose, was a foolish hope. I may at least assure you that both Gwen and I are perfectly well, and very far from any sort of excitement. I regret to say that Sophie is not so well as I should wish, though at any rate her health seems not to be growing worse at present.*

*I shall not sport with your patience by simply repeating facts with which I must suppose you are already acquainted, through Courcy's letter to Kergabet—it was not I who enciphered it, and in fact I did not read it at all, but its contents are not difficult to deduce. You may, however, be interested in a second angle of view upon those facts.*

She read this over, chewing thoughtfully on the end of her pen—a bad habit of her childhood, which she had taken up again under the strain of this visit.

*So, then: Sophie and some of her mage friends have located Gray, through some combination of spells which I do not at all understand, in the general vicinity of an abandoned castle on the island of Mull, off the eastern coast, which was once the seat of Clan MacAlpine. Circumstances suggest that where Gray is, we shall also find the several other foreign mages who have gone missing whilst visiting or residing in Alba, in the course of the past twelvemonth.*

*An acquaintance of Gray and Sophie's may be somehow involved in the business, which is a great consternation to Sophie, particularly because it was her brother who secured them the invitation to the University. She could not be questioned, having left Din Edin shortly after Gray did, allegedly on a visit to her parents; but the brother remains here, and has admitted quite openly that though he had been previously in correspondence with Gray, and thought the invitation an excellent notion, it was his sister who first suggested it. I do not believe he himself stands accused of*

*any wrongdoing, but he has been put under guard, lest he
attempt to communicate with his sister. I am sorry for it,
but I cannot fault the decision. The absent sister was also
responsible for engaging Sophie's daily woman, who as a
result is now also under suspicion—though erroneously, in
my view, for she seems quite devoted to Sophie.*

*Sophie believes—and it appears that Lucia MacNeill
finds her theory plausible, though I confess I cannot entirely
fathom it—that there is some connexion with an old legend
from the time of the MacAlpine kings, of a "spell-net" which
is attributed to Ailpín Drostan, called the father of Alba, but
which must have been the work of an entire cohort of mages,
not just one.*

*Donald MacNeill having once been convinced of the
accuracy of Sophie's information—*

And what a conversation that must have been! Lucia MacNeill's
exasperation had risen like steam from her explanatory note to
Sophie, which had arrived by one of her father's pages on the following afternoon.

*—called for the muster of the company of what we
should call royal troops which are quartered at Oban, and
sent his serjeant-at-arms (a cousin of some sort, in whom he
reposes great trust) to take command of them and to lead an
expedition to Mull (which lies within sight of the town) to
investigate the recent rumours that the old Castle MacAlpine
is haunted, and if possible to rescue the prisoners. Most
unfortunately however, the serjeant-at-arms was badly
injured in the course of the journey—he will recover, we are
told, though I fear the same cannot be said for his poor
horse—and the company commander, it appears, received
his instructions, disregarded them almost entire, and turned
a quiet investigative sortie into a full-scale assault.*

*If you were to suppose that His Majesty sent a troop of*

*the Palace Guard against, say, the Duke of Kernow, without
warning or parley and upon no evidence but the claim of one
of his sons, that some foreign mage had seen something
through a finding-spell, you should begin to have some idea
of the result. Only you must understand that the man so
attacked is one of two claimants to the chieftainship of a
clan which once ruled all of Alba, and not only that, but a
direct descendant of the kingdom's founder; and that the
politics and sensibilities (and, it appears, the magicks) of
our own factions at home are as nothing beside those of
Alba's clans and clan-lands.*

*It was, in short, a disaster—not only was there no
rescuing of prisoners, but I should not have been at all
surprised, if it had ended in civil war—the only redeeming
feature of which was, that in the course of it two of
D.MacN.'s guardsmen, sent as scouts, did in fact (or so
they say) find evidence of prisoners' being held there. I am
confident, therefore, that this is indeed a case of kidnap and
not murder, and that I shall soon have the best of news to
send you.*

Joanna chewed her pen once more as she considered this last. It
was not untrue, so far as it went, but she could certainly not tell anyone what, in fact, she meant to do next.

The council of war, so called, which followed the disastrous raid
upon Castle MacAlpine was, as Joanna had expected, entirely
unsatisfactory. Joanna was included in it—or, rather, her presence
was tolerated—only at Lucia MacNeill's insistence; and her gratitude
for that favour, and for Lucia MacNeill's earnest, if bizarrely
expressed, desire to help Sophie, allowed her to keep her countenance,
and her silence, in the face of what proved very strong provocation.

Donald MacNeill's serjeant-at-arms was in no condition to travel,
or to answer questions; his ill-fated second-in-command had taken to

the boats, and though he had sent in letters—a series of letters, each, or so said Lucia MacNeill, more defensive and self-serving than the last—remained at sea, in the firth between Mull and the mainland, with his troops. The recriminations now flying about Donald Mac-Neill's council chamber, therefore, were balked of their proper object, and thus accomplished even less than such post hoc strategic argumentation ordinarily does.

Donald MacNeill had dispatched a courier to the encampment to question the two guardsmen whose scouting report appeared to confirm the presence of prisoners at Castle MacAlpine, and the courier had this morning returned with his report.

"'While observing from the cover of the wood abutting the castle to the northwest, at a height of some ten feet, we saw a man in shackles,'" Lucia MacNeill read, her voice as clear and precise as though the words affected her not at all, "'and two men dragging him between them towards the castle walls, as though he could not walk. He was a small man, and his hair apparently dark. We could see nothing else of him but that he was dressed in rags.'"

Not Gray, then, but very possibly one of the other missing mages. Joanna glanced up from the handkerchief she was worrying in her hands, for lack of any useful task to turn them to, and found Lord de Courcy and his secretary exchanging a look which told her quite clearly that they had made the same connexion.

"'We followed them at a little distance. They entered through a postern-gate in the castle's northern wall. It was too small for more than one man to pass through at a time, and reached by means of a walled staircase, yet it was guarded by two armed men, and the staircase itself by two more. We therefore set a watch upon this gate for some time, in hopes of learning what lay beyond it, and of overhearing some watchword or countersign which might be used to gain entry.

"'Approximately a quarter-hour later, the same two men again passed out through the postern-gate, again escorting a shackled prisoner who stumbled badly. They spoke to the guardsmen, but we could not hear what they said. The prisoner did not appear to be the same as before, but we cannot be certain, as the night was very dark.

They entered the wood, but did not come out again while we watched there.'"

The assembled company waited for Lucia MacNeill to continue, but she only said, "There is no more."

Donald MacNeill bent his head and pinched the bridge of his nose between thumb and forefinger.

Joanna remained long enough to conclude both that Lord de Courcy could be relied upon to take the matter seriously, and that Donald MacNeill would not or could not act so quickly as she considered needful. Then, with a glance at Lucia MacNeill, she seized the chance of a particularly loud and vitriolic dispute between two of the Albans—both cousins of Donald MacNeill, if she read the insignia on their various accoutrements correctly—to leave her seat at the periphery of the room and slip silently out of the door.

"If you have been plotting to go haring off without me, you had best think again," said Gwendolen, folding her arms across her breast.

She had quietly dogged Joanna's steps almost since the moment of her return to Quarry Close, and now was standing firmly in the doorway of Sophie's tiny guest bedroom, blocking her way. Of course Joanna had not supposed that she should succeed in evading her; but she had hoped for a little more time to collect her thoughts.

"I take it that you mean to cross half of Alba all alone," Gwendolen continued, "and hire passage to the isle of Mull, and take Castle MacAlpine by storm?"

"Of course not!" said Joanna, stung into speech by her friend's mocking tone—which over the months of their acquaintance she had grown used to hearing directed at almost everyone but herself. "Storming Castle MacAlpine was an idiotic idea when Angus Ferguson did it, and I should be the queen of all fools to try it a second time, even if I had the men to do it with." His Majesty's guardsmen, indeed, were much more likely to pack her off back to London than to follow her orders. "And I am not such a fool, Gwendolen Pryce, and nor are you."

"What, then?" said Gwendolen, still sceptical.

"Obviously," said Joanna, "I intend to infiltrate by stealth."

Gwendolen frowned at this for a moment before translating, "Sneak in, you mean."

"Yes."

"You"—looking her up and down—"dressed like that."

"Well—"

"And when you have done your stealthy infiltrating, what then?"

Joanna scowled. "Well, I cannot know what to do next until I have seen the lay of the land, can I?" she said. "There is a postern-gate in the north wall—away from the sea—with two guards. The prisoners are brought in and out that way."

Gwendolen's eyes widened. "Please, Jo," she said, "tell me that your grand plan does not rely upon being taken prisoner yourself."

"I did think of that, at first," Joanna conceded, "but it will not answer; they are kidnapping powerful mages—for their great spell-thing, if Sophie is not mistaken—and I cannot even call light."

"Then you had much better let me do it," said Sophie.


The ensuing dispute quickly became a shouting-match, which Gwendolen (aided by her superior height) interrupted by taking Joanna by one shoulder and Sophie by the other, dragging them apart, and bellowing over their combined protests, "You shall neither of you do anything of the sort, if I have to lock both of you up in that wardrobe to stop you."

The three of them retreated to separate corners of the tiny room—so close together, still, that any of them might have reached out and touched the others—and glared, breathing hard.

"How can you think of doing such a thing, Sophie?" Joanna demanded, not for the first time. "You have scarcely left your bed since—"

"Have you forgot already how Donald MacNeill came by the intelligence that sent all those men out to the Ross of Mull to begin with?" Sophie retorted. "If done once, it can be done again—and besides, the nearer I am to Gray, the better I shall recover."

This last, at any rate, was true enough that Joanna could not at once find words to refute it.

"Wardrobe," said Gwendolen darkly. "Locked. I have three brothers and three sisters who will tell you whether or not I mean what I say."

Sophie glowered.

Joanna took several deep breaths, marshalling her thoughts, and at last said, "I cannot be content to wait for Donald MacNeill to put his house in order. Something must be done, as soon as may be, and we are the ones to do it." She turned to Sophie. "I had hoped to keep you safely out of it. That was always a vain hope, I suppose."

"We are neither of us renowned for keeping safe at home," Sophie muttered; Joanna pretended not to hear her.

"I am—I am willing that you should be of the party, if Lucia MacNeill will consent to share her magick with you. Otherwise you should be a danger to all of us, rather than a help. I am sorry to say it," she added, in response to Sophie's poorly concealed flinch, "but so it is."

It was not an entirely safe promise to make; still, Donald MacNeill's reaction to the first such undertaking had been such as, in Joanna's estimation, made it unlikely that he should countenance a repeat performance.

Relief and terror and hope chased one another across Sophie's face before a careful blankness took their place. "I shall go and write to Lucia, then."

Joanna watched her go, attempting to look encouraging whilst earnestly praying that Donald MacNeill might refuse to let his daughter anywhere near Quarry Close for the next month.


Sophie's letter to Lucia—in which she pleaded for a renewal of the MacNeill magick, so that she might continue her attempts to reach

Gray by means of a drawing-spell—produced a swift and damping reply, to the effect that Donald MacNeill had expressly forbidden any undertaking of the kind. The despondent mood into which Sophie fell as a result was not alleviated by a strong impression that Joanna was rather relieved than disappointed by this turn of events.

But hard on the heels of Lucia's letter came Lucia herself, again on foot and dressed as a University undergraduate, complete with a stack of codices and a quite plausible air of abstraction.

Sophie heard the knock at the door, but she paid it no heed until Donella MacHutcheon came into the sitting-room—where for the past hour Sophie had sat forlornly at the pianoforte, looking through sheets of music which she had not the heart to play, whilst behind her Gwendolen Pryce worked silently through the contents of the mending-basket—and said, "You have a visitor, Domina."

She looked up just as Lucia followed Donella MacHutcheon into the room, throwing back the hood of her grey woollen cloak.

"What—"

"If my father learns what I am about," said the heiress of Alba, cutting off Sophie's astonished protest, "I cannot say what he may do. I have almost no time; I pray you, let us not waste it in arguing. Come."

She gestured at the sofa, and Sophie swallowed her questions— *What do you here? Surely you do not mean to defy your father's direct command, only to help me work a drawing-spell? Have you guessed what it is I truly mean to do with your magick?*—and obeyed.

The rite proceeded more quickly this time, for Lucia did not pause either to explain herself or to seek Sophie's consent for each separate step. Again the borrowed magick surged through Sophie, swift and sharp and hot, but she was ready for it now, and gentled it down more quickly than before.

She looked up at her deliverer, hoping that her expression might be capable of conveying her gratitude, for she could find no words adequate to the task. Whilst Lucia was smiling at her, beginning to clean her knife and tidy her materials away, the front door opened once more as Gwendolen Pryce appeared in the sitting-room, pink-faced and breathing hard, with Joanna on her heels.

"Do you see?" she panted over her shoulder. "What did I tell you?"

"Sophie, what are you about?" Joanna demanded, reverting to Brezhoneg; as she drew closer, she exclaimed, "Your hand is bleeding! Sophie, what—"

Lucia frowned—whether because she could not understand the words or because the tone was only too comprehensible—and Sophie shifted into Latin to reply: "Is this not what you wished for, Jo?"

Joanna could not reasonably deny it—though *demanded* might be a better term than *wished*—but she looked as though she should have liked very much to do so, and Sophie's belly clenched: She had been right, then, that Joanna had never wished for this at all. That, in fact, in setting such a condition on Sophie's participation in whatever rescue attempt she might be concocting with Gwendolen, her aim had been to strand her sister in Din Edin, safely out of the way under the eyes of Lord de Courcy and her father's loyal guardsmen.

"I wished—that is, I thought—"

*Did you think, can you truly have thought, that I should send you off into certain danger to rescue* my husband, *and myself stay here and rot?*

Lucia had finished packing away her things; she rose to her feet with her arms full of books, saying quietly in Gaelic, "I must go. May your gods keep you, Sophie Marshall of Britain."

She bent and kissed Sophie's upturned brow; their shared magick flared minutely at the point of contact, like—

Sophie resolutely set aside the thought of what it was like.

"And may your gods smile upon you, Lucia MacNeill of Alba," she said.

Lucia straightened her back, pulled up the hood of her cloak, and sailed past Joanna and Gwendolen like a small, imperious ship of war.

"I am coming with you, Jo," said Sophie, the moment she heard the door close behind her visitor. "I beg you will not waste precious time in attempting to stop me."

"Sophie—"

"*No.*" Sophie surged up from the sofa, drew herself up to her full height, and fixed her sister with the most daunting stare she could muster. "You do not know me very well, Joanna Callender, if you thought I should sit quiet and safe in Din Edin whilst you risked your life and Gwendolen's for the sake of *my husband.*"

"And *you* do not know *me* at all," Joanna retorted, standing on tiptoe to glare directly into Sophie's eyes, "if you imagine me capable of dragging you into mortal danger when you are already half dead."

The worst of it was that Joanna was quite right—for a certain value of *right* which was calculated from prudence and logic and sober good sense, taking no account of constancy, or heartache, or love. She should regret this, she knew, when her borrowed magick faded—her mind might now be sharp again, the fug of melancholy cleared away, but after nearly a month's debilitating lethargy, her body could not recover its strength in an instant, and was running on pure nerve—but the very notion of leaving Gray to his fate, when she might have helped him . . . ! Not to speak of sending her younger sister into a danger which ought to have been her own to face.

But if logic were to be Joanna's weapon, then Sophie should try her hand at wielding it also.

"The closer I am to Gray," she said again, "the less I shall be 'half dead.'"

Joanna's silence was not concession, but neither was it an objection.

"And I am not helpless now," said Sophie, encouraged; "I can do things. Useful things. If the plan is not to be taken prisoner, then you shall need concealment; they will all be on the alert now. And," she concluded, carefully keeping the triumph out of her voice, "you are speaking of a journey all the way to Mull, and I am the only one of us who can speak Gaelic."

"That much is true, Jo," said Miss Pryce. She spoke slowly and reluctantly, and when Joanna turned to glare at her, she shrugged one shoulder and said, "I do not like the thought of it any more than you do, but . . . we have few enough arrows in our quiver, and I should be a liar if I estimated our odds of success any lower with Mrs. Marshall than without her."

*I thank you for that ringing endorsement, Miss Pryce,* thought Sophie dryly, but she held her tongue.

"That has nothing to do with the case," said Joanna furiously.

"It has *everything* to do with it, Jo." Sophie kept her voice low and even. "You need me, and I need you; and Gray needs all of us."

Joanna sat down at Sophie's desk (no one—not even Sophie herself—being permitted to use Gray's) and, after several false starts, closed her letter to Jenny with vague reassurances which, however, were not so vague as to raise suspicion.

*Or so I hope.*

"Well, it will have to do," she said aloud, and folded the letter up to seal it.

She looked thoughtfully at Sophie's paper-knife. After a moment, she slipped it into her pocket and went down to the kitchen to look for a whetstone.

Joanna woke very early next morning, after a restless night, and found herself alone in the Marshalls' spare bedroom. This circumstance was not unusual—Gwendolen was an early riser by nature as well as by habit and, upon finding soon after their arrival that Donella MacHutcheon did not generally arrive in Quarry Close until well after sun-up, had appointed to herself the task of making the morning tea—but Joanna's unpropitious dreams lingered, and she admitted to herself that she should have been glad of the tangible evidence of life provided by Gwendolen's quiet breathing on the far side of the bed.

She washed and dressed with brisk efficiency, descended the staircase (avoiding the creaky step, so as not to risk waking Sophie), and made her way into the kitchen.

"Good morning," she said, and stopped dead.

There was a strange boy sitting at the kitchen table, eating an apple.

They looked at one another for a moment—the boy nonchalant, Joanna silently frantic. Who in Hades was he, and by what magick, trickery, or violence had he got into Sophie's house?

Then the boy swallowed his mouthful of apple, gave Joanna a cheerful grin, and said in Gwendolen's voice, "Good morning, Jo!"

Joanna sat down heavily on the nearest chair, for her knees seemed no longer willing to do their office.

"Your *hair*," she said, without altogether intending it. Last evening Gwendolen's hair, plaited for the night, had hung down nearly to her waist, a dark rope against her pale nightdress; now her face was framed by a mass of loose curls, which softened its angular lines without at all detracting from the graceful curve of her throat. "How did you—"

It was astounding how well she carried off her masquerade: the hair, indeed, scarcely registered beside the confident set of her shoulders, the careless sprawl of her trousered legs, the rakish tilt of her head.

As Joanna stared, Gwendolen's smile faded. "Do you dislike it so much?" she said. "It will grow back, you know. If I only put it up under a cap, I should be forever in danger of the cap's falling off."

Joanna stood up again and went round the table to stand behind Gwendolen's chair. "It suits you," she said. "I should not have thought it, but it suits you very well."

"Oh," said Gwendolen, and Joanna discovered that her right hand had risen, without volition or indeed conscious thought on her part, to ruffle the soft dark curls.

Gwendolen tilted her head back, dislodging Joanna's fingers, and resumed her boyish grin, but Joanna fancied that it was not quite so insouciant as formerly. Then she pushed back her chair (narrowly missing Joanna's toes) and jumped up to attend to the kettle.

★   ★   ★

"You see the advantages, of course," said Gwendolen, when the tea was made and they were seated on either side of the kitchen table, drinking it. "In Alba, women may travel together unescorted as a matter of course, but in Britain almost never; your tale of Elinor and Harriet will be the more plausible for having their cousin George in the party, in place of Louisa. And George will be able to speak to people whom Elinor and Harriet never could."

"*Not* George," said Joanna firmly.

Gwendolen frowned. "Why not? I have just been explaining—"

"Oh! No, I did not mean that we ought to have Louisa instead," Joanna said. "But George is Gray and Jenny's dreadful elder brother, you see. Perhaps you might be . . . Arthur, instead? Or Denis, or Gaëtan?"

"Or Gaël," Gwendolen suggested, her mouth tilting up at one corner, "as I am wearing his best suit of clothes."

Joanna was surprised into laughing aloud. She studied Gwendolen's neat trousers, shirt, and coat—the polished riding-boots, she saw now that she was looking carefully, were Gwendolen's own. They were not a gentleman's clothes, exactly, but the lines seemed to be drawn rather differently in Alba; and where they were going, distinctions of this sort were highly unlikely to matter.

"I hope you did not steal them, Gwen?" she said.

"Of course not!" Gwendolen looked scandalised. "I asked very politely, and I gave him enough coin to replace them. And I did not steal that, either," she added, with a reproachful look at Joanna; "Lady Kergabet is astonishingly generous, and makes me a much larger allowance than I can possibly spend."

Joanna acknowledged this to be entirely in character.

"He was quite pleased with the transaction, in point of fact," Gwendolen continued, "for he has never liked this shade of blue." She tugged gently at the collar of Gaël's best coat. "Though I am not sure how he means to explain the alteration to Lady Kergabet."

This time, the smile she directed across the table at Joanna was no more than a crinkling-up of her dark eyes; but it made Joanna grin recklessly in return.

"Morgan," said Gwendolen after a moment. "That is the name I used when last I ran away dressed as a boy—but nobody in Alba knows it. Morgan Prichard. What say you, Jo?"

"Harriet, you mean," said Joanna.

"My apologies, dear cousin." Gwendolen's voice went slightly deeper and very slightly rougher about the edges. "Should you care to dance, Harriet?"

Joanna goggled at her. "By Thalia's masque, you ought to be on the stage!"

After all, however, if she were to be Harriet Dunstan again, she ought to do the thing properly. When Gwendolen held out her hand, therefore, in the best gentlemanly manner, Joanna took it.

At once she was swept into a sort of manic reel, danced to and fro across Sophie's kitchen, which left them both breathless and laughing. When finally they spun to a halt and dropped hands, and Joanna (in character as Harriet) curtseyed whilst Gwendolen (equally in character as Morgan) made her elegant leg, and they looked respectively up and down at one another, Joanna felt quite capable of facing down any number of inimical MacAlpines.

## CHAPTER XXVIII

# In Which Sophie
# Makes Herself Useful

*Loath though Joanna* was to admit it, it was true that the addition to their party of Sophie—of a Sophie, that is, perhaps not altogether herself, but certainly restored to something like it—was both encouraging and enormously useful. In the service of this cause, and with Lucia MacNeill's borrowed magick almost visibly thrumming in her veins, she was taut and focused, entirely free of both irksome doubts and tedious melancholy. It was she who had procured them seats in a mail-coach bound for Glaschu, under the names of Elinor Graham, Harriet Dunstan, and Morgan Prichard; she who had done the hard magickal labour of creating a seeming of herself, which should sit at the pianoforte for some hours as she ordinarily did, to be seen by anyone who looked in at the window; and it was thanks to her concealing magick that they were rattling along in a coach full of strangers more impecunious than themselves—not one of whom paid them any mind at all—before the day's guardsmen, Menez and Tredinnick (and thus Lord de Courcy), had any notion that they had so much as left the house.

The broad outlines of this part of the plan had been Joanna's, but she could certainly not have carried it off so well without Sophie—

Sophie who sat composedly beside her, knitting (knitting!) something on large needles with a soft, heavy wool, and looking nothing at all like herself.

When they came to their destination, they should again be relying heavily on Sophie's magick, first to slip unnoticed into Castle MacAlpine, and then to escape with—in the best case—five rescued prisoners, or—in the worst case—sufficiently damning information to spur Donald MacNeill to immediate action. Joanna eyed her sidelong, uneasy.

At their first halt—some three hours into the journey, at a posting-inn of vaguely unsalubrious appearance—Gwendolen sprang down from the top of the coach, attempting without much success to conceal her delight in being out of doors in the spring sunshine, behind if not astride a team of fast horses. Joanna rather envied her this outside position, for which she had volunteered when the number of passengers proved greater than could be accommodated inside; the interior of the coach was hot and close, and smelt strongly of damp wool and of the roasted chestnuts which several of her fellow passengers had been sharing out between them for the first hour of the journey. Equally she envied Sophie her unruffled calm, despite knowing it to be entirely fictitious.

"Should you like me to fetch you some wine, Harriet?" Gwendolen asked her, in English; and, turning to Sophie, "Elinor?"

Joanna's lips twitched; had Gwendolen been taking lessons from Lady MacConnachie's superior manservant, then? "At the next halt, perhaps, cousin," she said. "We shall walk apart a little; mind you do not let the coach depart without us!"

She took Sophie's arm and steered her away towards the least crowded corner of the inn-yard, swinging wide about a stack of crates each of which appeared to contain at least one deeply offended goose.

"What is it?" Sophie demanded, sotto voce, the moment they were out of earshot of the rest.

"Nothing," said Joanna, surprised; "I only wanted to ask whether you felt quite well."

"Perfectly, I thank you," said Sophie. She frowned. "Why?"

"Because . . ." *Because you look and speak and behave like a stranger, and you are so much better at it than you used to be, and it puts me quite off my stride.* Joanna lowered her voice. "Because this masquerade must be costing you a great deal of magick, and we cannot know how much or how little you may have to spare." Besides her own disguise, Sophie's concealing magick was also, more subtly, protecting Joanna and Gwendolen, by rendering them unremarkable and deflecting from them any unfriendly attention.

Sophie's face—or, rather, the apple-cheeked, befreckled face she had assumed this morning, together with a very slightly more curvaceous version of her general shape, and a riot of auburn curls—grew briefly introspective. "I think . . . I think we have no cause to worry as yet."

Joanna nodded warily. Sophie's expression, so often difficult to read, was now entirely inscrutable, cloaked as she was in the mysterious Elinor Graham.

The name worried her a little, too: *Elinor Graham.* Sophie had briefly been Elinor during their flight from Callender Hall three years ago; and Graham of course was Gray, whose Borders-born mother had once been Agatha Graham. "Is that not something of a risk?" she had asked Sophie, cautiously, on its first being proposed, but had desisted thereafter, in the face of Sophie's frosty stare.


In Glaschu Sophie procured both rooms for the night at a respectable-looking inn and—by way of a voluble half-hour's conversation in Gaelic with the innkeeper's daughter, of which Joanna understood no more than half a dozen words—the names of several boats known to take passengers to Mull.

"You mean ships," Joanna corrected reflexively, when this welcome news was imparted to her, in a low voice, over supper in the inn's common dining-room. It was an effort to avoid slipping into Brezhoneg, but a necessary one; to account for Sophie's serviceable but imperfect Gaelic, Elinor Graham must be a child of the Borders, and the others, who spoke no Gaelic at all, her English cousins.

Sophie's—Elinor's—mouth crimped. "No," she said, "boats. I hope you have neither of you any objection to fish."

Joanna chuckled at the mental image of the Princess Royal perching amongst some oblivious fisherman's catch; Sophie frowned at her with Elinor Graham's heavy auburn brows.

"I am sorry," Joanna said. "Pray continue, Elinor dear."

The frown relaxed a little—although she could still read in Elinor's hazel-green eyes Sophie's dread of being mocked or laughed at—as Sophie explained that the same trading-boats ferried cargoes—including fish—and passengers from the larger seagoing vessels that put into deeper harbours on the coast along the River Clyde into Glaschu, and goods and passengers out to those same harbours, and Joanna committed the names and descriptions of promising boats and their proprietors to memory.

"Morgan and I shall go and speak to them," said Sophie, when Gwendolen had gone to fetch back a jug of wine—and perhaps a scrap or two of gossip—from the barmaid.

"My going to haggle with fishermen will offend Morgan's sense of propriety far less than your doing so," Joanna protested.

"But you have no Gaelic, Harriet," said Sophie, "and they will have no English and no Français."

The look in her eyes said, more clearly than any words, *You could not have managed this without me.* Though Joanna was not entirely prepared to concede this, it was certain that they should have had infinitely more difficulty over the business, and she saw the wary tension fade from Sophie as this understanding passed between them.

"We shall all go," she said, by way of concession.

Joanna, for her part, did not relax until—having consulted with Gwendolen on the pretext of walking about the town, with Morgan for escort—they were safely ensconced in their modest bedchamber, behind a reasonably solid door and Sophie's wards, and she could at last look her own sister in the face once more.

★   ★   ★

They were up before the sun to pursue their quarry, and the ebbing tide found them seated on oilcloth-wrapped bales of woven cloth, amidst a small party of women somewhat older than themselves, on the deck of a tubby fore-and-aft-rigged craft bound for Dùn Breatainn, where they should attempt to find passage to Mull.

Their fellow passengers were apparently well acquainted both with one another and with the journey and its sights. Their voluble and unceasing conversation (or as much of it as Sophie could comprehend, for they all spoke very quickly and in an unfamiliar accent) revolved entirely around some set of persons evidently known to them all, and they seemed to take no notice either of the sun rising through a bank of brilliant cloud on the eastern horizon or of the faintly greening hills and tidy villages along the river's banks. From time to time, looking up from their knitting, they darted an interested glance at the Sasunnach strangers; Sophie's bland smile and concealing magick, however, prevented the glances' developing into anything further.

It was not safety, but it was at any rate something like.

Abhainn Chluaidh—the River Clyde, as the folk of the Borders named it—stretched wide and blue, and their tubby little boat ran on the tide with a fresh breeze blowing almost dead astern to speed it along. *Mother Goddess, bountiful and kind,* Sophie prayed, *great Abhainn Chluaidh and mighty Neptune, may it so continue.*

By the time the boat set them ashore at Dùn Breatainn, Sophie had learnt—largely by paying close attention to their conversation, but also by means of a few calculatedly diffident overtures of her own—that the Alban women hailed from Eilean Arainn, or the isle of Arran, and were bound for home. This was disappointing in that it removed them as a possible source of intelligence on the quickest and safest means of reaching Castle MacAlpine; on the other hand, it meant that they should soon be parted from Sophie and her friends and thus should not have time to become suspicious of them.

Dùn Breatainn, though much less populous than Glaschu, possessed a minuscule dispatch office from which one might send an express to Din Edin. Sophie visited it early on the morning after their arrival, and there deposited an express letter directed to Mór Mac-Rury, in which was enclosed a sealed note to Lucia MacNeill.

> *We are on our way to Castle MacAlpine*, it read, *as I
> expect you have guessed, and I have not the least idea what
> we shall find there. I beg you will find a way to send some
> manner of assistance. If the rescue does not come off quietly,
> I expect there will be fireworks, and the time for subtlety
> will be at an end; please, if there is any possibility of your
> managing it, get word to Angus Ferguson's company—
> though I hope he may not still be in command—that should
> they see or hear anything suspicious from the castle or its
> environs, they are to come at once in what force they may.*

Nothing might come of it, she thought with a sigh as she sealed the letter, but at least she should not have left the way untried.

The journey by water to Mull—requiring as it did a wide circuit about Arran and the long, narrow peninsula of Cinn Tìre, even before the voyage north through the sound—was the longest any of them had ever undertaken, not to mention the most costly. Sophie's repeated prayers to Neptune notwithstanding, the sea was choppy and the voyage punctuated by what the sailors called *little squalls*, which the latter took in stride, assuring Sophie and Joanna that the storms of winter had been far worse and appearing not to remark how little comfort this brought them. Joanna's typically stoical demeanour did not spare her from sea-sickness, nor did her outrage at the resulting indignities in any way alleviate them; Sophie, having found her sea-legs a little more quickly, was almost glad for the care of nursing her sister—though it meant spending much of her time belowdecks, where the air was close and none too fresh—for otherwise the slow passing of time must have pushed her close to madness.

The worst of it was that she could feel Lucia MacNeill's magick ebbing. At the same time, as the good ship *Muireall* inched closer to her port of call on the southern coast of Mull, she could feel her own magick stirring, but it came in fits and starts, and was not enough, not yet, even to begin to make up the lack. *No, that is not the worst of it: the worst is that we have had no reliable news since leaving Glaschu.*

They had inquired, of course; finding a ship bound for Mull, willing to take on three Sasunnach passengers of dubious provenance, and able to satisfy the requirements of respectable accommodation as well as the limitations of Sophie's increasingly thin purse, had taken more time than Sophie had felt they had to spare, the one side benefit of which was that the delay afforded them plenty of time for both eavesdropping upon and openly questioning every traveller they could find who had lately set foot on that isle. The accounts thus gleaned, however, were so various and contradictory as to be entirely useless as intelligence. There were shades and spirits haunting the old castle (as it was invariably called); there had been a pitched battle— riots—a rout of Angus Ferguson's company by men of Clan Mac-Alpine, or the other way about—pillaging and rapine—peaceful demonstrations—the accepted chieftain of Clan MacAlpine had been ousted by a rival claimant, or had shut that rival up in the old castle to keep him out of the way—the castle had been fired, and its forests burnt, or its walls had been levelled, or the force sent against it had been laughably inept—the people of the Ross of Mull were cowering in fright, or they were taking up arms against Donald MacNeill, or they were fleeing in fishing-boats, or they had welcomed Donald MacNeill's troops with open arms because all through the winter their clan chieftain had let them starve.

"None of them look particularly hungry to me," Gwendolen had said, when Sophie related this last.

"Perhaps," Sophie had replied thoughtfully, "those we have met are the lucky few who have succeeded in making their escape."

Joanna scoffed at this, however. "Donald MacNeill is not a fool," she said, "and he does not rely on rumour and happenstance for news of what befalls his subjects. If the folk of Mull had been starving to death by their clan chieftain's fault, you may be sure that he should have intervened long before now."

At Sophie's look of mild surprise, she added, "You do not suppose that your father—"

Sophie and Gwendolen had both hushed her then, for they were standing in the inn-yard in full daylight; but in the dark of a night aboard ship Sophie was a little ashamed to recall that she had required reminding that her father was not, in fact, a tyrant content to see his people starve.

Joanna whimpered almost inaudibly, curling herself more tightly towards Sophie in the narrow bunk they shared.

"Ssh," Sophie murmured, smoothing a hand over her sweat-damp hair. "Hush, now, I shan't leave you." Joanna had seemed a little better this evening—at any rate, the vomiting seemed to be over and done, to the great relief of all concerned—but now the physical symptoms appeared to have been succeeded by a terror of Sophie's abandoning her to . . . to, Sophie supposed, whatever horrors were plaguing her dreams.

*I wish I had been born a healer,* she thought, not for the first time, but perhaps at least she might do something about the dreams.

She reached gingerly for her magick, and found it sufficient for her purpose; leaning close to Joanna's ear, she began to croon the spell for dreamless sleep which Gray had taught her in the midst of a very dark night of her own, some years ago.

Gradually Joanna's limbs relaxed and her breathing slowed as she slipped deeper into sleep. And at last, though not for some time, Sophie succeeded in joining her.

The *Muireall* was hailed early one morning, as she emerged from a narrow channel between two islands, by a trio of young men in what looked very much like a fishing-boat, and shortly thereafter boarded by two of the same. They spoke Gaelic with the same half-impenetrable accent as the islanders whom Sophie had met in Dùn Breatainn; they swaggered and glared, demanded payment from the ship's captain for her passage into "the domain of Ailpín Drostan"— from the gobsmacked expressions of the crew, this was by no means usual—and commanded that all the passengers identify themselves and explain what business brought them to Mull.

Joanna was up and about once more, if a little thinner and paler than was her wont, and for some days now Sophie had felt the welcome flicker of her own magick reasserting itself, bit by infinitesimal bit, over the ebbing traces of Lucia MacNeill's gifting. She was better equipped than she had feared, therefore, to encounter a pair of large, impatient Albans desiring to know her business—though nevertheless thoroughly terrified by the experience—and by means of a wistful smile, the interminably rehearsed and therefore reasonably glib tale of Elinor Graham's mama, whose last wish it had been that her daughter should visit the birthplace of her grandmother, and the judicious use of her own mother's magick, she succeeded in persuading them to move on to the next party of passengers with no more comment than a gruff injunction to take care and to go nowhere unescorted. If, afterward, she leant rather heavily upon Gwendolen's arm, she hoped that this might be attributed to her own recent bout of sea-sickness.

Joanna had been expecting some sort of port—not one so large or so busy as London or Portsmouth, naturally, but something like the port of Douarnenez, where fishing-boats, traders' vessels, and private craft put in with some regularity, and a modest selection of inns stood ready to feed and house those newly arrived to the town or awaiting passage elsewhere. She had been ill for days and days, or so it seemed, and for much of the voyage she had longed for a proper meal, a proper bed, and a proper floor that did not rock and sway beneath her feet, to the exclusion of all else.

Instead, however, the *Muireall* stood off from a shallow bay on the south shore of the Ross of Mull, and those passengers whose destination this was were sent ashore in the ship's boats.

"Look," Sophie whispered, as she and Joanna leant their elbows on the taffrail, awaiting their turn to climb into the swaying boat. "There it is."

She pointed with her chin to the southwest, where a stone fortification—it looked tiny from this distance—perched high above the sea. Castle MacAlpine, then.

Joanna nodded.

Gwendolen, as Morgan Prichard, took a turn at the oars—acquitting herself rather well, and preening only a little at Joanna's pleased surprise—and as they approached the shore, she hopped nimbly over the gunwales to help one of the sailors run her up onto the stony beach, so that the ladies might disembark onto relatively dry land. Joanna remarked, with a pang of guilt at not having done so before this, that not since that first unauthorised gallop in London had Gwendolen looked so uncomplicatedly happy.

The three of them hung back to watch the rest of the disembarking travellers—a shopkeeper and his wife from Glaschu, come to visit the latter's elderly and ailing parents, and two sandy-haired brothers, island-born, who had gone to Din Edin to seek employ and found it did not suit them—make their way up the beach. To their left above the flat waters of the bay, a hill rose precipitately, rocky and rough, with turf and heather beginning to green over it and thin cloud drifting lazily across its seaward prow. As Joanna watched, a tiny figure appeared over the brow of the hill, followed at once by a greyish mass that ebbed and flowed around it, which after a bemused moment she recognised as a flock of sheep.

"Come along, Harriet," said Sophie, tugging at her elbow. "Look."

Joanna looked round and followed the direction of Sophie's gaze to where the shopkeeper was solicitously helping his wife along a steep, narrow footpath leading upward and inland from the rocky beach. Each of them carried a large valise in one hand, which made their progress slow and ungainly. The sandy-haired brothers were well ahead of them, and widening the gap.

She looked behind her; the little boat and its crew, rowing steadily, were already more than halfway back to their ship.

With Sophie and Gwendolen, at their own insistence, carrying all of their scant possessions, they turned their faces to the northeast and made for the path.

## CHAPTER XXIX

# In Which There
# Is a Change of Plans

*There was no* inn at Carsaig.

A public-house there was, at least, denominated the Drovers' Drum, and here Joanna and Gwendolen inhaled vast helpings of roast mutton and vegetables while Sophie, who was too tightly strung even to think of eating, sought the assistance of the publican's taciturn wife and rather exuberant daughter, nursing the mug of porter which the latter had pressed upon her.

"There's Rose Neill MacTerry," said the daughter to her mother, whose sole contribution to the discussion thus far had consisted in attempts to persuade Sophie to eat something. "Her youngest married an Arrain-man last summer and she's all alone now. Or Malveen MacUsbaig—but she's a Hearach, you know."

Sophie did not see in what way Malveen MacUsbaig's coming from Na Hearadh—what the British called the isle of Harris—could have any bearing on her own present difficulty, but it seemed impolite to say so. And perhaps she had misheard; the Gaelic of these islanders was not that of a Din Edin drawing-room.

The publican's wife looked directly at her, frowning. "You are Sasunnach," she said.

"My father was," Sophie said easily, thinking *I am Elinor Graham* as hard as she could. "Or half a Sasunnach at any rate, on his mother's side. I was born in the Borders. My mother was born in Glaschu, and her mother at Pennyghael."

"Oh!" said the daughter. "MacGille, was she?"

Sophie knew not how to reply to this; would it be the more suspicious to answer *yes*, or *no*? Pennyghael, on the far side of the narrow neck of land that was the Ross of Mull, had seemed the safest decoy destination—near enough to account for their wishing to go ashore where they had done, but not so near as to make a long stay in Carsaig convenient for their alleged purposes.

Fortunately the publican's wife ignored her daughter's question entirely. "But your cousins"—she gestured at Joanna and Gwendolen—"have not even so much claim as yourself to Alban blood. This is a bad time for Sasunnach strangers to be coming here. Have you not heard that Cormac MacAlpine is trying to raise the clan-lands against the chieftain Donald MacNeill, because Donald MacNeill is bent on selling his own daughter to the Sasunnach King, and Alba with her?"

Sophie blinked. *Cormac MacAlpine is trying to raise the clan-lands.* Was this useful intelligence, or yet more unsubstantiated rumour?

Behind her, the quiet sounds of Joanna and Gwendolen working their way through their luncheon continued unabated. *They did not hear that,* she reminded herself, *and could not have understood it if they had.*

"I had heard that there is to be a marriage between the heiress of Alba and one of King Henry's sons," she said, feeling her way slowly through what was abruptly become a sort of conversational fenland, liable to sink her to the neck in stinking mud at the least false step. "I have not heard any of the rest, and I confess I do not know what it means to *raise the clan-lands.*"

"It is Alban magick," said the publican's wife, "old magick and deep. Not for strangers' ears, or strangers' eyes. You had better have stayed at home, child of the Borders."

At this point her daughter intervened, feeling perhaps—as Sophie did—a little taken aback by her vehemence.

"I'll just take you up to see Rose Neill MacTerry, shall I?" she said, smiling brightly at Sophie. "Will your cousins come, also? Or will we come back for them later? It seems a pity to interrupt their dinner."

Sophie smiled absently in return. *Cormac MacAlpine is trying to raise the clan-lands. Old magick and deep—might that be Ailpín Drostan's spell-net, or Cormac MacWattie's magick of the land? And five powerful mages vanished without trace . . .*

"I thank you, yes," she said.

Rose Neill MacTerry, it appeared, lived halfway up the side of a mountain; at any rate, Sophie was feeling achy, dishevelled, and sluggish by the time she and her companion reached the gate of her small stone-built house.

The woman who opened the door to their knocking was a very little taller than Sophie, straight and slim despite the four grown children about whom Sophie had heard endless anecdotes in the course of the journey from the Drovers' Drum. "Teàrlag MacAlpine!" she exclaimed, prompting a very belated recognition on Sophie's part that she had come all this way with a girl whose name she did not know—and, it now transpired, a daughter of Clan MacAlpine. *Tread carefully.* "What brings you?"

Sophie caught Teàrlag MacAlpine's brief frown at Rose Neill Mac-Terry and wondered what it meant. A faint itching sensation tickled the bridge of her nose; she knew very well what *that* meant but could not deduce its source.

"Elinor Graham of the Borders," said Teàrlag MacAlpine, gesturing at Sophie.

"Are you so indeed?" Rose Neill MacTerry smiled pleasantly, but she studied Sophie in a way that Sophie did not altogether like.

"She has two Sasunnach cousins with her," Teàrlag MacAlpine continued; "my mother is giving them their dinner at the Drum. Elinor Graham asked our help to find a bed for the night."

"We did not know that Carsaig had no inn," Sophie put in; she was conscious that the admission made her seem careless and irresponsi-

ble, but the circumstances seemed to demand some sort of explanation. "It is only for the night; we must be on to Pennyghael tomorrow."

Ought she to mention payment? Would Rose Neill MacTerry welcome the notion of compensation for her trouble, or would it be an
insult to her hospitality? Impossible to say.

Rose Neill MacTerry smiled again. "There was an inn, once," she
said, "in the days of the MacAlpine chieftains. 'Twas named the
Sasunnach's Head."

Sophie shivered. At the same time, incongruously, she had to stifle
a yawn.

"Do you come in, then, Elinor Graham," said Rose Neill Mac-
Terry, holding wide the door of her little house, "and sit you down a
little."

Sophie could never afterwards remember exactly what happened
next.

"Sophie has been gone a very long time with that girl," said Joanna,
frowning.

Gwendolen blinked at her in the dim light of the taproom. "Where
did she say she was going?"

"I . . ." Joanna thought hard. *I am just going to see about a bed for the
night,* Sophie had said, surely more than an hour ago; *stay here and
finish your meal, and I shall be back directly.* It had not seemed suspicious
at the time, but it certainly seemed so now. "She did not say *where,* at
all, and she meant to be back directly. Which she is not," she added
unnecessarily. "And we do not even know that girl's name!"

The publican's wife had vanished at some point during their prolonged (and, it must be said, very welcome) meal. Joanna and Gwendolen went in search of her, and failing to find her, or anyone at all,
in any of the public rooms, behind the bar, or—to judge by the lack
of any answer to their repeated knocking—behind the door that
led to the private part of the house, they gave up on the interior of
the house entirely and circled about the outside of it, looking for any
sign of human life at all. The afternoon was well along by now,

LADY OF MAGICK 363

though there would be several more hours of daylight yet, to judge by the angle of the sun, yet the village seemed sleepy and unpopulated.

When at last they ran their quondam hostess to earth, it was by the sound of water sloshing from bucket to bucket; she was filling the water-trough for a pair of huge and weary-looking horses pastured at some distance from the public-house.

Gwendolen chirruped softly to the horses and slipped fearlessly between them to scratch at their shaggy manes. The publican's wife regarded this spectacle with some alarm, but upon seeing that the horses only whickered and nuzzled at the strange young man's shoulders, she appeared to decide that neither party was in any danger from the other, and went on emptying pails of water into the trough.

Joanna took hold of the last full bucket.

"'*S mise* Harriet Dunstan," she said determinedly, gesturing at herself with her free hand; "*dè an t-ainm a tha oirbh?*"

The woman frowned at her, and was silent for a long moment. "Morag MacGregor," she said at last, in a grudging tone.

"Morag MacGregor," Joanna repeated; and then, her meagre fund of Gaelic exhausted, she said, "will you tell us where my cousin and your daughter have gone?"

Morag MacGregor spread her hands and shook her head. "*Chan eil mi a' tuigsinn,*" she said. Joanna could not tell whether this meant *I do not know the answer* or *I do not understand the question*; but, she supposed, there was little to choose between the two, as in either case she should get no useful answer.

It was only a little longer, however, before Sophie and Morag MacGregor's daughter appeared in the distance, descending the steep hill behind the village.

"There, you see?" said Gwendolen, clasping Joanna's shoulder. In a lower voice she added, "How should you like to borrow these horses? I think one of them might easily carry any two of us."

Joanna controlled her initial startlement to give this notion serious consideration. "They do not look as though they should go very fast," she said doubtfully.

"No," Gwendolen conceded, "but they will know the lay of the land, and will not panic or put their feet in rabbit-holes." She looked doubtfully about her. "Are there rabbits on this island, do you suppose?"

"I should imagine so," said Joanna vaguely; most of her attention, now, was on following Sophie's progress down the hill.

She and her companion had now reached the foot of it and briefly disappeared behind the clutch of little stone houses that constituted the village of Carsaig; when they reappeared, they were within hailing distance, or near enough, and Joanna called, "Elinor!" and waved one arm wildly in the air.

"Harriet!" Sophie's voice came faintly back, caught on the rising breeze.

A little nearer, and Joanna's heart leapt, then plummeted; the woman striding along beside Morag MacGregor's daughter was not the buxom, auburn-haired Elinor Graham, but unmistakably Sophie.

"Mother Goddess," Gwendolen breathed, going very still. "This is a right balls-up."

"It is that," said Joanna, too poleaxed even to demand where Gwendolen had learnt such language.

She wished very much, at the moment, to swing up onto one of those enormous horses, kick it into a gallop, and pull her sister up behind her on the way to . . . well, to somewhere very far from this gods-accursèd village, at any rate. None of this was possible—quite apart from anything else, she should need a mounting-block the size of Glastonbury Tor to get aboard either of those beasts—but her pulse pounded with the need to *do something*, and her feet carried her towards Sophie as if pulled by one of Sophie's drawing-spells.

"Elinor," she said cautiously, as they drew level with one another, "are you quite well?"

"Very well," said Sophie. Her voice was even, her lips curved in a smile, but her dark eyes held Joanna's, wide and frantic.

Gwendolen stepped up behind Joanna, one hand splayed across her back. Half an hour ago, she should have shrugged it off with sharp annoyance; now she had to fight the temptation to lean closer, into the comfort of the known.

"Rose Neill MacTerry will give us a bed for the night," Sophie said. "Two beds, that is. And our supper." She half turned, gesturing towards the hill. "Her house is up there."

Squinting, Joanna could indeed make out what might be another of the little village houses, high up on the brow of the hill.

"Yes?" she said.

Sophie's brisk nod said *yes*; her anguished eyes cried *no*.

What did it mean that Sophie had let go the masque of Elinor Graham? And what did it mean that Morag MacGregor and her daughter were pretending not to have noticed the transformation?

Joanna gently took her sister's hand, ignoring the Albans as steadfastly as they were ignoring her, and turned to walk back towards the public-house, and their modest carpet-bags waiting under the shelter of the overhanging roof.

"Sophie," she said, low, as soon as she judged them to be out of earshot. "What has become of Elinor Graham?"

Sophie looked down at her, and once again Joanna's mind swam briefly as she struggled to reconcile the baffled expression on Sophie's face with the desperation in her eyes.

"She is bespelled," said Gwendolen, her voice low but sharp with impatience. "Obviously. *Why*, I have no notion, and I believe I had rather not. I think we must get away tonight, if we can."

She collected the carpet-bags and turned expectantly.

"Well?" said Joanna to Sophie. "Do we go?" She did not see that they had much choice; they must sleep somewhere, or, at any rate, they could not *borrow* Morag MacGregor's horses and ride away in broad daylight.

"Of course," said Sophie, smiling. Her fingers gripped Joanna's elbow so tightly that Joanna expected bruises in the morning.

"I know," she murmured. "I understand."

Sophie's eyes closed briefly, and when she opened them again the sharp desperation had eased a little.

\* \* \*

They trudged up the hill to the house of Rose Neill MacTerry. It was small, stone-built, with a heavy front door whose hinges creaked as it opened; Joanna reflexively looked for and marked all other possible means of egress. It was not immediately apparent why, as between this diminutive dwelling and the much larger one which housed the Drovers' Drum, Rose Neill MacTerry's house should be the one offered to guests; was Morag MacGregor hiding something, or someone?

Rose Neill MacTerry gave them a supper of bread, smoked fish, and a strongly flavoured sheep's-milk cheese; Joanna suspected this last of harbouring some noxious substance, but Gwendolen elbowed her and muttered, "We do not know when our next meal may be," and she succeeded in eating a few bites.

Sophie ate mechanically, her eyes fixed on some unidentifiable point midway along the scrubbed kitchen table. Their hostess, having set their meal before them, sat down to the spinning-wheel in one corner of her kitchen and made no attempt to engage them in conversation; when the meal was done, she showed them their night's accomodations—a small, square, aggressively spotless bedroom for the ladies, and a clean straw-tick in the attic for Gwendolen—and left them to their own devices.

Sophie sat down on the edge of the bed, smiling absently at nothing in particular.

"Elinor?" said Joanna, laying a tentative hand on her shoulder. "Should you like to take a turn about the garden with Morgan, before we go to bed?"

Sophie looked up at her, her eyes deep wells of furious anger.

Joanna blinked in surprise. Then she hugged her sister tight, bending close to her ear to whisper fiercely, "Good."

There was very little garden to walk in, and the slope was such that it was often more climbing than walking, but they were very near the sea, and for all that Joanna had lately conceived a considerable dislike of sea voyages, the wild salt smell and the glitter of the swell along the horizon were a comfort to her. Sophie did not speak—whether because she could not or because she refused to do so was difficult to discern—but her hand gripped Joanna's painfully tight.

"Can you get down the hill yourselves in the dark?" said Gwendolen. "I should think we shall have moonlight enough to see by—the sky is clear, and the moon nearly full—but we cannot risk a light."

"We shall manage well enough," said Joanna, frowning, "but what of you?"

"I shall be fetching the horses," said Gwendolen. Then, pointing down the slope, she added, "There is a stream there—do you see? If we ride along it—"

"Yes, I see. To hide our tracks."

They were keeping their voices lowered, but Joanna could not help frequently glancing about, in case of listeners.

"We shall have to leave all of our bags and baggage behind," Gwendolen added.

Joanna sighed. "What sort of idiot do you take me for?"


After bidding Rose Neill MacTerry a good night and shutting herself and Sophie into their bedroom, Joanna dug out her huswife and her warmest and least-beloved pelisse, and set about picking apart a seam. Sophie lay curled on the bed, watching her: placid face and raging eyes, her limbs relaxed and languid, her fingers curled like claws into the candle-wicked coverlet.

Joanna heard nothing to herald Gwendolen's departure and bolstered her courage with the notion of her having escaped the house entirely undetected. Having made her preparations—and, by necessity, Sophie's also—she blew out the lamps and watched the moon, peering at intervals through a small gap in the window-curtains.

Long before the moon reached the agreed-upon point in its trajectory, however, Joanna, peering out of the window for at least the hundredth time, caught a glimmer of light bobbing its way up the foot of the hill. It was gone again directly, but she crouched down on the floor below the window and exchanged her intermittent reconnaissance for a continuous vigil, determined not to repeat the mistakes of Angus Ferguson's ill-fated scouts.

Sure enough, before long the glimmer came again, and nearer; and again, and nearer yet: someone was climbing the hill.

Joanna dropped the curtain and scrambled to her feet.

"Sophie," she said, low, bending over the bed where Sophie yet lay, silent and unmoving. "Sophie, someone is coming. We must go at once."

Sophie's pale face turned up to hers, and her eyes were no longer terrified or angry, only unfathomably sad. "Go," she said. "You have no magick; it is me they want."

Joanna gaped at her. "We thought you were bespelled," she managed, after a moment.

"I was," said Sophie quietly. "Rose Neill MacTerry can see magick, you see, and she is in league with a man they call Cormac Mac-Alpine—he must be the rogue chieftain whom we have been hearing of. Morag MacGregor's husband and her daughter, also—I am not sure of Morag MacGregor herself, for I think she tried to warn us off."

"Sophie, what—"

"Hush, now. Listen. They spoke of Cormac MacAlpine's *raising the clan-lands*; they would not say what it meant, only that it was an old magick—*old and deep*, Morag MacGregor said—does that not sound very like the legend of Ailpín Drostan's spell-net?"

"Oh!" said Joanna.

"Yes. We knew already, that someone has been collecting mages, and we suspected what they might be wanted for, and now I think we know both the *why* and the *who*, and one part of the *how*. There are more mages unaccounted for than we know of, I expect." She shivered. "Teàrlag MacAlpine brings travellers here, so that Rose Neill MacTerry can see whether they have power worth . . . pursuing. I suppose there must be allies of Cormac MacAlpine in Din Edin, doing the same office—"

"Catriona MacCrimmon," said Joanna. *Oh, Sophie.*

"But they will not pursue you, Jo," Sophie went on, ignoring this, "or not at once, provided they have their prize." This with a little grimace of self-disgust. "Go and find Gwendolen—"

"Sophie Marshall!" Joanna hissed. "How can you—"

"Jo. *Listen.*"

Sophie's palm wrapped warm across Joanna's mouth; Joanna swallowed outrage.

"Go and find her. Wait with the horses at the bottom of the hill. And *follow me.*"

Joanna considered this scheme. She had not much liking for it in general, and none at all for Sophie's part of it in particular; but Sophie in this mood (as Joanna knew from long experience) was immovable, and as between the capture of them both, leaving Gwendolen in ignorance of their fate (and in possession of someone else's horses), and the capture of one, with two relatively well-informed rescuers to pursue her, the more rational choice was not difficult to see.

Joanna nodded, and Sophie let her go.

Then she surged up from the bed, crossed the small room, and crouched in the corner to rummage in her carpet-bag. When she rose to her feet again, she held something out to Joanna and said, "Here."

Joanna reached for Sophie's hand and was puzzled to find herself holding a tangle of silken cords and smooth oval stones. The puzzle resolved itself when Sophie said, "From Lady Maëlle, for emergencies."

"Mama's jewels?" said Joanna, disentangling one of the cords and looping it twice about her wrist.

Sophie's nod was just perceptible in the darkness.

"And have you kept one for yourself?"

"I have only those two," said Sophie; when Joanna attempted to give back the one she still held in her hand, she said, "I can shift for myself, Jo; you and Gwendolen cannot. Go, now, before it is too late."

"Be careful, then," said Joanna, hating the incipient tears that roughened her voice and made her breath come short. "May all the gods go with you."

They clung together tightly for a moment. Then Joanna wrapped a heavy knitted shawl over her gown and pelisse; tied a double knot in each of her bootlaces, and kilted up her skirts; and, having opened the window as silently as she could, climbed up over the sill and lowered herself carefully to the ground below.

Crouched against the south wall of the house, as deep in shadow as circumstances permitted, she watched the small procession approach the front door, which faced eastward and down the hill. At first only that little intermittent gleam showed its progress; as it drew nearer, however, she at last made out the tall, broad shapes of three men, dressed in the kilted plaid.

There came a quiet knocking at the door; the hinges creaked, and soft lamplight gleamed briefly on the flagstoned path. When she heard the door closing again, Joanna crept round the corner of the house, through the garden, and away down the hill; the moment she was out of sight of Rose Neill MacTerry's house, she ran.


Sophie eased the window closed behind Joanna and allowed herself a moment's frozen, agonising terror. Then she took a deep breath, let it out, and drew another, until the terror had receded a little; then, at last, she set about making her preparations.

First she drew down the bedclothes and arranged carpet-bags and cushions in the general outline of a sleeping body. Then, closing her eyes, she summoned up what magick she could.

In the darkness behind her eyelids she called to mind the curves and hollows of Joanna's body as she slept, curled beside Sophie in their bed at the inn in Glaschu; here the slope of her tucked-up knees, there the swell of her hip, here the fall of a chestnut plait over the curve of her shoulder. She marshalled the words of an illusion-spell and, murmuring them under her breath, shaped the magick to hide the cushions and carpet-bags under a semblance of her sister, breathing slow and steady in deep sleep. It was not so precise as the likeness she had made of herself before leaving Din Edin; but this time, in hopes of delaying its discovery, she gave her illusion no catch, no clue for Rose Neill MacTerry to follow. Silently she thanked Cormac

MacWattie for insisting that she learn this magick and begged his pardon for this deliberate lapse.

Finally she drew the bedclothes up again and, lying down again atop them, on the nearer side of the bed, composed herself to wait.

No more than a quarter of an hour had passed, or so she judged, when the tense breathing silence of the house was broken by a knock at the door—a strangely syncopated rhythm, which after a moment her mind's ear absently identified as the characteristic snap of a strathspey reel. An odd thing to remark upon, at such a time; Sophie let her mind focus on it, hang a melody upon that snatch of rhythm and build up harmonies around it, the better to keep up the pretence that she remained bespelled.

Since waking from that first baffling oblivion, she had puzzled over the nature of this spell for hours, locked within her uncooperative body, even her voice answering to someone else's will in place of her own. Only once had she experienced anything even remotely similar, and that was at the hands of the priests of Apollo Coelispex, who wielded the god's power in his name. This did not feel like that calm, suspended stillness, nor like the treacle-toffee grip of the spell known as Arachne's Web, but like a firm grip on the back of her neck, anchoring a chain which allowed her freedom of movement but could be pulled fatally tight at any moment.

Had she had the full use of her talent, she might have thrown it off, if not easily, then at any rate without material strain, but Lucia MacNeill's magick was ebbing, and her own not more than half recovered—and, besides, she could not silence the voice in her mind that murmured, *They will take you where Gray is.*

And when, hours into the early-falling spring night, the spell at last gave up its last grip on her, that voice only grew the more persuasive. *Only pretend*, it said, *only submit, and they will bring you within sight of your goal, to their own undoing. You are Ulysses in the belly of the horse; this is an opportunity not to be wasted.* Whether or not she had gauged their purposes aright, Gray's captors were collecting up powerful mages; Gray was still alive (Sophie ruthlessly quashed the new, unwelcome mental voice which tried to add the caveat *when last you were able to find him*), and thus, logically, it followed that whatever they wanted with Sophie, it was not her immediate demise. Joanna and Gwendolen, on the other hand, were not powerful mages, but *were*—or could be—witnesses who might carry tales, and thus were, at present, in more danger than she was herself.

Sophie knew very well what the others thought of her scheme of infiltration by surrender, and she had been prepared to bow to their wishes, but the thing was so close to being accomplished now, and if she could persuade Joanna to allow it, and to follow behind—

The door of Rose Neill MacTerry's spare bedroom opened quietly, and through slitted eyelids Sophie watched Rose Neill MacTerry herself step cautiously into the room.

"Elinor Graham," she said, her contralto voice so low as to be almost a hum of sound. "Come here."

Slowly, deliberately, Sophie rose from the bed and obeyed.

## CHAPTER XXX

# In Which Joanna and Gwendolen Experience a Setback

*The men did* not treat Sophie roughly or cruelly, though neither were they particularly solicitous of her comfort. She offered them no resistance; she was not appreciably stronger in body than she had been when they left Din Edin, and what strength she had, whether of body, mind, or magick, was better husbanded for whatever might be to come than wasted on struggles which she was doomed to lose.

She was escorted down the hill, therefore, in an almost restful silence, treading the same path which her feet had stumbled up and down so many times already since the previous morning, and boosted aboard a tall horse—brown or black or bay, though in the moonlight she could not tell which—after which one of her three captors swung up behind her, taking the reins in his left hand and tucking his right arm snugly about her waist.

It was at once an impersonal and a distressingly intimate gesture, and for the first time Sophie had real difficulty in maintaining her pose of pliant, unresisting stupor.

They spoke very little amongst themselves—perhaps they were as weary as she was—and she took care not to react to any of their words. She could not know what Rose Neill MacTerry (or, for that matter, Teàrlag MacAlpine or her mother) might have told them, but if they could be persuaded that she had no Gaelic, there was some possibility of her overhearing something useful.

The journey would not have been long as the crow flew (*as the owl flies*, Sophie thought, and gritted her teeth to keep her silence), but the terrain was craggy and rough, and their route seemed to lie always steeply uphill or down, except where the horses were forced to pick their slow way around the side of a hill, along a rocky outcrop. It was after dawn, therefore, when their little procession drew to a halt at the heavily guarded gate of a small castle.

Castle MacAlpine, such as it was, perched at the top of a rocky promontory, looking out to sea. Sophie and her captors had approached it from the east; to the north and west, a small forest—unexpected in this sheep-cropped, windswept place—pressed in towards its walls, its edges lit by the rising sun, dark and grey and brown and green with the full branches of pines and the just-unfurling new leaves of aspens.

The riders and the pikemen at the gate traded greetings with the ease of long acquaintance, yet still the latter demanded the day's watchword before signalling for the gate to be opened, and the former awaited its countersign before kicking their horses into motion once again.

Once inside the courtyard, they dismounted without ceremony, and Sophie's saddle-mate helped her to dismount as well, not roughly though quite without tenderness. She had not spent so much time on horseback for many months, and when he set her on her feet, her limbs wobbled under her and her knees threatened to buckle. The man whose arm had held her pinned against him all those long hours of the journey now wrapped big hands around her elbows, supporting her weight until her muscles and joints consented to do their work again. She risked a glance up at him, and before dropping her gaze again she glimpsed a ruddy-brown beard, a crooked nose, and eyes so deep-set as to obscure their colour.

"Steady," he growled, not unkindly.

Sophie registered, with a tiny flare of hope, that he was addressing her in Latin.

Joanna froze in her tracks and held up a hand to halt Gwendolen likewise. "I hear something," she hissed.

She could hear nothing now but Gwendolen's breathing and, in its interstices, her own. As soon as they resumed their stealthy progress, however, the sound tugged at the edges of her hearing again: faint, familiar, impossible to identify.

Not the borrowed draught horse they had left picketed at the edge of the wood; they had come too far from that point, now, for any ordinary horse-sound to carry, and had the horse managed to get loose, it should have turned for home, not followed a pair of strange riders. And not, she thought, the sounds of any creature native to this forest.

But footfalls, yes. Lighter than a horse's; heavier than a fox's or a deer's.

*A sentry of this castle, or a scout of Angus Ferguson's company. Neither is likely to welcome our presence here.*

The footsteps were growing louder. It was almost full daylight, even here amongst the trees; there was no time to climb up out of sight, and no other cover sufficient to conceal them. Now they should see whether Mama's charms against unwelcome notice could inded protect them.

Joanna stretched out her right hand towards Gwendolen; Gwendolen caught it in her left and held fast.

A pair of men, long-haired and bearded, emerged from between two pine-trees. They wore breastplates and vambraces of boiled leather, and helmets on their heads; one wore a sword on a heavy baldric, and the other carried a recurved bow as tall as his shoulder. Their gear and badges were not those of Donald MacNeill's troops; sentries of Castle MacAlpine, then.

Joanna held her breath. Gwendolen's hand gripped hers so tightly that her fingers were growing numb; where their wrists aligned, she felt her trembling and was reminded that Gwendolen had never seen Sophie's magick put to the test. Even Joanna herself, who had seen it more than once, did not altogether trust that the charms could prevent their being overheard, and so she could not risk any word of reassurance.

But for the present, at any rate, the magick held, and the strangers passed within half a dozen paces of them, apparently without remarking their presence at all. Joanna and Gwendolen watched them out of sight into the trees.

Gwendolen exhaled a long, almost silent sigh, and releasing Joanna's hand, she sank down with her back against a tree-trunk, resting her head on her drawn-up knees. For a moment, Joanna tactfully averted her eyes. Then she crouched beside Gwendolen in the leaf-mould, balancing herself with a hand on her friend's shoulder, and said quietly, "If we follow them, we shall have our way in."

The shoulder beneath her palm stiffened momentarily before Gwendolen raised her head. Her face was pale but resolute. "Lead on," she said.

They caught the sentries up at the edge of the wood, slipping out into the open just as their quarry approached the steps leading up to the postern-gate. The guards at the foot of the walled staircase made to bar the sentries' way; one of the men spoke a brief unintelligible phrase, and the guards raised their long pikes again and let them pass. When the sentries reached the middle step, Joanna and Gwendolen crept up behind them, slipped between the two guardsmen, and started up the staircase.

Another pair of pikemen guarded the postern-gate proper, at the top of the steps, and again the returning sentries were challenged, gave what must be a watchword, and were permitted to pass, with Joanna and Gwendolen unnoticed upon their heels. It was heady and terrifying, to see without being seen, and Joanna's heart beat so loudly and so rapidly that she half expected the noise to give them away.

Once inside the castle walls, Joanna tugged Gwendolen behind a rain-barrel and muttered, "Where do you suppose they are keeping the prisoners?"

Sophie was escorted into a pleasant sitting-room, where a tall man and a smiling golden-haired woman sat by a crackling fire. Her captors had bound her hands and stood either side of her, each with a hand on one of her elbows, from which she deduced that it was now that Rose Neill MacTerry's spell ought ordinarily to be wearing off.

The woman's eyes widened. "Well," she said, in a pleased tone. "How *interesting*. I had almost given up hope."

*Given up hope? Hope of what?* But she should not ask; much better if they thought her unable to understand them.

"Indeed," said the man. He rose from his seat and stalked towards Sophie, who now saw that he was even taller than she had supposed: quite as tall as Gray, in fact. "I had thought Rose Neill MacTerry over-optimistic; but unless I am much mistaken, this is the Sasunnach princess indeed—only a little later than expected."

Sophie's stomach clenched painfully, and her heart threatened to smash through her ribs. *They know who I am; I have walked into a trap.* She held her face and body still, however, and tried to think rationally: *This changes nothing. They covet my magick, that is all, and I sprang the trap of my own will.*

"Truly?" said his companion, leaning forward in her seat to study Sophie more closely.

"Oh, yes." The tall man smiled—a slow, secret, chilling sort of smile. This, Sophie was beginning to suspect, would be Cormac Mac-Alpine himself. "She imagines that she can hide it from me, but I believe she is more powerful even than that husband of hers."

*So, then: He can see magick, and he recruits others who can do so to spy for him elsewhere. Yes, that explains a great deal.*

But could also he see the remnants of Lucia MacNeill's magick threaded through her own? If so, he gave no sign.

Had Joanna and Gwendolen arrived yet? Had they succeeded in

gaining entry? *Great Janus, keeper of doors and gateways, smooth their journey.*

"Do you mean to try her at once?" said the woman. "She does not seem very likely to give trouble. Though perhaps that is only Rose Neill MacTerry's spell? I hope she will not become a spitting fury the moment it wears off."

Sophie did not doubt that she appeared, at present, quite incapable of resistance. She longed to prove their assumption wrong, but her task at the moment was to divert their attention from Joanna and Gwendolen's search for the prisoners; instead of struggling, therefore, she drooped against her bonds, forcing her captor to catch at her elbows to keep her on her feet.

"Perhaps," said the tall man consideringly. "She must at least be easier to persuade than her husband. I think, however"—and here his eyes lit in a rather disconcerting manner—"that I shall take this opportunity to fill the grove; we have enough sources now to do so, and I hope this may prove the turning-point in our journey."

Though Sophie had no more idea what these words might signify than if he had truly been speaking a language quite unknown to her, his voice came near to freezing her blood in her veins.

His companion visibly weighed the merits of this new idea and slowly smiled. "And perhaps the others will be more compliant, with such an example before them."

Despite herself, Sophie shivered.

"Go and make them ready, then," the tall man ordered; and, turning on his heel to face Sophie, he added, "and take her down there to wait." He spun sharply and strode towards the door.

A hand between Sophie's shoulder blades propelled her forward, stumbling, in his wake.

She tried desperately to *think*. If Joanna and Gwendolen were here now and had gone to find Gray and his fellow prisoners, then no good could come of the order to go and fetch them. She stumbled deliberately and was saved from falling flat only by the hard hands gripping her elbows.

"Wait," she gasped, as they set her on her feet again; she made sure to speak in Latin, though if she were correct in supposing that Catriona MacCrimmon had provided a full report on Gray and herself, they must know that she had at least a little Gaelic. "Wait—who is that man?"

The man on her left—he was not so very much older than herself, she thought, for all his large frame, magnificent beard and mane of russet curls—frowned down at her. "He is the chieftain, of course," he said. "The true chieftain. Cormac MacAlpine."

"And, and what does he mean to do with me? Why am I here?"

"That's for the chieftain to say," said the man on Sophie's right, a shorter, slighter fellow whose face narrowed down to a point.

He glared at his companion, and neither of them would answer any more of Sophie's questions after that.

Angus Ferguson's scouts had reported seeing the shackled men brought in and out through a postern-gate in the castle's north wall, which was reached via a walled staircase. There could not be two such (unless the scouts had mistaken their cardinal points), and it stood to reason (thought Joanna) that if one were required to drag from one place to another a heavily shackled man who could not or would not bear his own weight, one should wish to expend as little time and effort as possible in doing so. One would also presumably wish, if it were possible, to avoid the main courtyard, which must often be full of people—not all of them, perhaps, privy to all of the castle's most sordid business—and offered a variety of opportunities for attempts at escape.

They considered the possibility of lurking inside the gate, waiting for a prisoner to be brought in or taken out, so that they might follow; but this was perhaps not a frequent occurrence, and in the meantime, the gods alone knew what might be happening to Sophie. Instead, therefore, following their murmured conference in the shelter of the rain-barrel, Joanna and Gwendolen crept back along the wall of the courtyard and into the narrow passage through the curtain wall.

Gwendolen gave a little huff of triumph when they spotted the low door in the wall of the passage, leading to all appearances directly *into* the curtain wall. She tried the handle, found it locked, and shrugged philosophically.

"Do you mean that the wall is *hollow*?" Joanna demanded, sotto voce. "Surely not. A siege engine would—"

"No, no, of course not," said Gwendolen. "Did you never look at a plan of this castle, Jo?" She had knelt before the little door now and was peering through the keyhole. "There was one in that book of your sister's, which I thought you must have seen, though it was not a very good one, and if I remember rightly, there ought to be a staircase behind that door, to take us straight down. Now, keep an eye out for a moment."

Whilst Joanna sputtered in silent outrage at *I thought you must have seen it*, Gwendolen went on down the passage, more silently than a person wearing sturdy riding-boots ought to have been capable of, and out of her line of sight. Joanna had not had time to go more than halfway from outrage to panic before she was back again, with a smug smile on her face and something clasped tight in her right fist.

The *something* proved to be a ring of keys, which they tried one by one in the little door until at last, after half a dozen attempts, one of them turned almost silently in the lock.

"There we are," said Gwendolen, almost beneath her breath. "And it turned so smoothly—it must be often used."

Leaving the key in the lock, she turned the handle; the door swung open on equally silent hinges, revealing, indeed, a winding stone staircase leading down into the dark.

*Down, certainly; but not so very straight, however.*

"After you, milady," said Gwendolen, with a flourishing bow.

Joanna glared daggers at her as she stepped through the door.

Gwendolen stepped in after her, then closed the door behind herself.

"You are not leaving the keys there?" said Joanna, frowning.

"Yes, I am," said Gwendolen. "I do not suppose that they have got more than one set amongst them—indeed, if this castle has been abandoned for generations, they are lucky to have found any keys at all—and if that set cannot be found, someone will raise a hue and cry at once; but this way, each of them will believe that one of the others was careless. With luck," she added as she turned away.

Joanna chose to pretend that she had not heard this last remark.

The staircase had no rail or any other handhold, though fortunately it was so narrow that Joanna could easily keep one hand on each wall as she descended. There was almost no light, but someone had affixed a magelight lantern, shuttered almost to invisibility, here and there upon the wall; these gave just enough illumination to allow her, once her eyes had adapted to the near-total darkness, to make out the vague shape of Gwendolen descending the steps just ahead of her. The steps, and the darkness, seemed to go on forever, and the tight spiral made it impossible to maintain either her sense of direction or any notion of how far down they might have gone.

At last, however, they came to the end of their descent and peered cautiously out into a long, dimly lit corridor.

They crept along in silence, side by side. Just as Joanna was beginning to fear that it led to a dead end, the corridor turned sharply. She drew in a startled breath at the sight of two long rows of heavy, bolted doors, and nearly choked on the smell of rank misery.

There was a square window in each of the doors, well above Joanna's head and closely barred. As they passed from one to the next, Gwendolen stood a-tiptoe and stretched her neck up to peer through the bars, while Joanna, who could not reach so high even by following suit, shot back the bolts.

"What if some of these men are such as belong behind bars?" Gwendolen objected, when Joanna darted ahead of her and began wrestling feverishly with the next bolt.

"I don't care," said Joanna fiercely. The bolt yielded with a rasping scrape, and she crossed the corridor and set her half-skinned hands to the next. "I don't care, I don't care."

Gwendolen halted just behind her and clasped her shoulders, one in each slender hand. "I know," she said softly, warm breath at Joanna's ear. "You thought your heart hardened, I suppose, and now you find it as soft as your sister's. But you cannot help them by losing your wits, Jo."

Joanna drew in a deep, shuddering breath—she recognised dimly that she was growing used to the smell, which was both a relief and a new source of horror—and leant her forehead briefly on the age-darkened wood of the door before her. "Yes," she said, after a moment. "I understand."

"Good." Gwendolen squeezed her shoulders briefly, then released them, and went back to peering through the barred windows, one at a time—though now Joanna heard her shooting back the bolts as she went.

Joanna had nearly reached the last door on her side of the corridor, and was beginning to despair of finding Gray, when Gwendolen whispered, "Jo! Come here!"

She fairly flew across the corridor, and scrabbled frantically at the bolt until Gwendolen batted her hands away and shot it back herself. The door creaked horribly as, together, they eased it a little way open, and Joanna half expected a tumble of angry Albans to descend upon them, but no shout or footstep came.

Joanna slipped through the narrow gap between door and wall; Gwendolen followed her. Then they stood for a long moment with their backs pressed against the wall, while Joanna struggled not to vomit, weep, or howl.

*We shall be leading no triumphal procession from this castle, that's certain.*

"Mother Goddess!" Gwendolen muttered, as she struggled to heft Gray's broad shoulders. "He is heavier than he looks."

"He is not heavy *enough*," said Joanna. She shifted her grip around her brother-in-law's bony knees and lifted. "I believe they have been starving him." *Or he has been starving himself, like my fool of a sister.* The part of her mind that knew better than to speak its thoughts aloud whispered that it might be as well, for Joanna and Gwendolen could scarcely have lifted him otherwise, even working together.

Gwendolen huffed a breathless laugh that was half a sob, and said it for her.

They were not even halfway to their goal when Gray half woke from his stupor, drawing in a shuddering breath and struggling wildly—if ineffectually—against their hands. Joanna fought to keep her hold on his shins; Gwendolen muttered curses in Cymric, hanging on grimly.

Gray's eyes fluttered open briefly, then fell shut again. "No," he said, very clearly, though his voice was ragged, as though he had been shouting. His wrists and ankles, Joanna had been unable to avoid seeing, were ringed with abrasions, red and raw or scabbed over or sluggishly bleeding. "No. No."

"Gray," she hissed. "Be quiet. They will hear you."

"No," he repeated, but for just a moment his eyes opened again and looked into hers in sudden recognition. He blinked. "S-s-s—"

Somewhere deep down, Joanna was implacably furious; deeper still, she was sobbing with grief and rage. "Yes, Sophie is here," she said, her voice pitched low, calming. "But you must be *quiet*, Gray."

Another blink; a short nod.

"Can you . . . can you walk?" Joanna suggested, doubtfully.

Gray nodded again.

Joanna counted three, and she and Gwendolen lowered him to the floor; then she held out a hand to pull him up.

He staggered as he came to his feet but kept himself upright by leaning heavily on Joanna's shoulder. She slid her right arm about his waist—the difference in their heights was perfectly ridiculous, and most inconvenient—and Gwendolen, at her pointed frown, hastened to do the same from the other side. She at least was a little nearer Gray's height.

They made their slow and awkward way along the dim stone corridor in considerably less silence than Joanna had intended. If Gray had not been lying, exactly, in claiming to be able to walk, he had certainly overstated the case; his absurd feet dragged at the ends of his long legs, and the weight of him lurched from Joanna's shoulder to Gwendolen's at every shuffling step. How in Hades were they to manage that narrow, tightly spiralling stair?

Still, this slow and shambling progress was progress nonetheless, and Joanna was just beginning to believe that they might make good their escape, in spite of everything, when heavy footsteps sounded ahead and there loomed up before them a large red-bearded man with a lantern in one hand and a dirk in the other, and an only slightly smaller man holding a wooden cudgel.

The large man shouted something in Gaelic, of which Joanna understood nothing but which made Gray's bent head jerk upright. "No," he said.

"Gray," Joanna whispered urgently, "if there is any helpful magick you might do—"

"Shut *up*, Jo," Gwendolen hissed. "He is dead on his feet."

Then more footsteps—stumbling, unsteady—sounded in the darkened corridor; a lamp glowed behind Red-Beard and Cudgel, who turned, temporarily distracted, and Gray's weight lifted from Joanna's aching shoulder as he straightened to stand upright for the first time.

Joanna squinted ahead and bit back a curse; the unsteady footsteps, she saw, had belonged to Sophie, who stumbled ahead of a man with a face like a rat—all nose and teeth and bulging eyes—with her arms bound behind her, her head bowed, her ankles shackled with rope.

Gwendolen groaned, a low, despairing sound.

As Joanna watched in a sort of horrified trance, Sophie slowly raised her head. Her stumbling gait, the droop of her shoulders, spoke resigned submission, but her face was pale, her hair a fury, and her dark eyes burned.

Joanna knew that look of old, and it boded no good for Sophie's enemies—nor, when she came to think of it, for anyone in Sophie's general vicinity.

Gray said, "Sophie," in a whisper that seemed to shake Joanna's very bones; then, more loudly, *"Let her go."*

Joanna had only that moment's warning—just enough to dodge behind Gray, seize Gwendolen by the wrist, and yank her backward, out of range—before Sophie opened her mouth in a cry of rage, and the corridor exploded.


Sophie's head ached so fiercely that she could scarcely see, and the rest of her felt as though it had been run through a mangle, then loaded down with bags of wet earth. Swallowing back a groan, she flexed her hands—freed again; that was something, at any rate—and wriggled her toes, to confirm that she could; then reached for her magick, to see how much that furious outburst had depleted it.

"Oh," she whispered, horror-struck. There was nothing there.

She tried to think, to remember, but her thoughts were sluggish and woolly, and everything ached, and last night's supper was threatening to reemerge.

*Lethargy . . . nausea . . . weakness . . . . a prison for mages . . .*

"Oh!" she said again. She felt no better, objectively speaking, but there was a certain comfort in knowing what ailed her. And this explained, too, why Gray had been so difficult to find by magick; almost certainly there were wards on the castle, too, against finding-spells and scrying, but wards alone, she suspected, could not have withstood the drawing-spell she had worked with Lucia MacNeill's magick. A strong interdiction, however, would deaden the effects both of magick within its boundaries and of any spell seeking to pass those boundaries. And the interdictions on Castle MacAlpine's prison-cells, if they had been designed to contain powerful mages, must be very strong indeed.

What they must have suffered, Gray and the others! Some of them had been here many months.

It was not long thereafter that the door of her cell creaked open and the young man with the russet beard hauled her upright by one elbow, bound her wrists behind her back once more, knotted a handkerchief across her mouth, and brought her out into the corridor. As they crossed the threshold, Sophie's magick surged up again; the nausea ebbed, and the pain in her head began to subside.

She had no leisure to enjoy her freedom from the interdiction, however, for her captor half marched, half dragged her down the corridor, pushed her into another cell, and locked her in again. As she staggered across the damp stone floor, the golden-haired woman she had last seen in that elegant sitting-room—somewhere far above her head, now, she supposed—rose from her seat on a wooden bench and said in Latin, "The Princess of Britain, I presume."

*Oh, gods and priestesses!*

Sophie straightened her back as well as she could, raised her head, and gave the other woman a level look, refusing to humiliate herself by attempting to speak around the gag.

The golden-haired woman smiled. "I *am* sorry," she said. "We have not been introduced. I am Aileen MacAlpine; Cormac Mac-Alpine is my brother."

Sophie shifted her gaze to the wall directly opposite.

For some time there was no more conversation, for which Sophie was grateful. To her surprise, it appeared that she had been brought here not to be interrogated, but to be bathed. The water was pleasantly warm, the soap pleasantly scented with lavender. Sophie's skin crawled; she tried not to let Aileen MacAlpine see it.

This was some ritual, plainly, but in preparation for what?

Finally she was reclothed in a linen shift and a robe of rough un-dyed wool, her hair combed out straight and left to fall down her back and over her shoulders, after which Aileen MacAlpine drew a length of slender cord from a pocket in her skirts, bound Sophie's wrists tightly behind her, and knocked loudly upon the door to summon the guards.


Joanna came to with a ringing in her ears, a fierce ache in her head, and a warm weight pressing her legs into the stone floor; she could not move her arms. She blinked frantically for a few moments, trying to dispel the blurred darkness that seemed to be afflicting her eyes; then, swimming up into full consciousness, she recognised that the half darkness was real, her hands were tied behind her back, and the weight across her knees was a human body.

Panic surged; then the warm weight shifted a little, and Gwendolen's voice, rough but recognisable, said, "Mother Goddess! What did those sons of the pits of Tartarus hit me with?"

"Gwen!" said Joanna, half laughing in breathless relief. "Are you hurt?"

There was a shifting in the gloom; Gwendolen's weight lifted away, then settled again along Joanna's left side as Gwendolen shuffled backwards to sit up against the wall. "A spooked horse trampled me once, when I was younger," she said; Joanna winced. "This feels rather like that. And you, are you—"

"I am not much injured," said Joanna. "Apart from a knot on the head."

The room was growing lighter, by tiny increments, or perhaps her eyes were accustoming themselves to the gloom.

"What *did* they hit us with?" said Gwendolen. "Did you see?"

"No one hit us," Joanna said; after a moment's thought, she amended, "that is, I did not *see* anyone do so. There was an explosion—that was Sophie's doing, of course; I wonder that they did not see it coming, for I certainly did. Then I suppose someone must have . . . must have collected us from that tunnel, and brought us . . . here." *Wherever* here *may be.*

"And," she added, "we must have lost Mama's charms in the explosion, or they should not have seen us at all."

"*Explosion?*" Gwendolen repeated incredulously, ignoring all the rest of Joanna's explanation.

Joanna turned towards her, frowning. Did she not remember the blazing light, the overwhelming noise, the great *whoosh* of displaced air? She must have hit her head much harder than Joanna had supposed.

"Yes," she said.

"You!" a rough baritone voice called, in an equally rough approximation of Latin, from several yards away. "Be quiet."

Joanna followed the direction of the voice, and her heart sank as she discerned its source: a man's head silhouetted against a high, barred window.

## CHAPTER XXXI

# In Which Friend Is Not Easily Distinguished from Foe

*The red-bearded man* herded Sophie into line behind four other prisoners, bent-headed and grey-robed like herself, and roped them together at ankles and wrists.

This stumbling procession made its way along a half-lit corridor, climbed a steep and winding staircase—not entirely without incident—and after passing through a torchlit passage, through a postern-gate, and down another equally steep, but mercifully straight, staircase, plunged into the edge of the wood. At last they halted in a clearing roofed over with the spreading branches of elm and yew trees.

Here their path intersected with another, and they met a second, smaller procession of men in grey robes, also escorted by a guard, but not bound as Sophie and her companions were. Sophie raised her eyes to look into their clean-shaven, well-fed faces and saw none of her own terror and pain, but a solemn trepidation—and here and there, she thought, a glimpse of something like guilt.

Each of them was shortly bound to his own tree, arms stretched backward around the trunk and bound at the wrists; from her vantage point Sophie could see only two of the others, both men of middle years, starveling-thin and bearded, dull-eyed and resigned—but clean, and newly dressed in woollen robes, just as she was herself. She shuddered at the thought of Aileen MacAlpine's hands upon her, washing her like an infant—dressing her like a doll.

And directly across the clearing—no, the shrine; the ring of trees was too symmetrical to be anything but a deliberate planting—Gray sagged against the trunk of an elm twice as wide as he was, his eyes closed and his head lolling. So still was he that for a moment Sophie's heart seemed to stop; then his chest rose and fell, just perceptibly, and she breathed deeply, trying to summon calm.

*Focus. Concentrate.* The thin cord cut into the skin of her wrists; her shoulders burned with the pull of it, and through the stuff of the robe the rough elm-bark prodded at her spine.

"You cannot possibly believe that this will do you any good," she said—speaking in Latin, in case there might still be some advantage to be gained. "You have won some of these men to your cause, I collect, and I wish you joy of one another. But the rest you have beaten and starved, you have held under interdiction; if they have any magick left at all, it is not by any care of yours. What do you imagine that they can give you now?"

The tall man—Cormac MacAlpine, certainly—turned slowly on his booted heel to look at her, and a smile, thin and narrow-eyed, crossed his face.

"You mistake, Princess," he said; "the question now is what *you* can give us, and what price you are prepared to pay for the petty satisfaction of refusing."

He gestured carelessly, and the red-bearded man stepped to Gray's side, wrenched his head up by the hair, and held a knife to his throat.

For a moment the world went very still. Then Sophie's magick roared up like a live thing, cold blue-white and shrieking—nearly all her own, now, the borrowed threads of Lucia MacNeill's faded almost to nothing—and tried to obliterate everyone here present who might do harm to Gray. Sophie's rational self fought it grimly; she would not, *must not* repeat the disastrous outburst that had led to her mother's death.

*I am no murderess,* she told Cormac MacAlpine, quietly under the clamour in her mind, *and I shall not let you make me into one.*

And if Gray, or any innocent person, should come to harm through any action of hers . . .

It did not bear thinking of. She fought the magick down, down, into a still small pool of fury.

Cormac MacAlpine smiled again. "Indeed, Princess. That is precisely what we expect you to provide."

*Yes, he truly can see magick,* Sophie thought, *and it appears he has set his sights on mine.*

"And why should I oblige you?" she demanded, as though she could not see the reason perfectly well, bound to a tree in front of her eyes with a naked blade at his throat.

"You are not a fool," Cormac MacAlpine said; "kindly do not insult either of us by pretending to be so. We have in our hands both your husband and yourself, as well as these others; you hold in yours, for want of a better metaphor, the fuel which our enterprise requires. To provide it costs you nothing; to refuse . . . well, I have no doubt that you are capable of interpreting the evidence of your senses."

Sophie swallowed terror, swallowed rage. There was no help or guidance to be had here, no more knowledgeable and experienced person to tell her what she must do; Gray was in no state to help her. Whatever choices were to be made, they must be hers alone. *Lady Minerva, in your wisdom, help me to choose rightly.*

"You need my magick," she said, and was relieved to hear her voice emerge strong and steady. "For what purpose?"

Cormac MacAlpine narrowed his eyes at her. "What matters it to you, Princess?"

"If you know who I am," Sophie said, "then you must understand that I have loyalties and obligations beyond the merely personal." She closed her eyes briefly and swallowed again. *Forgive me, Gray.* "And I would hear from your own lips who you are, and what you intend, before I agree to lend myself to your . . . enterprise."

"Even at the cost of your husband's life?" His tone was less threatening than intrigued.

"You will not kill him," said Sophie, with a great deal more confidence than she felt.

"Will I not? Why say you so?"

"Because you have the talent of seeing magick in others." It was a desperate play for time, and the prize very uncertain; at present, however, Sophie could think no farther ahead than the next moment, and her only goal was to divert her captor's attention from whatever it was he wished to do with his captive mages, until Joanna and Gwendolen should succeed in . . .

In doing what?

*No matter.* "And if you have seen mine," she continued, "as you certainly did just now, you will easily imagine what your fate might be, were you to eliminate my motive for restraining it."

Cormac MacAlpine paced to and fro before her, thoughtfully; Sophie fixed her gaze on him, doubting her ability to look upon Gray's face without bursting into tears, or worse. Considered objectively, their captor was not difficult to look at—tall and straight, with gleaming auburn hair tied back from his high forehead, clear blue eyes set wide above a fine straight nose, firm jaw, and expressive mouth.

Sophie hated him as she had rarely hated another mortal being.

Gray had once taught her a spell to unfasten knots; whilst her captor's back was turned, she drew up the minutest thread of magick and muttered the words, two fingers pressing the one rope-end that dangled just far enough. But there was some other spell woven into the cord, which stung her fingertips viciously and set up a furious itching wherever it touched her skin.

*Magickal talent,* said Gray's voice in her mind, *is sometimes less helpful than you might suppose.*

Cormac MacAlpine turned suddenly to face her, hands clasped behind his back. "Your mother was Breizhek," he said.

Sophie regarded him impassively. Did he know what she had tried?

"And all know the tale of her petty rebellion. Does it never gall you, Princess, that you might have ruled a kingdom, had you been born a boy?"

"Never," said Sophie at once, with perfect truth. Many things galled her, in relation to her birth and upbringing, but having missed the opportunity to inherit her father's throne was decidedly not one of them.

Cormac MacAlpine's eyebrows flew up and his eyes widened briefly, perhaps the first uncalculated expression she had seen on his face.

"What has my mother, or my inheritance, to do with your purpose?" she demanded.

"Your pardon, Princess." The moment of uncontrolled reaction was past now. "I had supposed that your sympathies might lie another way than with your own oppressors."

Sophie's bound limbs were trembling in little helpless shudders, her arms flinching away from the rough elm-bark, and she fought to keep her voice from trembling likewise. "This enterprise of yours: Do you tell me that I am to sacrifice myself for a purpose of which I know absolutely nothing?"

The tall man studied her. Slowly, a smile curved his lips—a smile at once self-satisfied and hopeful. "Every great cause demands some sacrifice," he said.

Inwardly, Sophie groaned. It was as she had feared: They had fallen into the hands of a man possessed of a grand idea. Ought she to have answered his question differently, feigned resentment of her half brother Edward, who would inherit their father's throne in her stead?

She risked a glance at Gray. He had not stirred, but neither, it appeared, had the man with the knife.

"And I do not ask of any man a sacrifice greater than those I have already made myself. I have succeeded in the task set us by Alba and her gods—our gods. My father devoted the last decades of his life to mapping the great journey of Ailpín Drostan, by which he wove together the clans and clan-lands to make the kingdom of Alba, and my loyal clansmen and I, against equally great odds, have retraced every step of that journey, and renewed its paths with the blood of Ailpín Drostan's descendants."

Sophie's mind helpfully supplied an image of MacAlpine and his followers retracing their distant ancestor's steps across and about Alba with arms outstretched, scattering in their wake their own blood dripping from their fingertips. She repressed a shudder.

*How much blood would such a deed require?* Though Alba's territory was nothing like so large as Britain's, still it was a kingdom entire, and not a small one. *All those hills and crags. All those islands, and the passages amongst them.*

"I had not so many willing assistants as Ailpín Drostan," said Cormac MacAlpine; with a bitter little smile, he untied one of his shirt-cuffs, shoved the sleeve upward, and extended his arm abruptly, revealing to Sophie's appalled eyes a long series of parallel scars. "He is said to have made his journey in a space of months; ours was the work of many years. But success in this great undertaking is worth every step and every drop of blood, for thus shall we cure the disease that afflicts both Alba and ourselves."

Sophie was silent, this time, not from a wish to goad her captor into speaking, but because she could think of nothing to say.

"You worship the conqueror-gods, I conclude," Cormac MacAlpine said. He stepped closer and loomed over her as he folded down his shirt-sleeve and retied the cuff.

Sophie answered cautiously, as she had once answered Conall MacLachlan the butterfly collector, "I hope I give all the gods their due." Cormac MacAlpine's remark seemed an entire *non sequitur.*

"Say you so, Princess? And why should you owe anything to the gods of those who broke your ancestors to the yoke? The gods of Rome have no rights in your land, and still less in mine. And if your father supposes that either the people or the lands of Alba will stand idle while he thrusts his son into the chieftain's seat of Alba and his conqueror-gods into our shrines and wellsprings—"

"I am sure His Majesty has no designs on Donald MacNeill's throne," Sophie said, lifting her chin as she thought Joanna might have done in the same circumstances, "and why you, or the priests of the Cailleach, or *anyone* should imagine that he has the *least* interest in Alba's choice of gods, is beyond my understanding. My father may worship what you call conqueror-gods, amongst the many who are revered in his kingdom, but he has no yearning for conquest himself, that I have ever heard of."

"Oh, indeed not," said Cormac MacAlpine. He had begun to pace again but paused in his trajectory to fix her with a venomous smile. "He had rather conquer Alba in Lucia MacNeill's bed, as his forefathers conquered Breizh, than try and fail to win her on the field of battle."

It was a barb which many a Breizhek gentleman or lady—Sophie's own family perhaps especially—might have found impossible to swallow; as a goad to Sophie's temper, however, it was singularly ineffective.

"And your enterprise will prevent him?" she inquired. "How so?"

The smile grew gentle and earnest; Sophie repressed a shiver that had nothing to do with the chill night air.

"You need not fear that any harm will come to your family, Princess," Cormac MacAlpine said, "or to your kingdom. None here wishes any ill to your father, so he and his gods leave us to ourselves. Our quarrel is not with him, but with the false clan that would sell Alba in bondage to Britain." He nodded to himself, and Sophie had to stop her own head from mirroring the motion. "Donald MacNeill ought never to have sat the chieftain's seat; any effort to right what is wrong in Alba must begin by removing him from it, and all of his clan and get."

"And replace his clan and get with your own, I collect?" Sophie let her eyes drift briefly to Gray's face and found it yet slack and still. Layers of old bruises marked the skin of his bared throat, and from his temple blood dripped sluggishly, one drop to every three of Sophie's heartbeats. "Is this the service you give your gods?" she said softly. "Trickery, treachery, and the blood of captives too badly broken to choose otherwise?"

The quick flash of fury on Cormac MacAlpine's face, though as quickly controlled, warned Sophie what was coming, and she tried, too late, to turn her head aside. The attempt was a mistake; he saw the motion and shifted so that instead of striking her cheek, his open hand caught her hard across one ear, crushing the other against the tree-trunk at her back. For a moment she hung limp against the ropes that bound her, dazed by the force of the blow. When she regained her balance and shook her head, trying to clear her vision, both ears throbbed, and something warm and wet ran down the treeward side of her neck.

*If his gods do indeed crave the blood of captives, it seems they shall have mine as well as Gray's.*

Cormac MacAlpine's hand darted towards her once more; with desperate effort Sophie controlled her reflexive flinch. He did not strike her again, however, but caught her jaw in a bruising grip and wrenched her face towards his own. "It seems my judgement is awry," he said; "I thought you a woman of more sense."

For the space of a few heartbeats, Sophie let her magick well up, felt it stretching desperately towards Gray's, and with satisfaction saw her captor's eyes widen minutely. Then she thrust it down again, almost savagely, and keeping her eyes fixed on his said, "For a man who has no quarrel with Henry of Britain and wishes him no ill, you have chosen a curious method of demonstrating your intentions."

"You imagine that he will rush to avenge his beloved child—the same child he once sold away to the Iberian Emperor?" Cormac Mac-Alpine scoffed. "How little you know of the world, Princess."

Three years ago, this line of argument might well have succeeded; three years ago, indeed, Sophie might have made it herself. Now, however, she could not help thinking of the way her father smiled at her, affectionate and regretful; of the anguish she had seen in his face when she had come so near to throwing him off entirely; of the pains to which he had gone to ease her journey to Din Edin, though so reluctant for her to go at all, solely because she wished it.

Of Lord de Courcy saying of her father, disconcertingly matter-of-fact, that *whosoever threatens harm to his daughter may expect swift retribution.*

"I may know very little of the world," she said, "but it seems to me that you know very little of my father." *Or of me,* she added silently. "You thought it very clever, I daresay, to target foreign mages—their acquaintance in Din Edin could be convinced that they had left for home, and their friends at home that they remained in Alba." The slow drip of blood down the side of her neck was an irritating distraction; if only she could reach up and wipe it away!

"It was clever enough," Cormac MacAlpine said, "to bring us seven mages with no one the wiser."

*Seven?* Sophie blinked, trying not to show her surprise; Lord de Courcy had known of only four, apart from Gray. "Yet you did not foresee that if you kidnapped the daughter of a foreign king, the consequences might not be to your liking?"

The tall man smiled mockingly at her. "Ah, but I did not kidnap you, Princess," he said; "you came to me of your own accord, or as nearly as makes no difference."

"Teàrlag MacAlpine and Rose Neill MacTerry were acting on their own impulse, I suppose," said Sophie. "And your henchmen to whom they handed me over, helpless as I was. None of them were carrying out your orders."

"They were acting in the interests of Alba," said Cormac MacAlpine, sharply. "As do I. You have seen, of course, that the Cailleach herself has no love for Donald MacNeill or his daughter."

*What can he mean by that? But of course: the effigies, the priests' instructive drama.*

"I have seen that her priests do not," she said, "which is not necessarily the same thing."

Cormac MacAlpine leaned closer to Sophie and drew one finger gently down the side of her face, in dreadful mimicry of a lover's caress. "You will find that we have many allies," he said, "even in Din Edin."

Despite herself, Sophie shuddered.

A tactical error on her part, to let him see that he had distressed her. But so long as he was enjoying himself at her expense, he was neither forcing her compliance with his *enterprise* nor actively doing harm to anyone else. And perhaps . . .

Sophie controlled a little shiver of anticipatory triumph. *Perhaps he will be willing to part with more information, if he believes it will give me pain.*

"I cannot believe such a thing of any of my friends," she said—defiantly, but with a tremble in her voice which suggested (or so she hoped) that it was her own defiance that she could not entirely believe.

"Can you not, Princess?" Cormac MacAlpine purred. "And yet you claim to have *duties and loyalties beyond the merely personal.* You cannot pretend to be surprised to learn that others have such loyalties also."

Sophie could see nothing about this man to inspire loyalty; but then, she still knew almost nothing about him. And certainly there were many in Din Edin—and presumably throughout the kingdom—who were ill pleased with the idea of an alliance of marriage between Alba and Britain. "Such loyalties might be easier to comprehend," she said, "if I knew who you are, and what it is you are about."

He narrowed his eyes at her again, as though attempting to decide whether answering her implicit questions was more to his own advantage or to hers. Had she succeeded in persuading him that she was capable of sympathy with his cause?

He was wavering, yes—Sophie made her face open and inviting and, to her relief, saw him yield.

"I am the true chieftain of Clan MacAlpine," he said. "You know, I presume, some of the history of MacAlpine, and of how my forefather Ailpín Drostan built this kingdom from a rabble of quarrelling clan-lands. Among the other debts which Alba and her people owe to my ancestors are the beneficence of the Cailleach and the lesser gods of the land, and the present system by which successors to the chieftainship are chosen and confirmed. To hear the lackeys of Donald MacNeill tell it, it has been done this way since the gods first made men to live in Alba; but the truth of the matter is that it was Drost Maon who first decreed that his heir should be chosen without bloodshed, under the guidance of the Cailleach, Brìghde, and the lesser gods, and were it not for the example of Clan MacAlpine, the rest of them should be all still murdering one another in their beds, or over their wine-cups."

Sophie refrained from comment. Where, she wondered, did the spell-net come into this tale?

"Alba prospered under the rule of Clan MacAlpine," Cormac Mac-Alpine went on, "for the gods of the land blessed their reign. But those among the chieftains of other clan-lands who could not see things as they truly were, and sought only their own private gain, twisted the Moot of Succession—"

*To choose an heir from some other clan, I suppose,* Sophie thought, and was grimly amused when Cormac MacAlpine's next words were, "to place an interloper from Clan MacLeod upon the chieftain's seat in Din Edin."

He paused, expectant, but Sophie said nothing, letting the silence stretch out past the point of comfort.

Cormac MacAlpine smiled a thin smile with no mirth or friendliness in it—*I know what you are about, Princess*—and at last went on: "Since the chieftain's seat was lost to Clan MacAlpine, there has been nothing but misfortune and mischance in Alba."

This assertion in no way aligned with what Sophie had learnt of Alba's recent history, which—until the present crisis—had been characterised by growing stability and the gradual cessation of hostilities with most of her neighbours. Certainly, however, there was more than enough misfortune to go round at present.

"And you mean by this *enterprise* of yours to win back the chieftain's seat from Donald MacNeill," she hazarded, "and thus restore Alba to her former glory?"

He could not decide, she saw, whether she had meant this last in mockery or in earnest.

Before he could reply, there came a rustling of footsteps approaching from, presumably, the direction of the castle; Cormac MacAlpine's head snapped up, and he stepped towards Sophie and clapped a hand over her mouth, gripping her jaw hard enough to bruise.

Sophie considered biting him, torn between the savage satisfaction of paying him back in some small way for his cruelty to Gray and the near certainty that to do so would be to ruin any possibility of stopping him.

"Cormac MacAlpine!" a woman's voice called softly.

In the midst of her calculations, Sophie froze. She knew that voice, had heard it not long ago, in fact, when its owner had left her in Quarry Close with a stack of parcels in her arms, to find her house empty and her husband gone.

*But why is she here? She was going to Leodhas.*

*Unless, of course, that too was a deception.*

The hand dropped away from her face, and Cormac MacAlpine turned towards the voice and said curtly, in Gaelic, "What is it?"

As he was turning, Sophie drew as deep a breath as her bonds permitted, and threw all of it into a single frantic cry: "Catriona! Help us!"

Cormac MacAlpine spun again on his heel and glared at her. "Be silent," he hissed, reverting to Latin, and lifted his hand again as though to strike her.

Sophie managed not to flinch, but neither did she speak again.

The approaching footsteps quickened. After another moment, there was a rustling of branches to Sophie's left, and Catriona Mac-Crimmon herself, wide-eyed and pale, stepped into the clearing.

"Cormac MacAlpine," she said breathlessly. "I must tell you—"

Then her eye fell on Sophie, and she fell silent. Sophie stared at her in horror; Catriona's answering gaze conveyed a sort of paralysed disbelief.

Cormac MacAlpine gritted his teeth. "Well?" he snapped.

"I—" Catriona looked from Sophie to her captor in evident bewilderment. "Why is—what have you—"

Sophie caught Catriona's eye and turned her head deliberately to look at Gray, willing Catriona to follow her gaze. She must herself, she supposed, present a frightening enough appearance by this time, but the sight of Gray—gaunt and bloodied and insensible, with Cormac MacAlpine's red-bearded henchman still holding a knife to his throat—surely was entirely horrifying.

Catriona looked; then, with a sort of choking gasp, she looked away again.

Sophie reached cautiously for her magick, caught the merest thread of it, and let it go in a low, quiet hum. Though she had no reason to expect any success in what she was attempting, it seemed impossible not to make the attempt. *Look at us, Catriona. You may wish the success of Cormac MacAlpine's enterprise, but will you accept the cost?*

"Say what you have come to say, Catriona MacCrimmon," said Cormac MacAlpine. "I can spare no time to indulge your fits of craven scruples."

He appeared to have dismissed Sophie from his mind for the present: good. She did her best to show no reaction to his words or to Catriona's, though the latter certainly knew her capable of following a conversation in Gaelic.

"Never mind that," said Catriona. Her throat worked, and her slim hands clenched into corded fists. "What are you about?"

"I am about the business of Clan MacAlpine." His voice suggested that he was very near to resorting to violence. "Which does not answer to you, Catriona MacCrimmon, and never shall. Say what you have come to say, or be gone from my sight."

*Look at me, Catriona. Look at Gray.*

Whether because Sophie's gambit was succeeding, or because she had indeed not understood what Cormac MacAlpine was about until this night, Catriona gazed silently at Gray, then again at Sophie, and at length said stolidly, "No."

Sophie's heart leapt.

Cormac MacAlpine stared at Catriona. *"No?"* he repeated incredulously. "And what of your vows of loyalty, then?"

"I cast my lot for Clan MacAlpine," said Catriona, squaring her slim shoulders, "and for the healing and defence of Alba. Not for forcible confinement and slow murder."

She flung an accusing hand in Gray's direction. "You wrote me word that he had agreed to help," she said. "That all of those I sent to you had so agreed, or had been sent on their way. I have been travelling up and down Leodhas and Na Hearadh on your behalf; and what do I find, on the very day after coming to you at last, but that your sacred grove is become a torture chamber!"

"They are only foreigners," said Cormac MacAlpine. He had adopted a reasoning tone whose very ordinariness, in the present circumstances, made Sophie's skin crawl. "And most are Sasunnach, at that. We pursue a great end, a god-given task; we must not be dissuaded by squeamishness over the means. If these stranger mages have the power we need to heal our ailing clan-lands, yet will not give it willingly, are we not bound by our service to the lands and gods of Alba to take it by whatever method offers?"

It struck Sophie then how odd it was that he should be attempting to persuade Catriona, when he might so easily have overpowered her. Certainly he had evinced no hesitation in offering violence towards herself. Just as this thought occurred to her, an echo of stealthy movement made her turn her head, and she saw that the red-bearded man had abandoned Gray and was circling the clearing to approach Catriona from the far side, quietly, out of her line of sight.

Sophie coughed. Both Catriona and Cormac MacAlpine started at the noise, harsh and rasping in the night-quiet of the wood. The red-bearded man froze.

Having begun to cough, alas, Sophie found she could not stop, and what was left of her song-spell slipped from her grasp.

Then Catriona did an unexpected thing—at any rate, Sophie had not expected it, and by the look on his face Cormac MacAlpine expected it still less. "Take mine," she said, holding out both her hands.

Cormac MacAlpine stared. Sophie managed at last to catch her breath.

"I have magick," Catriona said; "not so much as she has, but certainly more than is likely to be left to him," with a jerk of her head at Gray. "If you have not killed him altogether, it is only by luck or his gods' own hands. But I have my magick still, and I will give it to the spell, if you will first let the unwilling go free."

*Clever*, thought Sophie approvingly, *to make him lay down his arms first*, before the true import of Catriona's offer dawned upon her and she gasped, "Catriona!"

Cormac MacAlpine gave her a look with daggers in it, and

someone—it must be the red-bearded man—cuffed her bloodied ear. Sophie closed her eyes briefly, swallowing a yelp.

Catriona turned on one heel and regarded her levelly, and shifting into Latin she said, "I have offered my magick in exchange for your lives. You had rather surrender your own?"

There was no particular affection in her gaze; indeed, Sophie saw, she had not been wrong to suppose that Catriona did not much like her. And yet she was playing along with Sophie's ruse; and yet she was offering—

Did Catriona understand, in fact, what she was offering to do?

"Catriona," Sophie repeated, "you must not—it is not safe—"

"That is very generous of you, Catriona MacCrimmon," Cormac MacAlpine interrupted, with a curl of his lip, shifting back into Gaelic. "But the spell needs more than you or I can offer it, my dear. The power of Clan MacAlpine, as you know, is sadly diminished since the days when the spell was wrought."

He gave Sophie a look of such thorough contempt as no one had directed at her since she left her stepfather's house, and added, "You surely cannot think that I would feed it on the magicks of strangers, had we sufficient power of our own?"

Catriona appeared to consider this.

At last she said, in the flat grey voice of one bowing to the inevitable, "Then at the least, let *him* go. Look at him; he can be of no use to you now."

There were footsteps approaching. *Rescue? Or more of Cormac Mac-Alpine's bully-boys?*

"I think not," said Cormac MacAlpine, who seemed not to hear them. "He is a hostage to his wife's cooperation."

Catriona scoffed, and he looked astonished and displeased.

"I see," said Catriona, her voice regaining some of its customary bite. "And are you finding it an effective strategy? Because, if so, I must say that your standards for success appear to be—"

As she spoke, Cormac MacAlpine's lips were drawing back in a snarl, his hand clenching into a fist. The unseen footsteps were growing louder; the red-bearded man turned his head, listening.

"Catriona," Sophie cried, desperate to divert attention from what she devoutly hoped was some sort of rescue party. "Go carefully! Whatever you have been saying to him, I fear that it is making him angry!"

As she had hoped, both Catriona and Cormac MacAlpine turned to glare at her; the red-bearded man stepped towards her, menacingly, then recoiled again at Cormac MacAlpine's furious "Look to your work, man!"

On the far side of the clearing, an unexpected flash of movement caught Sophie's eye. Her heart leapt: *Gray!* She nearly turned her head to look but, catching herself just in time, looked sidelong instead, keeping her face to Cormac MacAlpine and Catriona.

The oblique angle made her eyes ache, but she scarcely remarked it. Gray had raised his head—*Oh, thank all the gods!*—and was gazing at their captors with narrowed eyes, his bleeding mouth set in a grim line.

Once again Sophie's magick reached for his, leaping up with desperate energy—no longer bent on destruction, but simply yearning towards its other self—and this time she made no effort to restrain it. Was it only her wishful fancy that made her believe she felt Gray's magick reaching back?

He straightened slightly, and turned his head to meet her gaze.

## CHAPTER XXXII

# In Which Gwendolen Proves to Have Unexpected Talents, and Joanna Is Disinclined to Follow Orders

*Catriona! Help us!*

Gray struggled up towards consciousness at the sound of Sophie's cry, though the words made no sense to him. He opened his eyes cautiously, and his bafflement grew; before him stood Cormac Mac-Alpine and the man he had dubbed Ginger, and with them—*By all the gods, how comes this?*—Catriona MacCrimmon.

He could not have told how he had come to be in the yew-grove; his last clear memory was of staggering back into the interdicted cell, propelled by a rough hand to his shoulder-blade, and collapsing against the wall, after which were only confused flashes which might well have been hallucinations, for surely Joanna had not really been wandering the corridors of Castle MacAlpine with a smooth-faced boy from Cymru? But he knew at once that Sophie was near; nothing else could account for this abrupt change of heart, from despair to hope, from grim resignation to a heady, almost drunken relief. It was not mere freedom from the interdiction—though that, too, was as always a blessed relief—but a more positive sense of something healed that had been sundered, something restored to him that he had lost.

He pressed his lips together tightly, lest he yield to his instinct to call out to her, and slowly, painfully, raised his head.

Cormac MacAlpine and Catriona MacCrimmon were arguing in low voices—so low, indeed, that Gray could not hear what they said, though that might be only the effect of the persistent ringing in his ears. He watched them through slitted eyes, wary, but they appeared for the moment to be paying him no heed.

His magick was welling up now—sluggish and uncertain yet, but gathering strength apace—and the deep thrumming of it seemed to vibrate through his bones. And almost, almost, Gray could hear the high clear singing of Sophie's magick, so closely attuned to his own. If the sound in his mind's ear was yet indistinct, however, the direction from which it came was not.

Slowly, cautiously, he turned his head to face the far side of the yew-grove.

*Sophie!* He did not shout her name across the clearing, but it was a close-run thing. She was closer even than he had suspected—directly opposite him, and bound to a tree-trunk just as he was: the great elm tree, the anchor-point of Ailpín Drostan's spell. *Apollo, Pan, and Hecate!* Gray knew too well what that meant; did Sophie? Her face was ashen; blood stained her throat and the bodice of her gown; but her eyes burned bright as they met Gray's, and now he truly heard the singing of her magick.

It seemed an age that he gazed into Sophie's eyes, feasting upon the sight of her after long deprivation; but in fact only moments passed before an ominous silence announced that Cormac MacAlpine had registered the altered state of affairs amongst his prisoners.

"Well," he said, reverting to Latin. "How very interesting."

Gray turned his head towards the slow, speculative voice, and from the corner of his eye he saw Sophie do likewise. Cormac MacAlpine gestured sharply to someone outside Gray's field of vision, then paced towards them, graceful as a hunting cat.

A little smile was playing at the corners of his lips.

Gray's heart sank, and his belly roiled, and his attempts to channel his magick into some useful offensive spell were floundering and slow.

"Gray!" cried Catriona, slipping past Cormac MacAlpine to approach Gray's tree. She stopped just short of arm's reach and stared up at him. "Brìghde's tears! I thought they had killed you."

Gray gaped at her, still too baffled by her presence here—though his notion of their precise whereabouts was distressingly hazy—to parse the import of her words.

"Catriona," said Sophie again, and this time her voice held a warning. A warning of what? How in Hades did Catriona MacCrimmon come to be here? For it was apparent even in Gray's advanced state of befuddlement that she was not a prisoner like themselves, and surely no one would single her out as a rescue party.

Now more baffled than ever, Gray closed his eyes briefly and leant his head back against his tree.

When next he raised his head and opened his eyes, he saw Cormac MacAlpine standing tense and still, looking from Gray to Sophie and back again with narrow-eyed intensity.

"How very, *very* interesting," he repeated, at last; and then, speaking in Gaelic now, and quietly as though to himself, he said, "What manner of spell is that, I wonder? One without words, at any rate; we were not speaking so loudly that I should not have heard one of them saying a spell. And it must be *her* spell, for the boy has not used it before."

"Cormac MacAlpine," said Catriona. "I beg of you—"

"Pàrlan Dearg!" he barked, ignoring Catriona entirely. Ginger—in whose hand was a worryingly large and keen-edged knife—fairly leapt to attend him. "Keep this one out of the way."

Ginger—Pàrlan Dearg, then, which came to much the same thing—had neatly stowed away his knife and taken Catriona Mac-Crimmon by the wrists almost before the first outraged protests had left her lips, and he quickly silenced them by clamping his free hand over her mouth. "No spell-words," he said, jerking his head at Gray, then at Sophie. It was not difficult to imagine how quickly his grip on Catriona's jaw could become a fatal twisting of her delicate neck. She kicked furiously at his booted ankles, to no avail.

Cormac MacAlpine meanwhile had unsheathed his own unpleasantly familiar knife and was approaching Sophie. Her dark eyes tracked his every step, equally terrified and determined not to give him the satisfaction of showing it.

"No!" Gray shouted—or, rather, croaked. Sophie's head jerked towards him. He coughed wetly and tried again, this time achieving a sort of hoarse bellow: "No! If you must have blood to feed your horror-spell, let it be mine, not hers."

And it was the truth—yet not all the truth, for if he could do again whatever he had done on that other occasion, and so confound them . . .

Cormac MacAlpine smiled broadly, and Gray's heart sank still further. "The time for striking bargains is past, Graham Marshall," he said, his voice a silken murmur, and gestured at someone out of Gray's line of sight. "I shall have your blood indeed, however; yours and your Princess's both, and then we shall see."

Steel-Eyes emerged silently from the shadows beyond the clearing, and at a nod from his master, he approached Gray's tree, smiling grimly.

"Shut him up," said Cormac MacAlpine, reverting once more to Gaelic, "and make certain that he does nothing which he may regret."

Steel-Eyes nodded sharply, and Cormac MacAlpine turned away. Digging in the leather purse that hung from his belt, Steel-Eyes produced a large handkerchief, then another. The first he wadded up and, after a brief scuffle—which Gray inevitably lost—stuffed into Gray's mouth; the second he then tied tightly about Gray's jaw, forcing his lips and teeth apart, so that he was effectively muzzled.

"Now then, Princess." Cormac MacAlpine was unsheathing his gleaming copper knife. As before, he sliced his thumb and slicked the knife-blade with his own blood, but rather than cutting her cheek as he had cut Gray's, he bent close and stroked the knife's edge along the sluggishly bleeding wound behind her left ear. Then he cupped her jaw in his right hand, a hideous parody of a caress, and pressed the palm thus bloodied against the tree-trunk above her head. Sophie was rigid with revulsion, her face white and her eyes blazing, and Gray was not at all surprised when he felt the air about him stir, then bite, and finally howl.

Cormac MacAlpine frowned at Sophie, whilst Steel-Eyes and Pàrlan Dearg squinted suspiciously at Gray.

"Now," Cormac MacAlpine repeated, impatient, and Steel-Eyes left Gray's side, crossed the clearing, and disappeared behind Sophie's tree.

Temporarily unobserved, Gray tugged at his bonds as hard as he dared. The knots were solid, and the movement jarred his raw-scraped back and bruised ribs painfully, but perhaps if he could put enough strain on the ropes, they might stretch sufficiently to allow some hope of escape . . .

Sophie's arms fell free, hanging limp at her sides. Steel-Eyes reappeared from behind the tree and grasped her right wrist, holding her arm out straight; Cormac MacAlpine took her hand, sliced across the back of it, and squeezed it—to Gray's furious eye, not at all gently—and as her blood fell against the roots of the great tree, the hum of magick in Gray's mind's ear grew suddenly louder and higher.

Cormac MacAlpine moved to Sophie's other side and repeated his rite—less graceful now that he must do all the work himself, Gray noted, with a small and bitter satisfaction. The wind was so strong now that it whipped the branches of the elm-trees and scattered their few small leaves; and its howling mounted higher, a mad keening that Gray felt as well as heard, at the second infusion of Sophie's blood.

The tearing wind, the flying leaves, the whipping branches: Gray could not help recalling the story she had told him—half a lifetime past, even then, but made all too vivid by her halting, horrified recital—of her mother's sudden and untimely death. He saw the moment when Sophie recalled it also, in the minute shift of her face from terror and revulsion to the grim expressionless masque which meant that she was fighting hard for control.

He caught her gaze and held it. *You are not that child now, Sophie. Your magick does not master you.*

The wind did not die down, but it seemed to Gray that its frantic howling eased a little.

He followed Cormac MacAlpine's progress around the circle of trees as well as he could. How many other victims were there? He could see two; but to judge by their placement, precisely two trees to Sophie's left and two trees to her right, there would likely be two more outside his line of sight. The man tied to Sophie's right—a small fellow whose tangled hair and ragged beard were black—raised his head as Cormac MacAlpine and Steel-Eyes approached him; with a renewed shock of dismay Gray recognised his erstwhile University colleague Professor Maghrebin, of whom Sophie had been so fond, and who had been called away so suddenly—

*No. Not called away. Decoyed away and kidnapped, as I was.*

He saw, or heard, the rite repeated over and over, and felt the earth-blood-ocean smell of Ailpín Drostan's magick thrum a little stronger as each was linked into the spell-net.

*Why now? Why all together? These men have been here even longer than I—or at any rate some of them have been—*

His attention was wrenched back to his own predicament, when a businesslike grip on his left wrist—his arm having been freed apparently whilst his concentration was elsewhere, and tingling fiercely with the returning flow of blood—jarred the accumulated bruises and abrasions, and he choked back a pained yelp.

He knew of course what must be coming, and could think of no way out of it but *through*. The others must know what it was to which they had agreed, or had been forced, to lend their magick; did Sophie know it? Or . . .

Forcing himself to a discipline which he had not found necessary for years, Gray closed his eyes, slowed his breathing, and ruthlessly excised from his consciousness the raw pain in his wrists, the sting of the knife across the back of his left hand, the bite of rough elm-bark against the half-healed skin of his back—the scuffles and blows, the oaths and gasps—the keening of the wind, the tiny sounds of the woodland night—the voices, the tense heavy breaths of his captors—until the thrum of magick about him was so loud in his mind's ear as to drown out all other sounds, all sights, all sensations. He wished, not for the first time, for some of Master Alcuin's talent for the visual perception of magick, so much clearer and less ambiguous than what he could himself perceive.

The sound of it, the *feel* of it, was only half familiar. What could that mean? To begin with, that there was magick here which was neither his nor Sophie's. The magick of Ailpín Drostan's spell-net, certainly, for it had a smell of blood and chill air and the sea which he had felt before, but not that alone. This was . . . this was . . .

But his speculative probing was swept away in an upsurge of magick, or magicks—Sophie's and his own, and Ailpín Drostan's, and others which he could perceive but not identify—which seemed like to take off the top of Gray's head from below, and he came back to the physical world with a ringing thump and a deafening blur of shouting, panicked voices.

Joanna pressed her right shoulder against Gwendolen's, then at once drew away again, ashamed of herself. "Heard you that sound?" she whispered.

"Of course I did," said Gwendolen. "I should not be at all surprised if it had been heard in London. What was it?"

Joanna had not the least idea. But whatever it was, their guards had heard it also, and plainly it had alarmed them. They argued in rapid, low-voiced Gaelic, their voices gradually rising and their gestures growing more emphatic, and at last the elder of them barked a sharp order to the younger—the tone of command perfectly clear to Joanna, if the words themselves were beyond her—who rocked back, wide-eyed, and departed at a run.

Their remaining captor fixed them with a hard stare which said more clearly than words, *Do not test me.*

Joanna, however, had never been very good at taking orders from men whom she did not respect, and Gwendolen, the gods knew, followed instructions only when it suited her to do so.

When the guard turned away, they edged minutely towards one another, so that their fingers met behind their backs. Their captors had, presumably during their period of insensibility, confiscated Gaël's borrowed clasp-knife from Gwendolen's pocket and the hoof-knife secreted in her boot; their search of Joanna's person, however, had evidently been more cursory, and (as she had hoped) it had not occurred to them that she might have concealed a small paper-knife, honed to a murderous edge, inside the left sleeve of her pelisse, between the tight-woven wool and the heavy satin lining. Gwendolen, however, knew exactly where it was, and was just enough taller than Joanna—as well as being much cleverer with her fingers, which could set tiny invisible stitches to mend a rent in a muslin sleeve, and dance rapidly across the keys of a pianoforte, as Joanna's could not—as to have it out of its hiding-place and busy about the cutting of their bonds in what seemed very short order.

"There we are," she breathed, gathering up the cut ropes—or most of them—as they fell away, and pressing the handle of the paper-knife into Joanna's stiff, numbed hands. "Now, we must not let him see."

*As though I needed telling.*

She tucked the knife carefully back into the lining of her sleeve, and flexed her fingers cautiously, keeping her gaze downcast lest any sign of her present relief, trepidation, or furious calculation show on her face.

The guard paced to and fro before the door, pausing now and then to peer out through the grille into the corridor, or to glare down at Joanna and Gwendolen—torn, seemingly, between concern for his comrades and distrust of his prisoners. Joanna watched him from the corner of her eye and developed an idea.

"He is wild to know what is happening without," she murmured, when next she heard the minute creaking of the door as he leaned upon it. "If he thinks we are too ill to escape, or too exhausted, perhaps he may risk going to investigate."

Gwendolen did not reply in words but (to Joanna's immense and secret satisfaction) by coughing pathetically and slowly subsiding rightward until she lay curled in a limp heap upon the flagstones—her no-longer-bound wrists still concealed between her slim betrousered hips and the dressed stone wall.

When next their captor turned to look at them, another damp cough and a little whimper emerged from the heap.

Joanna debated briefly the relative merits of bolstering Gwendolen's charade by means of some appropriate theatre of her own, and of joining her in it. Which approach might their captor find most persuasive, or least suspect?

The natural, the obvious response in such circumstances would be that which had come so naturally to her when Sophie had been so ill during their visit to Donald MacNeill: panic, quickly suppressed; demands for assistance; an insistence that everything possible be done for her cousin, and that she herself take charge of the doing of it.

Natural, too, to demand that their captor free her hands for the purpose; and then he should realise—

Joanna groaned—her despair was only partly feigned—and let her head loll back against the wall, attempting to look as helpless and dispirited as possible, whilst still keeping one eye obliquely on Cormac MacAlpine's henchman. Could she, for the sake of facilitating their eventual escape, muster some tears?

She found that she could—that it was, in fact, disconcertingly easy. Her eyes stung, her nose prickled; her throat clogged, and she coughed wetly, her shoulders held rigid against the wall to preserve the illusion that she remained bound and helpless. She let slip the tight rein she had been keeping on the part of her mind which insisted upon imagining, in minute detail, what dreadful things might have happened to Gray during his captivity, and might now be happening to Sophie also; the nightmare images bloomed behind her half-closed eyelids, and a gasping sob tore from her throat.

Booted footsteps approached, heavy and slow. Joanna forced her eyes open, and through the distorting lens of brimming tears she saw her captor regarding her and Gwendolen with mouth downturned in an expression of bemused disgust. "Shut up," he growled, in heavily accented Latin, and prodded at Gwendolen with the toe of his boot. "Useless children."

It was exactly the reaction which Joanna had hoped to produce, and she was in equal parts elated that they had managed it and profoundly ashamed of the extent to which her play-acting was nothing of the kind.

A renewed commotion in the corridor—rapid footsteps, incomprehensible shouting—drew the Alban's attention away once more; he crossed to the door, peered out through the grille, and gave vent to what was unmistakably a string of curses. He glanced back at Joanna and Gwendolen—both shamming despair, resignation, and bodily weakness for all they were worth—and out through the grille again, and at last he opened the door and slipped out into the corridor.

Joanna's elation crowded out her shame, even whilst she heard the distinctive metallic *chunk* of a key turning in the lock on the far side of the door.

A long moment passed in tense, expectant silence. When at length no sound or movement signalled the return of their captor, Gwendolen sat up, shaking out her wrists.

"That was well done," she said. Her voice was prudently low, but she wore a broad grin, plastered precariously over a wild-eyed exhilarated terror. "The maidenly tears, especially."

Joanna scrubbed the sleeve of her pelisse (no longer very clean) across her eyes, dug her handkerchief out of her bodice, and blew her nose. "One does one's best with what the gods send one," she said primly.

Gwendolen climbed to her feet, a little unsteadily, and reached down a hand to pull Joanna up. Joanna reeled, light-headed, and was forced to lean one shoulder against the wall for a few breaths, so as to regain her equilibrium.

"He has locked the door," said Gwendolen, striding across the room to investigate. Her stride was half a stagger, but Joanna, equally unsteady on her feet, forbore to comment.

"Yes," said Joanna, rubbing her aching shoulders. "I heard him. What—"

"Give me that knife." Gwendolen cut across her, holding out an impatient hand. She braced one hand against the wall and crouched down to peer into the keyhole.

Joanna limped towards the door, taking care to stay out of line of sight from the grille and decanting the paper-knife from her sleeve as she went. She crouched beside Gwendolen, heaving a tiny sigh for the comprehensive wreckage of what had once been a simple but particularly becoming gown, and laid the knife in her outstretched hand.

"Gwendolen Pryce," Joanna breathed, as the lock snicked softly open, "I believe you have been concealing a very unsavoury past."

Gwendolen ducked her head. "That's as may be," she said, all the bravado gone out of her voice, and pressed herself upright, her back against the wall.

Joanna rose from her awkward crouch to the tips of her toes to peer out through the grille. The corridor appeared quite deserted.

"Well?" she said.

But Gwendolen was no longer beside her; glancing back over her shoulder, Joanna saw her hefting a small spade in one hand and a large long-handled broom in the other, as though weighing them against each other. After a moment she dropped the broom and swung the spade over her shoulder, for all the world like the Breizhek groom whose clothing she wore.

A sound like a thunderclap raised the hairs on Joanna's arms; she succeeded in keeping her composure, but only just. They opened the door just enough to slip through one at a time, and Joanna kept watch, her heart pounding unpleasantly, whilst Gwendolen again prodded at the keyhole with her paper-knife and a long sliver of wood, split off from the broken leg of an abandoned wheelback chair, which she then secreted inside her right boot.

"Done!" she said at last, and stood up abruptly, tucking the paper-knife into Joanna's hand. "Come along."

Moving as quickly and quietly as they knew how, they set off in the direction of the noise.

The corridor was deserted. Once out in the cobbled courtyard, they moved more cautiously, hugging the walls. But here, too, the sentries seemed all to have abandoned their posts, and Joanna and Gwendolen dared to break for the open and run towards what had now become a roar of unintelligible sound.

The postern-gate had been latched from without, but yielded without much difficulty to their determined application of Gwendolen's salvaged spade, in the character of a hatchet; the noise of this undertaking was such that had anyone at all been within earshot, they must have been discovered at once—yet no one came to investigate.

They stumbled through the gate and looked wildly about them for the source of the deafening roar that seemed to come from everywhere at once. It was nearing dawn; Joanna had had no sleep to speak of in what by now seemed like days, and had become thoroughly disoriented in their wanderings through the bowels of Castle Mac-Alpine—all of which might be supposed to explain, if not excuse, her mistaking the glow along the northern horizon for the sunrise.

Then the breeze shifted, and Joanna smelled smoke. She turned her head into the wind and saw the marks of milling footsteps taper off into a faint trail.

"There!" she cried, catching at Gwendolen's elbow, and took off running, following the footmarks towards the coppiced wood that lay to the northwest of the postern-gate.


The forest was not burning.

Or, at any rate, it was not burning in the usual sense, but lines of flame, bright and weirdly blue, ran along the ground beneath the trees. Gwendolen nearly trod on one of them; her squawk of pain, when Joanna yanked her back by the wrist, gave way to a startled *Oh!* when she saw what she had been about to do.

"Will we go over?" she panted. "Or go round?"

Joanna stood for a moment contemplating the line of blue-white fire that blocked their path. It snaked round between the tree-trunks, branching and joining like the tangles of rivers on one of Donald MacNeill's military maps; there seemed no way of going round it. She crouched long enough to feel about amongst the leaf-mould and grasped the first kindling-sized branch she came across; then, rising again, she reached out with it to prod the flames, ignoring Gwendolen's attempt to stop her.

The branch smoked faintly but did not ignite.

"Over," said Joanna, dropping it, and began tucking up her skirts.

"Jo—"

"*Shut up,*" Joanna hissed fiercely.

They crossed the first fireline at a running leap, and when this produced no worse effect than a sort of buzzing sensation, they forged ahead with more confidence and less care, towards what appeared to be the centre of this uncanny conflagration.

Joanna did not stop to think whether they were running in the right direction, or to consider what they might do when they arrived at the end of their present trajectory; her single goal, at present, was to reach her sister and brother-in-law, and in Joanna's experience the epicentre of some inexplicable catastrophe was always the most likely place to find them.

And, indeed, when at last she and Gwendolen, running hand in hand, burst through a tangle of bracken, between two closely spaced yew-trees, and into an unnaturally round clearing, Joanna at once beheld Sophie, glowing with furious anger and tied to the trunk of an enormous elm-tree.

Her first instinct was, of course, to dart forward and cut away the cords that bound Sophie at ankle, waist, and breast; the sharpened paper-knife was already in her right hand and her feet carrying her forward when at last the evidence of her eyes reached her conscious mind, halting her in her tracks.

Whoever might need rescuing in this wood at present, it was not Sophie.

## CHAPTER XXXIII

# In Which Sophie Makes a Surprising Discovery, and Lucia MacNeill Pays a Debt

*The first revelation* was that Catriona MacCrimmon had been right, and both Rory, with his talk of legends, and Cormac MacWattie, who would not opine on the truth or otherwise of that elusive phenomenon known as the magick of the land, entirely wrong; and the second, that Cormac MacAlpine had done precisely what he had set out to do.

Sophie could feel the branching tendrils of Ailpín Drostan's spell-net, great and small, immediate and distant, stretching in all directions from the hub of the great elm; could hear them singing in a thousand separate voices; could see their branching, intertwining paths.

Cormac MacAlpine had drawn power from every mage whose blood had been spilled in this shrine and fed it into a web woven through every corner of the kingdom. But the magick ran both ways: from web out through tree and field, stream and firth and loch, into the bedrock of the land—and from the land back into the spell-net. *The magick of the land, indeed.*

The magick channelled into the spell fed on her own, and fed it; it reached towards the faint thread of Lucia MacNeill's magick, and the two flickered and darted about each other like swordsmen testing one another's defences; then, as sudden and fierce as two cataracts meeting, they rushed together and flooded the pathways laid down in Ailpín Drostan's time, from the greatest to the least.

And Sophie, pinned at the hub of the spell, could sense the flow of that power—all shot through now with the bright red-gold flavour of Lucia MacNeill's magick; could see how, by means of her connexion to that magick, she might reach through the web and use it to heal or to harm.

At present, however, she could not think beyond the threat to Gray and their fellow prisoners. If Ailpín Drostan's spell-net worked in the way she suspected, there was work to be done—but first, the enemy at her own gates.

She reached carefully for her blood-bond with the great elm-tree, and through it to its companions in the grove; there was a long, fraught moment as the trees sought and tested the red-and-gold thread of Lucia MacNeill's magick that she yet carried, and she found that she could wield their roots and branches like an extension of her own hands.

"I have not done with you, Cormac MacAlpine," she said, and knew not whether she spoke the words aloud.

Not for years now had Gray seen Sophie lose control of her magick. On those prior occasions, the resulting physical destruction had been immense, and the danger to Sophie herself almost greater; but this time—

*This is no loss of control,* he thought, astounded; *this is Sophie wreaking deliberate havoc.*

And what glorious havoc it was!

He could see the branching lines of Cormac MacAlpine's restored spell-net now, ablaze in weird blue fire; when he closed his eyes, the lines of fire remained behind his eyelids, a bright tracery like the blood-vessels he had seen represented in healers' diagrams of the human body. The magelight lanterns hung about the tree-shrine blazed so brightly that they hurt to look upon, and tree-roots were snaking up through the layers of leaf-mould to wind about the ankles of Cormac MacAlpine and his men.

But the trees themselves remained untouched, and the men—though terror was writ plain upon their faces—entirely uninjured.

Every cell in Gray's body thrummed and fizzed with the mingled magicks—his own and Sophie's, well known and welcome as the touch of her hand in his; the unfamiliar flavours of their fellow-prisoners' magicks, struggling and uncertain; the chill salt-and-iron tang of Ailpín Drostan's spell, and that other presence, faint and fading, that tasted of pine forests and the cry of gulls, of rocky crags and the purple of heather, of fierce loyalty and a strong, determined love. Across the clearing, Sophie stood straight and tall against her tree, her eyes burning and her dark hair rising about her like Medusa's snakes.

She ought to have been terrifying, and in a sense she was, but the small part of Gray that feared what she was capable of was entirely overwhelmed by the heady mix of pride, exhilaration, relief, and fierce love. He caught her gaze across the field of fire and grinned, and after a long, startled moment, an answering smile, small and hesitant, curved her lips.

A moment later, the sound of breaking branches made him turn his head, just in time to see Joanna and a dark-haired young man of about the same age crash through the trees and into the clearing. Joanna started towards Sophie, then checked herself, staring around her with a thoroughly gobsmacked expression. She and her companion were both pale-faced and very dirty, as though they had not only run through the wood but also crawled up a chimney on their way to the grove.

"Joanna!" Gray called. He had to call her name twice more before she at last located him; then her soot-streaked face lit up with relief, and she ran.

"Gray! Thank all the gods! I thought—"

"Have you got a knife?" Gray demanded, cutting off her eager exclamations.

He spoke in Brezhoneg, as she had; the language reminded him strangely of Oxford—Oxford with Sophie—a life for which captivity had given him a strong nostalgia, despite its many imperfections.

With a startled grin, Joanna held up her right hand, in which gleamed Sophie's paper-knife, last seen on her desk in Quarry Close and now honed to razor sharpness, why? No matter.

"Good," he said. "Go and cut the others free—they will need food and rest and most of all a healer—I hope you have brought one with you?—and then Sophie, and then me."

Joanna bit her lip and dropped her gaze at the mention of a healer, from which Gray concluded that there was no healer in their party. Which party, it occurred to him now, was nowhere to be seen.

"Joanna—"

She held up the knife again and ran light-footed to the next occupied elm-tree.

"Your Alban friends took my knives, both of them," said Joanna's companion, in a conversational tone. He was real, then, this Cymric boy, and Joanna too apparently. He disappeared behind Gray's tree, and Gray could feel him prodding speculatively at the cords about his rib cage. There was something familiar about his voice . . . "But I expect one of them might have one to lend me in return."

"Not the copper one," Gray said urgently; "Cormac MacAlpine used it in his magick"—he waved his left hand, still sluggishly dripping blood, in the young man's general direction—"and I do not know what . . . what properties it may have. Ginger, there, has a perfectly ordinary knife, however."

Reappearing from behind Gray, the young man followed his gaze to Pàrlan Dearg, trapped in a coil of elm-tree roots and glowering furiously in an attempt to hide his uncomprehending terror. "I daresay he does," he said, and loped away to retrieve it.

*Who in Hades is that boy? How did he come here?*

But no matter; whoever he was, he had retrieved Pàrlan Dearg's knife and was applying it very usefully to the prisoner at Gray's left.

Once freed, the man staggered a few steps forward before collapsing to all fours, retching. Joanna's young man knelt briefly to speak to him, laying a reassuring hand on his shoulder, before springing up again to free the next prisoner.

It was Joanna who first reached Sophie, and in the fierce glare of the magelight lanterns Gray could see tears gleaming on her face as she crouched beside her sister, sawing at the ropes about her ankles. Sophie's face was grimly set now, and Gray suspected that she was wrestling with forces she did not entirely understand.

The last of the ropes parted under Joanna's blade, and Sophie fell forward—caught herself—stood for a moment breathing deeply, clasping her elbows—and swung wide about Cormac MacAlpine and Pàrlan Dearg to fling herself at Gray.

Joanna had pelted across the clearing behind her, and both she and her friend were now sawing industriously at Gray's bonds, but he scarcely noticed, and cared not at all, for he had Sophie in his arms again, and for the moment life could hold no greater reward.


Sophie clutched the folds of Gray's robe, her ear pressed to the rough wool over his heart, and squeezed her eyes shut. *Breathe. Calm.*

Gray was speaking to her—Joanna, also—but she could not hear the words, nor even discern in what languages they were spoken. In the grip of this magick that spoke to all of Alba, she was no longer certain even of the borders of her own body, and she had lost all sense of the borders of her mind, or of her magick.

One thing she had seen clearly from the moment of her absorption into the spell: Cormac MacAlpine might have remade its pathways, but he was no longer in control of its working, if indeed he ever had been. It was her blood, her magick, and those of the other prisoners, which had fed enough power into the spell to begin to bring it to life—Gray's that had completed the circuit—and that tenuous golden thread of Clan MacNeill magick, still clinging to her own as Cormac MacAlpine opened her veins, that governed its effects. The power now flowing through those pathways would never answer to Cormac MacAlpine, no matter how direct his descent from the great Ailpín Drostan. For he had fatally misunderstood the nature of the spell; it was not that the magick made the clan chieftain, or that the clan chieftain made the magick, but that they made and mended one another, through the will of the clan-lands and the people who inhabited them. The clans had chosen their chieftains, and the clan chieftains had chosen Donald MacNeill, and approved his choice of Lucia MacNeill as his heir; now Sophie and Cormac MacAlpine, the one unwilling and the other unknowing, had bound Lucia MacNeill's magick (if not, perhaps, Lucia MacNeill herself) into the ancient magick of her kingdom, as Cormac MacAlpine must have hoped to do for himself.

But in one matter he had spoken true; there was healing to be done in Alba. Through the web of the spell Sophie heard the blighted fields as dull, throbbing aches—tasted the emptied storehouses like the gap left by a missing tooth—felt the hunger of man and beast in dark and hollow silences. There was a tract of pine forest felled by drought, a flash of sere brown in her mind's ear; here a sheep-cote succumbing to some ovine plague, a hot insistent whine that tasted of copper.

*But if the magick will do my bidding . . .*

She had often wished for a healer's talent; if the gods (which gods?) had chosen this bizarre means of offering her that gift, what sort of ungrateful fool could possibly refuse it?

Hesitantly, wary of making some misstep, Sophie reached towards the nearest point of pain and poured her magick into it through the web. The pain did not disappear, but it eased a little, from sharp agony to dull ache. She flew along the lines of magick, somehow riding all of them at once—*I am my father's heir,* she heard Lucia Mac-Neill say; *my range is the whole of Alba*—singing the warped melody true again, shaping the power to fill the gaps and the silences.

When the well of her own magick threatened to run dry, she reached out for Gray—blind, deaf, and drunk, but finding him no less readily for that—and drew him down into a long, searching kiss; his magick rushed towards hers, and hers welled up to meet it, and she was out again amongst the clan-lands of Alba, making whole what Cormac MacAlpine had put asunder.

There was a paean and formal supplication to the Mother Goddess, which in Britain was sung each spring at the festival of Matronalia; it thrummed under the surface of her mind as she worked, and though the gods of Alba might disdain its origins, Sophie felt they might nonetheless appreciate its substance:

> *Lava quod est sordidum,*
> *Riga quod est aridum,*
> *Sana quod est saucium.*
> *Flecte quod est rigidum,*
> *Fove quod est frigidum,*
> *Rege quod est devium.*

She could not have said how long she swam the currents of the spell-web—it might have been moments or days, months or years. She might almost have been content to do so forever, for each hurt that she used her magick to heal—though in the full knowledge that it was not hers alone—was also a balm to the wounds left on her soul by every inadvertent act of destruction which it, and she, had ever wrought. But after some unknowable time, she found that the music of the spell had changed, relief and thankfulness rippling through it to crowd out the warped and discordant echoes so strongly felt at first; the fainter those echoes grew, the more Sophie grew conscious of the world outside the spell.

Gray's arms, solid and familiar, still held her fast. Gray's heart still beat steady and strong beneath her ear. But nothing else, she found when at last she closed her eyes to the aetheric Alba and opened them upon the earthly one, was as she remembered it.

It was full day, and a brisk northwesterly wind sent woolly puffs of cloud scudding across a clear azure sky. Cormac MacAlpine and his men had gone; the men they had kidnapped were disposed about the clearing, variously seated or reclining, but all snugly wrapped in clean woollen blankets and spooning up some sort of fragrant soup from wooden bowls. Beneath a spreading yew-tree, Joanna and Gwendolen, with blankets trailing from their shoulders, stood talking quietly with a puffy-eyed and tearful Catriona MacCrimmon. And all about them—Sophie blinked in astonishment, certain at first that her eyes deceived her, but indeed the ten well-armed young men and two slightly older women who now guarded the perimeter of the tree-shrine all wore the badge and gear of Donald MacNeill's household guard.

*Angus Ferguson's men, I could have made sense of; but how comes this to be?*

"Sophie," said Gray quietly. "Love, have you come back to us?"

His voice came from somewhere above her head; Sophie twisted awkwardly in an effort to look up at him and, finding it did not answer, sank back into his arms again. She was half sprawled upon a blanket, she found, her hips slotted between Gray's drawn-up knees—someone had found him a proper pair of trousers, it appeared—and another blanket covering her from ribs to toes; an almost embarrassingly intimate posture, save that no one had any attention to spare for their particular corner of the forest at present.

"Nearly," she said, reaching for Gray's hand where it wrapped about her shoulder, and spreading her own over it, her fingers slotting into the interstices of his. "Another moment; I can see now how to go on."

She tested her connexion to the spell-net and found it as firm as ever, but now that she had seen the magick from within, she could see too the way to break free of it—to free herself, and Gray, and all the others, without material damage to any. Reclining against Gray's chest, her head pillowed on his bony shoulder, she closed her eyes again to shut out the physical world, and reached after the thread that linked her magick to the great elm-tree. From there it was no difficult matter to trace the magick from tree to tree, and from tree to man, and to sever each thread that tethered one of the mages into the spell, and draw them all together with her own, through the heart of the great elm, and now . . .

The last trace of Lucia MacNeill's magick gleamed bright red-gold amidst the blue-white flower-petals that Sophie's mind used to represent her own magick—easily seen, and easily drawn out to stand alone. It was Clan MacNeill's magick that would feed the spell-net, and could command it; if, when that last thread returned to its source, it carried with it the full strength of the half-dozen links which Cormac MacAlpine had created, would that not close the circuit once for all? Sophie wove together the strands, her own and Gray's and Professor Maghrebin's and the stranger-mages', with the red-and-golden thread of Clan MacNeill; at last, when the plaited rope seemed to pulse with life before her mind's eye, she reached for her own link to the spell and, with a deft twist of a metaphorical wrist, severed it cleanly.

She fell back into her own aching, bruised, and half-starved body with a resounding, if metaphysickal, thump.

"It is done," she said, and, burrowing closer into Gray's arms, closed her eyes again and tumbled headlong into sleep.

"I cannot understand it," said Joanna. "Where can they have come from? Who summoned them, and when, and why?"

There were guardsmen everywhere: in the wood and in the courtyard, in the kitchens and the stables, on the battlements and in the cells below the walls. It was not that she objected to their presence—indeed, they had made themselves extremely useful thus far, taking Cormac MacAlpine and his henchmen into custody, bringing food and blankets and even a journeyman healer to the erstwhile prisoners—but it was baffling and inexplicable, and Joanna was not overfond of things she could not explain.

"They were on their ship, out in the firth, were they not?" said Gwendolen reasonably. "Surely they are come here for the same reason as ourselves, thinking the wood was afire. It must have looked it, from a little way offshore."

"No," said Joanna decidedly. "That is, I can easily imagine it, but these are not Angus Ferguson's troops. They are Donald MacNeill's household guard. *Household* guard. From Din Edin. It is no part of their business to take ship to Mull to put down a"—she waved a hand vaguely—"whatever this was intended to be. They ought not to travel at all unless—"

"Unless?" Gwendolen prompted, after a moment.

Joanna said nothing, however, for she was staring in open-mouthed alarm at the person, decidedly *not* a guardsman, who had just stepped into the clearing, pushing back the hood of her dark-green cloak to free a riot of red-gold curls. "Horns of Herne," said Joanna. "Lucia MacNeill has followed us here!"

"*Oh,*" said Gwendolen. "Well. Birds of a feather, I suppose . . ."

Joanna frowned at her, and she subsided.

The two guardswomen fell in behind Lucia MacNeill as she conducted a sort of makeshift tour of inspection of the late battlefield, pausing to speak to each of the freed prisoners. She spoke longest to Gray—Sophie being still so deeply asleep that it seemed nothing could wake her—and Joanna wished very much to know what they might be saying, but though she sidled close with that purpose in mind, the conversation was all in Gaelic, and her stealth availed her nothing.

At last Lucia MacNeill rose to her feet again, laid one hand briefly on Gray's shoulder, and began to make her way towards Joanna. Curiously, her route seemed to involve touching the flat of her right hand to the bark of each tree she passed.

"Joanna Callender," she said, halting before Joanna and reaching for both her hands.

Joanna unthinkingly reached back and was startled and a little alarmed when the heiress of Alba pulled her into a fierce embrace.

"You were very foolish," she said, when she pulled away. "All of you. Thanks be that Sophie sent me that note from Dùn Breatainn—"

"Which note?" said Joanna.

"To say that she was not sitting quietly at home, as we supposed—as though one small illusion-spell should hoodwink the whole of her acquaintance!—nor convalescing at the seaside, as she seems to have suggested to Rory MacCrimmon, but staging a landing on the Ross of Mull," said Lucia MacNeill, "and requesting me to get word to Angus Ferguson's company, that they might intervene if they saw 'fireworks.'"

"I see," said Joanna, who did not.

"But of course I could not trust anything of the kind to Angus Ferguson, and I am not myself empowered to relieve him of his command," Lucia MacNeill continued, which answered that question; "and so I had to come myself, with our own troops, whose commander can be trusted not to overreact. Though I confess," she added, with a little shudder, "I was greatly tempted myself to overreact, when we saw the whole of the wood behind the castle apparently afire."

"It did look rather like that," said Joanna. "But it was not fire at all, in the end; it was magick. And Sophie has sorted it out, I believe, for there is certainly nothing afire now."

"That is what you think," said Lucia MacNeill darkly.


"It was your magick that the spell wanted," Sophie explained, between spoonfuls of mutton stew. "Not Cormac MacAlpine's, and not even ours, truly"—she gestured expansively at the rest of the mages sleeping in cots slung from the ceiling of the spacious cabin aboard the *Malmhìn NicNèill*—"though it drank our power greedily enough, given the opportunity. But it was only because you had lent me your magick that it . . . came awake." She paused for another bite. "At least, that is my present theory."

"So, then," said Lucia MacNeill bemusedly, "whilst I have been blaming myself for giving you the means of putting your life in danger, you have been using it to set my kingdom to rights?"

"And to save half a dozen lives," Gray added, "for I think Cormac MacAlpine must have killed all of us sooner or later, and himself with us—though I do not believe he meant to do either."

Sophie flushed and looked down into her soup-plate.

"And now this . . . spell-net . . . is linked to me." Lucia MacNeill very evidently did not know what to make of this development, and Gray could scarcely blame her.

"I believe so," said Sophie. Now that they were speaking about magick and not about her bravery under fire, she was perfectly able to meet Lucia MacNeill's eye. "I hope it was not all my imagination," she said, a little wistful, "for it was a great satisfaction to me to help in such a way."

Gray slid closer to her on the narrow bench and surreptitiously rested his hand on her knee.

"If what you say is true," said Lucia MacNeill thoughtfully, "then you held the fate of the whole of Alba in your hands."

"I suppose I did," said Sophie, and took another mouthful of stew.

"And you might have done anything at all with that power," Lucia MacNeill persisted, "but you chose to use it to heal our wounds."

"Of course I did!" Sophie sat up straighter and put down her spoon. "Do you tell me that you should have done differently?"

"No, no!" said Lucia MacNeill. "I should have done just as you did, and counted myself lucky to have such a chance. But I am the heiress of Alba, Sophie; and you are—"

"Your sister, or nearly," Sophie said gently. "A welcomed guest in your home, as well as in your kingdom, and a student at your University. I was not born in Alba, Lucia, but that does not make me indifferent to her fate."

"No," said Lucia MacNeill, a little subdued. "No, I see that. But—" She hesitated, then plunged onward: "You gave it up. You held the power of life and death over an entire kingdom, and at the first possible opportunity, you chose to give it up."

Sophie looked genuinely astonished at this. "Of course I did," she repeated.

For some time thereafter, the three of them ate their mutton stew in meditative silence.

As well as magistrates' men to take charge of the prisoners, the *Malmhìn NicNèill* was met on the quay at Dùn Breatainn by the private secretaries of both Donald MacNeill and Lord de Courcy, each of whom had brought with him a carriage and driver for the purpose of conveying his charges to their destination. The difficulty was, however, that the distribution of charges and of destinations seemed not to be altogether clear.

The foreign mages were to remain in Glaschu for the period of their convalescence; Donald MacNeill had dispatched instructions for their proper accommodation, together with a purse of coin and the formal request that the local magistrates should hear their evidence as soon as they should be well enough to provide it. Mr. Powell had strict instructions from Lord de Courcy, who had in turn received them from His Majesty by way of Sieur Germain de Kergabet, that Joanna and Gwendolen (now respectably clothed in a sober travelling-gown from Lucia MacNeill's trunk) were to be returned to London with all safe speed—a course of action which Sophie regarded as eminently sensible, and Joanna as the height of injustice—together with an invitation for Sophie and Gray to return to London likewise, if they so chose. On the other hand, Ciaran Barra MacNeill carried both strict instructions to return Lucia MacNeill to Din Edin by any means necessary (though Sophie suspected him of exaggerating the vehemence with which the request had been delivered) and an invitation for Sophie and Gray to return to Din Edin as guests of Donald MacNeill, or to their house in Quarry Close, whichever they might prefer.

Mr. Powell had also brought Joanna's and Gwendolen's effects and a considerable stack of letters collected from Quarry Close—most of them directed to Gray, half a dozen to Sophie, and two to Joanna. The first of these made her roll her eyes, and she tossed it aside unopened; the second (in the direction of which Sophie recognised Jenny's hand) she slit open with an expression of trepidation and read through very quickly, before folding it up again and stuffing it into the very bottom of her reticule. Her face was pink and her shoulders hunched when she turned away to look out at the harbour.

A surreptitious glance at the neglected letter showed it to be from Roland. Sophie frowned thoughtfully, and refrained from rocking the tenuously balanced boat.

"What had Lady Kergabet to say to you, Jo, that made you squirm so?" Gwendolen inquired, sotto voce, as Lord de Courcy's coach rattled out of Glaschu.

Joanna hunched her shoulders and jerked her head at Mr. Powell, who sat gazing out of the window with a careful appearance of insouciance.

"She chastised me for taking criminally foolish risks with my own life, and with Sophie's and yours," she said at last, too low (she hoped) for Mr. Powell's ears, "and for frightening her half to death—as though Sophie's mad schemes were all *my* fault."

Gwendolen hummed sympathetically and tilted her curly head on one side. "To be fair, Jo—"

"And then she thanked me," Joanna continued, "and blessed me in the names of a dozen gods, for saving her brother's life, and told me—" She swallowed hard. "And told me that she should have been proud to be my mother."

"Oh," Gwendolen murmured. She inched closer to Joanna on the leather-cushioned seat, and clasped her hand, and said no more.

That night, however—Mr. Powell having grudgingly consented to a full night's halt, rather than another change of horses, because Lord de Courcy's coachman insisted upon it—she turned from the dressing-table and said quietly, "I have a confession to make to you, Jo."

Her tone—hesitating, almost fearful—froze Joanna in the act of unfolding her nightdress.

"H-have you?" she said.

Gwendolen ducked her head, as though studying her hands. Joanna, drifting closer, found herself studying them likewise: still long and slim and graceful, and now perfectly clean, they bore the unmistakable signs of their recent ordeals in new blisters, scratches, and ragged, broken nails.

The silence stretched out unbearably. "Gwen, we are good friends, are we not?" said Joanna at last. "Whatever it is—"

Whilst she was speaking, her right hand, smaller than Gwendolen's but similarly marked, had crept forward of its own volition and her fingers woven themselves into Gwendolen's soft curls. Now

Gwendolen's face tipped up towards hers, and her dark eyes were wary, troubled.

"Jo," she said, "have you ever been in love?"

"No," said Joanna at once, "and—"

"Nor have I," Gwendolen said. "That is—I had not—until we were caught and thrown in that horrible place; and then I could not mistake it."

Joanna frowned. Why should those words make her stomach churn? *I ought to be happy for her, surely.* But then, Gwendolen herself seemed more tense and anxious than happy.

"May I . . . may I ask who . . ."

"Oh." Gwendolen's lips twisted in wry self-mockery. "I hoped," she said, bending her head again, "I hoped that she might feel the same. But I see I was mistaken."

She spoke so quietly that Joanna was not altogether certain of what she was hearing. She dropped to her knees, feeling as much at sea in this conversation as though she had been attempting to comprehend some complex magickal working, to bring their faces closer to level.

"I am not sure I understand you," she said carefully.

To her dismay, rather than explaining further, Gwendolen flushed crimson and turned her face away, twisting nearly out of her chair in her attempt to escape. Joanna clutched at her knee, at her elbow, feeling obscurely that they ought not to be so far apart; Gwendolen subsided, but kept her eyes averted.

"Please," said Joanna, half ashamed of the urgency in her voice. "I daresay you think me very stupid, but—"

She could go no farther, however, because Gwen was kissing her.


For a long moment, Joanna sat frozen, with incoherent questions bubbling up in her mind like soapsuds from a washtub. Then the warm lips on hers withdrew fractionally, and without conscious thought she tilted her head and rose on her knees, chasing them.

Gwen's breath huffed out warm against Joanna's skin, a soft *Oh*;

Gwen's hands came up to cradle Joanna's flushed cheeks, her uptilted head. When they broke apart again, a long and breathless moment later, her eyes were wide and soft, and a dazed, delighted smile—an entirely new smile, such as Joanna had never before seen—lit her face.

"Oh," said Joanna, stunned almost speechless. "I—oh."

She reached out blindly; Gwendolen caught hold of her hand.

"Yes," she said.

They beamed at one another, holding tight.

In the end, having packed Joanna and Gwendolen very firmly into the ambassadorial coach with Mr. Powell—from whom they had extracted a promise to personally deliver his passengers to Lady Kergabet at Carrington-street and no one else—Sophie and Gray ascended into Donald MacNeill's carriage with Lucia MacNeill, Ciaran Barra MacNeill, and a shaken and chastened Catriona MacCrimmon, who had hardly spoken a word since going aboard ship.

"Are you quite sure you wish to stay, *cariad?*" Gray had asked Sophie that morning, tenderly cradling her bruised left wrist in his right hand, and examining a livid bruise on her temple.

"The spring term is scarcely begun," said Sophie stoutly, though in truth she was rather leery of what sort of climate they might find in Din Edin upon their return. "I have no intention of leaving my year's work half done."

And Gray had grinned at her, and clapped her carefully on the shoulder; and for the first time since his departure from Quarry Close, she found herself inspired to grin back.